Sampson
and Delilah

ARTHUR P. DAY

iUniverse, Inc.
Bloomington

Sampson and Delilah

iUniverse books may be ordered through booksellers or by contacting:

iUniverse
1663 Liberty Drive
Bloomington, IN 47403
www.iuniverse.com
1-800-Authors (1-800-288-4677)

ISBN: 978-1-4759-1774-1 (sc)
ISBN: 978-1-4759-1775-8 (hc)
ISBN: 978-1-4759-1776-5 (ebk)

Library of Congress Control Number: 2012907391

Printed in the United States of America

iUniverse rev. date: 05/19/2012

GARAGE

Thomas DiNapoli hated family problems. Hadn't he worked and slaved all his life to put himself in a position where other people worried about problems? Hadn't he earned the right to sit back, enjoy life a little, play a little golf, show up at charity events with a big smile and a check, flirt with women half his age and enjoy one or two of them in bed? Thomas sighed and sipped his Kona coffee. It was absolutely the best in the world, he thought, and let the flavor build in his mouth as he swallowed it slowly. Yes, business could take care of itself now. Sure he had to make decisions now and then and keep a firm hand on the rudder but people he'd brought up and trained could now take over. Families, though, never stopped demanding attention.

In the business world, you ran the numbers, and made a decision based on the facts, and what you thought would happen if you did A or what would happen if you did B. Thomas loved the intricate puzzle that was business, the negotiation, the plan, the execution and the result. Always be aggressive but never merciless. Always leave a little on the table for your opponent. That way, you did not have to be constantly watching your back and you could always go back and get it the next time. He had never forgotten his father's truism; be careful who you step on when you're going up because you'll meet that same person on the way down. It was a philosophy that had worked for him, made him rich, kept him alive to enjoy life.

With families, though, no decision was simple. There were seldom any real facts that were not influenced by emotional attachment to one person or another. No matter what he did, someone would not like it and not hesitate to say so. It was all very disagreeable and Thomas DiNapoli resented having to deal with disagreeable matters. He sipped his coffee again. It was getting cold. He should get a freshly brewed cup.

The trouble was his daughter, Lisa. He loved her dearly. His wife, Maria, had such trouble bringing Lisa into the world, and would have no

1

more children. Lisa was it and she had proved to be the equal of several children when it came to attention. Thomas pushed a button on the floor under his desk and set the delicate Dresden china coffee cup gently down on its saucer where it picked up the sunlight from the window behind him. Lisa had been an open, friendly, laughing child and had grown into a charming, sophisticated woman, unless she did not get what she wanted.

Thomas sighed as the door to the study opened and Janey came in from the kitchen holding a black lacquered coffee tray carefully in front of her He picked up his cup and waved it at her. Without a word, she placed the cup and saucer on the tray and replaced it with an identical cup and saucer full of steaming Kona coffee. "Thank you, Janey," he told her.

Janey smiled, nodded, turned and left the room as silently as she had entered.

The problem as he saw it was twofold. Lisa was spoiled rotten. Maria had doted on her only child as only an Italian mamma can. Nothing was too good for Lisa, no pains would be spared to provide for whatever she needed and, moreover, whatever she wanted. Thomas had to admit that he was guilty of this as well, but the consequences were not pleasant for anyone in the surrounding area when Lisa lost her cool. It was as if a Cat 5 hurricane had swept through flattening everyone in its path and leaving a trail of emotional wreckage. The second problem was men. As Lisa got older, she proved to be a horrible judge of them.

Thomas had tried several times to interest her in men he thought would make good husbands, solid, reliable men, professionals, with family money and good connections in the government or business. The two were rapidly becoming one in the same even as the politicians denied it. Washington was no less corrupt than Baghdad. There had been Terry Voccia, son of Bob Voccia of Voccia Construction, for example. The company was doing well. Bob was a big-time donor to the Republican Party and his company bid on and got a steady stream of lucrative government projects. Voccia had the reputation for finishing on time and on budget thus preventing any embarrassing, political fallout. He used union labor and specialized in projects where special skills were needed thus minimizing the competition. Thomas had been an early investor and had never regretted it. When the unions had gotten a little greedy, he had put in a word with the right people. The son, Terry, was Lisa's age, good looking, well educated, enthusiastic about working the business with his father. He absolutely idolized Lisa. They had known each other for years. What was not to like? It seemed like a match to end all matches.

The results had been disastrous with Lisa throwing off immense numbers of screams and insults. She would be dead before she even met a man her father had chosen. He was some kind of monster to try and foist these morons on her. Did he think that they were living in the nineteenth century? Terry was a friend, and nothing more. She did not love him and that was that. No, Thomas did not think that. His ego was such that he thought she was rejecting suitors because they could not, in her mind, match her father. Nevertheless, he would not be around forever and feared for her comfort and security when he and Maria were planted in the Old Oaks cemetery. She needed a husband. Every woman needed a husband. Thomas saw nothing wrong with that thought.

His daughter had, though. She had despised anyone he had tried to introduce to her. Instead, she continued to go through men like toilet paper. They might last a day, a week, a month or two. Thomas thought the record was five or six months but he was not certain. He sipped at his coffee, closed his eyes and leaned back in his chair. He hated family problems. There was always a maximum of grief and a minimum of profit, usually no profit at all but simply expense. The current boyfriend was a classic example.

When Thomas had first met Mark, Lisa had brought him over to the house for lunch. He had shaken Mark's hand and looked him in the eye and silently asked himself what could his daughter possibly see in this man? The man had the look of a sullen child and eyes that had no depth or feeling to them. His handshake had been weak and sweaty. Thomas knew a lot of men like Mark. Many such had worked for Thomas over the years and the current crop still did. They were the soldiers, the wannabe's who stood on the edge of the conversation and smiled and nodded their heads though they did not have a clue to the problem or its solution. When asked, they inevitably came up with a quick, bloody and totally wrong answer. They always saw themselves as being right on the edge of success, advancement, wealth and power. None of them were even close. They held their pride out like a shield. They would get into a fight over nothing and end up winning nothing. They were the brawlers, the con men, the sharpies who looked to take advantage of anyone they met and whenever they were a few bucks ahead, they would show up in expensive clothes wearing lots of jewelry and driving heavy metal.

Thomas had looked at Mark, shaken his hand, and taken his measure. This was a loser who was never going to be more than that. Thomas had been polite and avoided arguing with Lisa about Mark, but it had taken all his willpower to do so. He thought Mark would last less than a month or two before Lisa got tired of his constant need for money and attention. In the meantime, though, Mark was a problem and becoming a bigger one.

There was a soft knock on the door.

"Come in," Thomas called.

Artie Tagliemo came into the study. He was a square, block of a man with sandy hair thinning at the top and cut short, close-set dark eyes and a nose that had been broken at least once. "You wanted to see me?"

"Yes."

"What's up?"

"The problem we spoke of the other day? He's into me for ten large. He says he can get the money but it will take some time."

"You believe him?"

"Doesn't matter. Lisa still thinks he is a man among men. It's not a huge amount so I'm giving him a chance, but I want some eyes on him."

"Okay."

"If he makes good, fine. If not let him know that we are not happy about it. Nothing permanent, but if word gets out that he blew me off . . ." Thomas blew air through his lips and did not finish the sentence.

"Understood. I'll be in touch." Artie turned and walked out of the room.

Thomas shot his French cuffs and picked up the cup of rapidly cooling coffee. Artie was not much for conversation, a trait that Thomas appreciated. Artie simply got things done and done right.

Family problems were a pain. He had bigger tasks to attend to. Thomas DiNapoli put his coffee to one side and started in on a pile of reports in front of him.

E2 Main Street

She was in the hospital for the last time and that was a blessing. No glorious cloud full of angels singing hosannas; no gentle light through yonder windows with soft hands calming fevered brow or anything but the end of agony, the goodbye of withered flesh and tortured mind. *The woman stood in the doorway leading from the bedroom to the hall silhouetted by the overhead light fixture above and behind her. She was all angles and bones, sharp curves, small breasts barely visible under the powder blue peignoir. Her face was shadowed but the light caught the tangled mass of her hair kicking highlights into a glistening halo. I knew she would come in happy she was still alive. I sat on the bed and watched her.*

Johnny Walker sighed and looked around at the huge room that was the ground floor of the Hartford Public Library. He had done everything but what he had come to do and he couldn't help but think of his wife, Beth, in the hospital for the last time. He had checked out the people huddled over the banks of computers built into rows of desks like so many moles burrowing into the fecund earth. He looked down at what he had written and felt like screaming. It was shit. Pure deep shit. He who was full of death could not write about life. How ironic. Just when he really needed to finish the book at least to the point where he could compose a query letter. He crossed out the woman in the doorway. Maybe she was already in the bedroom. Lying on the bed. Naked. And the man was ignoring her. Why? Were they enemies? Maybe he has just rescued her from an awful death at the hands of a psychopath and she wants to thank him. Maybe the writer is a drone and a hack. Walker crossed out the whole page. It was impossible for him to write here even though it had been impossible for him to write at his house, now alone with all his memories of a wife and a life now gone or almost gone. Walker felt more alone than ever. The mole next to him straightened up and yawned widely in toothsome wonder. Good thing that wasn't a fart, Walker smiled to himself, or he would have had to evacuate along with everyone else in the immediate area. Need sustenance. Need booze. Need a new brain. On sale at Sears. Now fifteen percent off but not for men with liver problems or who are pregnant or might become pregnant. He wished he was. Then he'd have something to write about. Could call any publisher. Have a ghost writer do all the work. Laugh all the way to the bank instead of the other way 'round. Wouldn't have to try selling this piece of shit to pay the bills and now with Beth generating bills instead of helping to pay them. Oh me oh my oh.

People drifted up and down the wide corridor between a bank of computer kiosks and the area of computer desks. He watched them as he might storm clouds peeking over purple hillsides. At the end of the corridor a long desk served to dispense information, register books brought in and taken out. The desk bulged at the top in a modernistic outward bow that resembled the prow of a ship. The good ship Hartford, Walker thought, and watched a particularly ugly librarian stacking books behind the counter. Where do they come up with people who work in libraries? Must be a special factory that turns out great intelligence and not much else. The woman looked a little like one of his neighbors who would walk up and down the street on trash day thrusting her arms into the trash cans and bags with a look of single-minded purpose. Long, thin face, slash of a nose. Well so? You're not such a Casanova either Walker reminded himself. Fat little scribbler of me-too trash. You shouldn't throw stones, my man. At least she can look down and see her toes, if she has any. The thought made him smile until he remembered.

He had been a small, overweight boy of eight years dressed in neatly pressed khaki slacks and wearing a white shirt and shined brown leather shoes carefully tied. He walked slowly down the hallway filled with pictures of dead people. He felt their staring eyes watching and judging, critical in the pigmented stillness. He tried not to look at them and walked in the middle of the hallway for he was not looking forward to entering the room at the end of it. His father was waiting for him and the boy knew that when that happened and he had to see his father in THE LIBRARY he was once again in trouble. The door was partly open and the boy sighed softly, and pushed it the rest of the way.

"You know why you're here, don't you?" The man behind the huge desk was powerfully built and darkly handsome with an aquiline nose and brown eyes that sat in a broad expanse of tanned flesh with only slight wrinkles around the eyes and mouth. Brown hair was swept back in waves. He was, indeed, a fine figure of a man, one used to power and the use of it without the rectifying quality of humility, a person for whom the achievement of goals was the ultimate goal. His family seemed merely reminders of his mortality. He was the storm moving mindlessly across the land; the blue skies and sunshine behind and in front of him were something with which he did not have to deal and which, therefore, did not exist in the barren chamber of his imagination.

"Yes, sir."

"I've seen your report card, and I am not impressed. Not at all. You can do much better than B's."

"Yes, sir."

"You are not applying yourself. You are a Walker. We are a proud family that has always excelled in whatever we set our mind to. You have heard this before, but apparently you weren't paying attention. Do you understand me?"

"Yes, sir."

"Very well. Grounded for two weeks and extra work on History and Geography. You will also lose weight. You look like a little balloon. You disgust me. You may leave." The majestic figure behind the desk turned away to focus on more important matters.

Walker grimaced at the memory, disappointed that he still remembered standing there while the old bastard laid into him and went on and on about the family and their achievements and their honor blah blah blah. How often had food been withheld on the excuse that he did not need it and that it was for his own good. Countless the diets, the times of hunger and imagined starvation to lose a few pounds only to lose all the ground gained as soon as possible after the enemy had relaxed his grip on the food intake of young John, not Johnny, for that would be plebian and common, not something in which the Walker family played a part.

His mother had remained a mystery to Walker and was so to the present day. Walker had not spoken with her in years and would be happy to continue that silence until she could speak no more. He regarded his nurse, an Irish girl named Bridgette, as the true source of his upbringing. His mother had been a shadow figure who, when he had been in her presence, had talked of guest lists and invitations, charity events and board meetings. He remembered her as tall and thin, bending over his bed occasionally and staring down at him as if he were an alien being for whom she did not take any direct responsibility. As he got older, she became a person, but not a pleasant one or even one he would come to know, for she was rarely around. You really need to focus on what you're doing, John," she would tell him. "This is not some kind of trivial charade. This is life. It is cold, hard and brutal and if you don't accept that and act accordingly, you will not be in charge, but always be one of those people bleating about how hard it is." She was a woman with an agenda always in her schedule book and later in her computer. She ran everything wonderfully and made most people feel as if they had just taken part in a mud wrestling contest.

Cold she was and cold she is to this day he'd guess. When he left years ago, he had no regrets. They were probably happy as well. Lose the family embarrassment. He hadn't even thought of her in years. She hated Beth. Too plebian and Jewish to boot. They thought he should be a lawyer or a doctor. Yeah, well. Sorry, Ma, guess your one and only was not cut from that bolt of cloth. He'd be better off if he had been, though, and no mistake about that.

Walker looked to his right down the wide corridor that led to the row of doors leading out onto Main Street and that is when he noticed the man. Of all the people moving in and out on library pursuits the man stood out but Walker couldn't really say why.

He was a man of medium height with salt-and-pepper hair and five o'clock shadow. He had on dark slacks and a black polo-style shirt with a blue stripe running across its middle. He wore dark glasses and it was perhaps that which got Walker's attention. He had always looked askance at people who wore shades indoors.

The man slouched slowly through the doors and edged to his right where he would have a good view of the room in general and the information desk in particular. Something about the way he stood and stared fixedly at the desk gave Walker the creeps. Perhaps it was the set of his face or the way he stood apart from everyone else. Walker thought he was lucky not to be the object of the man's attention.

People were walking in and out in a steady stream, and were eyed by the security guard who sat at a little table just to the left of the doors. There sat a woman who looked as if she had just walked out of <u>Little Women.</u> An old man tottered down the center of the aisle clutching a green cloth bag with L. L. Bean imprinted on it in white letters and looking as if he had just come off life support and would keel over and croak momentarily.

As if to refute such a sight, behind him strolled a man who looked as if he spent most of his time in a gym. Broad shoulders, curling brown hair and beard, tiny waist. He reminded Walker of a coach he had known long before in grade school. Walker thought that this man's muscles must have been piled on top of each other. He held a stack of books in one giant hand that made them look like pamphlets. Walker grimaced and looked down at his own belly that flowed over his belt and pushed against the side of the desk. Never had much of a chance in that area either. Not that he didn't try when he was a kid. He tried and tried. Didn't like being one of nature's little jokes.

"Walker. Front and center." Coach, huge muscles that seemed to bulge everywhere even around his eye sockets eyed Walker with a basilisk stare. "Walker, you Druid, get over here."

And there he was front and fat and center but thinking that he had lost three pounds and was lean and mean, a calisthenics machine. "Yes coach." Front and center.

"Are you worthy?"

"Yes coach."

"Are you ready?" Now he remembered a smirk but then he saw encouragement and responded.

"Yes coach."

"Up the rope then, tiger."

"Yes coach."

"Right." He looked at the rope snaking up into the stratosphere and disappearing into the clouds above Olympus where the gods had their swimming pool complete with naked nymphs serving martinis. He knew he was screwed. Knew he was lost and then forgotten on the rope, at his house, in every situation that he could imagine at that age except maybe for Florence Gustaffsen who, if his ego allowed him to think it, was even worse off than he and smiled at Walker(oooh gross you pig) in history class (don't touch me I'll turn green and my dick will fall off). So he gripped the rope, and the rest of the gym class leaned forward as if watching "Casablanca".

He probably resembled Clarabelle the clown. His arms trembled. His chins wiggled, and his belly jiggled but his feet never left the ground. His face must have been beet red from the effort but nothing happened. Gravity was a greater force than his muscles. He could hear the other boys snickering between themselves. Embarrassment flushed his cheeks and burned in his gut like a hot coal.

"Okay, Walker" the coach said not unkindly in manner or mien. "Need a little more work on that. Okay, next up. You Gerdens. You laughed the loudest. Up you go."

Little Andy Gerdens, more snake than boy, rose up the rope like a fucking cobra. Walker stood to one side, breathing hard as Andy reached the large knot in the rope about twenty feet off the floor and hung there smiling and waving down at us. Walker wanted desperately to conjure a pistol out of thin air and shoot him off that rope.

Walker sat back in his chair and closed his eyes. What he needed was some inspiration, preferably liquid, but since he was here, maybe a little Lee Child or Greg Iles would loosen up his mind and get his prose flowing. Yes, he told himself. Yes that might do the trick. What a trickster. Sly Stallone and the Wiki Walker. He got up and walked over to the information desk where the lady he had seen was helping a student with a reference book question. A face of lines, up and down, not deep but defining, and lips with no lipstick, smooth, brown eyes but with little gold flecks. High nose thin, a slash that went with the lips. Not beautiful no, but

"May I help you, sir?"

"Huh?" Walker realized that the person ahead of him had finished. "Uh," he stuttered "mysteries. I mean where are they?"

"Mezzanine. Up the stairs."

He didn't hear what she said. In his head the harpies were swinging low sweet chariot. It was the fact that he was hungry, Walker decided and told her "thank you, ma'am" and, turning away, walked from the desk still deep in thought and feeling. Sure and what do you do now some deep voice echoed within the space between his ears. Be a writer. Never drop your pants in public. Unless you have a godlike gift and are young. Publish learned meaningless pieces. Write essays and hold literary teas. Speak nonsense and all will bow before your erudition. Quote Milton. Milton wasn't writing all the time. He probably drank tea when he was of sober state. Walker came back to the present with the feeling that he had, once again, made a fool of himself.

She laughed, a musical note no notes for it was really a trill, a rising series of notes much like that of a Pan Pipe, not shrill or unpleasant but sounding more of a welcome into the space of the person issuing them. Come in come in and be welcome stranger to the inn at the crossroads and rest your weary legs before the fire while your noble steed is taken in and fed on oats and sheltered from the storm. Come and hear the notes of my life for they are not those of war and savagery but those of peace and friendship.

Walker walking away was not the same Walker that approached, but Walker walking away had no idea that this was so. Instead he walked up the stairs to the stacks beyond.

The sun burned a hole through him as Walker stood outside the Travelers waiting for the E2 bus. He felt stupid and broken, an overloaded machine that had been reduced to a box of smoking junk. He looked down at his feet sticking out of the Teves sandals. Heat and earth, heat and earth, burned and buried for all he was worth. He fanned at his face with the notebook containing his manuscript. That was about all it was good for, he thought. Poor old man. Never did anything much with your life. Sired a kid you don't even like to be around now. There's something special. Worked as a cube rat for thirty years and your salary did not even cover everything and Beth had to go out and work though she probably would have anyway. Never much of a stay-at-home mom type. Just another itty-bitty life and getting meaner every minute and where the hell is that stupid bus? A person could die standing out here in the middle of summer with the concrete canyon walls surrounding him.

Walker stood in the sun scourging himself with savage ecstasy tumbling into the hot, dark depths of himself where he stood in judgment of his total inability to accomplish anything that might move the human experience along even one iota. He was just one of billions crawling in and out of their little hills, back and forth in a brief moment of determination, a spasm of hill building and food collection. He felt like lying down in the street and waiting for the dammed bus to come along and run over him.

He scratched at a bug bite on the back of his neck. It was probably infected and then it would turn cancerous and he would walk around with his head tilted at an angle until he died just before the earth itself exploded. Bastard bug. The thought made him laugh in spite of himself. All right, so he was never going to a great American author and he wasn't going to ever be rich but what the Hell. He could keep on trying. No harm in that was there and one never knew what might come along tomorrow or the next day, did one. No sireee Bob. You just never knew. A huge black woman pushing a tiny dark blue baby stroller waddled past, her eyes dark and incurious passed over him and moved on as if he was not even there. The baby, dressed in a pink sun suit, stared up at Walker with wide-eyed wonder. Walker smiled back. He could not remember anyone ever looking at him that way. Maybe Beth all those years ago but that look was one of love, or at least that is what he had named it and had returned it fourfold. Walker thought he had probably been wrong but it mattered little now.

The blunt blue and white front of the bus turned the corner from Gold Street and moved towards him with majestic deliberation. It was one of the buses that had been turned into a gigantic moving advertisement along its sides. This one had the face of a lawyer advertising his integrity and honesty in the time-honored tradition of ambulance chasing. A four foot face full of huge white teeth smiled out at Walker. Go on, it seemed to say. Get hit by a drunk driver. I'll get justice for you. I know how to deal with the mega insurance companies that want to settle for pennies on the dollar and I will win for you a big wad of cash but I'll take a big chunk of that, thank you very much and then Uncle Sam will want a big chunk of what's left so you'll be lucky to end up with enough money to pay for that new motorized wheel chair . . . Jesus Christ on roller skates. The air brakes popped as it drew to a stop and the doors swished aside leaving Walker staring into the belly of the beast and the thin, elderly uniformed driver sitting in the driver's seat. The man seemed both amazed and outraged at his own boredom and, turning his head slowly, looked at Walker as a Monitor lizard might look at a tit mouse.

And Walker was then possessed by an acute panic, a sense of fear and singularity that seemed to fill every cell of his body. The darkness of the bus's interior swallowed his thought while the driver's face turned into a huge grotesque mask with white hairs growing from the nostrils and deep set eyes the color of blood, glowing like red hot coals and filled with malicious intent. The whole bus seemed to reach out to suck him into its depths where it could deal with Walker at its leisure. He opened his mouth to scream but nothing would come out. Not a peep. His throat had turned into the Kalahari Desert and closed down upon itself. A low moan was the best he could manage.

"Hey buddy. You need to either get on the bus or stand back. Are you okay?"

The driver's voice sounded as if he were talking through a wad of cotton. Walker made a monumental effort and pulled himself onto the bus. He wobbled in front of the driver while he fished in his pocket for the monthly pass hoping that the bus and everything around him would settle into one place and stay there. He pushed the pass into the machine;

it beeped and spat it back out to him and he turned and, with what seemed a tremendous effort, lurched towards an area of emptiness in front of him. The bus started up again and he felt himself propelled forward and only by gripping the metal bars that ran overhead along each side of the bus for the standing passengers was he able to swing himself around and collapse into an empty seat with a force that left him slightly out of breath. He wondered what the fuck he had just experienced. Had he almost fainted? Heat stroke? It was certainly hot enough. Heart attack? He tried to normalize his breathing and settled for a panic attack. Everyone stressed out at one time or another. He probably just needed to relax and get something in his stomach. Food. That was the ticket. Too much sitting around fretting about the manuscript. As if to confirm his suspicions, his stomach rumbled gently.

"Excuse me."

Something jabbed him in the ribs. Looking to his left, he found himself staring down at an elderly lady who was jabbing him in the side with her right elbow and glaring up at him as if he had just been caught trying to cut into a long line at the movie theater. "What?"

"You're sitting on my bag."

"What? Ohh . . ." Walker looked down where part of the woman's bag disappeared under one haunch. He stood up and she pulled the bag onto her lap. It was small enough to be a wallet. No wonder he hadn't felt it. "I'm sorry," he told her and he sat back down staring straight ahead at a huge lady in tight-fitting jeans and a bright yellow blouse who had sat down on the bench seat that was directly in front of him and ran along the side of the bus. She was even bigger than he was, Walker thought with a sense of satisfaction. He sat up straighter in his seat, pushed his chest out and tried to bring his belly in. He wasn't really in bad shape after all. Not really. There were people who were worse off.

"Hey. Are you going to be sick?"

Walker turned and found that the old woman had shrunk back against the side of the bus and was regarding him with a mixture fear and suspicion. He couldn't help himself. He let out the breath that he had been holding and chuckled loudly. "No. Of course not."

"I see. Just pretending?" she commented.

"Ehhh?" Was the woman teasing him? He didn't even know her but there she sat staring at him with a punky know-it-all smirk on her lips as if he were wearing a straight jacket.

"You swelled up just like a blowfish I saw on National Geographic. I thought maybe you were pretending to be one." She turned away and stared out the window at the commercial dump that was Farmington Ave.

A blowfish? A BLOWFISH? Walker wanted to punch that wrinkled, sour, old face hard enough to put her through the side of the bus. He glared at her hoping that she would feel badly at having insulted a total stranger. She would be contrite and ask his forgiveness. He would be magnanimous, smile gently and tell her that she should not worry about it at all. Not at all. He probably had looked somewhat bloated. She did not turn her head, though, but looked out the window in determined silence. Bitch. Had she spoken with an accent? French, perhaps. They were a rude and arrogant race. No wonder she was such a CUNT. He might not be as skinny as some people but he was most definitely not a fucking blowfish. Walker thought about moving to another seat but found that idea embarrassing. He would be dammed and in Hell eating soy protein and lawn clippings before he would stage that kind of retreat. He made a show of opening his pad and studying all the blank pages until he came to the one on which he had scribbled in the library. Witty repartee, he thought. he needed a come-back that would even the scales. He stared at her malevolently but could think of nothing to say. Just like the rest of his miserable existence. He could never quite understand the world around him or respond in a way he thought he should. At parties he was always the one to blush at a dirty joke while forgetting any he might have known, dirty or otherwise. People would stop talking when he approached and start again when he moved away as if he were some freak winter storm in Miami. At work, he would sit at his desk and listen to co-workers chatting back and forth around him and not say a word not because he didn't want to but all the words he could think of seemed ill chosen and juvenile and he ended up smiling like a stupid asshole and saying nothing.

Blowfish. The word bounced between his ears growing louder with each passing bounce. He was a fat man in a skinny world. Fatso, blimpy, two-chins, lardo, pig, porky, pasta bowl, beach ball, oozo, hippo hips, among many others and now blowfish. Because of his weight, people thought him less intelligent, less capable of doing anything. He was certainly self indulgent and probably had horrible table manners. Doing things that others took for granted was an exercise in masochism such as bending over to pick up a magazine from the floor or loading the dishwasher. When he walked past, people whispered behind their hands. When he joined a group, they would look at him and then at each other. Uh oh. The walrus has arrived. At the company picnic (when he worked for one that considered employees to be revenue generators instead of cost drivers) no one even bothered to ask him if he wanted to join a softball team or any other team (except perhaps beer imbibing in college when it didn't matter what you looked like as long as you could chug). His whole life had been spent walking along the side of the road not because of his lack of wit or intelligence or because of a perverse personality that enjoyed fugues and satanic chants oh no but simply because of his belly, that massive protrusion of his body that he had long ago given up trying to vanquish losing both pride and money in the process. He had long ago accepted the quiet jibes and noisy jokes from the jocks standing around showing off their hairy muscles and flat bellies. It was the unintentional bigotry of those who considered themselves free of such displays of small spirit that still hurt way down behind the grins and shrugs. In his whole life he had only known one person who he had liked and respected both for what he did and what he said. In truth, Parson Bean had a funny name but was six feet five and a wrestler in college and built like a brick shithouse. Smart as shit, too. Rhodes scholar if Walker remembered correctly. Parson had come into a bar where Walker had been holding down one section near the wall for a while. He had come in flanked by jocks flashing his white teeth and neck muscles that could have belonged to a gorilla. He did not even have to say a word. The crowd of students jammed against the bar parted as if faced with a biblical miracle and Parson strolled up and leaned on the bar next to Walker. He looked to his left and found Walker investigating the color of the bottom of his beer glass.

"Hi. Name's Parson."

Walker did not at first realize that he was being addressed, and continued to stare at his glass.

"Hey. I'm talking to you." Parson nudged Walker in the side with an elbow.

Walker looked up into an all American steak and potatoes grandma apple pie road signs advertising Crest smile. "Hello."

"I'm Parson."

"I'm sure." Walker felt in his pocket for money he already knew was not there. Shit. Time to go.

"You're sure?"

Why was this guy still talking to him? "Yes"

"Sure of what?"

"Sure that you are what you claim to be."

Parson looked at him perplexed, perhaps even momentarily confused. Then he suddenly burst out in laughter. "Yes I am. And you are?"

"Broke."

"Well, broke. You're a fat fuck but you talk a good one as my daddy sometimes says." He wiggled an eyebrow and the bartender, who had been doing his best to ignore Walker, suddenly appeared in front of him. A beer for me and one for my friend, Broke, here."

"My name's Johnny Walker."

"How cool is that? Bartender, a black label for my friend the broke scotch."

Walker couldn't help himself. He started with a smile and ended up with a gut shaking belly laugh. He had a most unlikely friend. Now, forty years later, he still had fond memories of Parson. Last he heard, Parson was a politician. Go figure. Congressman from Massachusetts.

The woman next to him reached up and pulled the yellow cord. As the bus veered right and pulled up to the next stop, she got up, ignored Walker, and marched off into her own reality.

Walker sat there and stewed and ruminated and stewed and felt hunger pangs rumbling like thunder inside and wondered whether there was still a steak and that half bag of oven fries in his freezer. The meat would go in the pan with mushrooms and onions sautéing and the red juice just beginning to appear in delicate drops on top of the steak. Potatoes crisply done and hot from the oven with lots of salt and butter. Just the ticket. Walker felt saliva rising in his mouth at the thought. Memories of his recent encounter vanished as Walker determined to buy a steak at Vincent's market if he didn't have one at the house. His immediate future settled, he leaned back into his seat and gazed through the bus's window with a fair degree of equanimity. It would not last long but his ignorance of that fact served as its own tiny moment of joy.

E2 Caliban Street

The little red cape sat sulking behind a hedge of straggling bushes as if embarrassed by its sagging gutters and peeling paint. The short driveway sported grass growing in the cracks of the asphalt leading up to a carport that sagged at one end while threatening to come completely off the concrete posts at the other. Actually, Walker thought as he walked down the short street containing a hodgepodge of multi-family and single family homes set back behind the shade of maple and oaks, an occasional birch and one pine, the house felt nothing at all. He was just associating a state of being with it. There was no doubt in his mind, though, that his scraggly hedge that made the house look like an old woman with no clothes on. Tired, saggy, old house. It had looked that way for years not because they liked living in a rundown heap but the medical bills had begun to mount and money became very tight. Only the blue and white For Sale sign in the dirt of the front yard changed the way the house appeared to the world. Perhaps it was the sign that blew his good mood all to shit.

Sure. Blame the sign. Been there for a while now. Part of the landscape and will be there a while longer, he thought. It's not just the sign but all that went with it, all the stuff they'd accumulated and all the memories that went with the patchy grass in the back yard, the battered front door, the stained kitchen counter where Jen had tried her first chemistry experiment. Boy, had he been pissed. Now it was just an object and not a home, once a wife and soon alone.

Walker walked past the sign and turned right along the slightly tilted concrete sections that led to the two steps rising up to the tiny front porch. The twenty-year-old Volkswagen beetle in the driveway said it all. Jen was here. The car had probably been a maroon color in the beginning but it had been repainted a latrine green at some point and now both colors showed around the rust holes in the body panels and where the green was flaking off on the back engine cover. The bumpers were covered with stickers old and new, some pasted over ones already there. Simple signs for simple minds, Walker decided.

Feeling depressed and resigned, Walker stood on his own porch not wanting to go in but left with nowhere else to go. Maybe, he thought, he wouldn't go in. Maybe he would just sit on the porch in the old wicker rocker that left his ass hanging low and watch the day slowly die waving its cloaks and banners in a diurnal display of pyrotechnics pinking a red and gray and purpling and blue like a dancing girl from Vegas putting on her makeup. It is quiet here and it is still here and soon it will not be here. He looked longingly at the old chair, sighed softly, and walked across the porch.

Walker gripped the corroded aluminum handle of the screen door that guarded the peeling wood of the front door and turned the old handle, twisting down hard on the harmless metal turned back to look at the old sugar maple guarding the front yard with its gnarled arms waving silently at him. For decades it had been a provider of perches from where birds could sit and poop on heads below. BINGO. Right on a baldy, buckaroo. Ah and there a Catholic. Notice the red scalp. Strict they are. She shoots she scores. Two points. No birds today, though. Just the tree, green and airless seemingly painted onto the scene by an ill-tempered child with purloined paints. Ahh childhood. One could do worse than be a swinger of birches. He thought reading that as a child was the crux of the matter. Bend but don't break, Walker thought.

In front of him the front door opened with a muffled CHUMP. "Hi, Dad." Big eyes. Wide and blue tilted just a little. A fat face of puffs and domes of flesh plunging downward past the mail slot of a mouth to double chins that always seemed to be slightly dirty.

She had never looked much like him or Beth. Some long dead ancestor had their last joke he supposed. Hiding out among the genes and chromosomes and stepping up to give her blonde hair, now fashionably streaked and drawn back. It was so incredible that she would slide out of Beth with that hair. Beth, his black haired beauty on top of him, the brown haired beast. "Hi, Jen." And now Walker was hungry again and needed fiercely to piss but could not move. It was as if he were looking down at some small, pudgy guy who could not decide what he wanted to do and so stood there trembling with the need of the bladder but afraid to go into the house. How laughable. Like one of those Tom and Jerry cartoons. Jen had parts of both Beth and he as well in her stubborn will and need to determine all and settle everything and for that which must be broken. He decided to wait another minute no thirty seconds if she gave him that long.

"Are you coming in?" Jen pushed out through the door, her belly pushing out of her orange tank top and spilling over her blue jeans like some huge fish trying to get back to the sea.

Twenty-five, twenty-six, twenty-seven, twenty-eight, twenty-nine to hell with it. "Yep. Gotta run to the bathroom. Make yourself a drink if you want one." And then he brushed past her and through the living room to the little bath off the back hallway. He stood over the toilet but then nothing happened. Beth had been like that when they first told her, he remembered. She was feeling fine, looking good, walking and talking, drinking and eating. Walker stood holding himself, stretching it a little hoping to break the seal and finally the release, just a few drops at first. That bathroom had been the scene of so much pain. Beth had been fine and feeling great. Just a stomach ache, darling. I'll be fine in a day or two. No problem really and then the first stomach cramps had knifed her over, stabbing down into the guts of her and so quick that she could not help but scream. Staggering in to vomit He frowned and suddenly he peed, the stream hot and piercing and sighed with relief as it weakened, working its way methodically from the back of the bowl to the front. Compensate, compensate. We had tried but there was no compensation, no religion, no mercy nothing but the hospital beds and tubes and machines that whirred and beeped and pills that made a zombie seem lively in comparison. God was on vacation it seemed and no amount of prayer, pleading, shouts, denunciations, or whispers could change the course during the nights when he had held Beth as she screamed and writhed in my arms, a mindless, bulgy-eyed beast insensate and ineluctable.

Walker finished but stood over the bowl, his mind full the night and days and finally the final ambulance and he shook his dick feeling a mildly pleasant sensation as he did so. Get the last drop. Wear clean undies. What if you were in an accident and had to go to the hospital? What then? They would see all the yellow stains and what would they think of you then, Johnny boy? He could still hear his father's voice standing behind him always demanding. Walker pushed it back into his pants and zipped up with a quick upward motion and a pull at his pants.

"Dad? Are you all right in there?" came Jen's voice muffled from beyond the door.

"Coming right out." Walker looked at the wall in front of him at the line of fat white fishes rolling and trolling along in a line in the middle of a sea of pale blue wallpaper. They could not help or answer. They blued and moved through the lit depths immune to the emotional warps of the human race their very creators. Around and around the tub and the shower head and the cabinet they moved in their groove never up never down round and round in perfect stillness with perfect poise above the rushing waters and the noise.

Jen met him with a glass half full with Jack Daniels and two lonely ice cubes throwing off sparkles from their surface. "I thought perhaps you sat down with the seat still up and got stuck." She smiled that gamin smile that mixture of tooth and lip that had amazed and entranced him when she had been a child. Daddy, are you going to work? Will you buy me something and then that smile would dissolve his harshest resolve, dissolve all feeling of being used, dissolve parental sternness kneeling down before the laughing eyes and twist of tooth and lip. He would tell her that she need not ask for something too often for she would not get it and then instantly regretting his words as her huge eyes filled with tears the size of a swimming pool.

"No such luck," Walker replied. If there was still a woman in the house to bitch about the toilet seat, he would have been the happiest man on earth. He sipped at the Jack felt the acrid liquid sliding in moist warm darkness down and filling his entire system with a momentary glow. Even Jen seemed charmed and happy.

"Dad, I want you to meet a friend of mine." She turned back towards the living room and Walker, following behind her saw a bald head, deep green eyes above a leather vest and dirty jeans. The eyes glared out at him, phosphorescence in a dark pool. "This is Moses. That's not her real name, of course, but we call her that because she is so wise."

"Hey," Intoned Moses looking as if she were about to fall asleep on her feet

"Hello." Walker felt as if he had suddenly stepped into a movie set of explorers after they had been captured by aborigines. Moses had metal rings in both ears and through her nose. God only knew what other parts of her body were pierced. The very thought was painful. "So what brings you by today?" he asked the back of his daughter's head. He knew but he was dammed if he was going to be the first to come out and say it.

"Broke as usual." Had a job at McD's for a while but lost it. "Can you loan me a little to tide me over?" Jenny walked over to Moses, turned, put her arm around the girl and stared at her father as if daring him to say anything about the obvious. "How 'bout it?"

"What makes you think I'm rolling in cash? Why do you think the house is for sale?"

C'mon, Dad. I'm not asking for a bundle." She eyed him suspiciously as if he had just announced that they were going to play bank robber and she would be the bank. "I saw your light blinking so I checked messages. Couple from me. Someone named Sabrina left a message about selling this place. You should check your machine more often."

"Why?" Why indeed was he so anxious to hear her pleas for cash? Was he in a big rush to list the house? Nope but it would have to be done somewhere in a span of time that he didn't even want to define yet. Time enough to do that when time has run out along with choices and laughter.

"A question that echoes in the tunnel of time," said Moses.

"See what I mean, Dad? About Moses here?" Jenny hugged her friend and sighed in admiration. "She's just awesome."

Walker found he was feeling a little nauseous. If that was what passed for the wisdom of the ages, he should have no problem finding an agent for his manuscript should he ever complete it. "That's nice of Sabrina," Walker mumbled with noticeable lack of enthusiasm. God damn her soul though he really shouldn't for she is just doing her job and it is no one's fault that medicine and the human mixture of life and death are so dammed expensive. If I go in for a routine physical it costs over two hundred dollars and the blood tests probably another hundred and yes the insurance pays most or maybe even all of it but we all end up paying for it in the end cause there is no fucking free lunch out there not at all and Beth is dying long and hard of a disease that has flown by the insurance lifetime maximums as if they were a child's allowance and now the house must pay the devil or the devil will have his due. At least this way I can walk away with a few dollars. Enough to start again maybe but how one does that I'm damned if I know cause I'm not even sure I can do it all again without her. I really just don't know. Here we are sitting in the living room counting our pennies. At least I'm counting mine and Beth lies over there in Hartford Hospital intubated and wired for sound and doped up to the max and here it is as if nothing were going on. The old couch still sags. The blueberry stain on the faux oriental carpet is still there. All is normal but all is a nightmare in flux.

"So how 'bout it?" Jen reminded him. "We gotta split, you know?"

"So split"

"I need it."

Walker sighed. Why me, an inside voice full of self-lamentation asked? Well why not you came the reply. Why that mountain? Well, because I am here. How much to get rid of her for a while? And her significant other. Can't believe this. Can't picture them naked and entwined between sweaty sheets. Wouldn't do much good to bitch about it. Just make things worse, I imagine. Maybe if I give them something, they'll at least take a bath.

"So like how long does it take to sell a house?" The sheen of avarice reflected in Jen's eyes and pulled at the corners of her plump lips. Jen let go of her squeeze and came towards him as Walker reached behind him and pulled his wallet out of his pocket. "I don't mean to sound hard, you know, but soon they'll be some funds available, you know what I mean?" She took the twenty dollars that he handed her and went back to stand beside Moses. "I know Mom is costing a fortune."

"No you don't. You know nothing of that. All you know is that she is sick and that makes it very difficult for everyone." Walker told her harshly. "You have no idea. I know this little old house is history, but it holds a lifetime of memories for me."

"And for me. I grew up here, after all."

"Yes. You did." Somehow, though, Walker did not think that Jennifer's memory went back much further back than the last meal or job. He wondered with an almost physical feeling of sadness where he and Beth had gone wrong. What moment or moments had occurred that had so shaped their daughter that she should grow up to be a fat little hippie with slogans in place of common sense? Had there been a time when she looked up at them smiling and asking something and whatever they had replied had turned her in a different direction? Some small act or lack of action, some word or look, some deed or misdeed? Where do we start really and in what small space do our personalities and characters first spark?

Jen came to a halt and looked down at him. "Thanks for the loan, Dad."

"Yes, of course." *Some loan. I'll never see it back but nevermind.*

"Sabrina'll be over tomorrow night." Her eyes were so hopeful, a face of expectation that he could not disappoint even if he had a choice. "Dad, we need." She stopped and turned her head to the left to look out the picture window as if to gather her thoughts or gain a fresh perspective on her subject.

Walker saw the hardness of it, the set of her jaw and the crinkled skin around her eyes. The window broke her face into triangles.

"We need to talk about after."

"The sale," Walker finished.

"Yes." Wooden. A still life in oil daubs of white and green, red, ochre, royal blue, charcoal, pimento, burnt sienna, teal, copper, cornflower yellow. Streaks of gray. A blob blue eye looking out and in at light around and in. Impressionist style.

"I send money to the hospital, the doctors, the light company, the oil company, the electric company, the bank, Master Charge, Visa, Walmart, and the list goes on and yourself, of course. That's after Sabrina takes her cut and the lawyers take their cut."

His daughter brushed at imaginary flies. "I didn't mean that, Dad."

"No?" Walker knew what she meant, but he wanted her to say it out loud. He wanted to hear it for reasons that were long lost within himself. Vindication perhaps or revolt among the masses leading to universal conviction. Religion as a placebo not an opiate. Hope springs eternal. He sipped at his drink and stared up at Jennifer.

"Money is the root of all evil," intoned Moses walking up and standing behind Jennifer. "We should all work the land or what substitutes for it today and provide each for his tribe through communal efforts."

Walker stared at her in amazement. His daughter actually simpered, her cheeks spreading out like white sheets on a line. "It seemed to work real well in Russia," he sneered at Moses.

"That was mishandled, obviously," Moses replied. "Like totally blown, you know what I mean? Like all those guys in Moscow kept telling everyone what to do and everyone outside of Moscow told them to piss off, you know? But with the right leadership it can be cool."

"People just don't work well that way. Sharing is not an instinctive part of our makeup. It is something that has to be learned. And if you don't get anywhere after working hard at something, you tend to work a lot less hard at that something." Money, honey. Gotta have it. Love is not free. No man is an island; he's a traveling dick. She wants to move in with this idiot. Could be she already has and now is an official club member in good standing mooching off of others and sneering at the rest of the

23

world. They were part of the disaffected, human flotsam that drifts slowly along the edge of life most of them because they weren't well equipped to deal with their environment financially or emotionally but some because they pervert their surroundings and call the side street the main road and go around advertising this only to despise those who still think that the big wide street with all the shops on it and the churches at each end is main street. I suppose I felt like that when I was young. God knows I thought my parents were awful and my life was awful at least until I met Beth but I never threw out everything did I? So now I have to deal with the fact that my daughter is clinging to this dirty, ignorant cunt and thinks that she is on the cutting edge of societal improvement. "Believe me, communal living does not usually work out. The Israelis have the best model for that in the Kibbutz. There it is driven by necessity and is an integrated part of their society."

"Yeah, well look at you, Pops. What has all those years slaving away at a desk got you? You're still out on your ass with your hat in your hand."

He wanted to turn on the oven and stuff her in it. Horrible way to ruin a perfectly good oven though and I needed it working for the house to sell. "We did okay. We raised you, put food on the table and kept a warm, dry roof over our heads. I never had to walk around asking charity from people. And I do useful work and make a living from it, thank you very much." There. That should shut her up.

"That was nasty, Dad. You're not even trying to understand, you know? Like everyone works and everyone contributes. I just thought you wouldn't mind helping out a little but I guess I was wrong. I mean, you could, like, be a part of it, you know?" Her eyes brightened at that thought. "Like unofficially, right Moses?" She turned to Moses and then back towards me.

"Sure. Unofficially," Moses said her eyes snapping her contempt.

"Thank you, sweetheart, but I'm sure I'll be better off on my own." So much for steak tonight, he grumped as he remembered his empty wallet.

He did not mind being alone; in fact, he welcomed alone. Alone we come and alone we go. Hohoho. In sixty years lots forgotten but lots to yet forget. So much shit clogging up the pipes and filling all the memory cells with junk. Pot boilers read on the bus. Spy conquers alien menace. Menace complains to the department of Consumer Protection. What about junk food that tastes like crap, gives you indigestion and costs big bucks for what you get. He should make a list. Pages and pages in length. Things he didn't like. Things best forgotten. Probably turn out longer than any book. Bet there's lots of people that feel the same way. How about liberals shouting that it's all our fault people drive planes into our buildings? We should kiss their Arab asses and leave them alone to plan their next big gig. Is that fucking insane or what? They say we should get out of Iraq. Count to ten, turn around, put our hands up and walk away. That's a juicy one. Bet all the families that sacrificed a family member for our way of life don't agree with that philosophy. How about political lawn signs? Simple signs for simple minds. IMPEACH BUSH. Right. That's right up there next to outright treason in a time of war and sacrifice. Still it's their right to put the signs up. It's what makes this country great. Say what you want, well, almost. Banning Tom Sawyer from the public schools. Our public schools suck. A thicket of rules and regulations and bureaucrats who haven't the common sense to interpret them. Private schools same problem as the Catholics. Swear above but the flesh must out. Censorship. Best forgotten in all its forms. Insidious and evil. If all we have is what a committee believes is proper, then we will always be an uncivilized society standing on the edge of the cliff of barbarism. Lemmings. All people should not have to accept the opinion of the majority, sometimes just a vocal minority, Group think. You will be as we are or you will be punished. How far away from the edge of darkness are we when a seven year old child gets expelled from school for hugging a classmate who had helped him. Madness disguised as sensible discipline. Every single one of us is racist. Black, white, yellow, red whatever color you are baby you prefer your tribe to any other. There's not a person on this earth who naturally rejects the familiar and embraces the foreign. Acquired taste type of thing. We have to learn how to accept change and live with different kinds of people. Add to list of "Don't Like" raw onions, people with a phone seemingly permanently plugged into one ear, underpants in the summertime, people who don't listen to phone prompts, people who follow rules instead of common sense, telemarketers, telephone surveys, strong fish, weak coffee, lawn cuttings disguised as salad greens, ATM fees, debit card fees, and dealing with snow and ice.

"Hello. Earth to Dad."

Walker came out of his reverie with a start. "What? Oh sorry, just thinking," he told her. Well, forget that. This was no time for thinking about likes and dislikes except how much he disliked this conversation and how hungry he was and as his stomach rumbled like a line of thunderstorms racing across a placid sea. Walker envisioned a rib eye steak an inch or maybe an inch and one quarter with a strip of rich fat running down the outside and well marbled on the inside. Red juices just welling up from within the warm depths spurting out onto the plate where the pride of Idaho lay open beneath a huge chunk of melting butter. Walker looked at his empty glass and rose from his chair, a man on a mission.

"Damnit. This is what I mean. You just don't listen." Jennifer trailed behind as he went into the kitchen and opened the refrigerator.

"Curses," Walker yelled with his head in the freezer. "Almost nothing to eat." He slammed the door with a soft whummp. The motor at the base of the unit kicked on with a soft hum. "And yes," he said turning to face his daughter, "I do listen." He completed the turn and stared out of the kitchen window at the tiny litter strewn yard beyond the kitchen. It had become overgrown through the years, Walker realized. The hardy rhododendrons beneath the kitchen window almost obscured it now. Through the branches he could just see the tiny shed where he kept the mower and some long-disused garden tools and then the wooden fence marking the back boundary. Gotta get that trimmed, he thought. Maybe the new owner could do that. He'd get more money if he did it though.

Frozen beef tips in wine sauce. Walker made a face. For the executive on the run, a perfect solution. Eat tips on trips. Made with real beef. Walker held the small cardboard box in his hand feeling it begin to thaw in his hand. So much for a sizzling rib eye. No money for that now anyway. Nor in the future, he supposed. Oh well. Independence costs. Everyone knows that. "I know, Jenny. Just let it be." He pulled the plastic container of frozen meat and potatoes out of its carton and dropped it onto the counter by the white grinning face of the microwave. Chomp chomp. Instant meal. Yum yum.

"Are you going tonight?" Jennifer laced her fingers across her stomach. White worms wriggling in the kitchen light across her stomach and then back again. Like rowing a boat, Walker thought, finger paddles back and forth.

"Yes." And poured more Jack into his glass and taking a sip, feeling the liquor romping and stomping riding down the chute of him. Yes, he would go. He always went. Beth was just there like a fleshy altar laid out in white and long on white sheets and white flesh before which he would pray. It was the stuff of philosophers and all Walker could do was sit there before her altar and wonder what went on inside and wonder does she feel pain long gone he hoped. Please.

"She won't know." Sorrow in her blue eyes too.

"She may not hear, but know?"

"She won't."

"I don't know. There is no way to tell."

"We will pray. I pray every day."

"Thank you. I will tell her."

"She won't know."

"Oh ye of little faith, prayer a day or not." Walker watched his daughter withdraw and felt guilty that he had brought out that irony to no constructive purpose. Her lips thinned to a line like darkness advancing up a cliff's edge shadowed with tufted grasses. She'd had it as a child, that taking-my-toy-and-going-home look to her. All through school. She was sunny as a baby, though. He wondered what had happened? Walker sighed and tried to smile at his big child there standing with frown in place and arms akimbo. "Come with me?" he asked again.

"No thanks. I hate hospitals. Beside's I just went yesterday," she lied standing primly upright in the doorway. "Gotta split now. Thanks for the loan. Check in with you later and all that jazz."

Cute for sure she had been but no more and now like a bitch in heat following the other unwashed around like smell on a turd.

Walker wondered why he even bothered to ask as he stood in his kitchen with the beef tips dripping water onto the gray linoleum floor underneath the counter. To his left, spread open on the counter, was the Sunday Courant through which he had been browsing before taking his sheets of paper and leaving for the library. Some Democrat was getting a photo op criticizing the war in Iraq. Stupid bitch, he thought. Doesn't have a clue. Like to see her face if el Qaeda blew up the Golden Gate Bridge. Below that was a rant about all the wrong doings and failures of the president and the government he led. Easy to criticize. Like to see any of these dicks do any better. The paper was a rag without doubt and he should have chucked it before he left, but, other than that, the kitchen was picked up. Dishes washed and put away. No slime on the counters or trash on the floor.

Walker went back into the living room and stood in the middle of it staring out the picture window unable to move or even think. He had been turned into a statue. It was as if the emotional tides of his life had come in and gone out and left him behind on the shore bleached white and cleansed of all thought and pretense, motionless and emotionless.

When he came back to the present, he saw the small stack of typed pages that was the skeleton of his novel.

How long had he been working on this book, Walker wondered? What if no one liked the words he chose? He didn't like them and so why did he write them to begin with? Years of putting off and putting off and further and further off until he could not hear the sound of the words anymore and not see their power and beauty and shunned all but the most plebian use of them. He had chosen foreign fields on which to fight away from home and hearth. He wrote and discarded and wrote again trying to ignore the failures and blunders for the greater good being done by just the physical act, by the grace gained simply by doing it even if the result was garbage and he judged it so again and again but kept putting them down like shovelfuls of sand on an icy road. Slipped and broke his ass anyway. He was still getting back up, though. Dammed if he was not still getting back up. "I have to get ready," he mumbled to himself. He went back into the kitchen, held up the frozen dinner and turned back to the counter and the waiting microwave.

"Yeah, okay. Gotta make like the wind and blow, Dad. Catch you later."

Walker nodded without turning around hoping that his daughter and Moses would make it back much later and then felt guilty that he should feel so. Moses was a total loss but Jennifer. Jesus H. Christ on a crutch. There had to be something he could do to get her back on track. Money was always a problem but once the house sold maybe he could take a little of it, but somehow he doubted that money was the answer. He hoped it was just a stage of rebellion that she would grow through and come out okay on the other side. That thought was followed immediately by the realization that such a supposition was a lame excuse allowing him to do nothing.

A memory snapped across his mind, one of being stuck, yes years back when he had taken Jennifer into downtown Hartford to buy her mother a birthday gift at Foxes. They had gone through the paper together and found what Jennifer thought was the perfect gift.

He had taken his favorite seat next to the window on the left first row just seated with Jen beside him sitting looking out at car roofs, bar windows, asphalt, concrete, a woman in a white tank top talking into a public phone, two men arguing outside the army recruiting office, another man smoking outside the library extension, a little girl with a big backpack walking bent over, yellow stripes, white line, parked cars, more parked cars, car stopping to drop someone off, red lights, green lights, lamp posts, parking lots, empty soda cups on top of a full trash barrel, a building under construction, police car, Jersey Barrier, CL&P construction crew, work zone signs, new reflections in the window with an old reflection in the glass.

Beside them, a thin man who stank and needed a shave talked ceaselessly to himself in a language that might have been Middle Eastern. Walker stared straight ahead at the massive pile of flesh that vaguely resembled a man or maybe a huge bag with a wig on top. Like a bellows, he puffed in and out with the sheer exertion of living. He made Walker feel skinny. "Hoo ha," he said to everyone and no one in particular. "Hoo ha, it's a hot one today, Lord." A man sitting opposite him smiled showing a row of rotting teeth and nodded his head in quick time two by two.

The bus had pulled to the right like a giant beetle and huffed to a stop with a low grumble of its engine and the clacking of its doors opening. Walker hunched and shuffled as the man next to him got up and someone else sat down. The motor on the bus died almost unnoticed except for Walker and an elderly gentleman with thick, brown framed glasses and tiny white curls of hair around his ears and an expression of desperate disdain in his eyes. The driver punched the start button. CHUNGA CHUNGA CHUNGA. Nothing. He tried again CHUNGA CHUNGA. Still nothing. The driver muttered a curse and got on the phone to the dispatcher.

"Daddy, how come the bus isn't moving?"

"I think it's broken, sweetheart, and won't start."

"Well why haven't you fixed it?" Jennifer had demanded looking up at him with a deadly serious expression on her face.

"I don't know how," Walker told her.

"You know everything."

"No."

"Yes 'cause you're my daddy." She had clutched the scarf they had bought and scowled across the aisle of the bus at the opposite window as people began to file out of the bus to wait for a replacement.

Well he couldn't do anything then and Walker was not at all sure that he was going to be able to do anything now. Certainly not for Beth and probably not for their daughter either. He felt consumed by ennui so deep that he found himself barely able to move to the microwave to cook his dinner. While the machine hummed and heated, he walked down the short hall to his bedroom and, removing his clothes, stood naked before his God.

Walker sat staring at the metal bar running along the side of Beth's bed without the knowing or the seeing of it but aware that it was there. She lay in a long white line motionless still so still under the lights in *vox machina* hummmm and little beeps soft like a cat's paw on paper. Tap tap bleep bleep, a small form barely a white line under the sheets bleep.

> Our father who art in heaven
> Hallowed be thy name

Walker felt like some huge, bloated caricature of a monstrous idol. He brought his hand up in front of his face. Could they heal? Nope. Could they comfort? Hell no. They couldn't do anything but wiggle like sightless sticks under the fluorescence. Hold a drink or a fork. That's all folks. Come back tomorrow at the same time to see the five fingers exercise. Come one, come all. Hear ye, hear ye. Hold them up for though they know of words yet they are useless and hang down from the hand in shame yes and speak to the world of impotence and death. Oh my love, Walker chanted slowly and lowly rocking forward towards the bed and then back again. Oh my love my sweet love. No pain please. Walker bowed before the altar.

Walker could not help himself. Memories of his childhood flashed across his mind as if they were photographs. He could not understand why he would remember such things now. Surely, this was not the time, but, as if to increase his misery, memories kept coming to him. CLICK, CLICK next one please CLICK.

Fourteen year old Johnny Walker feeling strong and very adult the night of the dancing school finale and knowing Linda would be there. Ah fair Linda Coulter with heart- shaped face and page-boy cut of blonde hair, blue sky eyes and a smile that he knew she held just for him. How many nights had he gone to sleep thinking of her and wondering what she looked like without, you know, without any and would it be blonde yes he thought so and had turned his entire body rigid with excitement. He had struggled into his dancing suit that evening trying to get it just right with his father standing behind him to do the Windsor knot on his tie. So cool and Walker had looked into the bathroom mirror and saw a man staring back at him and so would Linda he thought mmmmmmmmm.

And they had crawled that evening of the finale creeping into the parking lot in a chain of cars like some sluggish multi-colored caterpillar that stopped every few seconds to let out a child or several of them scrubbed and rubbed and dressed in new gowns and freshly pressed suits hair curled and teased ribboned and Brilcreamed all looking very serious and not a little nervous coming out of the cars and into the view of their peers standing by the entrance to the old building and congregating in clumps in the lobby just through the double doors. Standing stiffly and staring at each other through the eyes of insecurity and discovery.

That included little Johnny, just as starched and jittery as anyone as he stood and looked around for Linda as parents started to come in providing a friendly audience for the foxtrots and waltzes and she was there, of course, looking like a dream in a pale blue dress with white lace at the neck and sleeves. The paleness of her skin seemed to heighten the effect of her pale blond hair falling straight to just above her shoulders. To Walker she seemed almost translucent as she stood under the candelabra in the lobby talking with a friend. A beam of light straight from above seemed to surround her and Walker felt goosebumps forming as he watched her clap her hands in delight as she responded to the other girl.

CLICK

Lighton lightoff waxon waxoff and the reality as the light over the bed next to Beth's goes on. Walker blinks back to the present and yes a floating piece of memory from a long time before but it was the first time he remembered seeing a girl as other than a menace. Walker smiled into the side of the bed, one that quickly faded in the tomblike silence of the room. Behind him a nurse swished away and the light went out again deepening the gloom. He stood and looked down at her; Beth seemed almost at peace were it not for the wasted skeletal face and the skin like wet newspaper that had dried in the sun. He had known it before, known himself before and now was engulfed in the fiery breath of his own guilt that he was the healthy one still standing able to think and laugh and cry and do all the postcard things that we do everyday automatically while she lay there barely breathing.

CLICK

And then he was in another room, this one painted snot green with a picture of yellow tulips framed and hung over the bed that occupied most of the space and in which the corpse seemed somehow shrunken and peaceful lying on its side as if asleep. Across the bed from him stood his mother. Yes just a gentle tap on the shoulder and he would open his eyes and reach for his glasses on the bedside table and see his wife and child. No sound came from him, no air in and out in and out; the bellows had stilled and the hearth had grown cold. Walker sat beside the bed, his head bowed over the body of his father and all that went through Walker's mind was

> Now I lay me down to sleep
> My hot rod parked across the street

And sleep you will, Dad, and may you be more gentle and forgiving in death than you ever were in life, you miserable bastard but I'll bet you're down in Hell now finding fault with some devil while I stand over your body with this lunatic verse running through my head

> If it should roll 'fore I awake
> Have mercy, Lord, put on the brake

Or maybe I'm insane and the verse should be incorporated into the Protestant hymnal along with all the tongue lashings and screaming criticisms and the times I was restricted to my room and the times I went without eating. I was never quite what you wanted in a son and had no idea why I kept coming up short and thought that it was my fault and that somehow on some golden morning with the sun shining and the birds chirping that you would give me a big hug and tell me you loved me but that never happened, did it? No and now I know that it would never have happened and mother is just as bad with her starchy code of conduct and what is right and what is wrong like the time I came home from school with a shiner. I was so proud of it. I had taken a soccer ball in the face and prevented the opposing team from scoring a goal. I was the hero of the moment. Good ol' Mom had me taken off sports because it was filled with lower class ruffians. No amount of pleading and explanation would sway her judgment or reverse her decision and there she was standing in that room looking down at the body of her husband as if he had exposed himself in public.

CLICK

And way back before dressed in their best bib and tucker, yesiree, Bob and hair all slicked, a little dab'll do yu and scrubbed till every pore

32

screamed for mercy and looked around for even a speck of dirt to attract. God forbid that he spill anything during Sunday morning breakfast because, as his mother never tired of explaining, they were going to visit the house of GOD and he would notice if little boys came to visit with bacon stains on their ties and even if HE might forgive such a sin his father would not. They stood silently like statues in a brown wooden pew surrounded by people standing with books in their hands in other brown wooden pews in a house mostly filled with brown wooden pews except in the front where some guy was chanting and the kids in the choir behind were standing in their brown wooden pews. Looking out of the corner of his eye, Walker would watch his father standing like a general reviewing his troops, solemn, with his stomach buttoned into his jacket with aloof authority that could only, in the Walker's mind, have been handed down from HE-WHO-HATES-BACON.

Above him the light filled and stuffed the air with velvet waves interspersed with dust motes dancing slowly in the beams of light coming through the stained glass windows where old men with beards and long sticks stood around waiting for something, perhaps a woman. Walker had spent many Sundays looking at the windows arching high above his head and had seen only one woman and she always looked as if her kid had come home from school with all "C"s on his report card but she knew that he was never going to bring his grades up and that was that. And then everyone would start singing, or at least pretend because standing beside his mother, Walker could not hear her sing but her mouth opened and closed like that of a marionette or a ventriloquist's dummy. Then Walker tried to sing a ditty he had learned in school until his father saw him and cuffed him on the top of his head. Walker was standing right next to the aisle. The priest was just finishing one of his long chants when this occurred.

"OWWW. Christ." Walker had let out a yell that would have curdled fresh milk and hopped into the aisle as fifty heads turned as one in his direction. A plastic toy pistol that he had stuck in the waistband of his pants under his jacket before leaving the house came loose and clattered down onto the stone floor.

> Our Father who art in heaven
> Hallowed be thy name.

CLICK

Linda shimmered like a blue diamond sparkling with her laughter tinkling and rising and falling as she walked into the ballroom with her friends. Walker, feeling like a great gray-green toad came solemnly behind her dripping drops of nervousness in his wake and feeling unnoticed and almost invisible, walked into the large dance area. Chairs for the dancers were set out all around the perimeter of the room while at one end more chairs had been established on a small stage, almost just a raised platform, where the parents could sit and watch little Susie or Johnny master the intricacies of the Fox Trot and the Waltz. By cunning design a girl followed by a boy would enter the room and walk around to where there were empty chairs and there they would turn and stand straight and still. Mrs. Finkleman, the dance mistress, walked to the middle of the room, held her arms out waist high and then let them drop and all would sit down in the chair behind them with a rustle of dresses and a low murmur quickly stifled by the Finkle.

Walker plopped, dropped, seated, lowered, ensconced, installed, parked and settled his big butt onto the folding metal chair in a state of gloom for he found himself seated, not next to Linda but Cornelia Watrous, she of the jaundiced eyes, sallow skin, flat chest, lifeless hair and depressing personality. Walker glanced at her and then quickly downwards at his shiny new black shoes that were already beginning to hurt.

Cornelia looked at him with adoration. "Hi, Johnny."

Eyes on shoes, hands sweating, tie choking him. "Hi Cornelia." On cue, everyone would rise. The Finkle's assistant, a gray haired beldame would play the piano and each girl and boy would assume the position and begin stiffly turning and marching until the piano ceased. They would then stand talking for a moment until the next dance began.

And where do the buffalo roam? Why directly across the room where a herd had gathered around Linda chatting and laughing, their tiny, dull-witted eyes constantly shifting from one to another and then onto Linda before repeating the cycle until the Finkle turned them all to stone and the piano sounded. Walker, thoroughly miserable by then, turned and stared across the room at her. His imagination took over and he would walk over to her and Linda would smile and take his hand and all the other admirers would take their seats green with envy at the success of the handsome jack in his new grey suit with the dark red threads woven into it.

CLICK

My God what a memory to have now when the lights have long since been turned off in that hall and the children of that night now grown and become parents themselves. How could he who now knew real pain remember all the imagined pain back when he was still checking the mirror to see if it had gotten any bigger. Will Beth make it through the night? He didn't know. The doctors had done all they could do and now it was up to He-who-hates-bacon.

Walker sat beside the bed with lowered head and fingers tapping on his knees looking up at random intervals to stare at her profile, the straight nose with the broadening flare at the nostril, the sunken cheeks and almost invisible lips, lips he had loved when first he saw them, loved and then trembled at the thought of love and so agonized in the immutable and eternal dance of fireflies as hormones and heartbeats stepped up the rhythm and caused the brow to furrow, sweat glands to produce, tear ducts to operate, penile blood vessels to engorge, muscles to spasm, speech to become unintelligible and clothes to constrict and now he touched those same lips and felt the cold stillness, the faintest touch of her breathing, the death-like fold and form and he was beset by the ambush of his spirit he could not understand or accept. Walker reached downwards through the seamless drift of generations such are memories of his dad curled into a slightly fetal position and then unfolding into youth. As we come so shall we go and back beyond to his father and his father's father and their parents and their parents and there was no way of knowing what unconscious fragment of instinct or experience or lesson learned or ignored might be part of what made him what he was for better or worse.

Walker sneezed and fluid began dripping from one nostril. Maybe he was coming down with a cold. Maybe the flu. Pneumonia. Dysentary. Jungle rot. He and Beth would travel to heaven together. That would be good. Beth had always been better at planning trips than Walker and much better at explanations. She could get him in. For sure. No doubt, absolutely, certo, positively and Walker positively pushed forward in the chair and felt his knees fold until they met the beige colored linoleum tile with the black squares on it. Looking down, he saw that he was kneeling on one of the squares. His knees felt foreign as if they belonged to some other body and he had merely borrowed them for a while. Big, blocky things they were, sheathed in a woven, tan material stitched together in China but made in Honduras from patterns sent electronically to the machines from computers in the States. He was still for a moment, head bowed against the side of the bed. His muscles began to ache from the unexpected position. Walker sighed with the memory of a younger, more elastic body and the fat old man he had become.

> Hallowed be thy name
> Thy kingdom come
> Thy will be done
> On earth as it is in heaven

Dear God in heaven, he prayed. I hope that you will hear me. I hope that you're there or at least you're near me. I have no beautiful prayer to speak in a language that your ears would tolerate. I am not pure or chaste or good and would not be even if I could, but, since I was created in your likeness, I assume you know that I came out slightly flawed like the majority of my fellow humans. I am not very good but I am sincere and I pray for you to spare my wife this day.

And there he was on his knees and suddenly felt the hard coldness of the floor and the chair pressing me from behind and the glare of the lights overhead and he could not help but wonder what kept him sitting in that dammed chair night after night beside a dying, unconscious body. Would Beth know? Maybe. Jen was right even though she had said that because she hated hospitals with their luminescent sterility and the smells of food and medicine and sickness; she hated everything that was controlled yet she herself was controlled by Moses and their friends. That had never occurred to her. Even as a girl she had hated doing anything that they asked of her so it had always been this way and he felt his breath rush out in a sigh of exhaustion and regret.

CLICK

There she was in a blue skirt with white flowers and a yellow blouse. She ran down the hill ahead of us. The soles of her feet were dirty and her arms were windmilling. She shrieked with laughter as she got to the bottom and ran onto the little beach by the lake.

"Jennifer. Stop that at once." Beth frowned behind dark glasses that seemed to hide half her face.

Our daughter turned and looked back up the slope at us, her face tightening into a blank stare, her eyes expressionless.

"There's no reason she can't run around and play, dear," he ventured.

"Do not tell me how to raise my child."

"Our child."

"Don't remind me, John." She wrapped her arms across her chest and strode ahead of him down the hill, alone, aloof, autocratic, imperial, manipulative, bitter, lost, judgmental, rigid, unyielding, intelligent, beautiful, honest, strict, scared, determined, embarrassed, vitriolic, charming, witty, piercing, sadistic, tightly wrapped, precocious, precious, unwavering, but human and not unloved.

Well Jen grew up and they grew older. He grew fatter, Walker admitted to himself. Ruth got colder and now she may be on the way to boss the heavenly choir and he was facing a huge hole where his life used to be and dear, sweet Jesus he have no idea what he was going to do or how he was going to do it. Putting a roof over his head was not going to be easy. He don't know if he could handle a cold water walkup or colonies of bugs but it might come to that, yes it might and if he wanted to be his own man he just might have to accept some discomfort but dammit if that is what it takes then he could do it. Yeah, sure, fat man, a little inside voice whispered. As soon as the going gets tough you'll be running for the nearest friendly face with hat in hand and foot in mouth and food dish held out in one hand and the other holding your blanket. You like to think tough but when push comes to shove you will undoubtedly be the original Chicken Little yes and you are and kneeling here changes nothing for either of us but just makes his knees sore as when he dropped that gun in church and then afterwards kneeling in prayer. He knew he would be in for it and all he could think to do was to ask God not to kill him and God must have heard, Walker smiled tightly, because he was still there and down on his knees again. This is ridiculous. Get off your knees and sit in the chair like a man or least like her husband. Do you think for a moment the great spirit in the sky cares what physical position you assume when your spiritual account is running on empty? If that were true it would be easy to eliminate human vices and infestations such as politicians where the worst of us run for public office and we manage to elect the worst of those. Walker was hungry again and wondered if there was a cafeteria in the place. There must be. Hospitals are seven by twenty-four. People always on duty. They'd probably have a hamburger. That would taste fine, fine superfine right about now. Big, thick ground sirloin with juices running out of it turning the bun beneath it pink and lettuce, tomato, cheese and bacon peeking out from underneath the big, fluffy bun on top and it wouldn't be complete without a stack of French fries golden brown and still steaming from the fryer with lots of salt and just a little vinegar dripped on them. If he believed that, he should grow wings. He'd be lucky if they have stale coffee and a dried up ham sandwich. The hamburgers are likely to be a tired little piece of leathery meat hidden inside a stale bun. Not a moment to spare. He would see for himself. Perhaps not so bad. Then home. Need sleep. Another day coming.

The air hummed through the vents over his head. Walker heard the clicking of some young lady, judging by the sound and tempo, coming along the corridor. He thought he could almost hear the rustle of her skirt and faint swish of the white stockings on her legs where they met between her thighs. There was no one else in the room but himself and Beth. Walker sat back in his chair feeling the weight of darkness outside the window and watching the still life reflection of the room in its darkened panes. A blurred reflection in the windows grew larger and the tap of rubber soles on the linoleum grew louder.

"Visiting hours are over, Mr. Walker." The soft, lilting tone of the night nurse surrounded him. How many times on how many nights in this and how many other rooms had he heard that? A dollar a pop, Walker thought and he'd be able to keep the house and pay off the bills. Different voices on different days and a multitude of windowed waxed floor nights in this and other sterile realities. Rows of eyes filled with pain and fear, sorrow for that which was lost or fear of the future. Apathetic stares of the forgotten ones, crammed into chairs or stretched out silently on their beds, flipped and changed twice a day like pancakes, watching the souless flicker of the television, mindless of the passing swell of hours and days, or mindful but caught inside a useless body as they were brought like dead trees down the wide muddy river into the vast nothingness of the human consciousness.

"Yes," he intoned as she walked past and stared down at Beth where she lay like a long, white cocoon. Walker stood up wondering what to do with his hands that had suddenly taken on a life of their own, flapping nervously against his thighs, his fingers closing and opening as if searching for something onto which to hold.

The nurse pulled the front of her white sweater across her chest with one hand while she picked up Beth's chart from its hook at the end of the bed with the other. Turning, she looked at him, head tilting slightly, eyes kindly with her rosebud of a mouth pursed. "No change, Mr. Walker. Get some sleep. If anything changes I'll call you." She held up her right arm and hand in the scout position. "I promise." She smiled slightly, eyes filling with empathy.

"Thank you, Nancy. I know you would, always would." And Walker turned within himself to face away and, heavy now, his breath in and out feeling as if he should stay or fell something anyway but with no feeling at all he found himself just walking towards the door and then through the doorway where the fluorescent lights in the ceiling killed his slow, bulky shadow. Silent and alone. Walker going out.

E2 Morning

Walker woke to the crack of thunder outside the window. God's grinding his teeth again, he thought. Probably can't sleep any better than Walker could. Be a downpour soon but that should cool things off a bit. Sweating all over the sheets. At least that makes them cooler. Should have washed them yesterday, though. Put it off. Put everything off except sex and cocktails and food and that has dwindled to cocktails and food. Sex had its day, though. Wonder how it all starts? Like a genetic thing gives us the instinct to procreate, but what about the rest of the time? Some people want it constantly while others hardly at all. Upbringing, maybe? Parents? Something more subtle? The old environment versus background thing? The first time he ever thought about his body was when, let's see, he must have been seven or eight anyway, and back then Dad wasn't the king handing down laws and punishments like some biblical leader but young and ambitious. Their house was a lot smaller too and he shared a bathroom with his Dad. He still thought that his Dad was without a doubt the finest man alive and probably held that opinion longer than most until his father turned into a stranger and Walker left their museum castle vowing never to return. Walker used to wake up in the morning when his father started singing in the shower. He would go into the bathroom and pee into the toilet and then the water would stop and his father would step from the shower and see Walker and say "Hi, squirt. How are you this morning?" and grab a towel. Walker would sit on the edge of the bathtub while he dried himself. Each hair in the forest of brown hair on his chest seemed to stand out and he would bring the towel down his back then between his legs. Walker remembered his fascination with this process. His dad's dick would flop back and forth. His testicles used to appear and then disappear into the folds of the towel. His penis was huge compared to Walker's and uncircumcised. Sometimes it would be small and scrunched up and hanging out of its hairy bed and sometimes it would be stiffer and redder with blue veins all over it; Walker used to wonder at the difference and he used to take a ruler to his own little peter to see if it was getting bigger. He was thrilled when he saw his first pubic hair, but he must have gotten his mother's genes for he never had much body hair, just a few on his chest and a little chain running down from there to his navel. Probably a good thing his father never knew what his little boy was thinking all those mornings. Walker would watch him lather up and scrape his face with a shiny metal safety razor then he would pat on some kind of liquid. "Another day, another deal," his dad would say to Walker as he turned from the sink. Sometimes he would stick his head out around the shower curtain and tell Walker to go to his room and get ready for school. He would go, but once he looked back and saw his father's dick standing out from its bed of hair dripping white drops. Even Dads get horny and that is something Walker could testify to. Was that where it all started with that initial amazed fascination staring at my father and knowing awe and something else, some other feeling that he could not put a name to or did it start before, before memory in diapers or back further in the womb, the dark place of life, the well head, the place of birth and death, blood and water, starting point of all spirit and body. What comes first he wondered, the body or the spirit, the first instinct or the first physical mass? What is the beginning? He didn't know and knew no one who did though many raved about the sanctity of life but they didn't know either for all their bombast.

Walker lay in his bed sweating as the storm approached. He lay on his back listening to the old house creak in the gusts of wind outside and know that he would not sleep again soon. His mind sees bits and pieces of the past, a kaleidoscope of fractured pictures and thoughts. The mind is the only force in nature that does not always heed the dictates of passing time. It is as if we could twist our lives like a strand of DNA looking forwards and backwards simultaneously part of ourselves and apart from ourselves.

Walker rose from the bed untangling from the sheet as he did so like some overstuffed mummy coming alive within the darkened depths of a museum. He stood streaming over the toilet grunting softly and then ran a comb through his hair and passed a toothbrush across his teeth. Should shave, he thought, but it is Sunday so to hell with it.

Coffee. Hot and black. Walker stood over the sink looking out onto the baked, brown square of yard in the back. He would need to get the house sale going. His talk with Jen the day before had jolted his sense of

41

imminent trauma, dislocated his serenity of place and time. He could no longer pretend that it wouldn't happen, Walker thought. Got to start going through and throwing out whatever he don't need. No money to store all this stuff and he probably doesn't need it or want it anyway. What is it someone said? If you haven't looked at something in six months you probably never will and should put it in the dumpster. The coffee pot sighed and chortled and then was still as if in mute agreement with him. Sighing, he poured it into a white ceramic mug with NO MORE MR. NICE GUY still faintly visible on its exterior. Gotta start somewhere. Might as well be the cellar. Walker went over and opened the cellar door and looked down into the heat of the darkness below. Ughh.

Holding his coffee ahead of him as if to ward off anything bad, he flicked the switch and the light went on below. Slowly, Walker descended.

At the bottom of the stairs he ducked his head and turned left into what had originally been intended to be a family room that Walker, with little experience and money had tried to create. Over a framework of two by fours he had nailed pine planks to make the walls. They had brought in an electrician to install outlets and two overhead lights but then the money had run out and the result had been a very dark, gloomy room with an unfinished concrete floor. Neither Jennifer nor Beth ever had used it and Walker had ended up using as a workshop for occasional projects and repairs. He had constructed a rough workbench on which was piled all manner of forgotten junk: a rusty saw, coffee cans containing old nails and screws, paint rags, window hardware from an attic window that he had been re-doing, a claw hammer with a cracked handle that had been tightly wrapped in black electrical tape, pieces of window glass, a can of green primer, a container of A-1 automobile windshield washing fluid, an angle guide for a saw, strips of quarter-round wood molding, a chisel, a can of 3-In-1 oil and a can of paint cleaner. An old portable workbench leaned against one wall. Green garbage bags were piled up against another wall next to the top of a hutch that they had not used in years. Into the middle of the room, he had swept a pile of dirt and small pieces of junk and garbage but had never bothered to pick it up. Walker flicked the light switch and stood looking around at this desolate scene. Haven't been down here in years. Way back he thought he would make furniture and sell it on the side. Hah. He'd made one bookcase for Jennifer and that was not what anyone would call fine furniture. Spent a lot of time on it though. Still have it up in her room. Holds a bunch of her junk. Dolls from twenty years ago. CD's. God, she must have hundreds. Walker was sure his daughter did not even remember all the items. Probably should just chuck 'em. She'd never know. Mutant Teenage Ninja Turtles. Never even miss them but was fanatical about them way back then. Fucking stinks down here. Smells like shit. Mice maybe. Need to air this place out before anything else.

Walker turned and left the room and went back to the other side of the cellar where a wooden door led up a flight of steps to the hatchway in the back of the house. He pulled the door open, unlocked the bar securing the hatchway doors and pushed them up and outwards. Heavy rain pelted him and Walker stood for a moment with his eyes closed feeling the heat of the coming day on his face. Guess I'd better start before it gets too hot, he decided.

Looking to his left he saw the end of an old camp chest protruding from behind the now open hatch door. Start at the beginning, he told himself, and, tuning to his left a few steps, he bent to pick it up. It was heavier than lead. What the hell was inside of it? The chest was black with brass banding and a large, brass lock. Walker pulled on the lock and it came up. The chest had not been locked.

Stacks of letters tied in bundles. Photographs, some in large heavy frames, piled on top of each other. The top photo showed a young Beth standing between her parents. They all seemed to be happy with big smiles as they stood in front of a small, spit level home in what was probably a community of such homes. Walker remembered when they had announced plans to marry. Beth's parents had been less than thrilled. No smiles that day, he thought. He looked at the picture under the top one. Another shot of Beth as a girl, this one had her sitting on the front steps of the house staring into the camera with a very serious expression on her face almost as though the photographer had been a policeman and Beth was trying to decide whether she was in trouble or not. She had always been serious, too serious Walker thought. Obviously, that was a trait that had shown up long before she and Walker had met. He picked up a pack of letters. The top one was addressed to her at U MASS and was apparently from her mother. He put the letters back in the trunk and stood over it thinking should take this up the steps and start a pile in the back yard. Old letters and pictures. She won't need them now and he didn't need them either. He picked up a thin series of letters held together with a string. Hmmm.

What's in these? No return address. A female friend or family member? Writing doesn't look female somehow. Maybe an old beau or a classmate or coworker. Walker tried to remember what Beth had been doing when they had gotten together but he could not. Could be interesting. Maybe she was part of an international spy ring. He tried to imagine his wife as a spy and chuckled softly to himself. Soldier, sailor, tinker, tailor do your best try not to fail her and if she's bad then simply jail her. He put the letters to one side of the trunk and pulled the trunk out from behind the door. Walker stood in his back yard puffing a bit from carrying the trunk up the stairs. He looked around slowly as if trying to decide where he should start his discard pile and then it down with an almost delicate motion beside the hatchway and ducked back inside as the rain increased.

He stood in the dimness of the cellar and wondered if Beth was dreaming or at some stage in between or simply trying to take one more breath and then one more breath and there is no time left for memory. Probably never know the answer to that one. She could wake up, though. The doctors think it's possible but only time will tell. He wondered what dreams she could have through the drugs and the pain, he wondered. Back to childhood perhaps. God I hope you are comfortable and you are dreaming colors bright and spinning like a pinwheel on a windy day. Perhaps we are all pinwheels in a breeze as some young god solemnly holds us up and then laughs to watch us turn, turn, turn. Beth used to relate that when she was a little girl, she was a naughty little girl, an ugly duckling who despised her brother, ignored her parents and terrified her classmates.

In one of her oral-history-of-Beth moments, she'd told of talking with her mother on the public phone at school in an attempt to get her mother to pick her up so that she would not have to sit on the bus glaring out the window like a thunderstorm in the making. A chunk of hairy flesh, and pimples with little piggy eyes by the name of Horton Foster, called Duke by his sycophants, sauntered up to the phone and stuck out his hand. "Need to use. Lose yourself, bitch," he told her.

"I'll be off in a minute." She stared back at him as if she were examining a frog in biology class.

"Now." He made a grab at the phone.

Beth pulled it back and his hand grabbed thin air. "Hey. Quit it."

Horton stepped into her face. "You looking to be even uglier than you already are, little girl. Give me the fucking phone."

Beth had yanked the handset so hard that it ripped out of the phone. Without even pausing in her motion, she brought the handset up and then down on Horton's head with a dull thump. The handset shattered into several pieces as Horton's eyes rolled up into his head and he went down on the floor like a bag of Jello. His hangers-on looked into Beth's eyes, turned and fled.

She'd told him of that incident often. It had stuck in his mind perhaps because she'd been punished severely for knocking the jerk unconscious for several minutes and she'd thought she'd had been the good person in that fight and found out that the big people didn't care who started it but only who put who in the nurses office and then in an ambulance.

Perhaps you are seeing that even now as I saw it through your eyes, Walker hoped. Over the years they'd fought and were close, fought and were apart until time ran into a wall. Walker stared into himself. Maybe he could share her mind still alive through his. Siblings were supposed to be able to communicate without speech or was that twins? Why not husband and wife? In some ways they had done so all along. He could always read her moods from the set of her face and the twist of her mouth, and he knew all the triggers that would set her off though sometimes he didn't give a shit and plowed ahead like a regular male asshole. There was always a part of her that was strange and unknown to him. Perhaps there was part of him that she did not know as well. Certainly there were parts of his life of which he'd never spoken, parts that would bore her, Walker thought, piss her off and so in his saner moments either forgotten or dismissed as past and done.

Garage

Mark McGuigan was not in a good mood as he drove up the New Jersey Turnpike towards the George Washington Bridge and Interstate 91 into Connecticut. He disliked leaving Lisa by herself, prey to some jerk trying make a play for her. Lisa had not been her usual bubbly self lately. In fact she had seemed downright withdrawn when he was around and that was another cause for concern and a further reason he was not enthusiastic about this trip.

Last night, in fact, when he'd told her that he would be making this trip on business and didn't know exactly how long he might be gone, she'd taken the news well, too damned well, in fact, and he had accused her of having another lover and things had gone downhill from there. Just thinking about that fight made him grip the steering wheel until his knuckles showed white in the reflected glare of the overhead lighting. He didn't know why he kept getting behind the eight ball. It was like some evil genie was always messing things up. No matter what he did or what he said, it always seemed to end up badly.

Lisa was a bitch, no two ways about it, but, at the end of the day, she held all the cards because of her old man. How'd he ever get into this mess?

He had been working away minding his own business without a care in the world. Okay, maybe things weren't that good. Bennie was always on his tail about being late and getting his work done. The guy was a supervisor and was bucking for manager and eager to show that he could boss people around. Bennie was a jerk. Mark had known lots of Bennies and they were always running around giving orders and acting like their shit didn't stink. You'd think the place was some super secret government project instead of a lousy health club. The club had windows between the outer lobby and the exercise area so that prospective members could see all the fancy equipment and imagine themselves looking like Schwarzenegger in a couple of weeks or so. He had been in that area helping a few old

46

wrecks work out when Lisa had come through the front door with her little gym bag that probably cost a grand and her hair all pulled back and tied to show she was serious about exercise. She looked like a goddess, Mark decided, a beautiful, untouchable goddess. He stood there and gawked at her until the old man on the weight bench started to weaken and Mark had to take the weight from him and set it onto the weight hold.

She signed in at the reception desk and then looked up and through the glass and their eyes met momentarily. She smiled slightly, a Mona Lisa moment, and Mark felt light headed and his cock sprang to attention not that it needed such motivation. Mark disliked work in the exercise area and would have given his left nut to work in the pool area where women wearing next to nothing were always coming and going. As if sensing this in him Bennie was not about to put Mark anywhere near the pool. Resigned to never seeing the woman again, Mark walked through the area picking up towels and putting hand weights back in their racks. You weren't supposed to bring drinks or food into the area, but people did anyway and the club was not about to make a stink about it. The recession had taken its toll and membership was down. He picked up a juice bottle and a couple of sandwich papers and made his way into the men's locker room where he stacked the towels in the used-towel bin and the papers in the waste basket. The room was mostly empty. Mr. Hirshbaum was getting out of his gym shorts and T shirt. Mark grimaced and turned away from the skinny hairy legs, tiny penis embedded in a mound of graying hair beneath the protruding belly. Ugh. Where was the goddess?

"Hello?"

"Well hello there. Is this the club guy?"

"This is Mark. I got your note." Her voice was everything he thought it would be. She had a low, throaty contralto that made the hair on his arms, among other things, stand up. In his mind, he saw her lounging naked on her bed, phone tucked into her ear and the Mona Lisa smile on her face.

"You saw me today. I saw you standing there with your mouth open. Good thing flies are not allowed in the club." She chuckled, a low throaty sound that almost destroyed him.

He swallowed and adjusted his pants to a more comfortable position. "So what can I do for you? I don't even know your name."

"Lisa"

"Hello Lisa."

"Hello Mark. Are you married or otherwise spoken for?"

He could hear the laughter in her voice and just a hint of something else. Mark could not believe his luck. He had no idea why Lisa would choose to contact him but he definitely was not about to discourage her. "Not married. No girlfriend," he told her. He would definitely be ditching his girlfriend, Mandy, that very night. She was starting to get on his nerves anyway.

"Join me for dinner. Portobello Restaurant. Seven o'clock. Don't be late. Ta-Ta." Lisa hung up and Mark stood there for a moment with the phone still held up to his ear. The goddess definitely did not beat around the bush. That made things much simpler he thought as he hung up the phone. No bullshit.

That had been the start. Mark honked his horn at a slow car in front of him. Okay, so maybe he had gotten himself in this situation. He could have said no but saying that was the furthest thing from his mind at that time. How could he have known that her old man was a power broker with lots of connections? Mark told himself that this was not his fault at all. Once again, he was the victim and not the victor.

He would come out on top, though. He would get the money, pay off the debt, and make sure that Lisa did not wander off with somebody else. After all, he was dealing with someone he knew, someone who would back down if he showed her a little steel and he had plenty of steel. Mark drove through the night burnishing his self-image as he did so. He was so occupied with Mark Mcguigan that he did not notice a sedan a car or two back but following him up into Connecticut.

E2 5:30 am Monday

It was not so much the light that woke him as the absence of dark. The difference slowly took over that part of his consciousness that bridges the gap between living and dead, between the cold, wet experience of reality and the dark warmer place of the unconscious tickling the former into awareness while the latter seeped slowly into nothingness. Ceiling. White, rough sand surface painted white with small crack in left, front corner. Getting hot already. It was like a blanket across his face and Walker could tell before he even opened his eyes that this was going to be a bastard of a day. Due to lack of interest, he thought, all Mondays should be cancelled.

Walker slowly turned his head to the right forced his eyes open and stared at the Sony Dream Machine clock radio on the small, battered, pine table beside his bed. He had used the table since childhood. It had been in his room by his bed, just a nothing-special table with four spindly legs that were carved in the shape of lions claws at their ends. He had discovered a hidden section in the one drawer. It could only be seen if you pulled the drawer all the way out. He had carved his initials in the table top and been soundly spanked by his enraged father. During one of its many moves, one corner had been chipped and numerous stains and scratches had appeared over the years. Currently, in addition to the Sony, the table held a small glass imprinted with the image of Ronald McDonald and containing a small sip of water, a Dumbo-the-flying-elephant lamp with a shade that was marred by a large, brown stain that looked like an eye where the light bulb had come to close to the shade, his brown wallet well worn along the edges and his company ID badge.

Walker closed his eyes and let his head roll back onto the pillow. He reached over and tapped the Sony to turn off the alarm. Another fucking Monday. He felt bloated and his bladder felt as if it would burst at any second but it was also obvious that relief would not be immediate. His dick was so stiff it hurt. It lay under his belly like a pine tree against a steep slope. Should I, he wondered? No. Better not. It would take too long and first thing in the morning I rarely make it anyway. Sign of age, I guess. Another fucking Monday. Phone call after phone call after phone call. Good morning, sir, good morning ma'am and what can I do for you this morning? Enrollment? Certainly just hang on while I transfer you to a specialist. You've already been transferred five times? So sorry. Can you count to six. No I can't help you. So sorry. Hold on hold on on onon and on and yes I can do that just be patient a moment sir and can you logon now oh good and have a nice day and have a nice day and week and year. It's another Monday.

Laughter, lots of laughter. That's what held this house together. There was laughter upstairs, downstairs, in the cellar, in the attic, in the bathroom reading words written on a white wall he'd put up alongside the toilet and in the bedroom late into a chuckle midnight mass moving on mass and then the sudden yielding smiling groaning stiffening and fingers moving. Laughter ran into and out of the doors like tides on a beach as Jen grew and ran and learned and hurt and learned some more and triumphed and phoned and agreed and rejected and cried and screamed and ate and fevered and slept and dressed and ran laughing with other girls who laughed and giggled and hid their mouths with their hands while looking at Walker with full neon eyes brimming with knowing innocence and laughter as they slept over and laughter as pillows flew and Ballou, their golden retriever, ran up and down the hall barking. Even Beth laughed back then but God must have limited her supply because she gradually ran out and then laughed no more.

Walker sat up on the edge of the bed, the wrinkled sheet, damp with sweat, coiled around him like a python. He heard the hum of a car passing by the house and then silence. Grunting with the effort, he pushed himself to his feet and walked down the hall to the bathroom, his penis still semi erect and waving in front of him like a divining rod searching for water.

The sky above the bus stop was stuck in neutral. It had a grey, metallic tinge from the smog and it seemed to flatten everything into a two dimensional landscape of heat and despair. Walker stood looking up Farmington Avenue at the oncoming traffic. Rush hour had barely started and already the broad avenue was jammed with vehicles. How many people were pointing at that fat little man standing by the bus shelter already sweating out his shirt. Hey, Mom, check out the Butterball turkey. Betcha he could wreck a set of scales, huh Mom? Stop it, Henry. That's not nice to say. Ahh Mom. Walker stood cooking in the juices of his paranoia. He wished he had an Uzi and could simply stand there and destroy everyone around him. Take that you idiots. He felt foolish standing there holding a little brown bag holding two BLT turkey sandwiches and a coke. In the past he would have had a decent if not great lunch at the company cafeteria. Their meatloaf and mashed potatoes were particularly good. They were best with an extra scoop of brown gravy and three of those ludicrous little containers of butter that restaurants love and their customers despise. The food industry has grown so enamored with portion control that it had relegated its customers to sitting there opening little packets containing a half teaspoon of bottom shelf butter, probably from government storage and dating from World War II.

Walker shifted the bag to his other hand and eased it behind his back. Expenses related to Beth plus the loss of her income had shriveled his paycheck until even a few dollars became a vital piece of the dam holding back insolvency. He tried to think positively. The sandwiches were good and thick with plenty of mayo. He had used a good brand of turkey and thick-cut bacon that made the soft lettuce and tomato stand up and dance on his tongue. Still, he could have been eating roast pork and oven-fried potatoes. Walker felt deprived and stood on the curb sullen, waiting.

The bus pulled up with a muted rumble and Walker pulled himself up the two steps into the interior of the bus. For handicapped people the driver would kneel the bus but Walker would be damned before he asked for that service. He would not make a stink about it because that would simply set him up for more annoying glances and sniggering whispers. He pulled out his pass and stuck it into the mouth of the machine. Another fucking Monday.

Carefully, he made his way down the aisle and sat down in an empty seat being careful not to squeeze the old woman sitting in the seat beside him. With half his ass hanging over the edge of the seat into the aisle, Walker rode into downtown Hartford in a state of high irritation.

That did not decrease as the work day began as he collapsed into his chair at his cubicle and slipped the headset on and prepared to log into the company's help line telephone system. He was used to helping people who rang through to him with problems and that was his job but a horribly poor telephone tree message system had many people pressing the wrong button on their phone and so most of his time was spent transferring calls to another unit on the help line, a part of the job he detested and attributed to having morons for managers.

"Good weekend?" Babs Smith sat in the cubicle behind Walker.

Walker shrugged. "Okay, I guess."

Babs nodded. "How's your wife?"

"'Bout the same," Walker admitted.

"It's very hard," chattered Babs turning towards him and looking as if she had just sat down on an Eskimo Pie. "My aunt had emphysema, you know, and it was very hard on everyone, especially at the end, you know, when she couldn't breath too good and needed 'round the clock care and, you know, it was really hard."

Babs had a pleasant manner over the phone, one with which people identified causing them to request her services repeatedly but her manner of speech off the phone left something to be desired, Walker thought. Sloppy verbal phrasing was probably the result of poorly educated parents and a tour through a less than stellar public school system. It was amazing, he thought, that so much was blamed on the schools when, in reality, much of the blame for a child's poor education lay with the parents. Inability to speak or write correctly and do basic math was laid on the school system and there was much that could be corrected there. As a country, we are conditioned to think that spending more money on the problem would resolve it. Politicians bought our vote by promising to spend more on education. This led to higher paid teachers and administrators but no better schools. Standards and testing were a definite step in the right direction but the root cause of poor schools were the homes from which the students came. If the parents didn't have the time or even care then the school was certainly not going to provide anything except elevated daycare services. Public funds were an invitation to corruption and incompetence. Walker knew of one teacher who was on long term disability and making her full salary. The school district was so poorly managed that they did not even know that this was happening until a federal audit was performed. Babs talked about her aunt whenever she thought about Beth so Walker was familiar with this little speech and simply nodded his head wishing that she would shut up and leave him alone.

"Isn't it terrible what people have to go through sometimes?" Babs chirped. "You'd think by now, they'd have a cure for all this stuff, you know? I was talking about it with my husband, Matt, and I said Matt, I said, the doctors are making a ton of money and for what, I ask you? They just seem to walk around giving bad news to people and then sending their bill to the insurance company and you can believe it's really huge and then sending you whatever the insurance won't pay for. It should be a crime, you know what I mean? I mean if no one can do anything and it's in God's hands then how come we get a huge bill that we spend the rest of our lives paying, you know?" Babs stuck out her lower lip in a pout that made her look like a hooked trout.

Skinny trout, though, Walker decided as he turned back to his computer screen. All eyes and mouth and not much between the eyes either. Still, she has a point. Wonder what our health system would be like if it was a pay-for-results system instead of a take-your-best-shot-and-pray system. That would keep a bunch of folks up at night, he'd bet. Beth had good doctors, though. Not their fault, but there is always a limit on the current state of human knowledge and after that it is up to God or fate or whatever lies just beyond our conscious horizon. He wished he hadn't brought the gun to church that day. Never really took to religion or went to church but if God is part of him, is part of his spirit or soul then He would know Walker did not dismiss Him but just the organized trappings of religion. He'd have to forgive Walker's thoughts too. Not always pure for sure. Bless him father for he has sinned and is sinning now. Wonder how Babs looks without clothes on. Nice breasts, certainly, and soft like Beth's used to be. Pointed nipples, I imagine. Small, pink aureoles. Pillow soft, pillow talk, pillow walk pillow caught. He would run his fingers lightly over them and they would harden and stand up at attention. So soft hard softhard like life like God hard. Supposedly made in his image wonder if God had a

The phone rang. Walker clicked a portion of his computer screen marked ANSWER and his work day began.

"Thank you for calling customer service. This is John. How may I help you?

Followed by strange voices on the phone. Soft, loud, musical, grating, half asleep, nervous, bitchy, arrogant, hysterical, demanding, pleading, erotic, nasal, inclusive, possessive, whispering, crying, laughing, singing, deadpan, staccato, accented, inflected, deflected, long-winded, lost from Ohio, Missouri, Georgia, Florida, Maine, Louisiana, Wyoming, Arizona, Colorado, California, New York, Washington and probably every other state in the Union and most of them had pressed the wrong button on their phones and needed to speak with someone else. "Yes ma'am,

I can reset your password. Out in California are your? Heard it's nice out there. Expensive though, I hear. Yeah. Couldn't afford a breadbox let alone someplace with a roof over it." The woman rattles on as he reset her password. Her voice is musical, up and down in pleasing cadence with just a touch of frustration left over from when she could not log on.

Walker saw her as tall with long, brown hair hanging in waves over her shoulders. A strong nose, maybe too strong for her to be classically beautiful but balanced nicely by a pair of large brown eyes. He could tell by her timbre that her mouth would be long and mobile, always moving up or down displaying her emotions as if she were writing them down on a piece of paper as they came upon her. Maybe in her late twenties or early thirties. Married but married long enough not to be thrilled by her situation any more. Love means having to live with shit you hate. Work and sleep, day after day. Casserole in the evenings with salad and hubby working the barbie on the weekends. Lying there once or twice a month while he made like a rocking horse on top of her groaning and slobbering ohyes yes yes unghnnnn yes almost oh God here it comes oh Christ and the final heave of his body and the feeling of his release inside of her as she lay counting out another day in the life and faking an orgasm that she had never experienced since a high school flame in back of her daddy's storage shed and then waking up and grabbing a shower and a cup of coffee and then to the office where her damned computer refused to let her log-on to the network. You're all set now. Have a nice day and the call disconnects and Walker waits for the next one sitting staring into his screen with a partial boner.

"Customer service, how may I help you?"

This job sucks. That call took two minutes and it is now two minutes later than it was before the call and now it is nine hours and eight minutes and only seven hours and forty-five minutes to go, baby, not counting lunch hour, yes, and the famous Walker sandwiches in which the tomato has undoubtedly turned the bread into mush. Well at least the bacon should still be good. Next time he should stick the tomato between the lettuce and the turkey to avoid the mush problem or maybe put the tomatoes in a baggy and put them into the sandwich at the last minute. Now there's a stroke of brilliance. Little extra trouble but a much better sandwich. Of course they might get mushed in his brown paper bag. Maybe one of those plastic sandwich containers. That would solve the problem. "No, Ma'am. I can't help you. Let me transfer you to someone who can." Now where did he want to consume this repast? At his desk? The post-prandial shock would be too great. Mmmm. Maybe the café. Not a good idea. Might throw financial discipline to the four winds and go for the roast pork and potatoes. Outside, perhaps. Nice weather but hot.

"Customer service. How may I help you? Yes, sir. Let me get you over to the right department." Let me get you over to the edge of a cliff and push you over it. Let me hit you over the head with a club. Maybe it will get your brain working again. I am so sick of these dildos choosing the wrong prompt. Does no one listen to phone tree messages anymore? HELLO OUT THERE all you morons. STOP CALLING ME.

"Thank you for calling customer service. This is John. How may I help you?" There's got to be a better way. He needed to get his book finished and sell it. More money. Maybe keep the house. Maybe lots of things. Think of all the pot boilers out there. He could write like that but he had to stop farting around and write. He could write during lunch. Even if it's no good. He could always change it. Time to put the pedal to the medal.

E2 12:30

The sidewalk was made of sun rising and falling slowly beneath Walker's feet with a pattern of old gum, cigarette butts, torn flyers, empty coffee cups and sundry liquid residues best left unknown. Pigeons strutted and fluttered among the humans, red eyes sharp and on the lookout for any crumbs that might escape a passing sandwich wrap or burger paper. People walked by him left and right like stick figures varying only in size and color as he struggled up Main Street towards the public library. Sweat ran in torrents down his face dampening his collar and dripping from his hair.

Ahead of him a large, rectangular, blue and white Connecticut transit bus waited patiently at its curb while people filed slowly in through the retractable folding front doors. It was an F1 traveling out to the projects by Albany Avenue and then back to Main Street; pulling up behind it was an E7 coming inbound from the UConn health center. Across Main Street a K bus pulled up to the bus shelter in front of the Congregational Church. Some of the people standing or sitting on the brown stone steps leading from the sidewalk to the church's entrance went down to get on the bus but most remained motionless, just colored splotches on the dark stone background.

Walker walked slowly past the open plaza that the Travelers Insurance Group had built over an underground parking garage. The center of the huge space was dominated by a glass and concrete dome shaped structure that served as an entryway to the main building on the left. On the right of the space, concrete planters held bushes and small trees providing shade for people sitting on concrete benches built into the planters. Along the side of the building were more plantings as well as smaller islands in between the two sides of the plaza. It was like an architectural rendering of a new building where the architect puts in lots of greenery and people walking around and sitting beneath trees so that the new building looks much better than it will when it is built.

The plaza looked inviting but masses of people had spilled out of the building during their lunch hour to enjoy the sunny, summer day. There was not a nook that was not occupied, no shade without a group of people eating, or listening to music from a boom box, lovers hugging and transit workers waiting for their bus to arrive so that they could start their shift. Walker found a little tune going through his head and hummed to himself past the plaza. Homeless wandering, hikers hiking, businessmen busying, bricklayers laying, readers escaping, judges judging, serious people frowning, happy people chirping, musicians playing, lawyers phoning, lonely people staring into the middle distance that was staring back at them, mothers walking kids, old people pushing walkers, policemen policing, security guards guarding security, poets phasing in and out, writers writing, teachers teaching, the ambitious reaching, the shrill ones screeching with others beseeching, sun freaks beaching, construction workers constructing and computer workers screening. Still dreaming words, Walker wondered what would-be writers did? Anything but writing as he could attest. Write stuff so bad that it never made it past his trash can. Write words that made no sense or were so trite as to be a competition for sugar. Well, that was going to change. He stopped humming. He felt a sense of determination and his stride picked up and his back straightened. Very military. Yes indeed.

He felt compressed as he watched the ebb and flow of human life on the plaza. It was as if everyone had stopped what they were doing and decided to form a mob with Walker at its center. The heat beat down and made him puff with the exertion of walking. Slowly, he continued past the plaza and across Gold Street to the Wadsworth Athenaeum that stood on the corner like a huge gray boulder in the middle of a stream. It's stone battlements and crenellations were solid reminders of the wave of Europhilia that swept through the upper crust of American society in the nineteenth century when whole castles were taken down stone by stone and moved to American soil. Walker could almost feel the archers and pike men staring down at him as they guarded the paintings and exhibits within. Wherefore art thou, Walker man? You cultural illiterate. We will defend the ramparts against the difference between Dali and Daffy. Stand back, you varlot, you cur, you peasant, you churl.

To the left of the old building as one faces it from Main Street is a narrow resting space of raised concrete planters containing shade trees above and benches below. This space had, as far as Walker could see from his position on the sidewalk, fewer people in it than it bigger neighbor across the street. The shade looked so inviting that Walker eschewed the air conditioned blankness of the library and went up the short flight of steps and onto the little side plaza next to the museum looking like Custer must have looked just before the trap was sprung. Here I am defending Fort Doom against the savage horde. Where is the cavalry? Oh, so sorry. They stopped for dinner along the way. SOL, baby. Have a sandwich instead. Walker looked at the paper sack he held. Mmmmm. Looks a little squashed. He sat down on the bench and pulled a zip lock bag containing a flattened sandwich from the bag.

"I don't think I'd want to trade places with your sandwich."

Walker looked up and found a familiar face standing in front and looking down at him, smiling a little, uncertain. He had seen her somewhere before but could not place her. Not at work certainly. He thought maybe the bus. Lots of faces there. Somehow, that didn't seem right, though. On his street? In a store? It was not a memorable face, somewhat plain in fact. The woman was probably in her fifties and on the thin side. Her eyes were brown and looked well used behind pouches of slightly discolored flesh. Her flesh was as white as copy paper. No outside activity for this woman. Muscles and skin sagged slightly from her jaw and he saw the faint track of a blue vein in her forehead. Where had he seen her? Supermarket? One of the checkers maybe? He tried to imagine her with a green apron and a name tag. Nothing. The seconds were ticking and Walker still had not responded. He looked down at the bag with the sandwich in it. It looked dead and evil. "I don't blame you," he finally told her and smiled. "Besides, I'd have a helluva time holding you in a bag in one hand."

The woman laughed, a momentary melody that started low in her chest and ended high, almost a bark but much softer. Her whole face seemed to soften, but it could have been the dappling of the sunlight through the shade tree in back of him. "You don't recognize me, do you?" she asked.

"I'm afraid not."

"The library on Saturday."

"Oh sure. The woman behind the desk." Walker smiled with relief.

"Yes, and you are the patron of the table in the center that has a dark stain on its front."

"I noticed that too. From coffee?"

The woman shrugged; her shoulders trembled slightly and she pursed her lips as if to blow a stray hair from her face. "Maybe a long time ago before they varnished the desk top." She smiled and stuck out her hand. "I'm Azalea Jones, but most folks just call me Zinny."

"Johnny Walker. My nickname's Agile."

"Agile Walker. How on earth did you come by that?"

"When I was a boy, I was a complete klutz. One day, I was walking along and tripped on an uneven section of sidewalk and split my chin open. My parents rushed me to the hospital where a doctor sewed me up. When I went to have the stitches removed, the doctor came bustling into the examining room and said 'My, my, and how is my agile walker doing?' I guess it just stuck." And suddenly Walker ran out of words and sat there wondering what to say. Good weather today. You like the summer? Hot, though. That's a pretty outfit. Is it new? It suits you. All the different ice-breakers he could think of fell dead at his feet. He didn't even know this woman, had just met her and already was feeling as if he had committed some gauche act that she would have the good grace to ignore but would later remember with a shake of her head and maybe oh my what a strange little man that was under her breath and then a quick look around to see if anyone had heard her. His tongue felt stuck to the roof of his mouth as he looked at her and fear caused his facial muscles to tighten up. He gripped his sandwich bag more tightly feeling the food inside squish even more between his fingers. He had talked with this woman but she was not behind the information counter now and she looked totally different and much better standing there with her close cut brown hair dappled by the sunlight filtering through the branches overhead. Walker wished he were standing behind a counter himself so she could not see what a fat old warthog he was.

"I see. Which chin?"

"I beg your pardon?"

"Which chin got split open?"

Zinny seemed genuinely curious and friendly, but Walker had spent too many years being hacked at and made fun of. He shrugged, angry that he had even thought he liked this woman. Silence was the only sound in their space, outside of which life, intelligent and otherwise, went on. It hung between and around them like darkness on the night.

"I blew it again," Zinny finally said, turning slightly away and speaking to no one in particular unless it was herself. She sighed softly and looked across the plaza at the side of the museum. Then she turned and touched his arm gently. "I do that, you know. I say the right thing at the wrong time or place or the wrong things just about any time. I never mean to be rude or cruel, but, as often as not, that's how it turns out. I shoot off my big mouth when my brain is full of blanks." She shivered and smiled in a self-deprecating manner. "When I was in college," she continued, "I told a friend that she was crazy to go out with her boyfriend at that time, that he was trouble and would dump her in a second. She married him and, last I heard, they were still together with kids." Zinny trailed off into silence once more. "I hope you'll forgive me. I meant no harm." There was a moment of silence and then Zinny looked almost shyly at him smiled. "You look as if I was standing here naked. Did my wig fall off?" Grinning, she reached up and touched her hair where it was parted and brushed back from her forehead framing her face. Walker smiled back and pointed to his real chin where a very small scar was faintly visible. Zinny leaned towards him and peered at his chin and Walker smelled apple and something softer and a whole lot more expensive. Something inside of him stirred slightly and opened one eye.

"Aha," she said. "The mark of the agile, by all that is holy," she intoned sonorously and made the sign of the cross in the air in front of her.

"You wear a wig?" Walker asked, amazed that he had been unable to tell.

Zinny giggled. "No silly. I was just joking." She reached into a huge black and tan leather bag hanging from her left shoulder and came out holding a Gala apple in her right hand. "My lunch," she announced and took a hefty bite.

The action shook Walker out of his daze and he pushed himself to his feet and gestured to the bench beside him. "Join me. Please. I am so sorry. I forgot my manners."

"Nonsense. We just met, after all." Zinny took another bite of the apple, shrugged her bag from her shoulder and sat tidily down next to where Walker had been seated.

Walker sat back down, and opened his sandwich bag, sliding the top down until the mashed mess inside was poking up from the plastic. "Is that all you eat for lunch?" Fine for her. Built like a dammed stick. I'll bet she eats a head of lettuce for supper. Snobby bitch. Probably hugs trees and bashes our country in her spare time. Walker smiled politely and bit into his sandwich while looking around the little plaza as if for someone he might know. Zinny took another bitecrunch of the apple. "So how's it going?"

"What?"

"The book."

"Book?" Walker stared at her blankly.

"Or whatever you were working on in the library."

"Oh. Yes, well okay, I think. Just a rough draft right now." Yeah and ninety percent of that still in my head but still it's there and it's gonna be great. I have to believe and focus. I don't care what anyone says. I'm going to do this. Walker's ego pulsed like a heart. His chins quivered. No sireeee don't have to be skinny to write and don't have to live in some dammed garret either and don't have to eat my mashed sandwich with librarians.

"Gotta start someplace," Zinny went on agreeably. "War And Peace started with one word and so did every other piece of writing."

"That you know of."

"What does that mean?"

Walker didn't know but he would be dammed and in hell before admitting so. "Just that."

Zinny rolled her eyes upwards. "Okay. I suppose so, but if there is writing without words, that would be thoughts or verbalized stories and not writing."

"So writing has to be physical?" Walker, having dug himself a man hole and finding no way to climb out of it, bit into his sandwich and sulked.

"At some point, I would think." Zinny replied.

"And if a tree falls in the forest and there is no one to hear it?"

Zinny laughed, full throated and rich. "Then no one knows or cares."

Walker looked at her and could not help himself but burst out in a loud guffaw, squeezing the mess of his sandwich even harder as he did so.

"Hah," he finally managed.

Zinny grinned. "Hah yourself."

Walker took another bite. Even mashed it didn't taste too bad. The bacon came through loud and clear. "So you eat out here all the time?"

"When the weather's good. The employee lounge at the library gets stuffy. Besides, I get tired of looking at the same faces day in and day out."

"Yep. I'm trying to economize". He held up the remains of his sandwich.

Zinny took the last bite from her apple and held up the core for his inspection. She rose and walked over to a concrete trash container where she dropped the remains of her lunch into its gaping mouth.

"I'd ask you to join me for a light repast but I see you have already completed your prandial chore," he joked and smiled up at her as she returned to her seat.

In answer, she reached into the cavern of her bag and came out with another Fuji. "See," she said as she sat down. "But I'm really not that hungry today. The heat probably." She put the apple back into the bag.

"Okay," Walker grumped. Snotty bitch. Thinks she's got an answer for everything because she works in a library. Probably pees library paste. I know women like that at work. Think their shit doesn't stink. Walk around checking their PDAs and talking into their Bluetooth headsets so it looks as if they are have a nonsensical conversation with thin air. Get one of them behind you and suddenly you think someone's talking to you and you turn around and there she is talking away a mile a minute and you're standing there with your thumb up your ass. They're always up on the latest twist of corporate America's move to destroy the English language. You don't talk with a person; you reach out to him. You didn't make a mistake; you rethink your figures. You don't move to a different plan; you transition to it. If you mentioned religion, it was to say that you had designated your bimonthly charity payment from your paycheck to something like children's relief or Catholic Charities.

"Are you Catholic?" he asked her apropos to nothing at all and immediately regretted doing so. He did not even know this woman and she might be insulted by such a question. In an age when everyone was considered a victim of one sort or another and political correctness of racial and societal terminology had taken the place of the Spanish Inquisition, when supposedly serious people were suing to have the word "God" and any other religious object or phrase removed from public buildings, when the Grinch went to court to have Christmas crèche scenes banned, one never knew what might be insulting. Like her question about his chins, he reflected with some degree of guilt. How ironic that it should now be his turn. "I'm sorry," he continued. "It's none of my business, really. Not important anyway." He looked away in some distress and then looked back at his new lunch partner.

Zinny's face tightened and her mouth became a thin line of uncompromising flesh. Her cheeks puffed outwards and her eyes crossed until she looked ridiculous. Suddenly, she exploded into laughter, rocking back and forth beside him like a maniac and Walker finding such glee infectious, could not help but join it. "No. I'm a woman," she gasped between breaths.

That set them both off again and they presented a curious sight to anyone who happened to come up the steps onto the plaza from the sidewalk and peer around the side of the enclosure; a fat, old man with closely cropped salt-and-pepper hair. a large gut and double chins rocking back and forth his face tilted upwards and his belly shaking with the effort and a birdlike woman sitting beside him with her mouth open and tears running down her face, left fist pounding weakly on one knee while the other leg bounced up and down with her glee.

"Oh boy," Walker finally managed to get out between great whooping breaths, "Oh boy, ohohohohoh," he ran out of breath and leaned forwards panting slightly. "Oh my," he finally managed to finish.

"I'm not terribly religious," Zinny told him with a straight face and then chuckled again, a low bubbling sound in the key of C.

"Well don't worry about it," Walker replied, "'cause I don't know any Latin. We had it in school but I've forgotten what little I might have known."

"*Vox populi.*"

"Is that a social disease?" He teased.

"No silly. It's Latin."

"Wow. I'm in the presence of culture."

"You betcha. I'm so cultured that I've practically turned into a mound of yogurt. I'm sorry I interrupted your lunch."

Walker suddenly realized that, not only was he feeling pretty good at that moment, but he had totally forgotten the remains of the sandwich he was holding and that was turning to mush in his hand. He slipped the mess back into its baggy and smiled at Zinny. "Don't worry about it. I don't." In another moment of clarity he knew that this was true. He had come for an hour of creative solitude determined to make progress on his book and he had failed. His failure had left him sitting on a park bench with an idiotic smile on his face and no thought of working.

It feels strange to be just sitting here, he thought. He wondered how she was feeling? Haven't laughed so hard in a long time. She looks happy too so he guessed that she had a good laugh as well. It's been a great lunch but he had to be getting back. What a shame. Be nice to sit here with her all afternoon joking back and forth. Beth never was one for joking much. Always serious about one thing or another. Wonder if she laughed much as a kid? Knowing her parents, probably not. They'd probably have gotten on with my parents. All of them so self righteous and full of themselves. Still, Beth and he had a few laughs like the time they'd taken Jen up to the Big E and she saw the huge draft horses. The look on her face had them both in stitches. Mommy, mommy look at the horse. He's as big as a mountain and she spread her arms as far apart as they would go and stood there with a look of wonder on her face. Good times, those. All gone now. Gotta go. Maybe stop by the library after work and go to the hospital from there. Strange how life changes going nowhere forever and then changing in less than a moment relatively speaking of course. He could be walking down the street eating a burger full of plans and reason, sound of mind and body and in a blink the food disappears, the plan is in the shitter and the even the street's name has changed and all he can do is keep on walking wondering whether, as he did so, whether he was meant to do so by the plan of some spirit greater than his own or whether he was simply a product of random chance, able to decide only on how to react but not to cause, in turn, a new reaction.

"You look so serious," Zinny remarked.

Walker felt a shiver run through his body and stiffen the hair on his arms. Had she guessed what he was thinking? Not possible. Even he was not sure of anything other than he had really enjoyed this time even though he had failed to write even one word but what to do with that feeling; ah therein lay the rub, he thought. Only a few blocks away his wife lay in pain and sickness. He had no right to be enjoying himself. Walker shrugged his shoulders trying to be polite. "Not really serious. Just enjoying the moment."

"Jees. If that's how you look when you're enjoying I don't want to be around you when you hate something." Zinny pursed her lips, looked sideways at him as if considering whether she had done the right thing or not. "You look as if your best friend had just shot your dog or something like that."

"Surely not that bad." Walker tried on a smile. That was it, of course. He shouldn't be enjoying the moment. Not with Beth in the hospital. What kind of monster had he become that he should like being with Zinny? He shouldn't even be talking to her let alone laughing and sitting here grinning and joking like some great fat fool. The thought of Beth and Zinny brought back memories of the past that now seemed almost irrelevant.

He remembered years before when he came home from work and Beth met him at the door and told him that someone had called and accused him of cheating. He wasn't and said so, but Beth didn't believe him. He was enraged that she did not. Stomped into the large closet that was their living room and plopped his ass on the couch. What a horrendous scene that was. They were still young then, and Jen was still a little girl, and they were possessed by the intolerance of youth that made compromise and discussion like a Rainbow fish of fragile beautiful colors that quickly disappear out of water. That some asshole would call her and accuse him of cheating pissed him off. That his wife would stand in the kitchen doorway of their tiny apartment and scream that she didn't believe him pushed him over the edge and he'd screamed back at her. Two hyenas fighting.

"Bastard"

"Bitch."

"Why would someone call and tell me that you've been porking his wife?"

"How the hell would I know? Maybe he called the wrong number or he's got the wrong person. Maybe someone doesn't like me or doesn't like you."

"Oh for sure. Some stranger doesn't like you. Do you know how stupid you sound?" She threw at pot of rice she was holding into his face, and Carolina brand rice sprayed across the room and suddenly there was little Jenny standing in the hallway leading to her bedroom staring at them with full-moon eyes and mouth agape.

"Jennifer, go back to your room please."

"But Mom."

Beth pointed in the direction of Jenny's bedroom. Jenny pouted and then disappeared.

"Maybe we should both cool down a little." he was looking for any little break in the rolling line of thunderstorms his wife had become.

"You'd better cool down real quick, Agile, or you'll be sleeping on the sidewalk."

"I've done nothing wrong, and I'll be sleeping right fucking here, thank you very much." We stood ten feet apart and glared at each other and then Beth turned and and disappeared back into the kitchen.

He'd disliked couches ever since and would take a chair whenever he had a choice. He wondered if Zinny liked couches? Probably has one that is covered in plastic printed with little yellow flowers. Wherever she lives is probably stuffed with ugly furniture. He'd bet she's was cat person. Walker hated cats. Filthy creatures. Tear up your stuff and then walk away with their tails sticking up in the air. Cute when they are kittens but then they grow up and stink up the house with their boxes and hair balls. He wondered what Jen was doing? Scrounging food or change probably or drinking McDonalds' coffee with her friends somewhere. What kind of life is that? Sooner or later, she's got to wake up and deal with reality. Does she really see herself doing this when she's forty? Christ, he had to try again. Got to convince her somehow that life is not some festering wound that won't heal. Money may not be everything but it's not nothing either. Didn't spend all those years raising her to have her live in a fucking gutter.

"Well, I need to get back," Walker told Zinny.

"Me too. Awfully nice chatting with you, "Zinny replied sounding both wistful and upbeat at the same time. She rose to her feet, smiled and waggled her fingers at him. "See you at the library, I suppose."

"See you there," Walker agreed and smiled back feeling somewhat relieved.

Zinny walked away towards the steps leading down to the street, a thin, erect figure that did not look back. Walker looked at the paper bag containing the remainder of his lunch and crushed it between his hands. Rising, he walked up the passage between the concrete seats and the museum and plopped the bag into a large, black wire trash container. It occurred to him that he might be hungry later but somehow that made no difference as he walked slowly back towards his building.

E2 5:30 PM

God, what a day. If ever Walker felt less like being on the receiving end of an analogue sound wave pushed across thousands of miles of copper wire and translated back into human speech at his end it was today. We have travelled so far along the technology highway and so quickly relative to perceived progress in past ages that we tend to become technology ourselves, living machines plugged into this net or that net or ARAPNET now the internet and existing on the flow of sound and sense from all parts of the industrialized world. He needed a Jack. Yes indeed. Ah, there it is. Strong and brown and now with a cube or two. Perfect. So for all the technology man still sighs with relief at the end of a work day in a comfortable chair with a glass in his hand, whether it be it mead or ale or port or scotch or bourbon or even milk, God forbid. Whatever floats the boat and gets us from where we did not want to be to where we want to be and let the memory of telephone calls slowly fade like the tattered remnants of a bad dream that flee even as you stagger to the bathroom sweating and trembling from the experience. Hard to forget that one guy though. What an asshole. Yelling and screaming about getting his problem fixed TODAY. Couldn't do it. Not with all the kings horses and all the kings men. Oh how the heaven's trembled as thunder rolled across the barren plain. Let me speak to your manager. No let me speak to her manager. This is totally unsatisfactory. I am surprised that your company has survived with this level of customer service and please transfer me to the local field office where I might find someone intelligent. Ah John, you sinner you, transferring that good and godly man to Dial-A-Prayer. Oh dear. Did he transfer him to the wrong number? So sorry. Really he was. Truly. Absolutely forever. He must have had a brain fart. Surely He-who-hates-bacon will keep that action in mind when next he saw Walker if indeed he did since he will probably still be listening to dickhead on the heavenly 800 line. Ah but Jack goes down as smoothly as a con man's spiel, warming its way as it goes. Warm as Zinny at lunch today. Didn't get any writing done and didn't mind a bit.

Good looking woman, and funny too. Liked the way she smiled as if she were opening up a view of some golden land full of sunshine where rosy-cheeked maids whistled as they milked contented cows and cowboys strummed guitars from the porches of haciendas. Made him forget everything for the moment. That kind of mind-opening smile. A Cinderella smile or maybe the smile of the prince when he found the glass slipper. Not exactly a raving beauty but she looked good sitting there in the sun eating her apple and chatting away as if we were old friends just met after a long separation. Walker liked the memory. None of this politically correct speech that turns us all into mindless drones buzzing soullessly through the hive and filling the air with monotonous languor. No touching. No sexual remarks. Don't get too close. Don't get too far. If someone reports you you're fired. Nice to get away from all that crap. We've turned into a nation of victims. No matter what happens to a person, someone else or something else caused it and they should be sued. A nation of ambulance chasers and class-action millionaires. Get through Podunk Law School and you got it made in the shade. Just find some unhappy soul and promise them that there is a price that will make that unhappiness disappear and you are just the person to wrest that money for them from the evil clutches of big business and big insurance and big this and big that. When in doubt, find an illness that lots of people suffer from and sue some major part of the economy for causing it, but it's no good thinking about how far our society has sunk over the years. Think good thoughts. Zinny with no clothes on. That's the ticket. Calmed him down right away. Nice breasts. Large. Probably still firm but soft maybe with pointed, little nipples. Sat for a minute with the phone offline and that thought filling his mind until it was so detailed it almost seemed real and he went back to work but not without getting a little stiff yes Lord and it felt good, too. Hasn't happened in a while sitting at work or anywhere else for that matter. What a treat lunch was. She's a real pistol. Good thing she's not a rabid follower of He-who-hates-bacon, Thought he might have put her off by saying that. Good laugh, though. Haven't laughed like that in a long time. Not much to laugh about recently, he thought.

When Beth and he were first together there was lots of laughter and the hot, wet dreams of youth just beginning to sense the totality of the human coil but the first time we met was not funny at all though looking back on it now he had to smile. It happened at the Durham Fair to which he had gone out of a sense of desperation. His dorm room had become a prison cell. He felt both depressed and crushed by the small room. He was sitting at his desk staring at Paradise Lost and not seeing a single word when Benny Simon from the room next to his stuck his head through the door and announced that he was going to the fair and did Walker want to come? He did. Milton got tossed into a corner and he'd run down the stairs behind Benny suddenly feeling as if someone had just told him he had won a million bucks or that the president of IBM wanted his services as soon as he was finished with school. His roommate, blessedly, had gone out the night before and not returned so he did not have to deal with him. Temporarily, at least, he was master of my own life and it felt great.

People go to fairs for many reasons. Some like the rock bands or the country and western singers. Some ooh and ahh at the tractor pulls and the chain saw contests. Others look at the livestock and food competitions or stick with the games along the carny rows. Moms and Dads like it because the kids have a blast cheaply. Lovers like it for the same reason and often don't even make it out of their cars. Some people just go for the sounds of the rides, the children screaming, papers blowing around and lines shuffling slowly forwards, tickets flying, gum popping, cotton candy billowing pink and green and blue, barkers barking, clowns strutting, prize bulls blowing and car horns honking. For Walker it was always the food.

He loved starting at one end of the food stalls and working his way down to the other end, particularly if there was a beer tent in the area where digestion can occur while a cold brew or two helped it along. French fries hot from the fryer glistening with grease and salt crystals, hot dogs (regular, kosher, foot long, Bratwurst, Weiswurst, Kielbasa, thick, thin, red, pink, multicolored, wrinkled, juicy) on a fresh bun piled with onions, sauerkraut and mustard, hamburgers with cheese and bacon, brown and shiny with grease tucked under a lettuce leaf and a thick slice of tomato and a pickle. That just makes the whole thing perfect. The tang of a dill pickle sets off the cheese perfectly. Only problem was that back then, you couldn't usually get bacon on your burger at these events. He loved bacon, though. Hickory smoked, thick cut or sugar cured or maple flavored. One could eat it all day long and it can be put on almost anything.

So he was walking around on an Epicurean tour of the Durham Fair when he spotted the epitome of fast food delight, an ice cream stand. What a perfect way to top off the full load of fuel he had just taken on.

Double scoop. Just what the doctor ordered. He marched happily through the crowd as parents gripped little children tightly by the hand and the older ones ran zigzag through the people laughing and yelling insults at each other. He watched the girl pile vanilla and chocolate into a large cone, handed over the necessary *gelt* and turned to wander off with his quickly melting treasure.

"Ohh shiiiit."

And found himself staring into two, large, brown eyes, and, looking downwards an instant later, two large breasts covered with the contents of his double scoop ice cream cone. A mixture of chocolate and vanilla was slowly oozing down her valley of delight. Shocked, he stepped backwards hitting the front of the Happy Farms ice cream stand as the girl brushed gobs of ice cream off her now stained and dirty blouse. "I . . . I'm so sorry," he stuttered staring at the damage with horror.

"Look at me." She held her hands up towards me, finger splayed wide open and a look of disgust on her face.

"Really. I am so sorry. It was very clumsy of me."

"You bet you are, you stupid shit."

Walker raised his gaze from the girl's chest and to his left and standing there staring at him like a prize bull in front of a red flag was Tom Beauchamp, Walker's roommate. Beauchamp's face had turned bright red and his eyes had gone small and piggy. He seemed ready to rip one of Walker's arms off and beat him over the head with it. He strode forward until his face was about an inch from Walker's. His breath smelled as if he had eaten a dead rat. "You're going to pay for that, Walker," he snarled.

"Of course." Walker pushed him away and turned to the girl at Beauchamp's side.

"I'll be more than glad to pay the cleaning bill." He gulped down a sudden wave of unreasoned fear that made his legs tremble. Unstoppable force meets stick of butter.

Tom grabbed a handful of napkins from the counter behind me and thrust them at the girl. "Here, Beth. Use these."

Beth dutifully dabbed at her blouse with the napkins without much effect. One breast was still chocolate and her white bra showed clearly through the brown wet stain. She was covered with Walker's food and he knew immediately that she was the most beautiful girl he had ever seen. He wanted suddenly to lean over and suck the ice cream from her breast.

"What are you staring at?" she demanded. "Oh, I know what it is. Little chubby lost his ice cream." She lisped. "Does he want Mommy to get him another one?" She ended with a hiss and a look of pure disgust.

Tom guffawed, moved over and took her by the arm. Walker turned and walked away to the sound of their laughter. He was half mad with self-hatred, embarrassment and fear. He swore that he would never have anything to do with moronic jocks and their brainless sluts.

Tom and he were just about exact opposites. Even then he was small, fat, ugly, bespectacled, insecure, and trying to glide through my life without making a ripple let alone a wave and then there was this big, athletic piece of mean with whom he shared a dorm room under stressful circumstances. Tom would come back from the bathroom, drop his towel and stand admiring himself in the mirror. "Perfection," he would tell Walker with a smirk tugging at his lips. Not a woman born who can resist it." And then he would run his fingers through the thick patch of hair on his chest and then grab his dick and wave it back and forth. "Take a good look at a real man, Walker. It's everything God forgot to give you or probably decided you weren't worth the effort." It was true that his was bigger than Walker's although, as Walker would later realize, Tom was not, as they say, hung like a horse. He simply thought that he was. At the time, though, Walker had simply turned and went back into his little bedroom and left Beauchamp and his ego alone. That was Tom. Probably still is. A strutting, preening, arrogant, bullying, thick muscled, intellectually lazy, good-ol-boy, conceited, hypocritical mass of young adult male. So Beth and Walker had met but not under the best of circumstances.

Walker wondered how Tom was doing? Still alive probably, but maybe not. They were no longer young, after all. He probably got aggressive with the wrong person. He had a bad temper and not a lot of patience. Walker hoped Beauchamp was a janitor or something like that. Hope he ended up somewhere getting fucked in the ass by someone twice his size. They were so dissimilar that they must have been paired as roommates because neither of them had the money to live off campus and nobody else wanted them. It's pretty much the same now. Don't give a shit about Beauchamp. Still scratching for money. Gonna have to sell the house to pay off the medical bills.

Life is like a pile of leaves tossed by a sudden burst of wind, swirled about in a dervish of energy and then left to drift again. He'd always wondered just how much people can influence their realities. Plot and plan, decide this or that, do this or don't. From waking until the temporary death of sleep they feel the master of their universe but each person's universe is different, each reality a different color. If he decided to get up tomorrow, will that be a good thing or a bad thing? Would the act of living put him in control or simply establish the myth of control. His first meeting with Beth was sheer accident as was seeing Zinny in the library.

Wonder what Zinny's doing now? On her way home or already home and making dinner or reading a book or gardening? Maybe napping in front of the TV. Wonder if she sleeps naked? Now there's a lovely thought. On her back, maybe, with breasts flattened by the sheet or maybe no sheet. Hot tonight. She'll probably sleep uncovered unless she's got an air conditioner. He knew he'd be sweating through his sheets. Have to wash them then. Wonder how she looks under her panties. Might be a lot of hair there. Saw some on her arms but that doesn't mean anything. She might, though. Nice to imagine her that way. Hmm. Not dead yet, he was glad to say. Thank God for small favors. Beth had a great bush. He loved to feel it against his face even when she was lying there stiff as a board and unresponsive. He loved her regardless right from the first time with that one chocolate tit.

F1 Bowles Park

Daylight sat dull on the window. Zinny Jones opened one eye, looked at the window, closed the eye, sighed and rolled over in bed getting tangled in her top sheet as she did so. The fan across the room pushed sticky, warm air against her face. The air smelled of exhaust and grease. It had probably started as a tangy zephyr in the Gulf but now it was old and stank and made her feel old and tired just breathing it.

She heard a muted snore from the bedroom next to hers and knew her father was still asleep. She might have a few minutes if she were really quiet, she decided. She would take her shower after he woke. She got off the bed and walked softly on bare feet out of her room and past her father's room where she stopped for a moment to make sure the air conditioner was still humming away. She then went down the stairs into the huge kitchen in the back of the old house. Zinny poured herself a glass of iced coffee from a pitcher in the fridge, sat at the circular wooden table with all its scars and marks, sipped at the coffee and tried to wake up. Condensation from the glass formed a small puddle on the table underneath it. She got up, carefully folded a clean dish towel to use as a coaster and sat down again. Putting the towel on the table, she picked up the glass, wiped up the small amount of water on the table top, put the towel back down and placed the glass in its exact center. *Alles in ordnung.* The glass in the window over the sink sparkled with the sunrise. A pipe somewhere gurgled softly.

What a shame, she thought, that she couldn't take this moment and stretch it like a piece of taffy over the whole day. See everything but dimly and sweet too. Could always take a lick of two if she was feeling in need of a sugar kick. When she was little it was sweet. Waking up early when the whole world was still asleep. Only the birds making little noises outside the window she would listen to their music for a minute and then slip into pants and a t-shirt, and tiptoe down the stairs and out into the back yard. The grass was a silver carpet of dew and she was queen of her own little world. She would jump on her blue swing with its white seat and rusting chain links and float into the heavens. Up and up and then down and wheeee free of everything. She would be beautiful and accomplished. Men would swarm around her with flashing white smiles and expensive gifts. Dressed in white silk and a powder blue satin gown, she would graciously wave them all away while waiting for that special someone to appear at her side. Nice dreams. Young girl dreams. Maybe a little fanciful even at that age but she did so love that swing set. As she grew older and the swing became increasing rustier and smaller, she still enjoyed sitting there while working through increasingly adult problems, mostly concerning boys with pimples and bad breath and hands that were everywhere. YUCK.

Sighing, Zinny washed out her glass and headed back up the stairs to begin her day.

"Hello." The old man lay on top of his bed, the top sheet tangled around him so that he looked as if he had been trussed and tied up with it. From under the sheet, a wizened, lined face still with a full head of snowy, white hair, stared at her blankly.

"Good morning, Dad."

"Who are you?"

"Zinny, Dad. Your daughter." This was not going to be one of his better days. Who was she indeed? The girl on the swing, the professional, the care giver, the klutz, the romantic, the scullery maid, the bread winner, the keeper of the hearth? She was the tomb. She was the womb. For her father, it did not matter anymore. His life was a series of moments each lived and then forgotten, each a miniature exposure of thought and feeling but unconnected by memory to the next. Like an infant whose memory has yet to develop, each moment was enough unto itself.

Zinny helped her father untangle from the sheet and, grunting from the physical effort, got him sitting up on the side of the bed. His underpants and the sheet below were soaked in his urine. Third time this week, she counted. Guess I'll have to get diapers. Don't need the extra expense and hassle but there no longer is much choice. Expertly, she helped him to his feet, pulled his underpants down in one smooth movement, and then let him sit back down on the bed where she finished removing the offending garment. "Okay, Dad. Up and at 'em. Another day begins." She tried to sound upbeat and cheerful but had no idea to what degree of success she attained.

The old man responded well. "Okay." He said and smiled, swinging his legs from side to side, quite happy to be sitting there on the wet bed. He had already forgotten what the woman standing over him had said.

"C'mon, Dad. Here we go." Zinny pulled her father gently off the bed and partially supported him as he walked across the room and into the bathroom where he sat down on the toilet and grinned up at her.

"Okay," he said

"Just sit there and try to go." Zinny made sure he was aimed downwards into the bowl. She then went into the bedroom and stripped the sheets from the bed. Thank God for mattress guards. She bundled up the sheets into a damp wad. She would take them down to the washer in the cellar when she went down to go to work. She heard the sound of water on water from the bathroom. Good. He would stay dry a while. Maybe he was even doing number 2. That would spare Rosy a dirty task.

"I'm cold." The voice was now thin and plaintive overlaying a core of paranoia, helplessness and despair.

"Coming." Zinny went back into the bathroom and there to wash and clean him and bring him out and dress him and sit him in his chair and bring him cereal and a cup of coffee that was mostly milk and sit there chatting gaily about the day ahead, about the weather, about the leak in the kitchen faucet, about the new taxes being debated in the city council, about the house going up for sale on the next block, about anything and everything except that she loved him but he would never know it and she felt as she had as a child when she had dressed her doll and sat her down to have tea with Zinny except her Dad's hair was different and he did change expression and speak on occasion.

Zinny walked out the back door, down the driveway and turned left towards the bus stop. Thank God for Rosalinda and welfare although she knew she shouldn't even think like that, but how else could she afford to have someone take care of her father while she was at work? Money under the table works wonders. Whoever said it was useless was never in Zinny's situation. God, she was a mess today. Hair like a birds nest and not neat birds either but the ones who have sticks and stuff sticking out everywhere. Everything wrong. She looked like a tramp. Need a hair do. Wonder if Suzie would have time on Saturday? Make note to call her this morning first thing and get it done. Sure, and what are you going to use for money? Got utilities to pay. Dad's medicines and everything else. Food if there's any left for it. Minor thing, that. Put it off. Now that's a laugh. Oh sorry, Dad. Ran out of money for food. Here. Chew on this weed that was growing in the lawn. They sell it in the grocery store as fancy salad greens. Hah. Everyone's got their hand out it seems. Might have to give up the old place. Oh sure, Zinny, old girl, and what about Dad. What are you planning on doing with him?

> Dear dad
> Poor dad
> We've hung you in the closet
> And we're feeling so sad

Some kind of children's rhyme, she thought. Forget who wrote it. Maybe someone like me saying oh she loves you but caring for you and paying for the house and everything and you not knowing what's happening around you and your life in firefly moments blinking on and then gone and yes there are times when she thought that it would be okay if she found him some nice place where he would be comfortable and there would be people dressed in whites and blues and pinks yes rainbow people smiling and caring but then she remembered the places she visited and the people she talked to and it tore her heart out to think of her Dad sitting in a strange room parked in front of a TV that he always hated with a bunch of other people whose families have given up and put them there in the middle of a plastic and linoleum palace smelling of piss and fear and cleanser and shit and memories that go so far back and are so tangled up that the beginning is really at the end where all the trains stop forever. She would come every day, of course, and maybe he would smile a little and say okay and she would hope that he would know her but she would never be sure and all the going away and coming to and from and to again and again would leave her wondering if he had any life when she was away or knew of times okay times when there was a moment of clarity and she would miss it. Then, too, she would be alone with just memories like morning glories beautiful when all is still and the first light sneaks along the streets and sidewalks winking at the departing night and bathing the flowers in a soft tinted light and the little flowers burst open in a passion of white and red and purple and then the heat comes and suddenly they are gone. Okay. The bus stop is empty. Hate standing around with other people. Look one way and nod, another way and smile. Good morning how you doing okay she would say and yourself and she would walk over to the paper machine to check the headlines. Bush says war must go on. The daily paper's a rag. Not worth reading but good as an excuse to walk away from the eyes for they are always watching, waiting, judging everything even when she was alone. She felt them. Some were friendly and some were strange and some were bad but they are always there. Zinny's days were filled with eyes. Eyes across the counter. Do you have? Do you know? Can I get? How do I? Where is the . . .?" What is this? Who was she? Maybe she was just going nuts. But no one knows about the eyes but her and she was not telling a soul. They did her no harm and she could live with them still she was glad the bus stop was empty. She would go and check books in and out in and out and out and in and to and from to and from.

The bulk of the Connecticut Transit bus rumbled up the street towards her and she tucked away her thoughts as the bus pulled up and she climbed the steps into its bowels. Two rows of eyes, patient, tired eyes staring thoughtlessly ahead waiting for the workday to begin. Watching.

"Hey, Zinny."

Zinny looked to her left and saw a tiny pixy-like face smiling up at her. "Hey Taneesha. How ya doing this morning? Okay?" Taneesha Evans was a commercial lines underwriter at Travelers and was dressed for the part. She had on a beautiful, light gray pants suit over a pale yellow blouse.

"bout so so," she said and shrugged.

Zinny sat down next to her. "Yes. Another day."

"Yes. Did you see the Oscars last night?"

"Nope. By the time I finished getting Dad in bed I was so tired that I just flopped myself, you know?"

"I don't know if I could do what you do for your father. Maybe I could. Maybe not. I don't know. My father took off when I was too young to remember but my mother always said, she said, Taneesha, darlin', yu gotta make your own way, girl, and don't let no one tell you different and I heard her. When I'm too old to carry on I hope my kids don't face the same problem that you are dealing with." Taneesha laughed, a throaty roar that shook her tiny body so that she looked as if she was suffering from poison ivy. She radiated the simple joy of a person whose life revolved around only three poles, her church, her children, and her job and who found a smile no matter how awful things were and she had known far too much that was awful in her life but she had the inner strength of belief that better things were coming and that was sufficient for her to plow through the water with dignity and humor.

"Amen," Zinny agreed as the bus swung onto Paton street.

"So how you doing these days?" Taneesha looked sideways at her companion. Zinny was no looker for sure but Taneesha had known her a long time and the girl had grown up to be a woman with some steel inside. Taneesha was glad to see it because Zinny had been dealt some bad cards. "You know if you need anything just give a holler. Your dad saved my life and a lot of others too and he did it without fuss or a fancy office or big bills to make one's blood boil. Yes, sir, he was a gentleman. I still remember when I was a kid and saw you standing there as a little girl holding those bandages up for him when he was patchin' up ol' Scotty Dilluth, that no-good drunk, and you looked so serious that I had a time just to keep from laughing out loud. It's undoubtedly a good thing I didn't because my mother would have had me standing up for a week."

Zinny smiled at Taneesha though she could not remember that specific event. Still it rang true and she remembered many other times standing by her father helping with his patients. Most of the time her mother would forbid her to go into the office that was built out from the side of the old, frame house. Your father is working she would say so run out and play and don't get dirty before dinner and out the back door she would run to her swing in the sky but every once in a while her dad would smile down at her and say hush now Liz the child is curious and that is a good thing and then my dad would stretch out his hand and Zinny would look up a mile of white sleeve to his big smile beaming down on my like the sun of all suns and then he would walk towards his office and the sunlight would be his halo in the window like a golden crown lying on a field of white. He would walk past cabinets with dark shattering glass reflections on rows of bottles lined up like toy soldiers praying 'now I lay me down to sleep' and Zinny would hold his hand and walk silently beneath him and then they were by the big brown table with its brown leather top that glistened with years of use and came up just to the level of her eyes and she would look across its top across the room to an open door leading to a rectangular entryway in which some chairs had been placed.

And there brown like the table and sitting quietly with a patient dignity all their own would be his patients and her father would be tall above her and with gentle voice 'Good morning, Mrs. Wilson and how are you? Not too well? I'm sorry to hear it. Do come in and I'll take a look' and Zinny would look up at the sea of white coat and above that the light above the table and see the long worms coming out of his ear and pressing the disk into the brown flesh and, head down, listening and moving it and listening and 'Take a deep breath, now. That's it', and then looking down at her looking up at the worms and saying 'well what do you think, Zinny?' and then up at the mountain on the table with arms like car doors and holding her wrist in one hand and looking at his watch ticking only I couldn't hear it but Zinny could see the huge brown eyes staring down at me and she would look into them and lose something or felt that she had lost something anyway and feel fear until she had got hold of her Dad's coat and held it to her. She would look across the table and there would be more, entering silently on foggy feet, a slow shuffle, quiet cough, and then sitting staring in at me staring at them across the table. "I think a little antibiotic should do the trick,' my father would be saying, 'and it's not too expensive, really. Here is a prescription,' and there would be the sound of paper being ripped off the pad, 'and that will be ten dollars, but you can bring it around later if you don't have it on you' and then he would nudge Zinny as the lady made her way through the doorway clutching the paper he had given her and Zinny would say "Next, please." And another one would come in and they would have big brown eyes sometimes pain-filled or perplexed or resigned or desperate knowing something is wrong and aspirin didn't help nor the neighbor down the hall or the mother in Birmingham and then hearing about the white doctor who lived a few blocks over. Some had been here before and Dad knew their names and always had a smile and a moment to chat and some were strangers whose eyes looked down at her as one might look at an exotic flower in a garden and they would nod and say 'Lord, chil' but you is the prettiest little girl . . .' and the mouths would break open into smiles, some white, some rotten before sitting on the table in the smiling of the light. My father treated all with a gentle respect, kind hands obeying the commands of a trained mind. That is memory at least for she was too young to know the reality of those times in his office but she didn't ever remember her father raising his voice but we choose to remember the best for if we didn't would there not be far fewer people in this old world?

Zinny had a feeling that when it came time to pay, her father would charge his patients some small amount and tell many of them that they could come back later and tell others such things as 'Well, I hear you make the best peach pie around, Mrs. Drummond. Why Lissy Thurmond was talking about that just the other day.' And they would smile and chuckle low and promise themselves to send over the best of all pies and they would laugh and the light world on white just smiling and watching and smilewatchingsmile.

She was young but not totally naïve. Like most kids, she was sure at one time or another as they grow up, she'd heard her parents arguing and she knew that what her father chose to do was not always easy nor popular with her mother and Zinny would lie in her bed and listen to their voices float up from below, a disembodied dream sound unreal and yet scary somehow so that she clutched her pillow and finally brought it over her head.

"It's all very well to have poor patients, Walt but you have to think of us too."

"I do think of you. Every day. We get by all right. I have patients who pay."

"Not enough. What about Zinny, eh? What about her education?"

"Shutup, Liz. Don't you dare remind me about Zinny. I know dammed well that she is growing up."

Sometimes their voices would be swallowed in the rooms of the old house and Zinny would sit beyond their room and swing up yes into the light white down and through the shouts thinking that she was big like the moon with arms as broad as a river and goggle eyes like the aquarium at school where

"Well you sure don't act like it. We made the mortgage last month only by skimping on the groceries."

"But we made it."

"Goddammit, Walt. Life is not always about just getting by. I love you but I will not raise our child in poverty just because these people need you. We need you too. Make up your mind."

The little colored fish went up and down turning to stare at her smiling what a cute little human and so frowning and looks like she is thinking all the time but no it was just Zinny swinging free in a mind terrible thing to waste up and down wheeee.

With a sigh, Zinny came back to the present and looked down the aisle towards the front of the bus. Heads in hats, heads in the heat so she turned hers and looked out at the heat waves blurring the houses behind the row of cars parked along the curb with their bald tires and hoods raised as if to sneeze. Here she was, she thought, but back then if life was emotionally complicated as judged from where she was sitting now, it was also simpler. No bills. No ills. Just a girl growing. So why was she still here? She was here and now because of her father obviously, but maybe that was how it was supposed to work out. Maybe all the big and little decisions that we make along the way take us in a direction that we would have taken no matter what. A fatalistic viewpoint, no doubt, but her father was still here. Zinny went through college on a scholarship and with help from her Dad so he won the argument in the end but of course that might be because her mother sickened and died else it might still be going on today well maybe not because of Dad the way he is but she could still remember him saying to me 'Zinny, these folks have little and need someone on their side. I just happened to be handy.' "But who comes first, eh?" she murmured to herself softly.

"Amen to that, sister," Taneesha said. "Why are you rattling around in that house anyhow? Get an apartment. It would be easier on yourself and your dad." Taneesha folded her arms across her chest, an immovable object full of stern solidity, patience and intelligence shaped by generations of being one of those apart sitting there on endless busses on thousands of seats worn by ten thousand butts and looking out at a shabby world where getting by while staying proud and independent is a constant struggle of being black in a white world where equal never quite comes up to equal but is always a little bit less than and sometimes a whole lot less than so that, after a while, it becomes easy to give up. There are those who don't, however, and those who just plain won't and Hell would freeze over and be taken by the Montreal Canadiens before Taneesha Reynolds moved one iota from where she thought she should be or anyone around her should be or do and like a rock she sat and stared at Zinny next to her.

"It's our house. That's why not. Dad never wanted to leave it even when he knew his memory was going. I grew up there. Know every piece of it inside and out." She replied to Taneesha. That wasn't the whole of it, though, she admitted to herself. Just the past week, she had walked along the second floor hallway and seen the faint tracks of her passage in the floor behind her. Must clean and dust and get this place shipshape, she told herself sternly but where was the time, and energy to do it? By the time she got home, and got supper for her father and herself she was bushed and it all got put off until the next day and then the next and suddenly the place was filthy and she was behind the eight ball once again and Zinny once more remembered the sight of ghostly passage of her feet on the floor but no one is there now, she thought. And no one has been in most of those rooms now empty but once ringing with laughter through the blue light of the sunsets in red and gold and stepping into her parent's room that was now hers and standing by the bed with its maroon duvet like an ocean at sunset yes and across from it the big shiny bureau with its brass drawer pulls and on top a white and gold clock with little black hands and a pendulum showing a star girl lying on top of a crescent moon. Back and forth, back and forth she would swing into the endless sky staring blankly out at the world with just a trace of smile under a mound of blonde hair. Tick tock, tick tock. She always looked happy with the sort of half-smile happiness when nothing much is going on but everything is doing its thing, no worries, and no clouds on the horizon. Zinny remembered standing by the bed watching the little girl tick tick and the black hands slowly move tock tock like no worry be happy and the light in the window lay upon the red sea sleeping on the blood water under the crescent moon.

Now Zinny tick tocked in her seat and stared at Taneesha while remembering the house still, strong, immovable, old in the way of age but full of life and lives where memories spooled onwards in a kaleidoscope of motions forward and back assed in the mortal way that imprints on cells slowly dying but the memories remain like weathered shingles shouldering aside the rains and winds. "Dad loves the house," she replied as if he had suddenly appeared in the aisle of the bus and was pointing out the window as his house disappeared behind them. "I think he still knows it, or knows that he is in someplace where he is supposed to be or where he wants to be. He seems happy to be there as far as I can tell," she finished feeling a little lame at having to admit that sometimes she could not even tell whether her father was happy or sad. It made her feel helpless and angry at the same time though she couldn't say what caused the anger. Maybe she would just have to kick the bus when she got downtown. "I don't know what would happen if I moved him. He might not take it well, you know what I mean?"

Taneesha nodded. "Maybe you're right. The old doc he's like one of the boundary stones, you know, that is pounded into the ground and you know it's not going anywhere anytime." Taneesha beamed and chuckled her understanding, a low, throaty purring sound like a large truck engine turning over. "I know there's a lot of folks would be upset if he moved and that's a fact."

Yes, thought Zinny, they would be. All those people who were young with my father, who worked at Veeder Root, Spencer Turbine, Otis, the Hartford, Travelers and all the offices and banks and insurance companies cleaning the floors and taking out the trash, cooking the meals and polishing the floors, line workers, assembly men, cashiers, janitors, cooks, landscapers, porters and waiters, those invisible people who helped keep the business of business in business. 'Morning, suh. How are you this morning? Looking like to be a nice today, yes suh.' And then going home to cramped apartments with squalling kids and everyone trying to make them bend over and take it where the sun don't shine and then the children growing up angry, better educated, looking to quickly change that which could only move in a slow, generational tide spreading up the sand further and further and then up and over the feet of those who would push it left or right and making a joke of those who would legislate human emotions both good and bad and still they lived in the old house. No window knew a rock, no lock a pick, no room a bullet hole while all around them guns spoke the language of death and destruction and the four horsemen rode out of a bloody dawn where babies bore gang markings and death passed out needles in the rank hallways of the projects. And this because of her father. He had turned away no one. He treated all who showed up in his office regardless of race or injury. The leaders of the burgeoning gangs in Hartford had all been his patients at one time or another as had their families, friends, and associates over a period of forty years. Now the old man, long retired did not need to worry about attacks from the vandals, thieves, druggies, whores, con artists, gangbangers, losers, pimps, homeless, bullies, and fanatics. The word was out and Zinny could not remember any attack on the house or its occupants. Unlikely as it was, she had once left the house and forgotten to lock the door. She had come back to find it as she had left it and her father sitting in his chair smiling and smiling as if he were in some West Hartford mansion surveying acres of tended green lawn and not his room with its peeling wallpaper from fifty years before.

What would it take, Zinny wondered as the bus pulled up to another stop, to end it all, to turn the house into a beggar's feast? Probably just leaving, getting out and leaving behind the iron pipes, peeling paper and torn linoleum, warped doors and worn lintels for the house is just the sum of its parts she reminded herself. Full of memories but those you could take with you. Dad could take no memories though. That was the problem. Sure a house is no more than timbers and stone built on a lot and perched over a dirt cellar that she hadn't been in for years but for her father it was all there was, his chair, his room, his window. No past and future. No memories to take, just the present, moment by moment. If they left would the new owners appreciate that? Not likely. Maybe no one would buy it. The area is a bad one, after all. Zinny realized that she might have major problems just selling it and there was no money to fix it up so the price would be way less than its value. Such practical considerations made her feel even less secure and she lapsed back into the past.

Where lines of black and tan faces standing in the yard, stolid, indifferent, possessed of patience so endless that to see it was to know the depth of despair that comes when you know that you are in play and there are no good endings and there is nothing you can do about it but stand and wait and look at the back of the person ahead of you as the evening ticks on the grindingly long work day sits on your body like a slab of granite. Zinny came back to the present with a sigh and stared to her left where the shoulder of the bus driver curved across the passing of two and three story houses lining Cornwall Avenue. "Can't stay. Can't move," she told herself softly but bitterly and felt her stomach lurch sending its contents back towards the entrance at which they'd already paid their fare. She swallowed hard and felt her innards settle down to their normal level of inconstancy. She farted softly and felt the push of her bowels against the seat beneath her. Later at work, she thought, well maybe. Make a good break anyway from the books and cards and web sites. Sitting there waiting and so life passes one bit and then pause and then

"Zinny, honey. You have lots of room in there. Rent one room out. It would help with the bills and with your father. The house big enough so you wouldn't feel crowded, know what I'm saying to you?" she asked Zinny agreeably.

Zinny turned towards her, excitement in her voice. "Yes Taneesha. Good thought. Yes, I'll think on that." Zinny sat back, aging and ageless in the mystery of her feelings, alone and universal.

F1 Main Street

"I still don't get it." The old woman peered at Zinny across the counter. "I click and nothing happens. It's broken. Like all the stuff around here. Every time you turn around something doesn't work. When are you people going to get your act together?" The overhead fluorescents glinted off her coke-bottle glasses making it seem as if she had two white holes in her face to match the thin white hair falling on either side of it and skin so thin as to be almost translucent.

"Don't worry, Mrs. Fuller. I'll be right over to help you." Zinny smiled in what she hoped was a reassuring fashion. The woman was determined to conquer the internet but she could never remember from one time to the next what she was supposed to do and was always upset when the unexpected screen popped up or she couldn't get to the one that she wanted. "Go and sit down, now."

"I shall wait right here," Fuller snapped. "You told me to do the wrong thing and now the machine is broken. You better fix it or I'll report you." She shook a trembling finger in Zinny's direction. "Maybe I will anyways."

"Sit down and be quiet," Zinny told her sternly. "You know better than to raise your voice in here.

"Hrummph," Fuller snorted. She crossed her arms and stood there glaring at Zinny.

"Please move to one side. I will be able to help you in just a minute," Zinny motioned the old woman to the left and looked for the next person in line. "Yes, sir how may I help you?" she looked beyond Fuller at the man standing behind her and extended a hand to receive the book he was returning, flicking automatically to the back cover and the date due card and then scanning the bar code and adding it to the stack on the cart behind her and then the phone rang and another person came up with a question and Zinny got back to Mrs. Fuller who by that time was in a high state of dudgeon and in the process of breaking her cell phone in an effort to call the chief librarian to complain. Zinny got the irritating old battle ax set on Yahoo Fashions and then back to the information desk for more calls and more books on carts and endless hands holding more books, magazines, articles, notebooks, paperbacks, reprints, xeroxs, journals, encyclopedias, dictionaries, index cards, menus, coffee cups, memos, bulletins, emails, transcripts, excerpts and just plain trash when they couldn't find a waste receptacle or simply were walking around holding it for the hell of it and were caught by surprise when she asked if she could dispose of what they were holding for them.

Midge Mallon, a friend and coworker, was sitting in the employee lounge when Zinny took her break. Midge was a small woman with big mud colored eyes, a small trembling pout of a mouth and the beginning of female pattern baldness. She always looked as if she were about to burst into tears and had come into this world with the expectation that someone would immediately slap the shit out of her. "Hi, Zinny. Have you heard the news?" Midge always had news but most of the time it proved more rumor than fact.

"I don't know. What news?"

"The politicians have cut our budget again. Three positions have to go." She looked at Zinny anxiously as if Zinny was in a position to decide the fate of those people.

Zinny shrugged hoping she looked secure and unconcerned. "I don't know. It's probably just another rumor. They're still arguing about the budget last I heard." She got a cup of coffee from the pot and sat down next to Midge. "How'd it go last night?" She knew the answer but it was something to say at least. Better than just sitting there like a dummy.

"He was very nice," Midge nodded her head as if deciding on a menu choice. "He's very smart, you know. Works at the Hartford as an analyst. Everybody loves him there. We had a great time. Really. The restaurant was really nice and he didn't even ask to go Dutch. I had the sole and he had chicken. It was really good."

"So you two got along okay, I take it?" Zinny knew where this was heading but knew of no reasonable way of avoiding it other than taking the most direct route through the swamp.

"Oh sure. I talked about the library here and he told me about what he does with computers. I didn't understand a word he said. He could have been speaking German or Russian or something but it didn't matter. He has a cute way of pushing his hair back from his face. We shared a chocolate mousse cake for desert. When he dropped me off, he said he'd call and we would do it again."

Zinny knew he wouldn't. This little play had only one act and it never varied. When Midge went out on dates, she invariably had an optimistic report of the man. He was invariably nice or friendly or cute and just as invariably, he never called her back. Midge would go from happy to concerned to dismissive to resigned until she met someone new and then the play would start all over again. Zinny felt sorry for Midge, but, thinking back on her own love life, she realized that she envied Midge a little bit as well. "Great Midge. I'm so glad you had a good time." She sighed inwardly and then took the plunge. "If he doesn't call, you know you could call him." She knew Midge would never do that either. Midge had gone out on a blind date the year before. Things seemed to go well and after a week or two she had called the man to suggest that they get together again. He had called her an ugly skag, told her to fuck off and not to call him again.

Midge's face tightened until she looked as if she were on the pot and having a hard time of it. "That's okay. I'm sure Chuck will call."

"Yes. I'm sure he will." Zinny always said that. She sipped from her coffee and looked at her watch. Almost time to go back to the counter. These conversations always depressed her. Midge was a friendly, intelligent woman with a good heart and absolutely nothing in the looks department. How long was she going to have to go through this before she met someone who saw beyond deer-in-the-headlights to the human being within?

Not that God had been generous with herself either, Zinny thought as she rose and disposed of her coffee in the little sink and threw the paper cup into the trash. Plain as plain could be, she reminded herself. Good thing Mom didn't call me Jane. All bones and angles like Dad. Mom's brown eyes but muddy, almost grey. An ugly duckling like Midge except I learned my lesson early and she hasn't given up hope. "Have you got stacks, today?" she asked her friend.

"Yes."

"Cool. There's a cart that was almost full when I went on break. It's all yours."

"Okay. I'll be out in a minute. You know, Zin, you should go out more yourself. If my social life isn't exactly fulfilling, if you know what I mean, at least I am trying. When was the last time you went on a date?"

Midge stood up. She looked so earnest and concerned that Zinny could not help but smile.

"If someone comes along, you'll be the second to know," she joked with Midge. "Right now, though, I'm doing just fine by myself. I've got my Dad to care for as you know so that doesn't leave a lot of free time."

Midge nodded. "I know, but hey, having only yourself for company all the time is not the way to go. I should know. You gotta break out a little even if it doesn't always work out." She twisted her face into a wry grin. "I know all about that one too."

Zinny left the lounge and walked towards the information desk still thinking about what Midge had said. It wasn't that she chose to have no social life. One had simply never developed. She worked. She went home and took care of Dad, went to sleep and then did it all over again. She wasn't avoiding men. They just weren't popping into her life as they did for Midge. She didn't go bar hopping or go to events like fairs and expos where she might meet someone. She simply had no interest in any of those things. She was a lot older than Midge too. That counted for something, didn't it? There just wasn't a whole flock or men her age hanging around waiting for her to pick one out. Didn't mean she had sworn off men, she told herself. Not at all. She noticed good looking men all the time in the library. It was no longer a place just for bookies and nerds and old folks, not with the burgeoning of the internet. She wasn't blind. When she saw a guy with cute buns she didn't turn away and sometimes caught herself thinking thoughts that just made it harder to get her job done.

Zinny came through the door into the area behind the information desk and looked around quickly to see if anyone had noticed that she was blushing. No one paid her the slightest attention. The room seemed smaller and more drab than usual. Zinny felt a chill run across her arms and quickly crossed them across her chest. She could not explain it but she was suddenly filled with a sense of foreboding and a strong urge to walk out of the place and never come back.

People were being helped at the counter. Midge came out behind her and started pushing a cart full of books towards the rear. Mrs. Fuller was still sitting at the computer scowling at the screen and muttering. Zinny took a deep breath, ignored her feelings, and plunged in and soon lost herself in the daily give and take of her job. When she finally had a chance to think about something else, she realized that two hours had sped by.

WOW. She pushed her hair back from her brow and turned towards the counter once again.

"Hi Zinny. Long time."

The sound of his voice froze her where she stood. She felt as if someone had pulled out a plug and the upper half of her body was draining out all over the floor. My God. After all this time. Can't be. Could never forget that voice even now. It's him, just an older version but it's him just strolling back into her life smooth as you please as if nothing had happened and he'd just stopped by to take her out to lunch or to discuss the price of oil or the current market. Time hasn't treated him well. Frayed jacket. Spots on his tie. Needs to wash his hair and cut it too. Looks like some Italian goombah in a Hollywood B movie only twice as vain and half as smart. "How may I help you?"

"Cut the shit, Zinny. Can't you even say hello?"

"Hello." Zinny looked at a grease spot on his chest and tried to keep her voice neutral and her emotions under control.

"That's it? After all these years all you can say is hello? Okay so we didn't part best of friends but I'm not a monster."

"When you're sober. Otherwise you fooled me. Listen, Mark. I know you didn't just show up here to say 'Hi, look at me. What a nice guy I am.' What is it you want? Money? I have none. You're supposed to be paying me, remember?" She finished in a bitter tone in spite of her good intentions. It was just too much to bear, she thought. As if things weren't tough enough, her ex has to show up. She felt her facial muscles tighten and, for a moment, Zinny thought she would burst into tears in front of him and the whole dammed library. Quickly she turned away, trying desperately to gain control while pretending to sort through a row of books on the cart behind her. She would not be a weak old woman. She would not. Zinny squared her shoulders, and turned back again.

"Don't be nasty. I could make a scene." Mark shifted from one foot to the other and sneered at Zinny through half-shut eyes as if he were trying to think and smoke a cigarette simultaneously.

"I could have you escorted out."

'C'mon, Zinny. Lighten up." His sneer disappeared and a smile with which she had fallen in love so many years before took its place. "When do you get off for lunch? We could talk then."

"One o'clock." An hour later than I actually eat, she thought. And now, suddenly, she had no appetite. She had nothing and they were watching her waiting to see what she would do and say thinking ohohohoh she is losing it now and she could feel their eyes all around her waiting just waiting wishing that they could see her fall and thus prop up their own lives a little bit. She could feel the goose bumps on her arms. A wave of nausea washed over her. What fun this is, she thought. Life's a blast as long as you can hold up. It was as if she had suddenly discovered that she had showed up promptly for a life or death appointment only to find that she was a day late. Suddenly, a piece of history was tearing up a huge hole in the pattern of her life, her job, her father. It just wasn't fair. Why couldn't he have gone off someplace and died? The world would have been a better place. Hell, Dad doesn't even know and, if he finds out, he still won't know because he will forget almost in the same instant that he knows but for that instant he will know and she would see it in his eyes and what she'd see would not be pretty. Then he will forget and that is the only good thing that can come of this. Zinny wished she was with him right now and could just sit in a chair and stare out the window all day. This was ridiculous and pathetic. C'mon, Zinny, Get a grip. She felt like road kill. She wanted to walk out of the library, start running and never look back.

"Okay. See you then." Mark turned and strolled off towards the entrance as if he were just another library patron.

Zinny worked to keep her stomach under control. "Take over my line for me for a minute, Betty? Would you?" she asked the broad-beamed friendly-looking woman standing beside her who was busily sorting books onto carts destined for various parts of the library.

Zinny lurched back into the employee area and hurried into the bathroom, and towards the grey rowed wall of stalls hoping desperately that one would be vacant no longer caring if others were and there within the gray-walled cathedral bent over the porcelain goddess, stomach lurching trying to bring up whatever was there, not much truth be told for she had been in a hurry and breakfast at best was a last minute thing often forgotten or relegated to a piece of toast or even bread with a glass of orange juice, but everything up and out, choking and coughing mindlessly, body doubled over in prayer. Now I kneel as if to sleep, my breakfast lying at my feet, and then staring at the tan goo and someone entering the stall next to hers are you okay in there oh yes just barfing to break the monotony. Yes, thank you. There's nothing left and Zinny rose to throw cold water at her suddenly blanched features and rinse a mouth tasting of bile and half-digested English muffin. What to do? What to do? She dried her face and tried not to see the expression on it. Pretend you're someone else, she commanded. It almost does look like that of a stranger's face with puffy flesh around the eyes and mouth than keeps sneaking in on itself. Oh, Mom, look at the woman standing at the middle sink who looks really sick. Works in the library, darling, what do you expect? Troglodyte. Impossible. Eyes like Joan of Arc when the fire got hot. Zinny took a deep breath. No more crying. Think, you stupid fool. Think. Can't run. Can't hide. Got to face Mark somehow. She marched back to the information desk. Onward, girl, onward Christian soldier marching as to war. Used to love that song. She would march around the yard humming it. "Doing okay, Betty?"

"Oh sure." Big smile. If Betty ever had a problem she kept it well hidden.

"Great. I'm taking off for lunch a little early. Not feeling too well. I'll pick up something at CVS."

"Yeah? Go ahead. Sure you're okay? You're as white as a sheet."

"Oh sure. Probably something I ate." or saw or talked to, she finished silently.

She walked out looking neither left nor right into the sunshine glaring off the library steps into the brassy sharp-edged day that glittered off the car windshields and stuck to her skin like a hot towel.

Zinny walked slowly down Main Street towards the museum not really knowing or caring where she was walking or why but just needing to be moving while she tried to grapple with a problem she thought was long past. She was in the present yet now, physically present, emotionally absorbed, a shadow link between what is and what was.

The heat burned the curiosity from her soul, leaving just the anguish of knowing that, whatever happened now or in the future would not be good. Zinny moved down the street, shadows flickering in her eyes and noises blurred into a cacophonous roar around her ears protected by their barrier of graying brown hair. Shadow world she found it but it was not real not really but Mark was real, wasn't he, and not a shadow when he stood there looking at her with those deep, dark eyes that she had found so soulful when she could not even spell the word but took it to mean anything within her sight that made a damp spot in her panties and caused her to walk with an unusual delicacy yes and so full of emotion and life and love when she envisioned herself an old maid who should be shot like a horse with a broken leg even though her roommate told her he needed a shave, smelled bad and had dead eyes, but what did she know, she who went out with a different boy every night, and anyway his eyes were not dead at all but drew her into their depths until Zinny felt as if she were falling into a rabbit hole and tumbling down into Wonderland where dead queens ruled. When Mark spoke she had felt as if winter snow had shifted under a suddenly warmer March sun and threatened to avalanche her entire being into a valley never seen before by man or woman. Wonder was the order of the day and awakening she knew that he would someday be king and they would rule as one in a sensible world.

It seemed as if the sun came up every day in order to give her the opportunity of waiting to see him, and then being with him, a warming of his shadow, and then missing his presence, his eyes, his looks, his moods. She knew better than anyone what she wanted and needed and, in the end would have, and that was the end of the chapter as far as she was concerned and if her parents or her friends or her ex friend roommate didn't like him it was simply that he was far too complex for them to understand. God, what a fool she'd been but isn't that part if not all of the definition of youth? Guess we all are at one time of another, she sighed. She couldn't imagine her dad being foolish but of course now he was making up for lost time. Mother Nature played a dirty trick on a man who was always neat and precise with everything in its place and a place for everything from stethoscope to daughter and now mindless incontinence.

Tell me, Dad? What should I do now? I know you warned me but I thought you were just being old and stupid. Turned out to be me. Will I be spending the rest of my life dealing with him? What if he finds out? God, don't let that happen. To have Mark see you in your present state would be awful. He probably wants money. He always wanted money. Always in and out. Just small stuff. Five here, ten there. Business is bad so he got laid off. Boss is an asshole. The job is a nowhere job. I'm a little short today. You got a ten on you? Pay you back next week. No problem no problem it was always no problem no

"Hi there, Zinny"

Zinny came out of her emotional fugue at the sound of a familiar voice. She found that she had walked into the shaded courtyard next to the Athenaeum and there, sitting on a stone bench to her left was the library patron with whom she had chatted. "Oh, hi there." She tried to sound nonchalant but it did not come off well.

"You look way sad. Care to sit and talk about whatever it is?" He took a huge sandwich wrapped in plastic from a paper sack and carefully removed part of the protective wrapping. He smiled up at her, a small twitch of the lips but quiet and friendly. "My mouth may be full but my ears will be open."

He wasn't exactly bouncing around like the Easter bunny either, Zinny decided. In fact, he looked worse than depressed, like a paperback that, having been passed through many uncaring hands, ends up in the trash with the covers ripped off and the pages twitching in the breeze. His eyes were dark behind fleshy bags of skin. His hair was whiter too than she remembered and fell onto his forehead in lifeless looking strands. He seems sad too, she thought, but he has nice eyes. He was looking as defenseless as she felt. "Nothing anyone can help me with," she told him and sat down next to him on the bench. "Agile, right?"

The man took a huge bite of his sandwich and munched for a little while before replying. "You have a good memory. Better than mine anyway." He finished chewing looking somewhat embarrassed.

"Zinny. Zinny Jones."

"Of course. Please forgive me."

"Nothing to forgive. I remembered your nickname only because it was so unusual."

"Doesn't really fit the man, right?" He looked at her and frowned as if he already knew the answer and didn't appreciate it.

Touchy, touchy. "Nope. Nicknames are strange that way. When I was small they called me goose. I hated that name and could never figure out why I got it." Remembering what she could of those long past days Zinny realized that the names they had called her had often been a lot worse.

"His face relaxed. "Hi, Zinny." He took another bite of his sandwich.

"Hi, Agile."

They smiled at each other comfortable that the other was safe, still fairly anonymous, and willing to talk about whatever came out of their mouths but able to get up and walk away should defenses start to crumble. Tiny little feet. Zinny felt as if tiny, little feet were walking across her mind tapping lightly on the icy surfaces with elfin patience, ahh yes those little knocks, coming as they did in staccato rhythm synchronized to the beat of her emotions. "You look a little down yourself," she ventured

"Yes?"

"Yes."

Walker nodded slowly as if to acknowledge the truth of her words. "Death in the family."

His face was a sinking, shadowed sun suddenly darkening behind the bank of strato-cumulus clouds behind his eyes. "I'm sorry," Zinny told him and meant it and saw that Walker somehow knew that the words were more than simply a polite way of expressing the inability to emote or describe the brevity of existence.

"Yes."

"A parent?"

Walker looked out beyond himself. "My wife."

"Oh no."

"She's best gone from here." Walker took a determined bite from his sandwich.

"Oh."

"No more pain," he continued after a moment's mastication

"Oh pain." Zinny repeated feeling like a complete fool. "Sorry."

"Walker looked at her and smiled. "It's okay. Really. So tell me why you were in such a dark study a few minutes ago." He took another bite. A piece of lettuce hung from his lip momentarily until he sensed its presence and licked it off.

"It's okay. Really nothing. Sometimes, the unexpected happens," she began in spite of herself and then ran out of words as her thoughts jumbled in a kaleidoscope and she felt herself blushing for no good reason. "I don't know. It's just one of those days, you know, when nothing seems to go right and the faster you run the behinder you get until you wonder whether you and the world would have been better off if you had just stayed in bed and cancelled the entire day for lack of interest. It's like finding a winning lotto ticket and rushing down to the claim center to find out that it expired the day before or something like that." She shrugged.

Walker nodded and took another bite of his sandwich. "Danger, life taking place," he said to no one in particular.

This made no sense to Zinny but it did not matter and they sat in silence for several minutes watching a school group pass by laughing and chattering on their way to the yellow blob of the bus squatting patiently by the curb. Two CT Transit bus drivers walked by, one gesticulating violently while the smaller one was shaking his head just as violently. Tweedle Dee and Tweedle Dum, she thought and wondered if she should say something more. Maybe she was just boring him as he sat there finishing his sandwich. Turkey and bacon on white, she noted mechanically. One of her favorites. Nobody liked listening to other people's troubles even if they pretended to unless they were family or really close friends and even then everyone had their own troubles, didn't they. She had listened to Mark bitch about everything for years, hadn't she, so she knew the feeling. "My ex just appeared," she said and then snapped her jaw shut with a click, once again afraid that she had said too much, gone too far and turned off the man with the soft, friendly eyes and the stomach bulging out over his legs. She felt embarrassed and wondered momentarily if Walker had noticed. Zinny didn't dare look, choosing instead to turn away and cough softly into her hand.

Walker chuckled softly, a low guttural sound somewhat like a truck engine idling. "As if by magic?"

Startled, she looked back at him. "Black magic, if that's what it was," she responded.

"Bad, huh?"

Zinny nodded and reached into her bag for her lunch, a Fuji apple that she had tucked into it on the way out of the house. No turkey and bacon sandwich, but it was better than nothing, she decided. They should put that as her epitaph. NOT MUCH BUT BETTER THAN NOTHING. Twenty-four point type. Times New Roman font scratched on a piece of old slate stuck into the ground above her bones, maybe just lying on the ground somewhere in the vicinity. She wasn't ready for her epitaph yet. Zinny took a fierce bite from her apple. Maybe her life was like her apple. People were always coming up and taking a big bite out of it. Not fair, not fair, not fair but if she wanted to feel sorry for herself, she dammed well would. Had Agile noticed her expression and interpreted it correctly? She hoped not, hoped that he would see only a woman, okay a middle aged woman, with whom he enjoyed talking. Men didn't notice much in that respect, did they? They weren't big on knowing what a person was thinking by how they looked, only how they looked. That thought depressed Zinny even more. She risked a quick look to her right but Agile was just sitting there staring off into the middle distance as if waiting for some preordained event to take place. He seemed at once resigned and somewhat aloof. "How are you coping?" She asked softly.

He did not reply but just sat there as if he had not even heard her. He was wearing a cream colored shirt. Crumbs from his sandwich had settled on top of his stomach. Zinny felt a sudden urge to move over a foot or two and brush them off. Taken together with a pair of badly creased pants he looked a real mess and she had to firmly resist the mother instinct.

"It's like an invisible weight inside me that keeps shifting around so that it pulls one way one day and in another direction on the next day," he finally replied. He looked down, hesitated, and then absently brushed away the crumbs. His voice held the desolation of wind blowing across a vast and barren desert.

"I felt that way when my mom died."

Agile nodded and crumbled the brown paper bag that had held his sandwich. "One day at a time," he said. "I was never divorced but we had our bad times, God knows and probably both of us swore many times that we would file for divorce, but it never happened. Doesn't make your trouble any easier, but I do know about trouble between spouses."

One day at a time, Zinny repeated silently. Why do we fall back on platitudes in times of emotional stress, she wondered? Some hoary saying that is disputed or denied at the risk of seeming callous or stupid. We look into ourselves and cannot describe the tidal flood of mud and debris that fills the delta of our soul so we simply use words that reassure, that pose no threat, that cannot be misconstrued and carry no hint of the emotional upheaval beneath: One step at a time, Sufficient unto the day, gotta break eggs to make an omelet, stiff upper lip, splice the mainbrace, I feel your pain, damn the torpedoes, stitch in time, measure twice cut once, miracles do happen, when in doubt drop back ten yards and punt, watch your back, silence is golden, brag is a good dog but holdfast is a better one. Simple words, just concise simple words hiding a whole range of experience and emotions. Bandages of our social existence. She really thought she could talk with Agile so why was she running around the edge of the swimming hole saying how nice the water looks. Silly old woman. Silly, stupid old woman. You who would know another must first know yourself.

"I supported my ex. I worked. He spent the money showing everyone what an important man he was and hopping into bed with anyone that took his fancy. He thought of himself as God's gift to womankind, though nature had certainly not given him any encouragement in that area." There. She'd told him but telling him did not make her feel any better. It only served to flood her memory with a series of pictures she had taken down off the wall of her memory and put away long before when things had been different or it seemed that way thinking back on it.

F1 Holcomb Street

The hallway is long. It divides the house in half from the front door to the kitchen. On the right, a staircase leads up to the second floor. To the right of the staircase is the dining room. To the left of the hall is a wide opening into the large, rectangular living room. The hall itself is dim at the best of times. There had been a light fixture mounted on the wall about halfway down but it broke long ago. Light used to come through two small windows on either side of the front door, but she'd put shades across them to maintain forgetfulness. Long ago as well there were pictures on the walls. Their marks are still visible on the old darkened wallpaper.

PICTURE FIRST, THE

Location: One foot to the right of the entrance to the living room, three feet from the ceiling and four feet from the floor.

Frame: Thin, sterling silver, now badly tarnished

Media: Color photograph

Description: The picture is a stock commercial shot of the bride and groom. She is dressed in a white wedding dress with a long train that sweeps and curls around her like whipped cream. She is looking up at her new husband and smiling. She has a good profile with a somewhat long, narrow nose balanced by a wide mouth full of white teeth. Her eyes are large and brown beneath thick eyebrows and a mass of curling brown hair that gleams and reflects in the light of the flashbulb. She is holding a piece of wedding cake as if she had forgotten exactly what she was supposed to do with it. She is caught in that once and timeless moment of the young when they are fully grown and at the peak of their physical attractiveness. She is totally happy and happily unaware of how brief that feeling will be. There is a sense of expectation in the way she looks at her new husband and the manner in which she extends the cake towards him.

The groom is dressed in a black tuxedo with a light blue four-in-hand tie. He too is young and slim, taller than the bride and standing very erect. His hair is black and combed straight back on his head and shiny with Vitalis or a similar substance. His features are regular with full lips and a slightly receding chin. His eyes are black and small. He almost looks as if he is squinting. His right arm is extended to take the piece of cake. It seems a rigid, almost a military pose as if in reaction to being told he was taking the whole scene too lightly. He is staring down at his bride with a set, somewhat dour expression as if this were part of a job that required him to be in such pictures every day. His left arm, furthest from the camera, seems to be around her waist.

Memory: Colors red and blue and white, of course, and after noon to night, of course and purple, pink and black, of course flashing through bits of laughter and consciousness of sounds and smiling Tims and Jims and Johns and Dons and Sallys and Bettys, aunts and uncles and cousins and nephews running around shouting and Mom helping me with the dress. Yes, dear it will fit. Lift your arms now. Ah how beautiful you look. She is smiling and talking a mile-a-minute but her eyes seem shadowed and sad. Perhaps she already knows of the malignant twist of chemistry that will take her life. But her only child is getting married and there will be no sadness today. All smiles and nods. A pin here. A pin there. Just a stitch or two. Perfect. You are a sight you are. Her thin face glowed in the light streaming in through the windows.

And after the ceremony I remember Dad smiling, walking through the house drink in hand saying Hi and Hello and thanks for coming wasn't it beautiful thank God for the good weather and everything else too. The Reverend did a good job, I thought. Yes the flowers were beautiful. My wife and Zinny picked them out with the florist. Yes the one over on Albany Avenue. Sara how wonderful that you and Fred could make it. And you brought the kids as well. Wow, have they grown since I last saw them. Time just flashes by, doesn't it? Seems like just yesterday. Did you get something to eat? The bar is across the way in the living room. Help yourself.

Kids were everywhere running in and out shouting and doing their best to turn their best clothes into rags. They invaded the kitchen for soda in orange and brown and green bottles and cans amid piles of pink and brown and white food in yellow boxes from the caterer and piles of canapés and crackers on trays and bottles of champagne held by black and white and flesh and flesh and more flesh with arms and faces swimming into sight and then gone and then the dancing swirling around and around watching sweat pop out on foreheads and under lips and noses and feeling it under my arms and between my legs as I swirled between different faces fleshy, thin with glasses, broad and red, white and powdered, pale without sweating, or cool but all smiling and you are beautiful what a wonderful wedding and Mark is so handsome we wish you all the best. The room was full of people and all of them looking at Mark and me, watching, always watching even with smiles and clapclaphands they never stop but I was ready and continued on as if I didn't know what they were doing just to frustrate them while we swirled around and around in blues and reds and purples and blacks, yellows and pinks, greens and teals.

And the sights and sounds of celebration: My mother raising a glass of champagne in a toast to Mark and Azalea for they are our joy and future. Her hand trembles slightly as she raises the glass. Her lemon yellow dress with white collar looks as if it had been made for someone larger. She had seen me through college and, despite reservations about Mark, her eyes sparkled with joy, and, ever so briefly, the lines etched on her face by time and worry and pain smoothed into the pretty young woman she must once have been and whom, she wrongly claimed, I took after.

The reception was winding down; my father motioned to me to follow his ohsofamiliar stocky figure to the little study off the examining room and then turning as the light reflected off his glasses momentarily exploding his head into fragments of rainbows as I stood in front of his old, battered desk with books and papers strewn carelessly across the top of it in seemingly random order as if he considered the world of science and medicine to be simply a different state of chaos wondering if anything that might result in a permanent stain had somehow gotten on my dress and if the roast beef had maybe been a bit too rare. It seems so trivial and child-like looking back on it but I had no way of knowing what was to come. My father looked across the desk at me and his expression was so sad for an occasion that was supposed to be happy that I could only stare back at him and wonder what on earth was wrong?

"I know you think I don't understand," he told me, "but I do. I think this marriage is wrong for you and for Mark. You come home from college one day and announce your getting married to a man you've only just met a few weeks before and about whom you know little except that he has nice eyes and likes his hamburgers medium well. He can know even less about you and yet he asks you to marry him. Maybe it makes me old fashioned in your eyes but I believe that you should know him better than how he likes his hamburgers and you find him attractive. From what little I've seen of Mark, I believe him to be weak of character. I think that he will always be somewhat of a boy pretending to be a man. You are determined, however, so I will not stand in your way." He sighs and picks up a piece of paper from the desk. "I've been putting a little money aside for this moment." He gestures out towards the rest of the house. "Some got spent on the wedding, but here is the balance. I believe a woman should have a little money of her own and so this is our wedding present to you. Put it away in your own account. You may well find a need for it sooner than you think."

He passed the check across the desk and then walked around and stared at me and I at him yet separated across the miles of age and the fact that I am in love, though more with the thought of marriage since I have not yet experienced the reality of it and have no clue as to the possible harsh texture of that fare and just stand there fading in and out of my father's face with his sad eyes and deep lines around his mouth beneath the graying mustache. "I hope he can make room in his life for you, Zinny, for if he can't you will never be happy," he told me as I stood there staring at him thinking all the while that he doesn't know Mark and he doesn't know me and we'll be just fine thank you very much. Just fine. I just know we will just know

PICTURE SECOND, THE

Location: On the wall opposite the first picture three feet from the ceiling and four feet from the floor.

Frame: A simple pine frame forty-five degrees on edge that has been painted a Chinese orange with black "antique" streaks in it.

Media: Pastel sketch

Description: The artist likes Japanese anime. In bold, almost careless strokes, he has created two figures on a motorcycle as seen by an ant from perhaps ten feet away. There is the huge, front wheel (cross country tread) under its mudguard that is gleaming and black. Sitting on top of the engine and gripping the handlebars with both gloved hands is an anime male with the distinguishing small slit of a mouth and extra large eyes. He is wearing leathers and a helmet with a red lightning bolt on its side. The character is looking out into the middle distance and is frowning slightly as if preparing to take on the bad guys who are out to destroy the world. A female character sits behind him with her arms around his waist. She too is wearing black leather but lacks a helmet. Perhaps she has not had time to put it on yet. Her hair is shaved on the sides and shaped into a Mohawk in the middle. Unlike the male, she is smiling and looking to her right as if talking with someone just outside the border of the picture.

It is a sketch of strength and beginnings, of a journey about to commence, of a challenge in the near future that must be overcome. The gleam in the male's eyes and the slit of the mouth suggest determination and the will to overcome fear and any other base emotions that he might feel as soon as he puts the bike in gear. One can almost hear the engine rev up and down as he impatiently twists the throttle. He is youth hot and eager and filled with the sense that he will be victorious regardless over what he must triumph. He will never die, never get sick, never find sagging skin under his chin and dark pouches under his eyes, a slumping frame and an ever limper dick. Not for him the monthly struggle with a mortgage and bills. No dead end job without hope for promotion. In his eye is the snap of decision and the aim of the eagle.

The artist treats the female much differently, catching in a few strokes an instant in time that seems to be always at the point of turning into the next instant. The female seems to be forever in motion and about to reach behind her for her helmet as soon as she has finished speaking. There is a timeless quality to the arch of her eyebrow and the turned up nose that suggests both innocence and enthusiasm for whatever fortune might present. She is happy about whatever she is saying or about the person to whom she is speaking or, more than likely, both. Behind her head, a few green and brown lines suggest trees and possibly the roof of a house, or perhaps a church. Such choices are we left with and, daily, make such distinctions for better or for worse.

Memories: I remember undressing, slowly as to not damage my wedding dress any more than it already sustained during the two hours of partying it had undergone. Below me, the sounds of the party continued with the trio of musicians pounding away with the Beach Boys and Beatles waltzes and fox trots for the older folks. From somewhere, probably the kitchen came the sound of glass breaking and a muffled curse. I remember smiling at the sound thinking that someone was having a bad hair day but it definitely wasn't Azalea Jones' bad day and that is all I knew and all I needed to know. I slipped on a pair of Levi's and an old pale blue blouse that I had had forever and loved dearly. Leaving the wedding dress on the bed in my bedroom, I went down the stairs to meet Mark. He was at the base of the stairs, drink in hand, smiling up at me with those dark, magical eyes of his. So, apparently was everyone else at the reception. The narrow hall was packed and people overflowed onto the porch and the front yard. So much for slipping away.

"What a party. Your parents did it up right, you know what I mean? Mark stood in the middle of the suite's tiny living room holding a bottle of champagne in one hand and a full flute in the other. He had taken off his jacket and his tie fell in two triangular shaped pieces on either side of his neck. His eyes were red and looked a little puffy but I thought him incredibly handsome standing there like a victorious James Bond with a weaker chin and smaller mouth.

He was weaving slightly back and forth and I realized that I had not seen him at the reception without a drink in his hand and a bridesmaid in his arms after our initial dance around the living room floor, but I pushed these thoughts back and went to stand with him putting my right arm around his waist, feeling the heat of him through the thin fabric of his dress shirt, and thought well of all the beautiful women he could have had, he chose me and only me and not them. I rubbed my hand over his shirt across his belly and a tremor ran through my body. So what If God hadn't given me a model's figure or features? So what if Mark wanted me and not them? A little voice within purred a warning that maybe he hadn't married me for my intelligence and warmth of personality either but I stifled it. I will tame Mark's ways and we will be a team and start a family and a life together. I felt him breathing in and out, in and out, slowly, steadily and a tremor ran through me and I felt a wetness between my legs.

How will it feel? Ahh the question of the ages. I thought Jen would know but my roommate said she couldn't remember. Some friend. Of course she remembered. Sure she had a different man almost every month but there was nothing wrong with her memory, damn her. All she said was the first time wasn't all that great but it got better. I hoped she was right and that I would not make a fool of myself. Jen had said that there was nothing to it and God knows she was experienced. Well beauty can do that and maybe people like me should hide in the stacks but here I am anyway. I wonder is my hair is still holding up and not flying out all over the place as it usually wants to do. Probably a rat's nest. It was really hot at the house with all those people standing around and moving in and out of the rooms laughing and eating and spilling their drinks and cigarette ash all over the place. I probably stink of cigarettes. Should go into the bathroom and shower and change but it's so peaceful here standing beside my man, my husband.

Mark turned and brought me to him in a bear hug and I felt his breath on the top of my head. His chest smelled of whiskey and tobacco and something else that I could not identify but did not like at all. I put my arms around him and hugged him back. "Finally, we are alone," he said and, putting his hand under my chin, tilted my head back until I was looking into those magnificent eyes of his even if they were bloodshot. We kissed and I felt his tongue in my mouth sliding around like a snake probing here and there and met it with my own. His hands came between us and began rubbing and pushing at my breasts.

The next few minutes were fragmented like a painting on a mirror that has fallen onto the floor and shattered. A piece here and a piece there like a prism in a light throwing strange shapes and colors onto walls and ceilings. His tongue, my tongue, the feel of his body against mine. It was as if someone had stopped all the clocks and all I knew of Mark was his body against mine and his tongue on my mouth. I remember putting my hands on his as he grabbed at my breasts so hard it hurt. There was a moment I felt the maleness of him as he pressed against me and I knew that my undies were wet as well. I could feel the heat and moisture between my legs as we held onto each other.

He started tearing at my blouse and suddenly I knew a fear such as I had never known before. Virginal jitters perhaps but suddenly I needed to slow down. I pushed Mark away. "Wait. Let me get ready."

"You're ready, babe. I can tell." He leered at me and reached for my blouse again.

"No. Wait. This first time. Let's make it special"

"Well, hurry up." He unbuttoned his shirt and let it fall to the hotel room floor exposing a chest full of black curling hair. My father had no chest hair and this was something I had not expected. I stared at it in fascination. It was thick and dark and a thick trail of it went down between his breasts and across his stomach and disappeared into his pants. What would it be like to run my fingers through it?

I tore myself away from this thought as Mark undid his belt and pants button. I turned to the suitcase for my nighty and when I turned back, he was standing there in the middle of the sitting room stark naked with his trousers and underwear puddle about his feet like ocean waves around the feet of Poseidon.

It was the first time I'd seen a man. Okay, I wasn't that innocent. I had gone off to college and shared my life with women for whom this was no secret. I had seen my Dad without a shirt, and, once, had seen him getting into the shower when the bathroom door had not closed all the way. I had heard descriptions and assumed what I hoped was a sophisticated and knowing air. I knew what a male penis looked like from a magazine my roommate had. She had left it open on her bed perhaps as a non-so-subtle hint that maybe her roomie could use a bit more of life's experience. There was also that abortion of a blind date in college. At that moment, I wished that I had taken the hint. I could feel my cheeks go red, and felt suddenly ashamed that my body should react that way.

Thick it was, not very long but thick with prominent blue veins along its surface and the mushroom-shaped tip slightly purple in color and sticking straight out from a large bush of pubic hair and it wiggled up and down slightly as if searching for something, and Mark stood there grinning and he grasped it in one hand and said "Now we'll have some fun, baby, and I'll show you what you've been missing all this time." and he steps towards me and took my hand. He put it on his dick. It felt warm and alive, a mixture or the knowing and the unconscious all in one piece of living tissue. I felt the pulse of it. It was strange and somehow repellent but I kept my hand on it and looked into his eyes that looked at me as if I were a fly in front of a frog. I moved my hand down slightly and cupped his testicles in their hairy sac. "Okay, honey. I'll be right out," and I release it and turned back and fled into the sanctuary of the bathroom.

And there I was, standing before the fogged mirror in the bathroom, my skin glowing from a shower so hot that the room is filled with steam and the mirror keeps fogging up. I felt clean and pink and even pretty as I dabbbed some perfume between my breasts and just a touch above my pubic mound. My nighty was pink and sheer and accentuated that fact that I had a pair of good-sized breasts that stood out proudly, their tips visible under the fabric. I left my panties on the bathroom floor. There seemed no point to them that night. Taking a deep breath, I turned, opened the bathroom door and walked into the bedroom.

He was there lying on the bed still with its coverlet on. He turns and rolled over onto me as I lay down beside him. Spreading my legs, I felt his dick but it was off target and I put my hand down there and guide it in.

The pain was sudden and sharp and I remember gasping and trying to squirm out from under Mark, but he would not budge and a subtle warmth flooded my torso and I tried to lie back and relax for that is what I thought I should do and then I felt him in me moving back and forth and I held onto his back as he pumped quickly, his eyes rolling back in his sockets, his mouth all over my face wet and panting, his arms on either side of me with their muscles quivering and his chest hair glistening with sweat and booze.

"Oh yes, baby, yes, oh God, c'mon, move with me, Jesus yes oh Christ this is good C'mon, Zinny, move your ass, oh yessssss. More, more, oh God, c'mon . . . harder . . . uhhh . . . harder . . . and he pounded away and I felt my mind separate from my body and float above us watching this consummation play from above as if it were happening to someone else. There Mark was pumping away between my legs. I had spread wide to help him. His ass crack widened and narrowed with his efforts. It is as if I were not there at all though I felt a slowly gathering sense of oncoming tickling desire that increased with every second and I felt my whole body start to burn. Yes, I thought, yes and I could do this too and now it is coming and I am

He suddenly went limp within me and collapsed across me as if he had been shot. "Goddamned bitch," he moaned. "All your fault. Should never have married a damned virgin. You stupid cunt." I couldn't believe what he was saying. I had never heard that kind of language directed at me. I thought I had been doing my best to help him. I pushed him off and he rolled over, already passed out and dead to the world and his bride. His dick has shriveled to a tiny inch of flesh almost hidden in his crotch. I reached over and gripped it between thumb and forefinger; he muttered something unintelligible and started to snore.

PICTURE THIRD, THE

LOCATION: At the other end of the hall, three feet from the ceiling, five feet from the floor and six inches from the doorway leading into the kitchen.

FRAME: Plain pine frame stained a light gray. Inside that there is a chocolate brown matt board, and a quarter inch of white matting around the inside of that. On the bottom of the wooden frame, there is a small brass plate with the following words inscribed: "The rain chased its feet down the street / and the south wind cast its net over the lily land"

MEDIA: Charcoal

DESCRIPTION: A nor-easter is raging. The figure of a woman is seen fighting her way through the wind and sheets of rain. Swift deft strokes of the charcoal suggest the force of the wind and the rain it drives almost horizontally from her left to her right. The woman leans into the wind, a fact nicely shown by the plane of her back and legs compared to the surrounding scenery. To her left is a street with a parked car facing the viewer. To her right is a row of bushes now tilting backwards with the force of the wind. Although her head is bent, obscuring her face, her posture demands that we recognize and admire her determination bordering on foolishness that brings her out in such weather. The viewer begins to feel at one with the posture and involved in the woman's situation. Why is she out in such weather? Surely she is not braving such a storm for a container of milk or a pack of cigarettes from the local 7-11 store. There must be some terrible event that motivated her to flee out into the elements, feeling safer in the howling wind and flying debris than where she was before. Perhaps someone is injured and she must get help. Perhaps the phones have gone out. The viewer is left with questions and almost wills the figure to come alive, to step out of the paper and tell what it is that caused her to be in such a scene.

MEMORY: "Bitch"

My head slammed back against the wall and suddenly staring at Mark, unable to comprehend what had just happened. My husband stood in front of me, eyes closed to slits and fists clenched, consumed by a rage the likes of which I had never seen before. It was as if someone had pulled a switch inside him tuning him from Jekyl to Hyde. It was the first time I'd seen him like this. The honeymoon in Puerto Rico had been smooth enough. Mark had seemed moody at times and would go off by himself leaving me to guess as to his whereabouts but there had been the beach and the shops, the tours and the boat rides, more than enough to keep me happily busy. I had never left Hartford until now and found everything to be new and exotic. I read the guide books and visited the sites. I thought that we had different interests and he should have the chance to do what he wanted and, I thought, we had both been in the beach bar too much, had enjoyed the golden days in an alcoholic haze and perhaps that explained the change that had come over him since we had come back. I had probably changed as well, I told myself. Since finding a job as assistant librarian with the Hartford Public Library, I had settled down to a routine that probably seemed dull to Mark whose only job so far had been the discovery of the nearest package store. He was the gardener who, having planted early beans, decided that they were pedestrian and that only tomatoes would suffice and then let the beans go to seed while waiting for tomatoes that he had never planted. I had suggested something in the medical field, a technician perhaps. I was sure my dad could help if Mark got the training and needed a reference. Mark informed me that he had a brain, that he was destined to be more than some hyped up flunky and that he would know when the right thing came along, thank you very much. He would disappear early and come back late, often with people he claimed as friends who had difficulty counting the number of fingers on their hands but who thought he was one of the area's leading business minds.

Was it true, I wondered vaguely, facing up at him looking face down, frown, fists balled? Was it me or mine or something I did or did not do or say that had brought this rage down upon me? I was backed against the wall; Mark was in my face with his glaring pig's eyes inches away and his fist grabbing for my nighty. "Mark, what . . . ?"

"Don't ever question me about where I've been or where I'm going," he shouted.

I could feel the floor shake and my body parts flopped and jerked like those on a puppet's strings. "W . . . w . . . wake . . . pe . . . pe . . . people . . . downstairs," I managed to stammer, and then "Stop . . . Please stop." Banging against the wall again and again until I could not even react and suddenly he stopped and spun away into the living room.

Leaving me flung against the wall, arms and legs outspread like a rag doll carelessly left behind by a child who had gone on to other toys and other stories. He had ripped my night gown and I noticed that my right breast was exposed, reddened in spots where his hand had gripped it through the thin cloth. I was still in one piece, I realized numbly, but my mind was traumatized, shocked by a revelation that it was having a hard time handling or even, in that instant of time, understanding.

"Good God, Mark. It's two in the morning. Where have you been?" He did not reply and I walked out of the bedroom and across the tiny living room to the kitchen where he stood at the counter making another drink.

"Shut up," he told me without turning around.

"I won't." I felt my own anger building like water behind a dam. "How do you expect me to react when you come home at two in the morning, drunk and mad? You've spent more time away from here than you've been here. Have you got another woman stashed somewhere?"

"None of your business," he muttered and took a sip from his glass.

I lost it then. I was scared and mad and I was determined that this would stop. "So why are you back at all," I spat at him. "Was your girlfriend smart enough not to let you near her? Is that why you're like this?" I flew at him arms flailing. I probably looked like a witch caught in a windmill.

He caught my arms and jerked me around and suddenly I was on my back with Mark on top pressing one knee between my legs and pulling at my panties. "You miserable bitch. I'll show you who's boss." His arm came down across my neck and then I felt my panties rip away and then he was in me grunting and rutting like a pig, drool coming from his mouth below his eyes full of hate.

I felt the hardness of the floor gouging my back as our momentum slowly pushed us across it. He was puffing from exertion. I knew he would be at it for a while. He never came quickly and sometimes not at all when he'd been drinking. Above us and over his right shoulder I watched the light fixture hanging from the ceiling. It shadowed his face and put his head in a circle of light and then, like a lunar eclipse, slowly moved away over his left shoulder. I tried to keep track of the time it took to do this but lost track and then I couldn't breathe very well. His arm pushed down harder and then even the light was spinning in circles.

E2 Caliban Street

Walker sat on the bus people watching, one of his favorite pastimes. Across from him sat a tall, black man sporting a day's growth of beard. The gentleman wore a black, windbreaker with the word INDIGO across the front in flowing script and badly creased, grey cotton pants. On his feet was a pair of white Nike cross trainers that were so white they almost seemed to glow. A donut man, Walker imagined, and on his way to creating a yeast-raised empire glistening with a sweet-glazed coating that melts in the mouth of the huge lady sitting beside him whose gargantuan thighs were wrapped in lettuce green polyester pants. She wore a white, tent-like structure over breasts that looked as though someone had attached two fifty pound mounds of Jell-O to her chest. Poor woman, he thought. Hard to get up, I'll bet, and hard to get around while everyone looks at you and sits next to you whispering about you and giggling into their friend's ear. The woman sat staring straight ahead, her legs apart, feet planted firmly on the floor of the bus as if she had been born in that position and would never move until the day she died. Her eyes were hidden behind wraparound dark glasses. She could be a venture capitalist, Walker decided, a wizard with the numbers. She could run down a spreadsheet as most people could run down a restaurant menu. She would have a mind like a steel trap inside that dissolving body. She is looking for new investments for herself and her investors in a wildly successful private capital fund. A chain of donut shops, perhaps, with sweet returns and plump profit margins. The gentleman next to her has come up with a winner for sure, donuts shaped like dinosaurs with shots for their eyes. Now all he has to do is find someone to invest in his idea, a chain of Dino Donut shops. Lines of cars will stretch for miles, each filled with kids waiting for their boxes or Dino Donuts and monster balls. Let's see, Walker thought. I need something more, a catalyst if you will. Sitting behind the woman is a teenage girl. Perfect. She is bent over as if in pain and whispering incomprehensible words into a cell phone that seems permanently attached to her ear. She is wearing a white T-shirt with DIRTY written on the front of it and baby blue clam diggers. She and the donut man get off at the same stop and her mode of dress so inspires him that he runs into her causing her to drop her cell phone. He picks it up. During the ensuing watch-it, excuse-me, so sorry, here let me help you, she discovers that he is looking for a manager for his first shop. She is delighted. Such a job would get her out of the back office of the financial firm where she now works whenever boredom and ennui do not cause her to fall asleep sitting in front of her terminal. In fact, she tells the man, her boss was the lady on the bus they just left. WOW. The coincidence of a lifetime says he, and, making the gesture of eternal peace, he chases after the bus only to remember that the new manager's cell phone is still in his pocket. He runs back to her, throwing away the chance of a lifetime, but returning her cell phone as an honest man should. Mister INDIGO at the bridge. Grateful to be once again able to communicate with friends, complete strangers and even a number that yields animal sounds that she claims is a rockin' music site, Blue Pants, suffocated by boredom but nevertheless grateful to the man for the return of her external oracular device, calls her boss and Dino Donuts is born. There are, of course, details that must be filled in, Walker tells himself, but bus trips, imitating art that imitates life, are short, smelly, often homophobic ones.

Walker came back to the present as a wide body in a teal jacket and wearing a red LL Bean backpack sat down beside him and then pushed to the left, squeezing Walker into the side of the bus. Asshole, he thought. Some people just don't give a shit. Irritated, he shoved back.

"Sorry, buddy." The man turned partly around.

"S'okay," Walker grouched less than generously and suddenly knew what his little fantasy story was missing. Thugster, the man sitting beside Walker, used to work for the donut man but was fired for stealing a stack of refrozen cherry turnovers that the donut man had been planning to give to all the people in his family he detested as Christmas presents. He is looking for a way to exact his revenge on Donut Man. He knows the girl as well since he has been sticking it into the girl's mother since no one younger, more able or more willing has presented herself nor is likely to do so. Thugster watches Donut Man and Blue Pants get off the bus together and is immediately pissed off to the second power, not only because he considers Donut Man inferior to himself and a cheap bastard to boot but Blue Pants will not even talk with Thugster.

Walker stared out the window playing with his new characters and a plot that involves them all with each other. This one had possibilities, he thought. Might even be better than the one with which he was currently struggling. That was a wonderful thing about public transportation in general and buses in particular. They presented an ever changing pallet of humanity with a sea of figures and faces unequalled elsewhere with scowls, grins, laughs, sneers, passive, impressive, worthwhile, blank, classic, misshapen, well fed, hungry, triumphant and defeated expressions that could change in an instant if something happened in front of the bus or somebody broke down inside of it. Once a man two rows in front of him had suddenly collapsed into the aisle and the bus was stopped while the ambulance was called. People either did not know what to do and sat staring dumbly at the man twitching at their feet, or they did not know what to do and crowded into the aisle shouting useless instructions at nobody in particular. The driver called into dispatch and an ambulance was dispatched while the bus pulled over and waited for it patiently.

To ride or not to ride. Walking was work and not an option. The car was expensive and parking even more so. You could end up paying a grand a year even with the company subsidizing part of the cost while a monthly bus pass cost half that plus there was no one to watch and no one to talk to but himself, decidedly boring company.

"Hey Walker."

Walker came out of his daze with a start, and found that his stop had arrived. Tony, the driver, must have seen him dozing off. "Thanks, Tony." Walker gripped the bar that ran across the seat in front of him and pulled himself to his feet. He lumbered down the aisle to the front door. "Catch ya on the flip side," he told the driver and eased himself down two big steps to the street as Tony brought the bus to kneeling position like a giant blue elephant.

The sun was still hanging in the sky, seemingly reluctant to go down and bring an end to the long summer evening. The street looked as it always did but he knew that everything was different because nothing stayed the same and even if it looked the same since he had last descended it was different. Walker stood for a moment by the bus stop just breathing, listening to the street breathing in and out, puff in puff out, there a new candy wrapper, a piece of gum on the glass of the shelter, pull in pull out. How many people listened to streets breathe he wondered. Not too god dammed many, he'd bet. His was a fat street. He could hear its heavy breath as the Briarcrest apartments on the corner pulled in another coating of smog to further dim its bricks, as a girl standing on the other side of the shelter flicked a cigarette into the street. Walker watched smoke rise from it for a second and then turned away, walking down the street to the end of the block where he crossed carefully with the light. He was no speed skater and you never could tell what madman behind the wheel might come roaring down the street.

Ahh. Red light. Sorry, buddy. You'll just have to wait another day to run me down. Big fucking Navigator. Probably thinks his name is on whatever road he decides to drive on. Sitting up there in his truck with the AC on and the music blaring. They should ban the damned things. The cretins we keep electing to Congress are much more likely to do away with mass transit. Let all the have-nots walk and keep the land tanks. Bunch of greedy idiots. They get driven around in their limousines and smile all nicey nicey for the cameras and issue statements that, at best, do no harm, and, at worse, cause war and recessions. The worst of us run for public office, and, in our collective intelligence, we manage to elect the worst of those. I'll bet they don't have to sell their god dammed houses just to pay off medical bills. Hell no.

Walker went slowly up the street towards his squat little brick house wedged between two Victorian era multi-family houses. Be sorry to see it go, he thought, and then grinned at his own understatement of his feelings. He would be sorry to burn a good steak, sorry to lose his wallet, sorry to have his manager rip him a new asshole for some misstep. Being forced to sell the house went quite a bit further than sorry. Have to start looking for a new place to live, he realized. It was not exactly a new thought but at times it startled him as if it were, as if somehow it would not be necessary, would be the sort of thing that happened to someone else but he admitted to such absurdity and walked on. The furniture was, after all, mostly old junk. He and Beth had financed a few pieces over the years such as bigger beds for Jennifer and new chairs as old ones became totally broken down, but most came from his apartment or hers and had never been updated since they had bought the house and moved in. There had always been a more pressing need for something even when they had gotten a little bit ahead. Jen had already taken what she wanted.

He should have a big lawn sale. Come one, come all. See the picture of the girl in the stall. Take it home for your bathroom wall, and how about that old wood chest, the one your wife would like the best. Four drawers in which to store her skirts, underwear and your cotton shirts, condoms, letters, watches too, just watch out who is watching you, old credit cards and business notes, lists of stuff you know by rote, grocery lists and things to do and for a price that's good for you.

The chest of drawers had been one of the first items they had purchased after moving into the house. They had purchased on credit because Beth had flatly refused to use the floor as the world's largest drawer. Come on, folks. It's a great chest with only one sticky drawer and for only twenty dollars a real steal of a deal, just one dead Jackson, folks. You can't go wrong.

Rummage through the flotsam and jetsam of a family's life. What a chance. Sift through the stacks of books he'd never read again but had an emotional hemorrhage at the thought of getting rid of. Sure, bitch about the price of that mirror that was in Beth's apartment and hung on the wall above her bed so that no activity would go unnoticed. Just for being such a cheap jerk, he would not come down one god dammed cent. Walker had to admit to his own hypocrisy. If he had such a sale, he'd undoubtedly feel differently and go running around the area posting TAG SALE signs and flogging his possessions for whatever he could get for them.

He hoped he knew himself by now, Walker mused. If nothing else, he knew the big difference between the tough guy between his ears and the marshmallow that he was in real life, like Zinny at lunch today really upset about her ex and all he could do was sit there and eat my sandwich and offer platitudes. She must consider him a real jerk, an old man who long ago has forgotten the rotten tricks that life can play on us, but she wouldn't think that knowing about Beth but still you must have come across as a real ass. Of course asses come in different shapes and sizes and she has a nice one. Enough, now, you dirty old man, clogging up your brain cells with such thoughts. Still, she does. Rather think of that than selling his house.

This pleasant comparison ended abruptly as he saw a car in his driveway belonging to the real estate lady. Shit, he thought. Well, there's no dammed choice; he had to do it so let's get to it.

Sabrina Deglace stood on the porch waiting for him. A fitful puff of wind blew her gray and green skirt first in one direction and then in another. A lock of brown hair stood straight up from the top of her head. She had one of those broad, soft faces that always seemed to be smiling. Coming towards her a person simply knew that Sabrina would have their best interests at heart and so it would be almost blasphemous to say 'no' to any of her suggestions. Her nose tilted up slightly and she had a wide mouth with full lips that invited openness and trust. Walker disliked her. He was unsure as to the root cause of this feeling thinking at first that it was just because he hated the thought of selling the house and would resent anyone involved in that process but he came to realize that the feeling went much deeper than her profession. He thought she looked down on him, despised him in fact for not having the time or resources to fix the place up and sell it for top dollar or even pretend to be engaged in a process that held only sadness and memories for him. He felt old and fat when he was with her, a broken toy cast aside by a willful child. Sabrina exuded the kind of physical and intellectual presence that caused him to dread any meeting with her.

This feeling had not been improved when she had appeared at his door at the godless hour of seven in the morning the Saturday past. At first he thought it was a dream or part of one. Someone was standing by his car beating on the roof with an iron bar. As soon as he opened the door to chase the person away, the man would stop hitting the car but would commence once again as soon as Walker shut the door to his house. Every time he stuck his head out the door, he could see rust flying off the car where the man was beating on it. BANG, BANG. Walker came awake with a start and realized that the pounding was coming from the front door. Struggling out of bed with a curse, he slipped on his tattered, old bathrobe, and padded down the corridor to the front door.

"Good morning, Mr. Walker," Sabrina stood on the front porch "You look half asleep. Did you get my voicemail?" Sabrina looked freshly washed, scrubbed, fed and so totally ready to face the day that Walker felt slightly ill just looking at her.

"No."

"Oh." She looked expectantly at him as if the man with the puffy eyes, unshaven cheeks and tattered robe was some nasty mirage that would quickly disappear to be replaced by a wide awake, rugged individual wearing a full tool belt and holding a bucket of soapy water. "Well, we need to get this house in shape this weekend. The broker's open house is Monday. Remember what we discussed a couple of weeks back? You were going to get everything cleaned up, picked up, and all the trash thrown out?"

"Vaguely," replied Walker and yawned, getting his hand in front of his mouth just in time. "Can you come back later?"

"Too much to do and not enough time to do it," she answered, and looked at him expectantly. When he just stood there she frowned slightly. "I'll wait here while you get dressed and then we'll tackle the house together. How's that sound?" She smiled.

"Awful," replied Walker and turned back towards the inside of the house.

He had worked on his knees and on his feet scrubbing and mopping, sponging and carrying out to the curb junk, boxes of forgotten stuff, and all manner of paraphernalia. There were boxes of books, bags of trash, broken tables, chairs, waterlogged containers from the cellar, dusty toys of unremembered origin from the attic, stacks of magazines, a grill with no legs, a broken air conditioner, badly stained carpeting with holes worn in it, a stack of jigsaw puzzle boxes with scenes from the Danube, New York and a waterfall in Hawaii, parts to a Barbie Dollhouse, a stack of 33 rpm records featuring such long past artists as Elvis, Patsy Cline and the Everly Brothers, Beth's favorite chair with the worn out covering and stuffing coming out of holes in the arms, a toy guitar with no strings, cans of old paint now dried up in their cans, a stack of pornographic magazines (Walker quickly stuffed these in a garbage bag while Sabrina was in the next room), and assorted old kitchen pots with missing handles or non stick surfaces that now stuck, dusty glassware and coffee mugs. Towards the end his knees ached and he started having visions of a tall stein of German beer with a hot pastrami sandwich on really good rye with strong deli-style mustard. As he sneezed in the dust of the attic, he knew in his heart that he would need three beers. One would merely wet the dust that had settled on him. Every time Sabrina announced that they were almost finished, Walker added a beer to the total. Scrubbing at the dirt on the kitchen linoleum under the direction of the ever cheerful Sabrina, he saw a mound of creamy coleslaw sitting alongside the pastrami. Cold, crisp cabbage mixed with a goodly amount of mayonnaise and a little carrot for color. MMMMMmmmm. Walker's imagination was driving his taste buds wild.

This must be what recruits in the army go through, he thought, but they are much younger and slimmer and their joints don't howl whenever they move. By the end of the day, he was aching and cursing and wishing he had told Sabrina to sell the place as is and not to fucking bother him. Just get rid of the place 'cause the money's going to other places and other people and so I don't care what it sells for. The trouble was that part of the money was going to Sabrina and Walker felt guilty that he wanted to lower her paycheck. She was working right alongside him, he reminded himself. Get on with it.

He felt an inflated sense of worthlessness all that long day as he played scullery maid and charwoman until, when he had given up all hope that she was human or at least retained a spark of humanity somewhere in the scuttle of her soul, Sabrina announced that she was mounting on her broom and departing for a showing and that he had better keep things as they were or she would visit the entire wrath of the apocalypse on him. He watched her striding briskly across his front lawn to her BMW 320 with an emptiness of spirit and exhaustion of body that begged the chicken and the egg conundrum. It was only fitting, he supposed feeling more resigned than jealous, that one who worked hard but managed only to run in place should watch the departure of one who worked hard and was promptly rewarded.

So now she stood once again on his porch, proud goddess of the roof and walls watching with benign interest as Walker made his way up from the sidewalk, slowly lifting one foot into time to replace it with one foot slowly lifting into time to replace with how many footsteps in a life or maybe even a lifetime, time permitting of course. How many times do we lay them down without thought or consideration but each step down is history and cannot be retrieved. Walker looked up at Sabrina from the head of the walkway and felt disjointed as if the past and present had somehow conflicted within him. "Hi Sabrina."

"Evening John. I would have called but I was in the area anyhow and decided to just pull in. If I'm messing something up, I will disappear and come back later. How are you today?"

"Monday's always suck. I'm okay, though."

Sabrina smiled in acknowledgement of that truth. "I've got an offer on the house so that should brighten your day a bit."

Walker smiled, slipped by her to key open the front door and then gestured her inside ahead of him. The heat inside the house was like an electric blanket thrown over them and Walker went around the living room opening windows and switching on a fan. "Maybe better to talk outside until the house airs out a bit," he said.

"Wheww." Sabrina turned quickly back to the relative coolness of the porch. "Good thing I brought an air conditioner over else no potential buyer would have made it inside." Sabrina stood on the porch waving her hand in front of her face as if she were trying to decide if the air was better by her left eyebrow or her right.

Walker stared at her wishing that a great puff of wind would come up and billow out her skirt. Bet she wears cotton undies, he thought. "Yeah. Guess we'll just have to put up with the electric bill. Want some ice water or ice tea if there's any left?"

"Thank you, John. Not for me." She settled into a dark wicker chair with a sigh as he disappeared back into the house, reappearing a minute later with a glass half full of Jack on the rocks.

Sabrina Deglace remembered the little girl in the worn dress who ducked through back yards to avoid seeing other kids after school, whose trips on the school bus were an exercise in torture as she imagined all the other children with new clothes and money in their pockets were secretly laughing at the ugly little girl from the poorer part of the town who brought her lunch in a Bugs Bunny box long after that had gone out of style and whose sneakers were badly worn. She had struggled and studied and worked her buns off, hustling seven days a week, carrying two jobs at first while trying to get the real estate career off the ground. There had been no time for men. There was no family now, but looking down at the Walkers' little patch of front lawn, she did not regret it for she had found something she could control and make neat and sometimes even beautiful and people asked her opinion and followed her directions, smiling and laughing when they saw the results and she bought her first investment property and then sold it for a good profit and bought another and rented that one and bought a third. She came to know the contractors, good and bad, the workmen and the goof-offs. She had local zoning codes memorized and knew many of the people on the town zoning boards. She was known for the good parties she threw two or three times a year and was sought after by bachelors and married men alike. Throughout it all, she never forgot the ragged little girl, never forgot the poor beginnings or the people with whom she grew up and so she never lost Kipling's common touch, for she never felt secure; there was always the next house to sell and the next deal to make.

She thought back to how this little yard had looked. There had been a straggling, dying rhododendron by the front porch, a sick-looking maple tree in the left front, and more patches of dirt than grass all over. The driveway had been badly cracked and out of level. There had been a feeling of vague despair when she had first walked up the uneven concrete blocks that formed the front walk, a sense that neglect had been ongoing but casual as the maple tree grew taller and children's toys appeared and disappeared from beneath it and McDonalds wrappers, old candy wrappers and newspaper had accumulated in the branches of the scraggly hedge bordering the sidewalk along with pieces of car parts, scraps of plastic, torn up parking tickets. An old tire had been left to the left of the walk as well as a metal cylinder from a bicycle pump and a three foot length of clothesline. The whole house had given off a sense of having been lived in but not with a great deal of pride and patience.

Well, she had changed all that, Sabrina thought with satisfaction and even pride. That was the yard before picking up and throwing out and raking and weeding, mulching, cutting, potting and planting had turned the space into a neat, sterile patch of grass and flowers. The walkway had been evened out and the driveway sealed. There was no clue left of the history that Walker and his family had left upon the space, its boundaries or geography. She looked now upon the bed of greenery now stretched and straightened with hospital corners and military precision and saw her imprint on the earth and was pleased and her mind turned inwards to yet another, if somewhat minor, conquest of place over space. Yes, all is well, she thought. *Sabby knows best as it should be and all the people will line up and their belongings with them march down the aisle and they will buy my houses for yet another generation and much treasure shall accrue unto me and I will be safe and apart from those who walk in the darkness and know not of joy.*

Sabrina relaxed back into the porch chair. Walker was just another client and yet not, and she was slightly irritated to feel this for she prided herself in not becoming emotionally engaged with her clients or their property. Line 'em up and shoot 'em down had been her theme, but, sitting in the chair looking out at the heated street beyond the yard, she couldn't help but think of the man sitting beside her, of his air of silent, lonely endurance as if he had fought a battle and lost and, having lost, just kept on walking eyes down and lips set in a sunset line of patience. With his wife gone and the house on the way out, he'd scrubbed and painted as best he could but always with a quiet about him, a zone of still life and air almost dead behind his eyes. Of course, he said he was trying to write. Maybe that was what made her see him apart from the rest. She had never known one. Sabrina sighed and looked to her left at Walker.

118

"Two hundred and seventy thousand, conditional on the inspection," she told him.

Walker took a sip of his drink. "That's a lot lower than what we asked."

"Yes." Sabrina watched him closely. The man sat with his glass of whiskey staring out into the street as if she hadn't said anything at all, as if she weren't there at all, as if nothing was there at all. She looked at the chair in which he sat. The vinyl had long since cracked and been patched with brown duct tape until it looked like a highway into whose cracks black tar is squirted until it looks like a gray river full of black snakes.

Walker looked back at her, his face set in planes and angles so that it seemed a paperboard cutout with two little black dots for eyes. He seemed at once sad and determined as if he had solved a difficult problem only to expose an even greater one by solving the first and so amazed, not yet ready to give up, but amazed anyway that he was still at the bottom of the slope that he had thought he'd climbed. "Disappointing," he said.

"There will be others, I'm sure," Sabrina reassured him, knowing that she spoke the truth. The house was small, but neat and clean and the price was right for a single family home right next to downtown.

"Yes."

"It's a game of patience," Sabrina reminded him, undoubtedly unnecessarily.

"Yes."

The haunted face encased in its jowls and chins glared back at her, "Time," she said. "Anyway, give it some thought. We can always counter offer. The buyer will probably expect us to do that. It's all in the game." If she could get him to counter for ten less, she thought the buyer might go for it. "Ten less might do it," she told him. The buyer's agent had been encouraging. Young yuppies looking for their own place close to their careers. No kids. Perfect. Sabrina knew she could get this done, would get this done. Time to move on.

"It's low."

"That's what I told their agent. Much too low, but I'm required to pass it on to you anyway.

"Okay." And it was okay for Walker knew that Sabrina was full of steaming effort and force of will so strong that he could not understand it but only recognize its existence with a feeling of joy that such a force was working for him and around him and even beyond him as she threw the same effort into other houses where other people sat and considered and checked the cards they'd been dealt. Walker looked at Sabrina sitting next to him. "I'll give it some thought."

He sat there thinking three hundred was not too high for a solid house, small and, okay, dated Sabrina says but solid and two seventy would be okay but two fifty after mortgage and loans and her commission he'd have one seventy and owe the doctors twenty and the hospital one fifty well you can't get water from a stone, a truism if a little dry and worn down by now and he couldn't bring Beth back and they'd garnish his wages. He couldn't afford the house even before and that was possible only when Beth was working in those good old days when Beth and he were getting along but now he was between a rock and a hard place. Thank you, Lord, for Jack Daniels. We grow up between walls that we take for granted with no worry about paying for them just growing and taping pictures of heroes to them and then posters of musicians and hairy singers and thumbtack license plates and Yankee cards and Lion King cards. We stand and gaze with amazement and growing self possession at walls where our dreams spread out like Monarch butterflies gliding in colors along the surfaces of our lives in which we think we are immersed in each moment, looking behind us at the cloud of dust we raised now billowing out and dispersing on the sour wind, we realize we have hardly lived at all. Later we get older and buy walls of our own we do not see the sticky part of our lives that comes off on the walls as we paint them or paper them, gouge them, tear them down, put up new ones, spackle them, nail them, screw them, tile them, scuff them, run into them, stain them, spot them, spill stuff on them that will rot them, write on them, fight between them, lean on them and raise kids within their boundaries and all during this time we leave our memories like tape sticking to them at random angles and heights. Later we find them and judge them incongruous and invaluable, arrogant in their grip upon our senses and now I have to put a value on them, a tribute to Mammon that stuff may be sold so that other stuff may be bought and so the walls must change but how much sticky stuff remains in me to attach to the new walls? What is this and what is it worth and worthless and more or less worthwhile suggesting time but timeless and thus worthless for he was tired and could not think but maybe only crying as men must when faced with themselves in the darkness of their minds.

"Do you think they'll come up if we counter offer?"

Sabrina shook her head minutely. "It wouldn't hurt to try."

"They could say no and walk away. No telling when another offer will come along," Walker mused more to himself than Sabrina.

"Do think about it. Let me know tomorrow. You've got my number."

"Yes." Walker smiled thinly stabbing his right forefinger in the air as if punching the buttons on an imaginary phone. "Dial 1-800-Dumpit" he added with a trace of bitterness.

"It's not easy, I know." Sabrina had seen this scene thousands of times and somehow, she had never gotten blasé about it.

"No you don't."

"You're right, John. I don't know your particular feelings. You said you wanted to sell your house. Over the past few weeks you hinted that you do not feel you have much choice. I have been in positions where I have found myself without much choice. It is not any fun at all." Sabrina replied softly, her eyes kind, her mouth shaped into a small moue as she stared at him.

Walker looked back at her in agony, his eyes blasting out upon a world no longer his with the very air closing about him like a vendetta, seeing only the inevitability of the road set before him. "I will call you tomorrow," he told her.

Sabrina rose, majestic, billowing, status cumulus on sunset air. "Fine. Have a good evening." And she glided out of her chair and down the stairs to the walk below as a golden galleon might glide into a phosphorous evening sunset.

Walker sat staring at the street, wrapped in that particular silence that comes when company is suddenly gone with nothing to pick up the slack in their absence. It almost seemed as if he were about to think of something or someone but could not. Emotional constipation. Walker smiled into the twilight and farted hugely. Silence stinks, he decided and, as on every evening since walking away from the newly turned earth, he got up and headed out to the corner bar.

It was called the Road's End with its walls of dirty knotty pine darkened by a patina of decades of smokers. There were tables with glass tops over more wood that provided the means to rest a glass and get a grip and feel the satisfaction of the overwhelming human urge to belong and avoid the dark, lonely interstices of life. There were pictures of Willie Pep punching his way through life and Mayor Mike talking his way through it. There was a dark mahogany bar rescued from an old Hartford hotel torn down years before. A mile of mirror was mounted behind rows of colored bottles that reflected in the overhead recessed lighting making the room seem twice its size.

Mike McGonley ruled this little kingdom from the end of the bar nearest the door. Draped in a glistening tent of starched white cotton behind fire engine red suspenders, he dominated the bar and the entire place simply by his physical appearance. It was as if the air itself was empowered to circulate by the vast, rhythmic bellows of his lungs, gently pushing the white expanse of his chest outwards before releasing it to get ready for the next effort. The flesh of his face was folded and re-folded below the sparse, white curls of hair that clung precariously to the sides of his head. It rose from the almost invisible collar of his shirt. It swirled around the fleshy knob of his nose and eyes that resembled two raisins in a bowl of pudding. It did not seem possible that a man of his bulk would be able to move at all but move he did, gliding up and down the length of the bar as if he were standing on a motorized platform. Bets had been made on that very possibility but no one was ever allowed behind the bar to prove or disprove it. Mike, when asked, would merely shake his head.

Bottles, glasses, ice, fruit for the occasional pilgrim all flew into his hands as if by magic and the results would appear before the customer moments later gently set down upon a white cocktail napkin with ROAD'S END in dark green Times Roman eighteen point letters. He was at once proud and embarrassed by the napkins for he had ordered them in smaller print and they had come back like this but he had not considered the printer's mistake a show stopper and anyway he had gotten more for his money and who would care, after all, if the letters were larger or smaller and if they did care why he could just turn the napkin upside down. Most of the regulars didn't look at the napkins anyway unless it was to get a fresh drink. Still, it seemed to bother him, as much as Mike could ever show such an emotion. It was like a spot on his bar or a dirty glass and he promised himself to find a new printing firm when he reordered.

No one knew from where Mike had come. Billy Boynton, the oldest beer-soaked seat warmer in the joint, liked to tell how he had stopped by Dugan's one day for a small sip before going about his business and dammed if Dugan's sign wasn't being lifted off the brick front of the bar and there being nothing wrong with the sign that he could see and knowing that Dugan was tighter with a dollar than an old maid's hole why he just had to stand there a moment and watch with his mouth open wide enough to catch flies by Jesus and then of course he had to find out the facts of the matter and so he strolled inside and be dammed if Dugan was gone and Mike was standing behind the bar and maybe even smiling though it was hard to tell, wasn't it, what with his face being so large and all so when it moved it wasn't always easy to say what Mike was feeling now was it? Billy had taken his usual seat and waited for his usual beer to appear before him and the space before him remained empty forcing him to the not unreasonable conclusion that, indeed, the bar was changing hands and had there ever been any doubt about that fact it lasted only until he had called for a Bud and Mike had promptly placed it before him and told Billy that Billy should now exchange one dollar and a quarter of U.S. currency, please and, even though the beer should have been free on account of the bar changing hands, Mike stood there staring at him until Billy pulled a couple dirty, crumpled one dollar bills from his left pants pocket and grudgingly handed them to Mike who took them by the corner with two fingers and glided to the cash register to make change. With a look of perplexed wonder on his face, Billy related how insulted he'd felt when Mike refused to put the bills in his register, putting them to one side instead to be dealt with at a later time.

Billy swore that he had never seen the likes of Mike before and so Mike must have come from New York which everyone knew was a cold, heartless place that bred bartenders who could stand around denying good customers a free morning sip and still think well of themselves, by Jesus it was so and Billy swore to it with a tone of injured indignation.

John Jurgins, a supervisor for the Hartford Department of Public Works (or pubic works as he liked to joke) and another of Dugan's regulars who had managed to transition to the new bar, had frowned and begun what appeared to be another of his pedantic discourses. "Let us ignore Mr. Boynton's self-serving rant and review the facts as we know them. Number one: It is well known the difficulties of moving such a great weight along roads not designed to hold such. Number two: (he held up three fingers and then got one to go down where it belonged): The change of ownership, as Billy had enthusiastically described, had been sudden. Number Three: It was well known that Dugan hoarded the first nickel he'd ever made and had found that one by accident in the gutter where he was doing deep knee bends and other invigorating calisthenics. It was, therefore, obvious that Dugan had planted an apprentice seed in a pot behind the bar so that he could retire while someone else he did not have to pay did all the work but the seed had grown so quickly and so fast, that Dugan, in fear of his wallet, had fled, leaving Mike in control.

"Jurgins, you're so full of shit it's a wonder that you don't leave a trail of it behind you while you're busy picking it up in front of you on parade days," cackled Billy. "Say, now, maybe you do and that's your secret. You create exactly what you pick up thereby accomplishing nothing and that's why they made you boss."

"Ah, Billy, Billy, Billy." John sighed. "I heard you were seeking gainful employment the other day and you were checking out the classifieds, but, though I hate to be the one to disillusion you seeing that I am one of the very few people who will still speak to you, I have to tell you that the pictures on the walls of the stall in the men's room do not constitute classified ads regardless of the angle from which you view them."

"Oh. That's low, low I say." Bill had turned towards Mike. "Settle it and be done. Where do you come from?"

Mike stared at him as if they had all been standing on a crowded bus and Billy had cut a noisy and very smelly fart. Mike filled a glass with Coke and took a sip. He looked back at Billy but did not answer.

"The man of mystery at the Road's End," John intoned. Billy laughed. Mike just stared.

The scenery was setup and the actors were in their places when the curtain rose and Walker entered the bar from stage left blinking his eyes from the sudden transition from sunny heat to dim coolness seeing momentarily nothing but dim shapes leaning on the bar and one huge shape at the near end as the light from the door behind him caught the mirror and the reflection in his eyes prickled light around his skull shooting shadows speckled at the bar as he hesitated and then found a stool to the left as the shadows turned into Billy and John, the former small with long, greasy-looking salt-and-pepper hair and at least two days growth of beard. Billy had on a gray baseball cap with DIESEL stitched onto it in large, red letters, a blue work shirt with dark stains below the breast pocket and Levis that were obviously old and well worn. These were in complete contrast to his shoes, a new pair of white Nike cross trainers.

John was the taller, strong-looking with just the beginnings of a paunch. His brown hair was cut short and bristled up from his head in short, brow hairs. Sometime in the past, his nose had been broken and now leaned to the left; that made him look slightly piratical, an effect that was completely dispelled by his large, brown eyes and the beginnings of a double chin that made him look more like a Bassett hound than a pirate. He had on a white shirt that was wrinkled and had obviously been through a day's use. His pants were dark and he wore black shoes that needed a shine. He leaned on the bar with both hands around his beer mug and seemed tired and somewhat dejected.

Mike turned his head slightly as Walker came in, a movement which Walker understood to be interrogatory. "Bud," he said and chose a bar stool to John's left as Mike placed a beer with a perfect head on a white Napkin with ROAD'S END printed on it. Walker pulled out his wallet and put a five on the bar. Mike rang the sales on an old fashioned manual register that must have dated from the early part of the last century and placed the change in front of Walker. The whole transaction took a matter of seconds. Walker was amazed. "How do you do that?" he asked Mike who simply looked at him and wiped the top of his spotless bar with his spotless white bar towel.

"He is a man of few words," John commented.

"As in none at all," snickered Billy.

"Isn't that a drawback in your line of work?" Walker asked Mike. "The bartenders I have met are pretty chatty people, always ready to exchange a word of two across the bar when customers feel like talking. I suppose it's like being a barber in that respect. However," he raised his mug in Mike's direction, "may the exception prove the rule."

They sat in silence for a minute, a small group of lonely men hunched over the bar except for Walker who could not hunch too much due to his paunch and Mike who might go on a hunch but was all paunch.

"The world is going to hell," Billy announced while staring up at the TV screen currently showing CNN and a youngish looking man with lots of hair explaining something about Iraq with a picture in the background showed people picking through the rubble and body parts of yet another car bombing. It was bloody and graphic but somehow sanitized and removed from reality by the medium. The talking head looked appropriately somber as he read off the latest atrocity from his teleprompter.

"Let me guess," John replied. "It is your mission in life to help it along as much as possible."

"I have nothing to do with it. It's the government that's making this mess," Billy replied indignantly

"And what mess are you talking about?"

125

"Look at the goddamned tube if you don't you read the papers, you ignoramus, John. How can you ask something like that?" Billy got off his stool and walked down to the end of the bar opposite Mike. He picked up a newspaper left there by a previous intellectual and held it up with a flourish. EXPLOSIONS RACK IRAQ took up the top two inches of the first page. He walked back to his seat with it and slapped it down onto the bar between John and himself. He had obviously been on his stool for a while and was full of alcoholically induced indignation. He nodded his head up and down and stabbed a less than steady forefinger at the headline. "What are we even doing in that god-forsaken country, I ask you? What have we accomplished except to kill thousands of our boys and make everyone in that part of the world hate us? It's a crime, it is, and Bush is the criminal in chief if you ask me. Every month you see thousands of people marching around and burning our flag, and we probably deserve it for occupying Iraq." Billy nodded his head for emphasis and sat back down on his stool. He seemed totally secure in his belief that he had just uttered an incontrovertible truth and there was, therefore, nothing left to be said

John belched loudly. "Mike, you'd best see if this little man has the price of another beer and feed it to him. Maybe it will keep him quiet. Everyone knows that Bush is being controlled by Big Oil and that's why we're there. If Iraq didn't have any oil, we wouldn't have given a damn if Saddam blew up everyone. Nobody did anything when he wasted all those people up north, now did they? Just look at how we busted ass in Kuwait. The whole country is a postage stamp floating on an oil pool. If it weren't for that we would have let Saddam have it."

"Yeah. Cheney is taking orders from the oil companies and you can bet your ass he's making a fortune under the table."

"Oh, bullshit," Walker said. "We have no need for their oil. We do have a need to avoid any more attacks like 9/11."

"This country is all about oil. Make no mistake," John replied.

"Maybe, but we don't invade other countries to get it."

"So you say, but I say Bush is a damned murderer."

"Bush has kept us safe. That's the primary job of the government, after all. All the rest is just gouging us for taxes."

"You are so wrong, my friend. You need to get with the program. We have no business in Iraq. There were no weapons of mass destruction. Bush just flat out lied about that."

"Yeah? Hey listen. He thought there were weapons. A lot of other countries thought there were too. So maybe Hussein got them out and into Syria or someplace like that. Ever think of that? If you were president and all your intelligence people told you that Hussein was building something very nasty over there, would you just shrug it off and say well maybe he does but I'm sure that the same guy who gassed a big part of his country wouldn't use them against anyone especially this country 'cause they love us so over there. And how about Iran? There's a bunch of sixteenth century nuts over there with twenty-first century weapons. You just want us to give them a Coke and a smile?"

A fresh beer appeared in front of Walker. He looked up into Mike's face and could have sworn he saw a smile. "That's on me."

"You're a vet?" Walker guessed. Mike nodded and went back to his usual position.

"He must have been smaller," Billy commented. "He'd take up the space of an entire platoon all by himself."

"Shutup, you rude little shit," John told him. "My brother was a vet."

"Bite me," Billy replied.

"He was a vet, but that has nothing to do with why we are in Iraq, now does it?" He turned towards Walker. "It's all about oil and Bush's ego. He was bound and determined to finish up what his father failed to do and so he went and got us involved in a civil war just like fucking Vietnam. If we'd simply turned Afghanistan into a parking lot *pour l'encourager les autres* and left it at that we'd have been better off."

"French, no less. I think you are misguided if you think kissing up to the Arabs is going to make us their friends."

"I never said anything about kissing. If they want to spend their time killing each other and putting another Saddam into power, I say let them go for it. Aint no nukes over there. Bush was just using that as an excuse."

"Oh that's nice. Just stand back and let them have at it until the entire region blows up into World War Three. You want to wait until they start killing us and each other over here?"

The front door opened with a tinkling peal of laughter and two women entered the bar. The one on the left was five feet five inches tall. She had white blond hair cut page-boy style, a long narrow nose that separated two deep-water blue eyes. Her complexion was pasty and this pallor was reinforced by the fire engine red lipstick and purple eye liner that she used. She carried a large black leather purse over her right shoulder. It was decorated by purple and silver sequins that sparkled in the bar lights. She wore yellow skin tight clam diggers and a black tank top with clam-shell cleavage that barely concealed her breasts. She had on white Zanottis with stiletto heels.

The one on the right must have been at least five feet ten inches tall. She towered above her companion even when she slouched as she was then doing. She had brown hair done in a butch style crew cut. Her nose was broader and had a turned up pug tip to it that gave an unexpectedly cheerful cast to her features. Her mouth was wide and full-lipped but she wore no lipstick. She was wearing Levi jeans and a peasant blouse with designs sewn in green and red thread. It was her laughter that announced their arrival the Road's End. ". . . and he is probably still looking under the table to see if I'm there 'cause if he got down that low, he probably couldn't straighten up again," she was saying as they entered.

The shorter one squinted into the dimness of the room. "Raise the flag and salute, guys. The A team has arrived," she yelled while waving one hand above her head as if waving a flag. "Drum roll, please, maestro."

"Clash of cymbals," her companion called. "My name's Lorna Dune."

"And I'm Elsie Moon," the tall one supplied.

They chose two stools to Walker's left and looked down the bar at John and Billy. "Two Bud Lights, my good man. My, what a lively crowd we have here today. Did we interrupt something important? Were you guys playing pocket pool and bragging about imaginary conquests?" Lorna smiled impishly.

Billy cackled. "Why do you want to know? Are you girls on the hunt for a nice cue ball or two?"

"Hey, hey watch what you're saying in mixed company," John frowned at Billy who seemed totally unrepentant.

"Whatch'a got, hotshot? One or two?" Elsie turned and winked at her companion. "Doubt anyone would want to find out." She took a pull from her beer. "Now this gentleman here," she put an arm around Walker's shoulders, "at least doesn't look as though he's spent his life on a park bench." She looked at Walker. "You haven't, have you?" Walker shook his head, somewhat bemused at this exchange. Elsie pursed her lips, made a kissing noise in his direction and returned to her stool. "My associate, here," she threw an arm around Lorna's shoulders "and I are on a research mission for a school project."

"Oh sure," muttered Billy staring down the counter at them," and I've just come from my job with NASA."

"Yes," Elsie ignored him. "We are on the cutting edge of social progressivism that categorizes all human beings and their positive and negative actions in order to delve into the very core of modern civilization, taking into account such factors as the increasing complexity of the machines we build in order that they can build more machines and accounting for the tremendous increase in communications velocity and media churn through the axis of American knowledge workers that causes the dissolution of traditional family values and bonding patterns."

"Oh boy," John remarked shaking his head. "What the hell did you just say?" Billy farted loudly but said nothing.

Elsie giggled and clinked glasses with Lorna. Walker finished his beer and started on the one Mike had put in front of him. "Yep. Look at all the people who walk around with a cell phone in their ear. They talk as they walk, in their cars, on the bus, on the train, in bars and restaurants, in toilets and elevators, supermarkets, dress shops, vet clinics, lumber yards, McDonalds, Max on Main, toll booths, park rides, hiking trails, carousels, corridors, office cubes, candy shops, drug stores, and probably a few while trying to get their rocks off for all I know."

"I'd like to be at the other end of that conversation," Billy remarked to no one in particular and no one in particular paid him the least attention."

"Do we have that much more to say to each other?" Walker continued. "Has our society been so conversationally stifled that we now cannot stop the flow that technology has started? I'm thinking we simply regurgitate the same thoughts over and over again."

"Or we find ourselves having to make decisions faster, absorb action and reaction faster and compromise the personal parts of our lives to the point where we become inextricably intertwined with work and play. We no longer have privacy in our personal lives because friends, family, coworkers, bosses and even complete strangers can call us or email us or text us any time they feel like it. We have become so networked that our value system has changed," Lorna said.

John nodded his head. "My Susie is always on the phone. I think her head is permanently tilted to one side, know what I mean?" He shook his head in mock wonder. "First thing in the morning, she's on with her friend Charlene and they're talking back and forth about clothes they saw, or a sale coming up or some such nonsense and they're still talking when I come home from work nine hours later. I once asked her if she spent the entire nine hours on the fucking phone and she got all pissed off. We had to get one of those unlimited plans just to keep the phone from wrecking our budget. I don't really mind, though, 'cause if she wasn't on the phone with someone, she'd be in my face about something or other, know what I mean?" He grinned and waved his glass at the two women. "Here's to sociology and all that crap," he announced.

Walker pulled on his beer and considered the sad state of his bank account. Payday was a week away and he would probably have to borrow part of the small amount left in his home equity loan to pay the doc bills that were stacked up on his desk because the collection agency was ready to blow up his house if he didn't give them something towards the surgeon's bill. They would, at the very least, garnish his wages and that would definitely collapse the house of cards that was his financial system. Fuck it all. He would take the best he could get from the people making the offer and go from there. "A Jack chaser for this beer," he told Mike and then went off the deep end, "and a round for the house." He grinned and waved his arm to reinforce his desire. "Do you ladies carry a cell phone?" he asked Lorna.

Mike seemed to move slightly and beers appeared in front of each customer. There was a chorus of muted thanks and a series of mugs raised in his direction.

"To cell phones, mobility and instant invisibility." Walker drained the shot of Jack and sat back feeling the liquor warm in his gut.

Lorna held up her cell phone that immediately started to play the William Tell Overture. She pushed a button and then another. "New screen saver," she exclaimed and held up the tiny screen for all to see. On it, a half-naked woman sways her hips from side to side while her breasts bounce and jiggle.

"Hey, is that you?" Billy asked and got off his stool to have a better look. John looked as if he had smelled something long dead. Walker finished his shot. Mike put another in front of him.

Lorna snapped her phone shut in Billy's face. "Go away, little man. You couldn't afford it."

"Can too." He pulled a crumpled dollar bill from his pocked straightened it out and waved it above his head.

Elsie laughed. "Oh my God. Last of the big spenders. Hey Diamond Jim, want change from that or what? That wouldn't even buy you a peek into an old lady's bathroom when she was in the shower."

Lorna handed her damp cocktail napkin to Billy. "Here you go, my good man. Suck on this."

Walker grinned. "Well this isn't exactly the ad where two people sit in bathtubs suggesting that sex is imminent as the sun sets on a happy, happy, joy, joy world."

"I think that's a goofy ad. What does he need Cialis for if he's going to sit by himself in a bathtub? I think one of them should get out of their tub and climb into the other tub."

Walker shrugged. "The sponsor would probably have a stroke. Scared of offending some soccer mom somewhere."

Lorna nodded her head. "I can think of all kinds of interesting things to do in a tub but it does take two most of the time. There are some techniques though . . ."

Walker turned back towards John. "About Iraq."

"Oh pooh. No politics. It'll give you a rash between your legs," Elsie said as she got off her stool. Waving her hands sinuously above her head and swaying her hips in an imitation of the Arab belly dance, she chanted to the tune of "I'm A Little Teacup";

> I'm a little Arab
> Dressed in white
> Trained from birth to kill
> Everyone in sight.

She bumped hips with Walker and then John.

> I'm a little Arab
> Dressed in black
> Please put my body parts
> All in one sack.

John clapped and whistled.
The girls bowed. "No applause. Just throw money."
"Down in front," John yelled.

Lorna pulled her shirt up to her neck exposing her left breast. "How's this, cowboy? I have a wardrobe malfunction."

John banged his beer down on the bar. "Well done."

Walker stared at John with a blank expression on his face. "Lorna has a beautiful breast and now that breast has become part of my past and future and will influence me in ways I cannot even guess at."

Lorna bowed deeply. Elsie clapped and whistled. Walker downed another shot of Jack and stumbled slightly against the side of the bar. "When Beth was around, we used to have many discussions on this topic, I do assure you. We would argue the philosophy of time and humanity."

"Who's Beth?" John asked.

"Sorry. Beth is my wife," he paused, looking a little confused. "Was my wife. She died." For a moment he was sober, and in his eyes the pain of loss and the eternal human question of why flickered and spun and then was gone, replaced by the numbing depressive effect of the alcohol. "Yep," he continued lugubriously, "Passed on, kicked the bucket, croaked, bit the big one, passed away, travelled on, crossed the river." He stared down at his reflection in the mirror finish of the bar but a stranger looked back up at him, a sad looking fat man who had nowhere to go and now no one there to accompany him on the journey.

Lorna and Elsie walk over and drape their arms around him while humming the "Song of The Volga Boatman". Walker looks up at them and regains his sense of the absurd. Smiling, he puts his arms around them. "Okay, okay. Me big into feeling sorry for poor old Johnny. Poor old man is on the road again." He raises his beer. "Here's to the sorry part of me. May it take a long hike and never return." Lorna bent slightly and kissed him on his cheek. Walker patted her butt with sodden affection.

John swayed slightly but rose to his feet. "Speaking of wives, I'd better get back to mine. See ya later Mikey." Mike nodded and polished the bar as John pushed his way a little unsteadily through the door.

Walker stood as well. "I too will affect a departure that will brighten your night in such a fashion and I would like to state that this is absolutely the best bar in the whole fucking world and you girls are the epitome of genteel womanhood, the absolute poster children for gentility of spirit and civility of manner." He patted Lorna on the butt again.

Elsie reached down and groped him. "Oh my," she said in a little girl's voice. "Is that a tumor? You should be careful lest it grows."

Walker grimaced. "I hope you ladies will excuse me but right now I have to pee so badly I could explode." He walked a crooked path along the bar towards the rest room in the rear.

"What a funny little man," Lorna remarked to no one in particular.

"Seems nice, though. Whaddya think?"

Lorna shook her head. "Not a chance. He'd just pass out on you. Besides, you said you hated balling fat men. Like riding on a balloon, you told me."

"Oh, I don't know. He didn't feel that small to me."

Lorna laughed sarcastically. "Feel his wallet and not his dick. You had your hand in the wrong place."

"You're right. Let's blow this joint." They walked out the door as Walker made his way out of the bathroom.

"Whooa. Where'd everybody go? I couldn't have been that long even though I must have pissed at least a quart."

"Left. Not to worry. They weren't worth the sweat on your asshole," Mike replied in a surprisingly high pitched voice for such a large man. "Just a couple of working girls cruising for action. Must be slow on their corners tonight."

"Wow. You speak." Walker felt immediately embarrassed that he had said something so stupid and demeaning. It wasn't like Walker was so perfect either, he reminded himself. He'd had too much to drink and shot off his big mouth. If hot air were money, he'd be living like his mother. The evening had been going so well and then he had to go and make a fool of himself.

"When I choose to," Mike said.

"And that's not often, I think. Sorry," Walker mumbled. "I didn't mean that the way it sounded." He slid quietly onto his stool and pulled his wallet from his pocket and pulls out the solitary bill that is in it. "Just enough for one last shot, soldier."

"How did you know?"

Walker shrugged. "The way you stand. Your eyes. Just instinct perhaps."

Mike moved slightly to his left and brought up a photograph, glanced at it briefly and then passed it across the bar to Walker. It showed a group of young men standing around a pile of sandbags, probably a bunker or gun position, Walker thought. Did they call them hooches back then? A black marker line pointed at a skinny young man on the far left. He was wearing jungle cammies that draped on him. He was slouched slightly forward staring at the camera. He had no cap on and showed brown hair in a military buzz cut. Looking closely, Walker noticed the little black oak leaves on his uniform. The man seemed at once part of the group and yet apart, as if a tree leaning out from the edge of the forest. He had a slight smile on an otherwise serious face that seemed to imply that somehow he had found himself in the middle of a gigantic bad joke and was just waiting for the punch line.

"Another lifetime," Mike told Walker. "A different realty that is best forgotten as much as possible, a dance between life and death in a soggy hell Dante could never have imagined."

Walker nodded as if he understood but knew he didn't, couldn't understand, had never been in that position and would never be and yet knew somehow that triumph over fear, the desperate feeling that the next second would be the last and then amazement that it was not. For a moment he experienced constant terror that seemed to go on forever and then he was back sitting at the bar feeling like an old dried out husk, cold, insensate, incapable of thought or movement save for the drops of sweat that had appeared on his forehead and the slow settling of the hair on his forearms. "You use words most would not."

Mike stared at him. Mike wiped the bar. Mike stared at him. Mike shrugged.

Walker stared at Mike. Walker sipped from his shot glass. The two were silent.

"I can't possibly empathize. No way of knowing what you went through. You've got my respect, though. Now and forever. You and everyone in the armed forces past and present." Walker raised his shot. "Thank you." He downed the remainder of his Jack and nodded towards Mikes vast bulk. "War wounds?"

"Shrapnel"

Walker got to his feet. "'Night Mike. May God be with you."

"and with thy spirit," Mike responded.

Walker bowed towards the bar. "AMEN."

Walker went slowly out onto the slowly cooling sidewalk, head down, stride not quite steady, mind drifting back to when anything seemed possible, when youth had seemed unending, when Beth had come to him.

E2 Hartford Before

A much younger Walker stood in the shadows just inside the Civic Center central court. He felt relief and disappointment in alternate waves as he watched traffic hum past on Asylum Avenue, like rosary beads in gnarled hands constantly moving. There were few people around. Good, he thought. This is probably just another bad joke. HA HA. Let the little fat nerd chase shadows. Well okay. Just as well that nobody had shown up. There was that project he needed to work on for his job and he could get some of that done before dinner.

Walker's stomach rumbled and he tried to remember whether he had enough money in checking to go out to dinner. Maybe that new Hungarian place. Goulash with lots of paprika and some good German beer? Walker began to salivate just thinking of it. He could almost see the big chunks of rich beef bubbling in its savory sauce. Still, he felt letdown that the meeting had not come off. When it came to girls, he was, he knew, woefully lacking in the tools necessary to turn on the proper combination of wit and charm that would attract them. Physically, he was even less prepared. Blame it on the goulash. Walker smiled grimly. In fact, he was a walking, goddamned disaster if this aborted date with Beth were any indication. If he had been Adam, God would not have had one thing to worry about in the Garden of Eden. The snake would have bitten him.

It was the same way he felt when the clerk pushed Walker's lotto ticket into the machine only to have it promptly spit it out and into a trash can. Even though you know you have a minimal chance to win, hope always springs eternal and he and millions of others always figured that they would hit it eventually. So it was when he saw the note pushed through the slot in his mailbox, just a plain white envelope with his name written on the outside in a flowing feminine script. On the inside was a simple white piece of cardstock. "Hi, John. I found you through a mutual friend. Long time no see. You may not remember but you bumped into me by accident at the Durham Fair a couple of years ago. I was with your roommate at the time. I am hoping that we can renew old acquaintances. I hope you will meet me at the Civic Center court at 4:00 PM", and it was signed Beth Danzinger.

He had barely met her. Walker, completely befuddled, stared down at the note. He had dumped ice cream down the front of her dress. She had sent him the dry cleaning bill and he had sent her a check for that amount and a few words of apology. He had long ago chalked the incident up to one of his more disastrous encounters with the opposite sex and forgotten all about it. Obviously, she had not, and who was this mutual friend? Beauchamp? Walker doubted that his former roomy knew Walker's address. Walker had heard that Beauchamp was in New York and good riddance to him. Walker was intrigued - astonished, but intrigued and he knew that he would have to be at the appointed place on time even if she never showed up, even if this was some kind of joke that she or someone else was having at his expense. He lifted the note and took a sniff. It was slightly scented and the smell reminded him of a time years before, when he had gone with his mother on a shopping trip. This had not been by choice, of course, but he was making the best of it and trying to get his mother to buy clothes that he liked instead of those that she considered proper. Mom had stopped at the perfume counter at Fox's Department Store. The lady behind the counter was tall and thin and dressed in a black dress that made her skin seem like an ivory statue like the ones he had been studying in school. When she bent forward to touch his mother's arm with a sample of perfume, Walker had gotten a glimpse of a large, white breast inside an equally white bra. The smell of the moment had remained with him and he had smelled it now as he stood in the tiny vestibule of the apartment building and he smelled it now in the Civic Center watching people walking by getting on with their lives.

"Hi John."

Walker almost came out of his skin so hard at he been concentrating on the people in front of him that the voice from behind him had been a shock. He whirled around to find Beth standing there looking a little startled herself at the speed of his turn.

"Sorry. Didn't mean to startle you," she smiled and then giggled a little.

"Oh no. I mean of course not." Walker stumbled to his usual awkward, verbal halt, sure that he had committed some faux pas and embarrassed at his own lack of response. He wished he was invisible. Start again. Take number two. A better entrance this time, yes? No tripping over your lines like some snot-filled little dick. Enter the hero, tall, aquiline features, flashing Spanish eyes and greet your heroine fair who stands now awaiting you with shallow breathing and pointed nipples. Right, he told himself. On with it. "Good to see you," he told her and saw a flicker of something within the depths of her grey eyes, but she smiled serenely.

"Shall we walk?" she suggested and shifted her little, blue handbag to her other arm.

"Oh sure. That sounds good to me." And Walker meant every word for now he did not need to talk only to walk looking into the windows of the shops as they strolled down Asylum towards Main. He walked on her right so that looking at the shops also brought her breasts into view. There seemed to be more jiggle than he remembered but then she had been mad and stained with chocolate. He felt fine and walked the walk of an elephant in a protected preserve, huge, amiable, and unafraid, in constant migration for food, lord of his kingdom. "You look great, Beth. I was afraid, you know, after the last time we met." Walker cursed himself for bringing up the subject, but part of him was curious. This girl didn't even know him really. Just that one chance meeting and not a good one at that. "So why now? I thought you had forgotten me long since. Maybe even thrown away that shirt." He grinned and looked sideways at her.

Beth smiled back, dazzling Walker who would have walked into a lamp post had one been in his way at that moment. "I never forgot," she said. "I don't know why that is. I was surprised and then mad. You looked so sad and shocked at running into me like that and dumping ice cream on me. Once I got over being mad I couldn't forget you. There was something about you that made me feel as if we had known each other a long time. Plus the guy I was with was a real asshole." She giggled again.

"He was my roommate."

"Oops. I'm sorry."

"Don't be. He was a jerk. Thought he was a real Romeo."

"Uh huh, and wasn't too shy about getting his way, if you know what I mean." They walked on for a minute in silence. "Like I said, I never forgot you. When I found out that Tom was seeing other women, well we had a big fight. He beat me to the ground. I am nobody's punching bag. I left and came back to my parents' house. Shelter from the storm, so to speak. That was a few weeks ago and last week I ran into Charlie Connors who said he knew you and I got your address from him and here I am, a wee lost orphan abandoned on a doorstep." She pulled the corners of her lips down and looked at Walker with her big grey eyes.

Charlie Connors had grown up on the same street as Walker; they had played back and forth between the houses as they grew up. Charlie had gone off to a different school and a different life but through the years he had called occasionally to keep in touch. "What is Charlie up to these days?"

"Married. Child on the way. He works for an insurance company. Some kind of manager, I think, or maybe junior manager. I don't really know but he was part of a group of people in a bar in New York when I came in with a group of co-workers and that's how we met. I told him the story of the ice cream and he said "Wow, I know that guy", and we went from there. They walked silently on for a moment. Beth stopped and looked into a window. "I can't imagine wearing those, can you?" She pointed to a pair of hiking boots, thick and heavy looking with bright red laces.

"Nope." Walking with Beth was the most hiking that Walker had in mind. If she had pointed to the same pair of shoes that he was wearing at that moment, his answer would have been the same. No screw ups, he thought. Not now. Not ever again. "Those are for people who have somewhere to go and plan on getting there. I have already arrived."

Beth took his hand and squeezed it and Walker squeezed back and they walked on, flesh on flesh, two shadows dimly blending, one thinner already slouching and one taller, much wider, short legs working out from the body and back in again in the duck walk of the heavy. They were two dots of color on a canvas of dots, bobbing heads, moving metal blobs, blended with all the others around them cajoled by sign and culture to consume and replace, bombarded by media to live for the moment. Crunch all you like. If it breaks, chuck it. Not worth repairing. Two for the price of one, my friend. Buy now for tomorrow the price goes up. They went down the street, two shadows slanting on a human sundial.

Walker felt the warmth of her hand, smaller even than his own chubby paw, and the feeling was that of a stiff drink after a period of abstinence permeating the spirit and suffusing the body with its tingling warmth. He found himself hoping she would never let go and they would continue walking until they ended up in the Connecticut River a quarter of a mile in front of them. He had been down so long, he thought, that this was surely his moment, his time to stand tall in someone else's eyes and even though this all seemed so improbable as to be a dream, he was not about to reject Beth for her sudden appearance in his life. She squeezed his hand again and he felt his dick stir in its cotton cocoon. Some part of him sat inside and waited with ghastly humor for the whole thing to collapse, for Beth to turn and castigate him, slap his face and stride off into another story in a different life. This could not be totally what it seemed, the nasty little voice within him said. What could she possibly see in him that she would throw herself at him? Where was the guy watching this and waiting to run out of some building and announce that it was all a good joke? Not for him would be the beautiful women in scanty outfits sipping tall drinks by shadowed cabanas. He was no Beauchamp with good looks and rippling muscles driving the latest sports metal from Germany. The voice went on and on. Walker pushed it away savagely. It didn't matter. She was with him this moment and that was all he cared about.

They ate at a restaurant that night. It was not McDonalds. Not even close. It was called Charbonneau's and it was quiet and dim with white tablecloths and quiet waiters in black bowties and red sashes. The paneling smelled of money and the menu read like a Dummy's Guide to French Eating. He sat and looked at it and hoped and prayed that his master charge card wouldn't be rejected. Beth's smile surrounded him and he adored her as she ordered clam chowder and fried filet of sole. He felt like a homeless man who finds a winning lotto ticket, a moment of revelation and clarity that he had never known before and even the smallest movement or feeling seemed to have tremendous meaning that could never be duplicated.

He saw how happy she looked sitting opposite him in the dark booth surrounded by maroon leather and walnut paneling. Every part of her seemed to glow. The lights glinted off the waves of her hair sending little glints into the space between them. She seemed happy to be with him and laughed and chattered away while he sat over his veal Françoise and fell in love. The flesh of her large breasts that showed in the scoop cut of her blouse amazed him. Walker realized he was staring at them and had to consciously pull his eyes away and look at her face instead where he found that she had noticed his interest. He felt his cheeks go red with embarrassment but then she smiled and it was all right.

"This is wonderful," Beth said.

"It's a nice place. Glad you like it." Walker picked at his potatoes *au gratin* and nodded his head. "I've wanted to try it for a while but never had a good reason to until now."

"That's a really nice thing to say. You are a lot different than your former roommate."

"I hope so."

"You are," she reassured him. "What do you like doing when you're not working?"

"I read a lot. Everyone from Hemingway to Stephan King. Eclectic. I write some too but it hasn't come to anything yet. How about you? Any hobbies or stuff like that?"

"I like to swim, I guess. Pretty boring, huh?"

"Not at all." He could not put a name to it. He did not think love or lust. The only thing going through his mind was an image of Beth swimming naked and the words don't ever stop. He realized that he had been eating like a Tom Jones, shoving the food in while staring at her while mumbling something from a full mouth so that he sounded like someone who had lost his false teeth. His glasses had fogged up so he took them off, stuffed them into his pocket and grinned out at his blurred world with its white globes of light and dark pools of table and date.

She's here. Sitting here with me. Don't care a bit. "You are delightful. Wonderful." Romeo, you scoundrel to speak of this in some foreign tongue. Onwards, yes. He mumbled to himself.

"John. What in the world are you talking about?" Her voice concerned not with his gibberish but with her inability to understand.

Yes. Good on yer, sport, Walker thought. Get off politics, religion. Talk a little nonsense. "Mock me not, Juliet," he said. "Beauty flows through your eyes and life from your thighs."

"You are crazy," Beth giggled, hands fanned in front of her face.

He felt a sense of oneness, of fulfillment, of being. He sensed that he could say almost anything and it would be all right. Ah mighty king Thebes lies at your feet. Conquer now thyself. Such visions. She would despise him if she knew what he was thinking. She sits there smiling, a drop of salad oil shining on her lower lip sinking into the soft tissue. He would lick it off and kiss the lip ever so gently. If she only knew, she would rise in one graceful motion of leg and torso, sling her bag onto one shoulder and stride away with no further words, only an expression of scorn, hurt, ends of her lips curling up. Caught in the moment, Walker sat mutely in the glow of Beth's incipient friendship.

"Is that a poem?"

"Not yet. It could be."

"Wow. I didn't know you were so talented."

"I'm not. I was just spouting words. Words are good but I'm no good with them. Hence my day job continues unabated. Answering the phone. Solving problems." He shrugged.

"I was not great at English. Math, though, was always fun."

"You're a mathematician?" Walker looked at Beth with awe.

"I teach it."

"That's great." He caught the waiter's attention, got the check and they walked out into the summer.

Beth slid into a position close on his left side. "Thank you for a wonderful dinner," she told him and leaned into Walker slightly as they walked through the front door of the restaurant, brushing her breast against his arm as she did so.

Walker strolled slowly back down the street towards his house, remembering that first date as a man blinded in an accident might remember the colors of the world before. He still had no idea what had made her contact him and, after all these years, it made no difference at all. Even back then, he thought, it had made no difference. They ended up at his apartment and he still could almost feel the touch of her lips as they came together in the tiny living room.

Her lips were so soft and when he felt them on his they opened and he felt the soft warmth within as his tongue found hers. He remembered that it all had a dreamlike quality at that moment and he kept hoping he wouldn't wake up as Beth ran her hands up and down his chest and arms and then hugged him so hard that he felt as if something might give way within. He ran his fingers along her arms feeling the soft hair there, like silk or velvet. The embrace ended and they looked at each other.

"Hi, there," Beth said and felt beneath Walker's belly to where his cock had stiffened to the point where it hurt. He felt it lurch upwards as her fingers traced its outline on the outside of his pants.

Walker reached out and ran his left hand over her breasts pushing them slightly upwards and then down again. Beth sighed. "Oh that feels so good." He quickly employed his other hand in the same labor. They kissed again and then broke apart. Beth reached up and undid the top button of her shirt and then another. The white fabric of her bra showed in the space. Walker stared at it in fascination. Hesitantly, he touched her breast with a forefinger feeling the soft flesh yielding to his slightest pressure. Beth undid another button.

Walker was stunned by her beauty. Even years later, the memory of that time seemed as clear as if it had just happened as she slowly undressed until she stood naked. In the soft light of the summer evening, her body seemed to expand and contract in the dim light of the one lamp in the living room.

An almost iridescent glow seemed to emanate from her black hair as it curled down onto her shoulders, black on white, and from her breasts with their large, dark aureoles and pointed nipples thrusting proudly out towards him as if daring him to hold them, heavy in their promise. Instead, Beth held them, moving them up and down gently, a soft smile or eye closed lust on her face. Walker continued downwards. She was a little thicker in the waist than he would have thought looking at her dressed but slim all the same and he was hardly in a position to judge, he thought, and he was much more interested in her navel. A thin line of soft, black hair ran from just below it down into a large mass of curling black pubic hair that trapped his consciousness as surely as an mechanical trap set for a bear. He could not stop staring at it, lush and full with just a hint of her sex below and between her legs showing through the coarse hair. He felt his erection ratchet up another degree and was surprised to find himself as naked as Beth.

Suddenly, he was embarrassed by his fatty, pointed breasts and protruding belly pushing out over his sex but it was too late for that, he knew, and Beth did not seem to mind he saw with relief. She reached down and gripped his cock encircling it with two fingers and gently stroking up and down, barley touching the super sensitized flesh, driving him mad with desire. Walker knew he was close to cumming and that would be a complete disaster. Hastily he stepped back. As if sensing his plight she let go but ran one finger down the length of his shaft and then caressed his balls snuggled up tightly in their fleshy sac. She turned and walked through the doorway into his bedroom, the cheeks of her buttocks moving gently up and down, the flesh dimpled by the shadows from the window.

Even now, after all the intervening years, the memory of the first night with Beth had given him a partial erection and Walker put a hand in his pocket and rubbed it gently as he neared his house.

"Lie down," she had ordered, and without a word Walker lay down on the bed while Beth stood on one side slowly running her hands lightly across her body. Then she climbed onto the bed and sat down astride him with her rear just inches from his face. She had a small, almost delicate anus surrounded by soft, black hairs. "Oh God, he groaned and licked the dark mass of hair and the hot, moist flesh of her vagina that filled his vision. He felt her whole body tremble and then she took his cock in her mouth and Walker groaned and felt the first tickling sensation in his groin and knew he was approaching orgasm. He thrust up at her more urgently, but, instead of responding, Beth stopped what she was doing and reversed direction until she was over him face to face. Walker felt her guide him into her and, for perhaps the first time in his life, knew what heaven surely was.

E2

Walker opened his eyes, and, not without effort and some reluctance, pushed himself up and swung his legs out until he was sitting on the side of his bed staring at the old, yellowed flower patterned wall paper on the wall ahead of him. What to do what to do for I grow old and will wear my pants legs rolled. Bah. I will be as morning bright. Walker sighed and stretched. I must find a new place to live, he thought. New roof, new truth. I must sell this hall of memories and walk away, like the ground fog on a summer morning. Away with the old, the tired, the almost forgotten but not quite but sticking deep in the memory, inexpugnable, almost spiritual.

Walker stood up and with the flatulence of age, let out a long, noisy fart. Sighing again, he walked across the room scratching his crotch and hoping his morning hard on would go down so that he could pee. Make a list and check it twice, he thought as he stood over the bowl. He must contract Sabrina and have her make a counter offer. He must find a place to live. Cheap place to live. Very cheap place to live. He did the math in his head for the hundredth time. It always came out the same. After settling the medical bills and home loan and taxes and everything else, there would be a few thousand left over. Enough for emergencies, but he needed to find a place that he could afford on his wages. If he had to use the money left over from the sale, he would be in trouble again sooner or later and probably sooner. He brushed his hair, looking at the bloated face in the mirror. Damned fool, he thought. Goddamned stupid fool. You should have stayed home and become a fucking lawyer like a good little boy.

Walker sat in the small kitchen, a cooling cup of coffee to one side, the Hartford Courant classified section spread out before him. He would start with the paper, he thought, and if that did not work out, he would go to one of the agencies that specialized in apartments. With a sigh, he took a sip of his coffee, folded the paper neatly and turned to begin his search.

My God in heaven, what they're getting for tiny boxes. Walker stared morosely at his roast beef sub with lettuce, tomato, and extra mayonnaise and can of diet coke from a nearby Blimpies shop. Bunch of crooks that's what they are. One tiny bedroom, living room with kitchenette for eight hundred a month five hundred square feet, a fortune for a shoe closet and that's just the beginning. Security references. Check with my wife, dickhead. She'll vouch for me. Cash up front. No smoking. No pets. Damage deposit. First and last month's rent. Shit. If you do more than stand in the middle of the room and breathe, you'd better have some long green in your hand. Some of the bathrooms were so small I would have gotten stuck and starved to death while taking a shit. One had mouse droppings in the cupboards. The agent for another looked like a kid earning summer wages. Whaddya think, pops? Pretty nice, huh. All cleaned up and ready to go. Whaddya say? Got someone coming in to look at it this afternoon so you gotta act fast. No pressure, you know, but this is a prime location. The units move fast, know what I mean?

Walker bit down angrily into the sandwich. Prime location, my ass. That dump had been ten minutes from the bus line and right next to the projects. Good luck getting home in one piece. Downtown, they had wanted twice the rent for the same amount of space and everything net of utilities. Jesus H. Christ on a crutch, he swore softly to himself. On his salary, it would come down to a choice between shelter or food. Whatever was left over from the sale of the house would not last long at this rate. Well John aka Agile Walker was not selling himself into homelessness and that, as they say, was that. Period. John looked at his sandwich and pushed the remains back into the bag that had already turned dark with grease. Shouldn't waste the money, he thought, but can't stomach the thought of it. He walked past the bus stop towards the library. Maybe Zinny would be there. That thought cheered him up and he swung the bag almost gaily. One of the dwarfs off to work. Hi-ho. Hi-ho. Was there one called Fatty? Hi-ho. Hole hi. The modality of the senses. If we do not see but yet feel is that a bigger reality than if we see but it makes no impression and just goes by accepted but forgotten? Perhaps we can at least stray from sense to common sense. If you hear him but do not understand then was he was expressing himself poorly or merely engaging in arrogant and pretentious twaddle. If he were a man of sense then doesn't both sense and cents decide between thought and twaddle? Intellectual masturbation. So many critics suffer from it. Pass the bone, Fido and onwards to bookville and

Zinny. Nice woman. Face kept popping up inside his mind. Like the way her mouth twists when she smiles and the way she looked at him as if she knew there was more to him than that.

Ah here we are now up the newly laid steps and through the newly hung doors and into the newly finished library. So where is Zinny? Walker stood inside the library looking towards the information desk where Zinny would normally be. It was Saturday, after all, he thought. Maybe she doesn't work on weekends. No worky no payee. Ah so, you lazy, scabrous Gaijin. Hephaistos arise. Where would she be? He approached the young, snotty looking girl behind the counter.

"Azalea? Oh no, sir. She is not working today," the woman said, young lips splitting over pearl white teeth and youthful breasts that would not even make up a proper handful.

"Oh too bad," he told her. "Perhaps I could leave her a note?"

"Certainly, sir." Blonde hair above a teal blouse that showed the faint outlines of the bra beneath. "and your name?" She looked up expectantly, her pen poised above a piece of memo paper.

"Walker. Just Walker is fine. Add lunches. She will know."

The girl made a note on the paper. "Certainly," she started and then stared at him, her hand flying up to hide her mouth, her eyes widening momentarily. "Excuse me just for a second." Slim teal turning into the back room behind carts of books by James Patterson, Margaret Cuthbert, Tom Robins, James Clavell, Howard Costain, Nelson DeMille, R.A. Salvatore, and Larry Bonds to keep senses damped and pots boiling and there a Stephen King, yes, look deeper into yourself and you will find . . . tales for the intelligent, a treasury of great poetry, Sailing Ships of the world for your coffee table, "The Stanger at Winds Point", romance novels with young men with huge muscles bending over a beautiful woman at sunset. Toilet paper for your rosy red hole. Walker stood reading the titles while waiting for the smiling woman on the cover to return from the orient with rice paper and diaphragm.

Ah there she was coming through the doorway, brown slacks slipping through the opening past the carts of books being returned or simply being, her face toothy with smile. "She left you a message," she told Walker handing a plain white envelope across the counter.

"Thanks." Walker smiled mechanically, accepted the envelope, and retreated from the line of people towards some neutral ground where he could sit. There was a place at a table where an old lady sat staring down at a newspaper and sighing softly. The war goes on. People are dying. Sigh. Was man ever thus? Sigh. For country. Sigh. They all hate us. Sigh. But still. Shake of head. Glasses pushed up upon hearing a noise. Rustle of paper. Wrinkled flesh jiggling. War is hell on time, on flesh. Time to do that? Oh yes, well tomorrow, then. Still, she could have turned to Current Events. Walker sat down across from her fingering the envelope. How could Zinny have known he would be by? Why would she leave a message on the chance that he would be asking for her? Was that good or bad? To open or not to open?

Walker stared down at the envelope as if to dissolve it and lay its contents onto the table in front of him. How could she know? He didn't even know. Just in case, in the event of, should it by chance occur, accidentally, karma, or fate or whatever you choose that she decided to write it to say that he should not bother her any more or that he had a book overdue, or that she would take it as a favor if he used another library. Well, she thought enough to write it. How bad could it be? Walker stared down at the envelope a moment longer and then lifted the flap and removed the single sheet of twenty pound copy paper inside.

> *Dear Agile. I enjoyed our talk the other day. It is not often that I find someone with whom to talk and one who seems genuinely interested in anything I say. I hope I did not bore you to tears (better than boring you to death, I suppose, for then I would have no chance to apologize. LOL) but if I did, I hope to have a chance to improve on that initial failure. I have that small personal problem that I mentioned the other day and may have to take some time off so you may not see me for a while. I did not want you to think ill of me should that come to pass.*
> *Zinny Jones*

Oh boy. Walker sat with the note in one hand staring into the space over the head of the old woman across from him. Well he'd enjoyed it too, he thought, and here he was looking for more and now this note. What kind of personal problem? Her ex husband? Could that problem be me? No. She cared enough to write it. Of course, she could be a compulsive note writer and spend her free time writing notes to any and all that she knows. Note to husband—Bring home milk. Note to self—Stop at ATM. Note to kid—make your bed. Note to kid? Maybe not. She looks past the age. Forties. Fifties maybe. Well kept for all that. Hasn't given up on herself. Not like Walker. He'd let himself go so far that down looks like up. Got get a grip. Get serious about a diet. Stop making excuses. Starting today, right fucking now. Walker nodded his head as if to seal the deal with himself. She definitely has an air about her. Seems to enjoy life. She didn't want him to think ill. Old fashioned phrase. Haven't heard that choice of words lately. Out of use today. Why would he think ill of her? Hope that she is okay. No telephone number. Sounds like the problem is not as small as she states. None of his damned business, of course. Still, human curiosity. Would it be smaller than a breadbox? Than a button, than my problem? Zinny doesn't seem like the panic type personality. Least he didn't think so. Small problem might be a big honkin' mother of a problem. Hope she's okay but what if she's not?

Walker found that he could no longer sit still. Holding the letter in one hand he bounced out of his chair so suddenly that the woman across from him looked up in sudden alarm. Masher, cad, druggie, rapist. Startled he saw all those thoughts flash through her eyes. "Sorry. Didn't mean to startle you," he told her and noted a look almost of disappointment on her face. He smiled vaguely and moved away from the table. He walked up and down the broad central aisle automatically folding the sheet of paper and then unfolding it again. What to do what to do? What could he do? The woman was almost a total stranger. One nice meeting in the park. Zinny Jones. Maybe she had the flu and would be in bed for a couple of days, or sitting in front of the TV gulping aspirin, fruit juice and Zycam, sneezing nosefulls of germs all over her living room. Beth's illness had begun as bouts of indigestion. That thought did not help Walker in the least. He forced himself to think differently. Maybe her parents had called with a problem and she had gone to fix it. His parents never had problems like that and would not have called him in any case but his parents were not exactly average, Walker thought. Maybe she just needed some mental health time and had taken vacation time to go and blow some bucks in Atlantic City or Foxwoods. He knew people at work who did that. Then why the note? If it was something trivial, she would be back in place in a few days and he would see her whenever.

Walker came to the end of the space between the rows of desks and looked up to find himself just to one side of the information counter. "Excuse me."

The woman looked up, face formed in an automatic question mark. Eyebrows mostly penciled in rose up. Mouth colored with Flamingo Sephora pursed. Kiss kiss. "Yes, sir. May I help you? Oh it's you again." No change of tone. A specimen on a slide that has suddenly reappeared. Okay, guys. Who duplicated the slide and forgot to check the sequence?

"Thank you for delivering the note from Zinny," Walker paused and knitted his brows as if trying to remember something. "Zinny, Ah,"

"Jones."

"Yes. That's it. Thanks." For once in his life Walker was glad that his body and his face were such that few people took him seriously. Playing the fool could be useful, he thought. "Bit of a senior moment, there." He grinned sheepishly as if caught masturbating in the men's room. "You wouldn't happen to have her address, would you? She seems to have left it off the note and I don't have it with me."

Eyebrows down. Face setting into officious lines. Teal defending. "I'm sorry, sir. We're not allowed to give out that information."

Made sense. Suppose he was a murderer or a rapist or a spurned lover. Still, he felt disappointed that he could not get at the information so easily. Teal of the set features looking down at the counter. Finnegans Wake. Hah. The end as the beginning but incomprehensible as are most beginnings in the end. Poetry amok amongst blood work. "I'm sorry," she told him.

"Quite all right. Good security, I'm sure."

The woman looked relieved and rubbed the forefinger of her left hand softly with the right(Like a lovers cockstrokestroke, Oh God) "Yes. Really I wish I could."

"Thank you anyway."

"Sure." The woman smiled and looked at the person standing behind him.

Walker made his way towards the front of the library stuffing Zinny's note into his back pocket as he did so. He still had to find a place. The house would be sold and in a few weeks he would be out on the street. That had to be his priority, Walker reminded himself. Home as in shelter from the cold as in hearth and home. When he was growing up it was not a home but just a place where he knew no want, had no fear of not having his bedroom or his clothes or his food. Fear of Dad. Yes, but that was a different fear, a fear of displeasing the man who was his father, not fear of being in a shelter surrounded by people with no money and nowhere to go but he would have money, at least enough to find a place and that is what he must do even if he didn't like it. Can always move later so stop being so dammed picky. He wonderd about Zinny, though. Why would she bother leaving a note if she didn't like him but with no address or phone there's not much he could do. Walker wanted to help her but he was like an enuch in a brothel. He should have faith, he guessed, that God or whatever force was above and beyond his control (call it what you will) was not going to let anything bad happen to her. Right. Just like nothing bad happened to Beth and the good fairy is guiding Jennifer safely through a world full of hopheads and ratfucks. Someone is dealing with all this, though. He felt every time he did something and looked back on it later and said well would he have done the same again and he would have to answer yes at least most of the time and even when he didn't answer yes he thought the end result would have turned out the same. Call it God. Call it life. Whatever it is, take care of Zinny. Please. Amen.

Anyway, one last place to visit today. Hope this one is it.

A feeling of impotent uselessness slithered through his mind and coiled and twisted around those problems. He stopped just before the revolving doors of the library ignoring the people coming in, the security guard behind his little desk. His head felt as if it would explode raining bits of trivial knowledge and limited intelligence all over his surroundings. He had to do something, anything. Move forward now.

The sunlight held him in a forest of black dots and orange flashes as he walked down the steps onto Main Street. The afternoon wore on him like a pair of tight pants, binding and constricting, numbing his senses as he made his way along the flat, heated sidewalk as the occasional car drifted by, seemingly propelled solely by its wish to be elsewhere. One more appointment and then home, thank God.

The man stood in the doorway with an old, blue cardigan draped across his bony shoulders. His eyes were as dark as the night. His hair was white and stuck out from his scalp at random angles as if trying to flee. He looked at Walker through the pale fence of the afternoon as if Walker had told him that it was snowing. "You're Walker?"

"Yes. I had an appointment at one to see the apartment." Walker smiled in what he hoped was a friendly and reassuring manner. If he liked the apartment it would be a big help if the super liked him.

"Follow me," the man told him and turned back onto the building past a row of battered mailboxes built into the wall on the right and up a flight of stairs. The walls were covered with wallpaper that must have been fifty years old. The paper had faded red roses as its pattern and was torn in places where people had banged their belonging into the wall as they moved into the apartments. There were dark stains and spots at random places along its length. By the time they got to the top of the stairs, Walker was puffing and trying not to pay attention to the dirty steps on the staircase. How many thousands of people had walked up these stairs ahead of him puffing or groaning, running up, staggering up, walking ahead of a partner or behind one while uttering sweet nothings or cursing or mumbling or trying not to sick all over the stairs. Walker was certain that no one who had walked up these stairs in the past had left any tracks on the beach of life. The thought depressed him somewhat but he had made the appointment and would see it through. He wondered if the old man ahead of him still thought about the ladies or maybe no longer thought about much of anything except keeping his job as super in this run down building.

The old man stopped before a door and fished in his pocket for the key. "It's small but it's clean." He opened the scarred door and pushed it open. It had a moonlike surface bumped and abused by thumbtack holes, nail holes, marks from tapes of various types (Doris—I will be at Mom's; Andy—get fucked) and a peephole in the center of it. Hello. Who are you? Oh yes. Do come in. I just happened to have some tea brewing. Pre cell phone. Medieval communications. No instant gratification. Just graffiti gratification. A door covered with clues to a history of the granularity of human relationships. Did Zinny live in an apartment? Somehow he didn't think so but he couldn't say why. It just felt wrong. Married again? Ugh, Walker grimaced. Probably. He shook his head trying to change his thought and walked past the old man into the apartment.

A large, double hung window faced him at the end of a rectangular room. At the far end to the right of the window, there was a door, and to the left another door. Bedroom and kitchen, he guessed. Well at least the kitchen wasn't part of the living room as it tended to be in more modern apartments. That was something he liked. He had grown up in a house with a separate kitchen and had spent his adult life in a house with a similar layout. We are creatures of habit and guardians of our past, he thought as he looked around the empty room, at the windows with noticeable grime on the outside and dust on the inside, at the wooden floor with various spots, stains and marks from spilled paint, at the ceiling with nice moldings along the edges but in need of a fresh coat of Ceiling White latex. In the center of the ceiling two thick black wires with their ends taped off came through the ceiling. A light fixture at some point, Walker realized.

The heat in the room was like a physical force that pushed him backwards into memory. He had just been a boy, already heavy, stomach stretching out, wearing his favorite Brooklyn Dodgers tee shirt, playing pin-the-tail-on-the-donkey at Eddie Moore's birthday party. Hot then too, flesh pressing, shoving, screaming. Nono wrongway sweating into the blindfold screams filling his ears nono colder, warmerwarmer shrill heat beating at him, sweat streaming down his cheeks, determined to make the pin, water pouring from his flesh like a water buffalo as he turned feeling towards the target so paper so muted hands no touching him pushing screaming on way and then another and all he could see was the heat and all he could feel was the piece of paper in his hand until suddenly he felt the ground beneath him, felt himself sitting, looking up at the faces above him, Eddie, Betsy, Sammy, Joe minimum eeny meeny miney moe hey what happened to the fat kid, yeah Johnny. He sorta fainted and sat down just before he was gonna. Oh yeah, Johnnie Walker from Eddie's homeroom. Whatta jerk. My mom says his parents are rich. Whatta piece of crap. Sitting down like a old woman. Fudge face, butter ball. dipshit.

"Pretty messed up," he told the man.

The super shrugged. "Nothing a little dusting won't fix," he replied with a gap-toothed smile. "I'll show you the rest." He marched across the room, "Bedroom and bath through here, he walked through the right doorway and, reappearing a moment later when Walker did not follow him in, walked across the room and into the left hand door. "Kitchen in here." He said from inside the other room.

Walker went across the living room and stared through the window. The sky took on the color of rotted meat and the air in the apartment tasted of iodine and despair. He turned through the doorway into the tiny kitchen, really no bigger than a closet. His parents had clothes closets that were bigger. On the left was an old refrigerator that hummed loudly. He opened it to find mold growing on the shelves. Obviously the super had just turned it on for this inspection. Next to it a small four burner stove. Opposite that was a sink in the middle of maybe six feet of counter top. Dark brown, knotty pine cabinets circled the room on three sides overhead. All of life requires sustenance, he thought. Could do a steak in here. Looks well used. There's a line of yellow grease running down the side of the stove. Lines of anchovies dancing with breasts a jiggling and wiggling and will no one applaud? Think Zinny might. Oh get a life, Walker. She has one already, you fat fool. "Includes utilities?" he asked.

"Only heat." The old man stared at him. "Eight hundred's a good price. Could get more for it if I fixed it up a bit."

Walker snorted. "It's a rip-off. Does the water even work?"

The old man looked wounded. "Of course it does." He turned and twisted one of the faucets in the sink. There was a loud pop and then a clanking of pipes that vibrated the faucet and a thin stream of brown water fell into the sink below. "Hasn't been used in a while but it will come around."

Walker snorted. "So will Christmas."

"You want it or not? There's others waiting to look at it."

Take it or leave it. It was always the same. God I hate this Walker thought and walked out of the kitchen and stood in front of the window again. I wore a hat upon my head within its bounds is something dead. Hah. Stray thoughts ran across the front of his mind like tumbleweed in a fifties western. He knew he should take it whether he could afford it or not. Time was almost up and a hotel would cost him at least as much and probably a helluva lot more. He looked down at the street below him at a sweep of people and cars, houses, streetlights, and thought of food, steak would be nice, and women, Beth smiling in the backyard as Jen ran towards her laughing and yelling 'Mommyyyyyy.'. Those had been the good times, or at least he remembered them that way for they came before Jen grew into a sullen, rebellious adolescent and before the illness began. House memories. Work and sleep, work and sleep but always someplace to call his own, a place of permanence and solidity where he could find a reason to keep on keeping on. Now, nothing permanent, not his, not anyone's except whoever owned the building. Where he stood others had stood and watched the street and the cars and the people but the window for certain had been cleaner, the cars smaller and more bulbous in appearance, the people with hats, a gentler age where space didn't mean Cape Kennedy and no one had electronics stuck in their ears.

Walker's belly appreciated and depreciated, rising and falling in even waves before the window sour and dirty rising and falling in the sun motes of dust floating still in the oven air as he pondered the inescapable fact that he would be paying far in excess of what he would be getting. Take it or leave it. The phrase ran in circles through his head and it was not so much conscious thought as a sense of being, of the ebb and flow of his life and those of the lives around him, much like the pace of his breath itself, heavy, steady like lovers in a full moon, in and out, pleasure pointing muffling sighs. The tickling of time within him served to bring him back to the window where he confronted the moment. "No." he replied, and felt the lifting of something thin and heavy that had rested within since the old man had first opened the door.

"Okay." The man shrugged and stepped out of the kitchen and across the living room with a measured, somewhat unsteady gait. "Your loss," he grumped without turning his head as they walked down the stairs to the first floor hallway.

Following him, Walker sneered at his "loss". Losses such as this were a good thing, he thought. He felt hungry and wondered whether he should walk up the street in search of a snack or head directly home to the waiting refrigerator. Pretty quick he'd be reduced to quarter pounders at the nearest choke & puke. Whoopee. Maybe he was just too dammed fussy for his own good. Walker decided to just go home and stop at the local grocery store on the way and buy dinner. He wondered if he could get old Fernando to cut him a couple of thick pork chops. The thought made his stomach rumble and he hurried across the street to the bus.

F1

The clouds looked like bullfrogs. They puffed darkly, curling and churning out rhythmic strums in the still sky, wet and shady a half mile away from the house so long ago in what seemed like some other woman's childhood, half shadowed in dappled grays and greens of lily pads and foreign seas caught up in the grinding roar of pirates on an island shore. Sighing, Zinny looked away, down from the sky to the land where cars replaced pirates and houses replaced frogs and problems did not gradually disappear into the blue but came back to sit on your shoulders and make you feel miserable. Cloudy frogs were part of a childhood and had no place in the concrete and asphalt life that she was in.

He would come. She could no more doubt that feeling than she could deny her own being and she felt the fear and despair of the past times forming in a tight ball in the pit of her stomach over which she now held her hands as if to ward off what she knew could not be avoided. Fear of the known combined with fear of the unknown caused Zinny to blink away tears of rage. After all these years. She had almost forgotten that part of her life, almost put it into a trunk in the attic, closed the lid and walked away. Dealing with her father was more than enough for her to handle. Zinny worked up a terrific session of feeling sorry for herself as she sat on the sagging front porch of the old house.

The street seemed to rise to meet her. Florence Tippin from the upstairs apartment at number eighty-five walked past, looked up to where Zinny was sitting and waved. "How you?" she called.

"Hot," Zinny replied and waved back.

Florence laughed, big tummy all a jiggle. "Sure 'nuf is. Stay in the shade, hear?"

An older, black Buick went by slowly, seeming to drift without sound through the heat rising from the asphalt in waves like some huge beetle on a rock.

A slight breeze tickled a few leaves in the maple tree in the front yard, and they waved in languid acknowledgment as if the heat were too much for them as well. Zinny sighed and sat back waiting for Mark and wishing that she was having a tooth extracted sans anesthetic instead, remembering the disaster of the day before.

After talking with Agile, she had stomped back to the library at one thirty. What right did Mark have to show up in her life again, his mouth full of sneer and his eyes stripping her as he looked at her across the counter? He had been standing in front of the library so that she could not avoid him.

"One o'clock, huh?"

"I have to work now, Mark. I have nothing to say to you so just leave me alone."

"Sure." Mark stood there in her path without moving.

"Please, Mark. I can't afford to lose this job."

"Bullshit, you sniveling little liar."

"I'm not like you." Zinny snapped. "I work for a living instead of bumming off of others." That had always been his problem. Mark knew with absolute certainty that he was destined to lead from above. Working one's way up was not part of his plan. When they had been together, he never kept a job very long and that was always someone else's fault. They were the small people who just did not understand him and were jealous of his good looks and intelligence and spent their time making him look bad. The man had no clue.

"Cmon, Zinny. We got off to a bad start here." He smiled at her with those eyes that had driven her crazy years before.

She looked at him as one might look at a cobra before it rose and spread its hood. "What do you want? Run out of victims?" Her stomach knotted. Had she gone too far? Public place, she reminded herself. No worries but he had no . . . stop it. Damn him seven times to hell.

"Listen, Zinny." Mark stepped towards her until his face was inches from hers. She smelled the hot sourness of his breath. "I didn't show up to argue with you in front of this place."

"I don't know why you bothered to show up at all." Zinny looked into those big brown eyes that she had long since found to be dead with unexplored depths of cruelty.

"We need to talk. Pick a time and place or I'll just hang around." He smiled then, cat sure of certain victory that Zinny would not want that no no.

"Tomorrow then. At my dad's house about eleven."

"Gotcha." He pointed a finger at her as if he were holding a pistol and clicked his tongue bang, bang. Done deal on the morrow.

And she had walked back into the library through the doors of glass past the security desk on the left where Henry sat and nodded at her nodded at him past the row of computer desks hiding more computers where people bent over as if in prayer past the wide staircase leading to the second floor stacks and finally past the information desk to her tiny cubicle in the back where she sat wrapped in rage and despair staring blindly at the screen in front of her unsure whether she should fish or cut bait, fight or flight, realizing that Mark would always come back like a cancer that had been in remission and what about her father who could not just get up and trip lightly down a yellow brick road. Trapped she was and the realization clawed at her senses so that the computer in front of her blurred and the papers on her desk turned into a grayish white mass. She dabbed at her face savagely with Kleenex. Dammed old woman. Crying about it won't do you any good now. Get it together.

Zinny made her way back to the bathroom to repair the damage, scrubbing her face with cold water, brushing at the always stubborn hair, inspecting the result. Lifeless looking brown with streaks of gray. YUCHH. Okay, okay, she thought. Take it one step at a time. It may go better than you think. Maybe he was just in the area and gravitated to her out of some sadistic sense of the perverse. Maybe he has mellowed. Maybe there's ice water in hell.

She stood in front of one of the sinks staring at a stranger in the mirror and wishing that she was back talking with Agile. Something about the man. She needed him or needed to see him again or needed to think that she needed him and suddenly the truth that struck her blindly from behind her eyes like some menstrual shotgun blast from her inner piece of certainty. What if Agile showed up tomorrow and found Zinny was off and what if Mark's appearance caused her to take days off the following week? What then? Zinny dried her face, and marched out of the bathroom, eyes slits of determination. Azalea is moving on, girl. Deal with it, with him, with it all. Take the bad and handle it; take the good and hope. Take the rest of your life, girl, one baby step at a time. For now, just finish the afternoon. Breath in. Breath out, in and out in and out inandoutandin. POOF. Take that. Fate, you bitchy sister spinning your strand. Zinny would stand tall while you finger your yarn. She'd leave a note for Agile just in case. Betty was on tomorrow and she owed Zinny one for helping with her - well never mind.

Now, Zinny sat on the porch and waited. Looking to her left down the block, she saw him ambling, shambling slowly legs swinging in and out and shoulders swinging in his usual fashion. Confident, aggressive, in-your-face, buddy do I have a deal for you. He needed a shave. He needed more than she had been able to give or wanted to give for that matter. Zinny frowned watching him as he came through the heat morning waves rising from the asphalt and leaf hot trees.

"Good morning." He smiled, raised his hand a little and then let it drop.

She tried to smile, felt her face stretching into some kind of mask. Hoped for the best. "You're here. What do you want?"

"Such bad manners," Mark sneered, "but you never were much for polite conversation, or anything else for that matter. Why is that I wonder?" Eyes flat, hands loosely at his sides, body shifting slightly in the light. Tiger crouching, heat striped, prey sure.

"What do you want?" Zinny wanted him out of her life now and forever. She was no longer his wife and she was dammed if she was going to stand there and make pleasant conversation. She was a woman, not a snake charmer.

"Nice house. Always was. Your dad made a good choice." He looked it up and down, side to side, a real estate agent sizing up a prospect. "Solidly built. They did it right back then." He came up the steps onto the porch and stood facing Zinny on the porch.

"So?" Zinny knew what was coming but dammed if she was going to hand it to him. All his life people had been handing things to him and he had always taken for granted that this would continue and even now, well into middle age, he thought that all he had to do was ask and it shall be given.

"Let's talk money, Zinny."

"I have none. I told you," now feeling impatient with this whole charade and needing to be done with it all. "If I had any money would I be working for a perennially broke, fifth-rate bureaucracy in a third rate city?"

"You've got this house. Even in this location, it's worth a bundle, I'd guess."

"It's my father's, not mine. Even if it were, it needs work and would take years to sell." Zinny cursed herself for even admitting that it could be sold. She had power of attorney but that, at least, she could keep from Mark.

"Not if the price is right. We can work out a deal." Mark grinned and winked at her.

"Get lost, Mark." Zinny felt the world collapse around her shoulders, a noose suddenly tightened, choking off all thought of life. "My father doesn't want to sell. So that's that." She felt the heat rising in her bones, a flame tearing her mind out of her flesh. Mark's face floated in front her, distorted into some gigantic dragon with bulging eyes and gaping jaws.

Marks eyes contracted squinty cold and snake dead. "You're such a liar, you frigid old cunt. Your holier-than-thou dad must have been in his fifties when we married and that was thirty odd years ago. I'll bet he's drooling in his oatmeal right about now. Shall we go and ask him?"

"Take another step towards the door and I will call the police." Zinny brought her cell phone out of her pocket and held it up. She was so scared that she felt faint. He legs trembled and she worked to keep from bursting into tears.

Mark held both hands up in front of him in a sign of mock surrender. "Yep. I'll bet he's a vegetable if he's even still living here and you've got power of attorney. So here's the deal. I need one hundred thousand dollars and then I'm outta your life for good. If I don't get it, I'll hang around and make your life hell and don't bother calling the police. I've been around and I know lots of ways to drive you up the wall and your father too and nothing they can do about it. Until it sells, you give me one grand a month for living expenses."

He stared into her with those lifeless eyes and Zinny knew that he would do exactly what he said. When they had been together, he had not hesitated to demand whatever he wanted and he had backed it up with his fists. That he could be more subtle but just as hellish this time around she had no doubt. Once those eyes had mesmerized her like a long stretch of flat highway. No longer. Nothing there. None, zero, zip, nada, *niente*, forget it, pass on that, but now there was only a bulging knot of despair inside her. Where was she even going to get a grand a month to pay him off, let alone sell the house.

159

The thought horrified her even more than his initial demand and she turned away from him abruptly to avoid giving him the satisfaction of seeing her reaction. Mark would not fade into some sweat tinged recollection of a nightmare. He was not some peripheral evil at the edges of a psychic breakdown. Mark smelled the only thing that had ever meant anything to him: money. He had married her to get it, and, when it turned out that her father was not one of those wealthy doctors, he had used her instead to satisfy his crumbling masculinity. The divorce had been one of disappointed avarice for him and total relief for Zinny. So now he had obviously run his string and was back for a big second helping, the asshole. "Get out." She told him softly without turning around.

"I'm not in."

"You know what I mean."

He grabbed her left arm and spun her around to face him. "Okay, but I'll be back. Shall we say in a few days for the first little installment? If you don't have it by then I'll be glad to help things along." He smiled at her, turned and walked down the steps and along the street towards the bus stop, legs moving in and out, shoulders rising and falling in the shimmering heat.

E2 Caliban

Walker sat on a Sunday porch deep shadowed back to the left of the front door where it jutted out into the porch area. Walker loved his Sunday porch because the street was quiet and he could watch the tilt and sway of life. An occasional car rolled by. Rap music floated out from a second floor apartment across the street. He felt slightly doped up and snoozy, full of scrambled eggs and good thick-cut bacon. He thought about taking a sip from the cup of coffee on the little table beside him but the effort seemed too great. It was that kind of morning. He wondered whether it would be worth getting the morning paper. Too much trouble, and the paper was full of Democratic politics anyway. Always depressing.

"Hi, John."

Walker came out of his reverie with a start, almost upsetting the chair that he had tipped back against the side of the house. "Morning, Celia," he answered the woman who was standing on the sidewalk in front of his gate. Celia Monroe was a thin woman of indeterminate age though Walker judged her to be in her fifties. She had lost her husband the year before and now smiled and waved at Walker whenever she saw him.

Her hair stirred slightly in a phantom breeze. "Hot one today," she remarked. Her hair was brown and curled and she kept pushing it back from her face. "It's too hot in my apartment but not much better outside." She brushed at her face again as she squinted up at him. "You look comfortable."

"Not so bad in the shade," Walker agreed. She seemed so small and wilted standing there, flotsam on a river large, spinning slowly through the eddies. "Come sit," he invited and gestured towards an old faded grey chair on the other side of the small table.

Celia stood for a moment, hand on the gate and the other hand waving in front of her face. "Thanks." She walked up and sat down in the chair with a quiet sigh, "Quiet now."

They sat and listened to the street, the hum of the traffic from Farmington Avenue, the BLEEP of a horn. The rap music from across the street had stopped but music was still coming faintly from somewhere, someone yelled something and then stopped suddenly. There was no sense of urgency or time, no feeling for the finite, resting however briefly in the old cunt of the world. Celia sat slouched in her chair. Walker watched her brown eyes in their fleshy bags travel left to right and then right to left as if she were watching a tennis match. She seemed nervous. Granted, he was just a man she occasionally passed on the street. She knew him by name but that was about the extent of it. "Trouble?" he asked her softly.

She turned towards him. "You have a child, don't you? I remember seeing one in your yard in past years." Walker was surprised at the question and it must have shown on his face. "I'm sorry," Celia clutched her hands together in a knot. "I didn't mean to bring up a sensitive subject."

"Not at all," Walker assured her. "Yes. I have a daughter. All grown, now, at least that's what she assumes." He trailed off and took a sip from his coffee. The street seemed different, somehow. Perhaps the thought of Jen had changed his mood to one of restless discontent. Perhaps, he reflected, that showed he was having sympathy pains with his daughter. She was about as discontented as a girl could be. Girl? Hell she was almost thirty and was still living the counter culture existence of the young and pimply. Walker thought, not for the first time, that she would probably never change to any life style that came remotely close to the one he had. Well, his wasn't all that great, right now was it?

"I have a child. I'll bet you didn't know that." Celia continued. "A son. I had him when I was very young."

Where was this leading, Walker wondered? He hadn't known about her son but why tell him now? "I didn't know," he told her more to be making noise than for any other reason.

"Yes well he came for a visit for a day or so. I hadn't seen him in years." Her hands clenched and unclenched, tightened and twisted like worms in a can. "Children can be such a trial," she announced to no one in particular.

"Yes they can," Walker agreed to that same nonperson.

Silence.

More silence. The sound of coffee cooling and breaths breathing. Two people trying to either get into or out of a conversation without knowing which way they wanted to go or where they would be after the act of going.

"So I'm not the only one with problems?" Celia asked

"Does a bear shit in the woods?"

Celia laughed. Walker grinned, suddenly feeling better, certainly happier, than he had felt in days and for no more reason than a neighbor's hearty guffaw. Her laugh had struck him as funny, done him a good one, tickled his funny bone, and he was so ready for it after his futile search for an apartment and Zinny's vague message of some problem.

"If I see one, I'll have to ask him," she rejoined.

He pushed himself to his feet. "Want some coffee?"

"Thanks"

Walked disappeared inside and reappeared a minute later with small black lacquered tray holding a white china coffee cup, a brown fired clay sugar bowl and a quart container of milk. He set this down on the table, lifting his own cup out of the way as he did so. "So what brought you past my gate?" he asked as it seemed not only an obvious question but the only words that came to him at the moment. It was a morning for the obvious, obviously.

"Heat." Celia added cream and sugar to her cup. "The fan in my apartment doesn't do much. It's probably as old as I am. I guess I got tired of sweating all over the couch and decided that outside would be better than inside. I came down the street and saw you sitting there." She shrugged. "We met at Stop & Shop a while back. That's how I know your name. So anyway, I figured I'd say hi and how you doing and what's happening and so on but then I guess the heat got to me 'cause all I could think of to say was hot one, you know, like maybe I was Leonard Medicus, that weatherman on Channel Three with all the radar and stuff. I noticed the FOR SALE sign and I said to myself, you know, I'll bet they just got tired of being here and having to lock everything up and being afraid to walk outside at night. I'll bet your wife is happy, you know, leaving and all that, and going somewhere safe, you know just about everyone that used to live here is gone now. My Tom and I talked about it lots of times but then he took sick and died, you know" She sighed lugubriously.

He knew not and Walker sat with coffee listening to the sound from beside him as one might listen to a waterfall or Musak in an elevator or while waiting with a phone pressed against one ear to see if a live human being would eventually come on a line that was computer controlled, witless, arrogant and unafraid of human needs and frustrations. Suddenly the noise beside him changed, deepened, no longer laughter. He came out of his stupor and looked at Celia who had bent forward onto her knees and, with her face buried in her hands, had begun weeping. What the hell? Walker was thrown for a loss. "Celia. What's the matter?"

"Ahhmm . . . sssorry . . . so sos so" Her shoulders heaved and she went silent. Deep breath in, and then another. "So sorry. Thought I had everything under control. No problem. Walk and talk. All of a sudden . . ." She stopped her head shaking slightly back and forth still buried in her hands and then looked up through reddened eyes. "I'll be on my way. Sorry to trouble you," she told Walker and started to get up.

"Sit down," he told her not certain why he'd said it but dimly aware of a need, a reason to believe that his part of the intricate, human dance involved this woman so obviously needing someone, even a stranger, with whom to share some part of herself if only for a moment before retreating into her time and place and separating her orbit from his. He got up and pushed her gently back into her chair where she seemed to shrink into a small, wrinkled ball covered with thin fabric. Walker could see the outline of her bra through her blouse and was immediately irritated for doing so. He sat back down. "Sometimes, we all need someone to talk to." He felt slightly absurd saying that, as if being trite was somehow obscene.

"I don't know where we went wrong," Celia said almost to herself. "We taught Jason all the rights and wrongs that I suppose everyone tries to teach. Be honest. Don't lie. Don't steal. Don't cheat. Be a good boy. Help your father. Help your mother. Do your homework. Do you want to grow up stupid? Don't do that. You will grow up with your eyes crossed. Wash out the tub after your bath. What a disaster area. Pick up your room." She gestured helplessly. "He showed up a couple of days ago and introduced his boyfriend, or significant other I guess you call him these days." Celia stopped, bitter, betrayed by morality and her sex, alone on a blasted plain with dusty tornadoes spinning across her mind, robbed of grandchildren, the propagation of the line negated, the intimate craving of male and female somehow short-circuited.

What to say in the face of such desolation? Walker remembered years before, still in childhood, still in school.

When he stood outside Mr. Hillerman's door and hoped that he had picked a moment when no one else was around to see him. Looking to his left he saw that 'Dodger' Parker's door was open and his room was empty. Johnny could look straight through the room through its door out past the Senior porch to the quad and beyond that the Fairfield Prep's field house and football field. Good. Dodger was always teasing him about his friendship with Hillerman, calling Johnny an ass-kissing teacher's pet. Well Dodger was off somewhere making someone else miserable.

"Come in, Johnny. Come in." The door swung open and Mr. Hillerman stood there in a white, crew sweater and chinos looking very preppy and scrubbed with his sparse, blonde hair combed back and his large blue eyes set back behind a mass of wrinkled flesh. He was a skinny man who always seemed to be in danger of falling on his face. His face was weathered, deeply lined, comfortable, and friendly, a gentle old dog who wagged his tail and whom everyone loved on sight. At least Johnny had. Mr. Hillerman was his English teacher as well as his dorm master and Johnny had immediately recognized a fellow book enthusiast. When describing a part of a particular book, a speech he had to have made hundreds of times before to mostly deaf young ears before Johnny heard it, Mr. Hillerman's eyes lit up; his whole body seemed to come alive, legs moving and little pot belly shaking. With him as a guide, Johnny walked the back roads of rural Mississippi, watched the people of Dublin come alive, saw the carnival come to town, and as men prepared to fight the Japanese and then marched off to do so. Always just across the line from the world of his imagination, Johnny jousted and toasted, made flip remarks and subtle comebacks, imagined the shadowed figures in darkened bedroom though that was somewhat distorted by total lack of experience. Nevertheless, he read Lady Chatterley's Lover under the covers by flashlight and got a huge boner.

"Thanks, Mr. Hillerman." Johnny entered a short hallway almost totally taken up by a large desk strewn with papers and flanked on either side by dark green filing cabinets. Immediately to his right a doorway led into a galley kitchen, and just beyond the desk, another doorway into a small living room. Straight ahead was yet a third door that Johnny supposed led to Mr. Hillerman's bedroom. He followed Mr. Hillerman past the desk wondering whether his latest paper might be one of those on top of it. He tried to sneak a look but did not see it.

The room reminded Johnny of his own bedroom at home. Bookshelves full to overflowing lined the far outside wall that faced the quad. On the opposite and interior wall was an old couch. Opposite it and set out in front of the bookshelves slightly was an even older but comfortable looking easy chair of some indeterminate gray fabric. To the left of the couch was a small fireplace in which a cheerful little fire was blazing.

"I found the book I was telling you about," Mr. HIllerman said and handed Johnny a thin paperback.

"Thanks, Mr. Hillerman." Johnny stretched out on the floor in front of the fire and opened to the first page of James Jones' The Pistol and was soon lost in the plot and the characters. He heard Mr. Hillerman moving around behind him but paid no attention. The toilet flushed and then Mr. Hillerman was lying on the floor beside him. Putting down the book, he turned to his right and found himself staring into the face of his friend just inches away.

"You know, Johnny, there are only two things that mean anything to me," the teacher began, "literature and you."

Johnny felt Mr. Hillerman's hand on his back softly moving up and down, almost stroking and, abruptly, Johnny instinctively knew that this was not just a friendly pat on the back, that it was a prelude to something else. He felt a moment of panic and his body went rigid as Mr. Hillerman continued to stroke. What to do? Something hard pressed against his leg. Johnny felt a hot flush rise on his face and then his body went cold and goose bumps broke out on his arms. Taboo, he thought. Yes, that kind and what to remember adults saying about it man love deep in the shadows dark figures doing bad things and fingers wagging no no you cannot must not will not do that you will grow up bad oh God now what but no answer came but he said he cared most and cannot even finish that thought because then I could not have to admit and how can I avoid him he is right.

The phone on the desk in the hallway rang, rang again. "Oh damnation," muttered Mr. Hillerman and rose to answer it.

While Johnny lay on the floor, his body like a steel rod, shocked, instincts battling without form or thought, will paralyzed, Oh God I must get out of here now move, move.

"Yes damn it. What is it?" Hillerman's voice came from the hallway.

Now up and Johnny rose forgetting The Pistol seeking only escape out "Gotta go now, Mr. Hillerman." Flung over his shoulder as he stepped past his teacher and through the apartment door into the safety of the common hallway oh thank you, thank you and he ran down to the end of the hallway and left into his room and throwing himself onto his bed, a boy thrown into the middle of a four-way intersection with no lights and no signs. The chubby little boy lay there trying to figure it all out while hitting his pillow with his fists.

"I wouldn't be too hard on yourself," Walker told Celia, the memory of that day so long ago still in his mind. "Sometimes it just happens. Nobody's fault really. Just life."

Celia nodded without speaking. They sat in silence for a moment. "You ever have to go through that with your child?" she asked. "What would your wife say?"

"My wife died."

"I'm so sorry. Guess you've got enough troubles without hearing mine." She snuffled and took a sip from her cup. "When I was young, there was nothing like this, at least where I grew up."

Walker nodded. "Hard to know what to do, sometimes," he agreed. He looked down into his coffee and saw death and sorrow and felt angry that he should feel so just when he thought he'd put it behind him. He tried remembering something pleasant of value. He had gone back to his friend, later, or course, but he had gone back and shared books and talk of books and those who wrote them and Hillerman's bed. Walker still had a vivid memory or lying beside Mr. Hillerman and holding his cock and suddenly Hillerman had stiffened and groaned and something had come out of the tip and run down over Walker's hand. Walker had thought he had caused damage but Mr. Hillerman had reassured him. 'It's okay, Johnny. Don't worry. Everything is fine. Just fine.' And they had laid like that, body to body as the yellowed light of an aging day had filled the room with a light so soft it could have held a feather forever aloft. Well, Celia still had her son, gay or not, and he still had Jennifer. Always something to be thankful for even though Jen thinks I live under a rock and that she alone has the key to understanding and spiritual enlightenment.

"I'll be on my way," Celia said and rose to her feet. "Thanks for the coffee and listening to me. Helps to have someone around to do that sometimes." She walked down the steps towards the sidewalk as a beat up old Volkswagon rattled up the street from the direction of Farmington Avenue. Its shocks were obviously gone as was the exhaust system and it trailed a cloud of burnt oil behind it.

Walker saw the car and sighed. It could only be Jennifer. For a moment he thought about going down the street with Celia but dismissed the thought as it was born. He would have to deal with this sometime, and he supposed that now was as good a time as any.

"Morning Dad." She called from inside the car.

"Jen."

"Howsit hanging."

"Sunday morning hanging low."

"Cool." The car died with a sigh of relief and the creaking of hot metal. Jennifer walked up the steps and plopped herself in the chair recently vacated by Celia. "Hot today. Got any beer back there?"

"Nope."

"So what's happening with the house."

"I sold it."

"What?" Jennifer sat straight in the chair and stared at her father. "When did this happen? How come you didn't tell me."

"Couple of weeks ago. I close the end of next month."

"What did it sell for?" Jen's eyes sparkled, avarice showing in every line of her face.

"It doesn't matter," Walker told her curtly. The money is mostly already spent to pay bills."

"But there'll be some left, right?"

"Not much." Walker walked back inside and sank into his easy chair in the living room. "What is it that you want, Jen?"

His daughter strolled into the doorway and stood there staring down at him while leaning against the door frame.

"So where you gonna live?"

"I'm looking for a reasonably priced apartment."

"There's lots of those in our area."

"I mean an apartment with functioning heat and utilities. Not an abandoned building.

"We don't live in a derelict."

"Next thing to it. I drove past your building a while back. Not for me, thank you."

"You don't like me, do you and you don't like my friends either especially Moses."

"Sometimes, I don't like you just like there are times when you don't like me. That's okay. We're both adults and can handle that, but I love you and do not like seeing you pissing your life away. I have seen lots of people like Moses and they are only out for themselves. She will get rid of you in a second if it suits her to do so." Walker sighed, got out of his chair and walked into the kitchen in search of ice cubes and a little Jack. He hated these conversations because they always ended with Jennifer stalking off and then continuing the status quo that had been the core of the argument in the first place. He wondered for perhaps the millionth time if there was something different he could say or do that would change the situation, but short of disowning her and therefore making it all that much worse, he could not think of anything. Walker came back into the living room with his glass.

Jennifer had not moved so much as a muscle as far as he could tell. "You don't like Moses because she's gay."

Ah the trump card, he thought. Mr. Hillerman floated across his mind. "That's just bullshit. I don't care who she sleeps with. Well, of course, I do for I wish it weren't you, but I have no objection to lesbianism, just to Moses and people like her. I do care that you seem unable to see that the course you've chosen can only lead to disaster. And I care that you are her partner and say that you love her but you refuse to see how little respect she has for you other than your ability to come here and bum money off of me." Maybe he should get Moses to meet Celia's son. That would be interesting. Maybe they could all sit around in a circle and make faces at each other. Maybe they could all get naked. Hello. The circus is in town. He took a long pull of his drink and looked at his daughter. There was so much of her mother in her, all that stubbornness, almost willfulness, paired with a temper that did not take much to set off.

"Yeah, right. You're just pissed that I'm living a cleaner more honest life than you ever did. Even when I was growing up it was always rules this and regulations that. It was like growing up in a fucking barracks with a sergeant on my ass constantly. You could spare the money. You're just too dammed cheap."

Good God in heaven, he thought. Here we go again. He had never been as Jen was, had never flown at his parents in such a way, but he had felt the same feelings. Perhaps she had inherited them from his mother, okay so the hippie didn't resemble the icy autocrat but underneath maybe the fire burned with the same degree of heat. Must be why they got along and grandma paid. The thought angered him, exposing what he considered a weakness. Beth had not felt that way and had won in the end. She had always won. Walker admitted to himself and took another sip from his drink. She had won because he was weak and hated to fight about anything and had put up only the barest beginnings of arguments. Jennifer turned to leave and Walker realized that he had once again lost this argument. "Jennifer." He called.

She turned.

Walker gave her the money in his wallet.

She took the money and turning left without a word

Walker felt the air of her passing as if someone had blown softly on his cheek. She would get over it, he was sure and a tiny voice in the back of his mind said that yeah maybe she was pissed but should disaster strike she would be there.

Fall-backs are good, he decided, as he picked The Hartford Courant off the small, somewhat fragile looking cherry side table by the cream-colored couch and walked back out on the porch holding his drink in his right hand and the paper in his left, very appropriate for the Courant, he smiled, settling into the chair again. Ahhh. Good chair always has been. Let's see. The mayor accused of using contractors' services free of charge. Hartford fails Department of Education audit. No surprise there. City's governed by a bunch of people with no fucking clue. You'd think the politicos would hire good professionals and then raise the money they need to do the job. City is too small that's the problem. Not enough people and business to pay the tab. Between a rock and a hard place, that's Hartford.

Walker eased back, tipping the chair against the wall of the house, paper spread onto his knees and the Jack in his hand. Too much for a Sunday. Try to relax and everyone beats a path to your door. Won't be my door much longer, though. Must find a place soon. Flip through the paper. Car ads, lingerie, home improvement, local news, sports, real estate, classifieds yes take a sip and work your way down the listings. Ah, there's the one I saw two nights ago. What a shit pit. And that one's still on the market. Overpriced or at least I thought so. Nice space though. Pay for location he supposed. View of skyline between buildings across the street. Orange sky with the buildings like burnt fingers sticking up from the hand of the earth.

Stop dreaming, you clown. Focus on putting a roof over your head. Would be nice to have one, nicetohavenice, useful, don't you think? Bigger than a breadbox. Let's see. Mmmmm. Large bedroom, kitchen privileges, parking. Might do the trick. Not an apartment, though. No privacy. Still, it might do. Probably an older home. A big room would do, especially if there was a place for storage like an attic or cellar or something. Depends on the landlord though; always does. Make or break a situation like that.

Walker sucked on his glass, passed his lips across the amber orange surface below the crystalline method of his consciousness. Drink think drink think, no think. All get it on now, get on down, man, I say get on down. Call the number. This had to work out. He was so tired of the whole effort. Finding shelter shouldn't be that hard on body and soul and wallet. Okay. Settled. He would call about the room. It would just be temporary, after all. Just until he found a place he could call home. Walker put his glass down on the table. He would call. Yes. Maybe. Definitely.

Out Of Service

The old man sat and waited although he had no name for this activity. He simply was. Daylight poured like champagne through the flute of the window spilling across the floor and the walls on either side. He watched the window. The glass was dirty and there was a fly on one pane by the ancient lock. He saw but did not know. Black fly on gray glass crawling and then gone away. He watched the glass. It seemed to wave at him. It wore a yellow dress and smiled light at him, holding him in its arms.

"Oh, Dad. You're all wet again."

Face.

Lots of lines. Brown eyes blocking light. Shadow face white like cheese curd whose face he should know. It says dad so must be someone who. Blue panes of glass full of sky. Someone pulling at my face and pushing on my back and I am up on feet whoops little weak but up then bathroom slippers flip flop flipflopflipflop and suddenly my plastic pants drop onto the floor and then I am looking at my penis, bent left.

"Hold still, now, and I'll get you fixed right up."

And standing I am a beam of light but why am I naked down below. Hands are on me. A rag slides between my legs like a warm snake. It cuddles my dick, slithering up and around, pushing it to one side and then the other. Tick tock, like a clock, flip flop, feels so good so don't stop. "Okay," I say into the lady in the light with the touch so soft and the smile of clouds.

"Okay, Dad. You're good to go. Sit back down."

Arms come and then go away and I walk a little and then feel the familiar grip of my chair. The woman walks in front of me holding a cup of something in her right hand. She stands in the window, half in shadow, half shot by the beams looking out at the light full of blue speckled in it like a fawn. "I don't know what to do, Dad. I know you can't understand me but I need to talk with someone or I think I'll have a breakdown of some sort." Her voice cracks like dead branches underfoot. Then I know. Zinny, yes, my daughter, and in trouble. I need to talk to her, and understand the problem. I can help her. She rides the wind of her thoughts down through the window to the light beyond. She is pale, the color of cream, still and thoughtful.

"Zinny," I say and somehow know that it is right, that I am right and she is right.

She whirls around to face me, her eyes widening. "Dad, you know me." Her mouth trembles and she seems about to burst into tears.

"What is wrong?" I say. "You have problems. I heard what you said. What is the problem?" I push at my chair in an effort to stand with her but my strength is gone and I sink back into its cushions.

"He is back," she tells me through slitted lips, fleshless, almost nonexistent. "Mark is back. Do you understand?"

Mark is back. The memory of a man with bad eyes comes and I feel that he is somehow bad, somehow part of the problem, part of what has crumpled Zinny's face like tissue paper. "Mark." I say and then the memory is gone. The woman stands there looking at me. "Okay," I say wanting to say much more but cannot remember what she said. She seems familiar and I feel I should know her but don't.

"He wants money. He wants the house. He . . ." she stops and flops her hands up and down in frustration turning back towards the window. "Never mind, Dad," she says. "Just never mind." Her voice is soft and purple with despair, overtones of anger, sewage dumped in a once clear mountain pool. Admission of waste and destruction.

"Okay." Light is back now. The whole window laughs gaily and lifts her skirt for me ahh if only I was younger but the light is there and carries me off into the blue coffee mug, bacon frying, a whole room with white cabinets and lines of black faces, a child singing somewhere outside the window ring around the rosy, ring around ring around, dim hallway and a large brown face full of fear eyeballsrolling lawd lawd sunlight through a tree hot water and bandages for a deep wound, that door banging shut, half a smile, breast in the moonlight softly shifting, soft boiled eggs, scary masks and candy bags for UNICEF, Mommy and Daddy said I could no, no not yet please, snow on the drive and bright balls sparkling in the light, the old black bag with little pockets of hope, pink pills, alcohol, can I Daddy? Hills of bills, bitter lips like acid spitting words at me, Korean hills bare and frozen Chosin, people in need, her eyes bitter, we need, lines of people, silent, patient everlasting amen, that little yellow dress so cute when she would come down the stairs and then kneeling in the pew, head bowed, face hidden by her curls. Now I lay me down, so sure that she could talk to Him, clear in her innocence. Read her a story sitting on the side of the bed almost falling off, loved Mickey Mouse Club. Nice when the human dilemma can be reduced to a catchy phrase, good for kids, nothing serious, red wine on Saturday nights and afterwards making love with the moon coming through the window. She had a great bush. Knew how to use her hands too. Sunset fingers lightly stroking while another probing down below.

F1

Zinny came out of the room propelled by a sigh and started down the stairs to the ground floor. The wooden steps were scratched and worn and creaked on risers in a similar condition. It's amazing I don't creak like that as well, she thought. Can't afford to fix them, though, more's the pity.

She paused halfway down the stairs and then turned and stared back up at her father's room. He had come back for a minute. He had asked about the problem. Such times were becoming increasingly rare but he had actually seemed to understand her. She habitually talked at him, sometimes for hours knowing that she would get no response but this was one time she hoped he came back far enough to realize the trouble they were in and he had looked alert and focused and then just as suddenly he was gone, wrapped in a mass of twisted, useless neurons, just totally off somewhere that no one could reach him. Wherever he was, Zinny thought, it could not be a very bad place for he was sitting up there with a little smile on his face as if he had just pulled off a nifty practical joke and was waiting for her to discover it and scream.

"Good morning, Zinny."

Zinny turned back and there was Viola Thompson looking up the stairs at her. Viola with her huge, moon face and bulging brown eyes and seemingly unlimited supplies of laughter, a woman who put in sixty hour weeks at Beldens Laundry and still came over on the weekends to lend a hand cleaning and taking care of the old doc. "Hey, there, Viola. How's it going?" Zinny smiled and finished descending the stairs.

"Can't complain. Don't do no good anyhow." Viola chuckled and Zinny could have sworn the entire house vibrated. Viola beamed at her with a gold-toothed three hundred degree smile. Her massive body rocked gently. "Ah tol Ozzie he better behave himself and pick up dat place cause I'd be here." She nodded. "Ah think ah put the fear in him, yesm, so I did".

Viola's husband, Ozzie, could not have weighed more than one hundred pounds dripping wet. Zinny could not imagine him doing anything that would upset her. The picture in her mind that such a conflict presented was so ludicrous that Zinny could not help smiling in spite of the problem she was facing. "If I were Ozzie, Vi, I think I would have stood at attention a long time ago."

Viola laughed a laugh great and booming and surely of Grand Canyon quality. "That man doesn't fear anyone except maybe the good Lord himself and then only on Sundays when the Reverend gets worked up and the girls is singing and screaming. Then he comes home full of the spirit and wants to start another baby." Viola waved her hands in front of her face as if to cool it down and raised her eyes and stared at the ceiling. "He's just a devil man, that's what he is," she finished fondly.

"He must have deviled you a lot. How many kids do you have now? Ten?"

"Yes and they all got a bit of their father in them. Gotta slap 'em upside der heads sometimes to keep 'em in line, you know what I mean?" Viola slapped at the air with one meaty hand and grinned. Then her face clouded over as another thought took over. "Hey Zinny. When I was walking down here I saw a white dude standing across the street looking at this house like he want to set it on fire. He looked plain mean, you know, and I said to myself oh Viola, girl, that honky means no good to no one. I looked at him and he looked at me and then turned like he didn't want me to see his face, you know, but I seen it anyways and it was mean looking, you know, jes mean." Viola shook her head, her expression grave, and then headed down the hall past the old dispensary to the kitchen.

Zinny felt as if she had not slept in days and suddenly been asked to climb a cliff. Damn him, damn him to hell, the psychotic bastard. Did he think she could just snap her fingers and produce a suitcase full of cash for him? Gritting her teeth, she strode across the little entry hall and peered out one of the two, tiny windows on either side of the door. The sidewalk across from the house was deserted, but he would be back, she knew, again and again and again.

"Is this man causing you trouble?" Zinny whirled around and found Viola standing there with the vacuum cleaner in one hand. "Because I can make him go away. All the help you and your dad give to folks 'round here, I can make him go away real quick. My eldest is no dammed good for much. He's a gangbanger, you know, but he be good for this." Viola nodded in emphasis.

Zinny could not deny that she was tempted. Snap her fingers and make it all go away. There were several gangs in the projects and some very nasty people who she had no doubt would be able to handle Mark and a hundred more like him but that was not something Zinny wanted on her conscience. She wanted to be able to sleep at night and consigning her ex to possible death would do nothing to aid that desire. Anyway, if they just roughed him up, he'd show up at the library and there would be hell to pay. If she could just come up with some money, someway, somehow. If someone rented the room, maybe she could give Mark the rent money and he would be satisfied at least for a while. She wondered how badly he needed it and when. She could use all the leverage she could get. "It's all right, Vi. Don't fret on it. I'll take care of it."

"Well if you change your mind, you just let me know." Viola strode into the living room holding her head and the vacuum cleaner high.

Zinny closed the door and slumped against the dark, polished brown wood. What a waste, she thought, and what a mess. She left the door and walked slowly down the hallway to the kitchen. Just that morning she had been full of hope and confidence, certain that things were finally going her way. She had placed an ad in the Courant "Room for rent . . . Kitchen privileges . . . parking." She had studied the money asked for similar lodging and priced hers a little lower. She and Viola had scoured the room, washed the windows, put fresh paint where it was needed and a new shine on the old wooden floor. It had really looked good, she thought. Fresh and clean and ready for a renter to fall in love with. She had even walked her father into it in the hope that the sight would bring him back a little. He had looked around blankly and spoken his benediction. "Okay," he told her.

The day she put the ad in the paper she had found in the closet an old baseball, yellowed by age and Vaseline, the threads worn with use. She had stood there with the ball in her hand, her mind a thousand miles away on that distant planet we know as childhood. She had been such a tomboy, so eager to play baseball. She had begged and, for her tenth birthday, had received a brand new outfielder's mitt and baseball. How she had loved that mitt, smearing it with Vaseline and putting it under her mattress at night with the ball wrapped inside to form a pocket. She practiced at first with her father and then with Ozzie Thompson whose mother suffered chronic pain and was a frequent patient at their house.

"Everyone knows girls can't play ball."

"I can too."

"No you can't. HEY, that hurt. How come you hit me with the ball?"

"How come you didn't catch it?"

"No fair, Zinny."

"Was too."

"Okay, smartass. Try and catch this."

"Hey, why'd you throw the ball into the street?"

"You're supposed to catch it."

"No fair."

"Na na na nanananana." Bronx cheer.

"Ozzie Thompson, you play nice with Zinny or I'll whip your butt, hear me?"

"Yes, ma'am, but she . . .".

"OZZIE!"

"Yes, ma'am."

And so it began and she found that she really could play ball. She was all legs and arms, pole thin and full of energy. She found that she had a knack for arriving at the exact spot she had to be in order to catch the ball and she had the speed to do so. Zinny loved the feeling of the ball smacking into her glove's webbing and the exhilaration she felt after making a flying catch that Ozzie did not think she had a chance in hell of running down. She could hit as well. Though she would never be a slugger, she found out how to hit the ball to whatever spot she chose. Ozzie would pitch and Zinny would aim for the orange crate that was second base or the old tire that was third. She still felt a flush of pride remembering when Ozzie suggested that they walk down the street to the vacant lot next to Albertson's grocery store where there were always kids looking for a pickup game.

Tony "Bigface" Scrutchens was there and another kid they called Webs and they were picking teams with a great deal of yelling and gesticulating.

"Yo, Oz, man. C'mon. You be with me," Webs called, picking Ozzie as soon as he spotted him coming down the street. Zinny followed Ozzie in the direction of Webs. "Hey you, girl. Get outta here now. This ain't no game for girls, hear?" Webs frowned at her, his thin face scrunching up until he looked as if he suffered from constipation. He stood there, hands on his hips, capo di tutti capi.

"It's okay, Zinny. You can join Tony. He's short one."

"No I ain't." Bigface looked around and spotted a younger kid standing on the edge of the lot. "Hey you," he shouted. "Come over here."

"Hey Tony," Ozzie yelled. "That sucker ain't even got a glove. How he gonna play? Take Zinny here. She good man. I wish Webs could choose her."

"Shiiit. He don't want her either. She just a girl."

"Don't matter," Ozzie replied, stubborn now that his ability to judge players had been called into question, but looking at Zinny anxiously as if she might suddenly say something and start a riot.

Zinny remembered the empty, desolate, blasted feeling in her gut as she had stared at the groups of boys standing there in the empty space with its surface of hard packed dirt and patches of dry sickly grasses littered with papers, bottles, tin cans and cardboard. Their expressions had ranged from hostile to amused to curious to simply blank stares as only children can accomplish. "My ball is practically new," she'd said tossing her birthday gift into the air and catching it without even looking at it.

"Don't matter. Go on. Get outta here."

She'd walked back to her house alone. Now, standing by the front door she felt just the same as she had decades before. She didn't even want to think of the number.

Even so, she wished she was once again ten years old with all the huge problems that ten-year-olds face. At least they didn't have to talk with prospective renters. What a horror this day had been.

First through the door was Mr. High-And-Mighty, tall and broad, black as night, wearing wraparound shades and a suit that must have cost a grand. He drove up in a white Mercedes that sat gleaming by the curb, almost blinding Zinny with the reflections off the chrome. Well at least he can afford the rent, she thought as she opened the door to let him in. Behind him, another black man got out of the driver's side of the car and stood there looking around impassively while working a cigarette out of its pack.

"I called about a room." He told her in a bass voice that sounded as if it had started in the pit of his stomach.

"Yes. Mr. Smith?"

"Yes."

"Come in." Zinny stepped back and Smith pushed into the hallway, almost filling up the small space. He looked around and sniffed. "So this is it?"

Zinny tried on a smile. C'mon, girl, she thought. You need this. You need this so just smile and smile even if the situation already seemed to be heading south. "Yes. This is it. Your room would be at the top of the stairs on the right. If you'll follow me, I'll show it to you."

"I need privacy. Does it have its own entrance?"

"Just the back door in the kitchen."

Smith sniffed again but made no move towards the stairs. Zinny suddenly saw herself sharing the house with this man. The thought did little to reassure her. He could obviously afford whatever he wanted so why look at renting a room? "Maybe you should consider an apartment," she suggested.

"Don't need no advice from you," Smith growled. He turned and marched back out the door leaving Zinny standing on the stairs staring at his departing back and breathing a sigh of relief. Probably wanted someplace cheap to stash a mistress. Whatever's fair. Someone will like it. Bound to. No problem. No problem at all. Didn't like him anyway. Nothing but trouble.

But next came the nickel-and-dimer, a tiny, birdlike, elderly, white woman who marched up the street from the bus stop and presented herself at the door by leaning on the door bell as if her life depended on it. "I'm Mary Dickens. I called about the room," she announced in strident tones when Zinny opened the door. She glared at Zinny as if Zinny had denied the accuracy of her statement.

"Yes indeed." Big smile. Hundred watt. Today is the first day. She's just scared. Strange house. Black neighborhood. Can't really blame her. Probably the only white face on the bus and at her age. Paranoia strikes deep. Make her feel at home. Should do the trick. "How nice to see you, Mrs. Dickens. Do come in."

"It's Miss." Dickens walked into the hallway with energy that belied her age. "Where's the room?"

"Right this way." Okay. Be rude you old biddy. Take the room and I won't care whether you're Miss or Mrs.

Dickens stared around the room as a drill sergeant might regard a new batch of recruits at Fort Dix. "Needs painting," she grumped and turned to look at the four newly washed walls, "and the floor needs to be refinished."

"They aren't that bad. I washed the walls and the floor. You can repaint the walls if you wish." She'll probably paint them black, Zinny thought viciously and then regretted it. Stop being so gloomy.

"Then I'm taking it out of the rent and I will not pay asking price with the floors in their present condition. Look at these windows." She marched across the room and pointed at the offending woodwork. "There must be thirty coats of paint on them. They will need to be redone. I'm sure they let in a terrible draft." She turned and stared at Zinny. "What about kitchen privileges? I don't need them so that should lower the rent. No private bath either. Where is it, by the way?"

Zinny wanted to slap her. She bore down, however, and, leaving the room, pointed to her left a few feet down the hall to where the bathroom, door open, was plainly in view. She assumed that Dickens made it to the house alive only by not talking with anyone. "I'll deduct the cost of the paint, but that's the best I can do." She told Dickens.

"Well, if you ask me, you're asking way too much for this dump, but okay, let's go look at the kitchen. If it's like this room, I'll need to call the Board of Health."

Yeah, well good luck to you with that. What a dippy bitch this woman is. I don't want her in my house now even if she produces a giant wad of twenty dollar bills. Zinny walked ahead down the stairs and into the kitchen, a large, old kitchen but clean. She stood to one side as Dickens walked in behind her and looked around at the knotty pine cabinets and Formica-covered table in the center of the room. Next to the door on the opposite wall was a strip of pine with pegs for hanging coats. Zinny stared at it, trying not to look at Dickens, and remembered all the times she'd sat underneath those same pegs trying to get her rubber snow boots on and struggling with all the buckles and fasteners. They never gave up easily.

"Well, at least the fridge is modern."

Hard to believe that she isn't complaining about something. Anything. She probably wakes up in the morning complaining about the fact that she woke up. Good, sweet Christ. This woman could turn sugar into salt. Maybe I should report her to Dominos. A sweet cheat. Zinny had to smile at that thought and suddenly felt almost light-headed and free. "Yes. Even the stove works plus we offer hot and cold running water and a thingy in the bathroom that you can sit on. We weren't certain that we wanted to get rid of the outhouse but, after trying out the new technology, we're glad we did." Another hundred watt smile.

"Well, you don't have to be sarcastic. I just try to point out a few things that are obviously in need of work and you start sassing me. I think it's terrible that the younger generation has no manners. It's a sure sign of lack of parental control. You should be ashamed of yourself." Dickens turned and strode down the hallway to the front door. "Good day," she called without turning around and slammed the door on the way out.

After that, two other prospective renters had come and gone with no result. Zinny's nerves were frayed and her temper short. There was nothing left of all the hope with which she had started the day. God, she could use a drink, maybe two, she thought. *Wonder if there's any of the wine left. Probably turned to vinegar by now. Dad used to like Jim Beam. Kept a bottle in the sideboard. Mom disapproved but she didn't remember them ever fighting about it. He would swish the cubes around with his finger, wink at me and then suck on his finger. I always winked back and smiled. Our not-so-secret secret sign. Is there still a bottle there? Don't remember. Been so long. Don't know if I could handle whiskey, now. Like sex. Been gone so long I wouldn't know it anymore. Funny how we don't even think about something for a long time and all of a sudden it pops into our head as if we had been thinking about it all along. Well, bourbon and sex are two things I don't need.* A picture of Mark walking towards her in the bedroom flashed through her mind. Zinny scowled, determined to think of something else other than impending disaster. She pushed herself from the door and walked slowly back towards the kitchen and the tea kettle. A quiet cup and then up to check on Dad.

BRRRRPP

Zinny was so startled that she almost dropped her teacup and sloshed some of it onto the table in front of her. Now what? Friends and neighbors would use the back door. No more appointments that she knew of anyway. She went back down the hallway and looked through the security eye on the door.

Pink, fleshy face obviously just shaven for there was red streaks along the sides and chin, pug nose and glasses in front of deep-set blue eyes or rather eye that was looking back at her. It was a familiar eye, somehow. No threat, she felt and yes friendly as a face she might think of before she went to sleep after a day of good fortune and accomplishments. Stepping back, Zinny pulled the door open. "Yes?"

Well, hello, Zinny. Remember me?"

"Good God." Her hand flew instinctively to her mouth. "It's Agile. What are you doing here?"

"I came to see about a room to let. I called the number in the paper and left a message a little while ago but I guess you haven't checked your machine recently." Walker smiled at her. "I miss a lot of messages like that myself."

"I'm so sorry. Please forgive my manners, or rather lack of them. Do come in." A true one-hundred watter. Suddenly the whole day seemed better.

Walker came through the door and turned to look into the living room on his left and the dining room to his right. "Nice house," he told her. "Feels lived in and friendly and soft around the edges." He beamed at her. "Small world, isn't it?"

"Indeed it is. How are you?" Zinny suddenly remembered the purpose of his visit. "Oh Lord. I hope everything is okay. I mean here you are looking for a room so where were you living before?' She thrashed her hands in front of her. "Forget I said that. None of my business really."

Walker laughed. "Don't worry. I've sold my house and couldn't find an apartment that I liked so I thought well maybe, since I'm on my own again for the first time in many years, I decided that I would look for something small and simple until I get settled somewhere else. Less upkeep and bother."

"Yes. I remember you telling me about your wife. So sorry." And Zinny genuinely felt a sense of sorrow all the way through and through for though she had never known Walker's wife she was beginning to know Walker and she was beginning to realize that some deep instinctive part of her was also part of him. She had seen the pain in those eyes buried behind their discolored fleshy blankets, and had felt a sense of loss as well. Suddenly, she felt an anxiety attack coming on. Would Agile like the room? She wondered whether the people who had been through it today had tracked dirt on the floor or left marks on the walls or wainscoting. Had she cleaned the bathroom? She couldn't remember. Oh God. The toilet. Had she run the brush with that blue stuff around the inside? Maybe not. What would he say about that? What would he think of her? Won't show it to him, she decided. Unless he wants to see it, of course. Jesus, my hair's a wreck. Maybe I should run up quick and run a brush around it but I can't just leave him standing here in the hall. He looks so alone, somehow, as if he'd come from a world where there was no one but himself, like he was walking along a road and came around a bend and there was nothing there and so he turned back towards where he'd come from and there was nothing there either and so he just had to keep walking trying to be brave and figure everything out and so came to a door, my door. "Would you like to see the room?" she asked, pushing her fears down, determined to give him her best.

"Oh, sure," Walker replied casually, as if he had almost forgotten what he had come for.

"Watch out. The carpet is a little loose." Zinny pointed down to a where a corner of the carpet on the hall floor had flipped over on itself. *Maybe, he's already decided against it,* she fretted as she turned towards the stairs. *Couldn't blame him. I must be an ugly sight. Thank God Viola was here this morning and cleaned up a bit. Place looks neat anyway.* "Right this way." *I can hear him coming behind me. Solid. Measured. Comfortable tread. Wonder how he looks naked? Is he circumcised? Probably. All the fashion now, I think but you never know. He's older like me and things were different back then. Thank God he can't read my thoughts. Walk right out and call the police. I like men with just a little body hair. Mark was a bear and just as vicious.* "It's not huge but it's clean," she said opening the bedroom door and gesturing Walker in ahead of her. *Oh hell, he's not even walking in, just looking in at it as if he was viewing a python at the zoo.* "You can fix it up however you like it."

"How much."

Zinny swallowed hard and somehow found her voice. "Six hundred a month, but that includes all utilities, a shared kitchen and parking." She plunged ahead. "Also, if you like sitting outside on nice days the backyard and terrace are right there. There are plastic chairs and a little table. I sit out there a lot." She shut her mouth, suddenly aware that she was beginning to babble. *Well, yes, I used to sit out there a lot when Dad was still mobile and sentient. Now I worry about what he's doing. Has he wet himself or worse? Is he sitting in his chair or has something disturbed him? Sometimes when the phone rings he tries to get up and answer, a Pavlovian response, and ends up on the floor staring at the radiator and saying okay but it never responds and he doesn't care but just lies there saying okay until I show up and make everything okay. Oh God. Agile's not even looking at the room. He's looking at me and why is he doing that? Have I got dirt on my nose or something like that?* "Would you like to see the kitchen?" *Keep him away from the bathroom at all costs. Things are not looking good here.*

"Certainly."

He has a great smile. Spreads across his face like a sunrise on a Vermont postcard. She couldn't help but feel better just looking at something like that. Back down the upstairs and "Here it is. A little dated but everything works."

184

"Well that's the main thing when it comes to a kitchen," Walker told her pleasantly.

Zinny stood there and knew that she wanted Agile to take the room more than anything in the world since her father had sickened and declined and she had prayed nightly for some miracle to halt the progress of the disease. Just to have someone else in the house, and not just any someone. She suddenly understood that if she rented out the room, it would have to be to someone who would be able to handle occasional scenes with her father. Whoever rented the room would have to know about Dad, and here was Walker. Okay, they hadn't known each other very long but what she knew she liked. Thank God one of the others hadn't taken the room, but how would he react when she told him? Zinny wiped her face with her hands in a storm of anxiety.

"Are you okay?" concern tightened the skin around the corners of his eyes.

"Oh yes." She dropped her hands and looked across the space at him. Now that push came to shove, she felt almost calm. It would be or it would not. "There is one thing you must know."

"Don't steal the towels?" Walker suggested, a smile playing with the corners of his lips, concern still in his eyes, trying to lighten her mood.

Zinny smiled, one that disappeared quickly under the strain of her feelings. "No, No. Not that. It's my father, you see. He has Alzheimer's so you might hear strange noises from the room next to yours every so often. You might hear him saying "okay". Sometimes he gets a bit loud. I don't think he means to be. It's just the way it comes out. There's nothing wrong with his vocal chords." She trailed off. She knew she sounded anxious and probably looked anxious but she couldn't help it.

"Strange sounds, heh?"

"Yes." Zinny tried to tie her fingers together in a knot.

"Ummm. Well, let me think." Walker looked up at the ceiling as if for inspiration. "My wife made awful sounds when she was sick and dying and I probably don't sound too great when I've had too much to drink and am snoring like a bear, so I think if you can cope with the snoring, I can cope with your dad. Thanks for letting me know, though," he finished and grinned at Zinny.

Zinny felt her whole body go light with relief. Yes, there was a God. "You're welcome," she replied.

"Let me think on it over the weekend and I'll let you know on Monday or maybe call before then. Would that be okay?"

"Oh sure. No problem." She'd hold the room until hell froze over or Mark came at her if it came to that.

"I know you can't stop showing the room but I need to make sure of something first."

"Sure thing. Just let me know. I don't think the room will be rented this weekend, so don't worry about it."

"Great." He walked across the room to the kitchen door. "Can I get out this way?" he asked.

"Of course. I'll walk around to the front with you." What was that something he had to check on, she wondered, as they walked down the steps. Another room or apartment, probably. Damn. Zinny felt like grinding her teeth in frustration. Why couldn't he just say 'yes, I'll take it'? Maybe there was nothing he had to check on. Maybe he would walk away towards the bus stop and she would never see him again.

She watched Walker as he walked a pace or two in front of her down the driveway with her house on the right and Jason Horad's multi-family on the left. Agile walked without the fat man's waddle, putting his feet straight out in front of him and swinging his arms slightly. White hairs grew down his neck and disappeared into his shirt collar. Was he like a lot of balding men with nothing on top but a lot down below, she wondered. He turned to face her where the driveway shook hands with the sidewalk.

"Thanks for showing the room to me. I know you weren't expecting me." Sunlight reflected off the top of his head.

"You're more than welcome. Let me know as soon as you can. Would you like a cup of coffee or tea before leaving? My manners are so bad. I should have asked when we were in the house." Zinny felt as if she was gushing and stopped, feeling awkward and exposed as if someone had told her a dirty joke during church service.

"Rain check?" Walker asked.

"Oh sure."

"Thanks again. You really look good today." And then he was off and walking away down the street. Zinny stared after him. He thought she looked good. That thought kept bouncing around in her head. She lightly touched her hair where it curled around her ears and the hint of a smile softened her lips. He thought I looked good, she thought again. So he said, so said he and I the ugliest broad around look good oh yes he said and I could tell he was serious and not just joking around and trying to be nice and butter up the landlady. He wasn't making fun of old Zinny of the many angles and lifeless hair and ugly eyes but yes I am looking good and thank you, Agile, oh thank you for kind words. Please call back. Call back soon. Oh my God. Dad. Forgot all about him. Probably wet by now. All my fault.

Zinny turned, distracted, and hurried up the front porch steps and into the house and, a moment later, from inside came the faint "Okay."

E2 Caliban

It was a summer night in the New Hampshire woods. Although he could not see it, Walker knew there was a huge full moon above him because the fields around the house were easily visible as if lit up by floodlights. Fireflies hurtled up and down in an exhausting manner. Crickets made rude noises in the long grasses. Walker felt truly at peace with the world within and without so that his body was tall and lean, strong and ready. He stretched his arms above his head until his joints creaked and then turned back into the room clicked off the one small lamp near the door.

She lay on the bed with her back towards him covered only by a sheet, her shoulders just a pale sliver of flesh in the moonlight. Walker felt an almost immeasurable tenderness like a physical knot in his chest as he stood at the doorway of the bedroom watching the almost imperceptible rise and fall of her breathing. From down the hall, Jenny coughed and then was silent. All the years with all the tears and laughter enveloped him. Not much laughter lately, though. Beth had become self-absorbed, almost morose. Still, Walker felt the magic of her naked back puddled in shadow by the moonlight. He would go to her and they would be as one and become momentarily what they had been in the beginning.

He stepped softly across to the bed and put one hand on her shoulder. The jolly red giant between his legs was standing at attention ready and, God knows, more than willing. He ran his fingers along its length and felt a spasm of pleasure.

What turned to face him, though, turned his guts to jelly. It was a woman's face but contorted into a rictus of agony. Shriveled, skeletal arms reached out to him, clawing at his shoulders while eyes without a spark of humanity in them stared up at him. She thrust her face up at him, opening a mouth filled with rotting yellowed fangs. He could feel its rank breath born in the deepest swamps of human depravity. He smelled the fecal stink of the sewer, of rotting bodies left in the sun, of gangrenous wounds in some jungle swamp. Walker tried to turn the thing back over and away from him but it clung, dead yet still alive, it's jaws clicking open and closed like a rusting gate on crumbling hinges. "Darling," it crooned. "Darling, darling, darling." It puckered the withered flesh that had once been lips and thrust its face into his.

Walker did not know for how long he had been screaming but only that he woke up sitting in a wrecked bed amidst wet sheets screaming at the far wall of his now not familiar bedroom after a nightmare about his now no longer wife. Sweat poured from his face and for a moment longer he was seeing everything doubled. His arms were stretched out in front of him as if to ward off an attack. He did not know how long he had been holding them out like that but, ordinarily, he would not have had the muscle strength to do so for more than a few seconds. Somehow he knew that he had held his arms extended for a far longer period of time. He felt his heart racing in his chest as he sat in the bed panting.

As his breathing slowed and his nightmare faded, he slowly swung his legs over and sat on the edge of the bed. Jesus, when was this going to stop? Again this nightmare over and over just when thought it was gone for good it came back and tore him up again. What time is it? Christ. Still dark outside. Feel like someone took a two-by-four to his whole body. Hot in here. Should turn on the fan. Might get back to sleep. Probably not, though. Sunday morning coming down as the poet said. Adrenaline still pumped up. Feel wrung out but wide awake and all fucked up. Gotta piss. First things first.

Walker stood up and shambled into the bathroom and stood over the bowl holding his cock between thumb and forefinger and awaiting nature's pleasure but all that came out was a loud fart and pressure in his bowels. The curse of advancing age. Sighing, he turned around and sat down on the toilet. Big and slow it feels like. What was on for today? Not much. Wow. Imagine seeing Zinny yesterday. Wonder what the chances of that are. One in a million probably. Got to give her a call. Didn't know why he put it off but it seemed like a great solution at least temporarily. Good idea then. Still good now. Go for it. Closing in a week. Shit. Still had stuff he needed to clear out and then rent a van or something to move over to Zinnys. Oh it was hard just edging out so don't push. Let it stay there a bit. That's what I'll do today, then. Have breakfast and then finish clearing out the attic. Ahh, there it goes. Must be the tacos from last night. Not too spicy and the ice cream Sunday was good too. Might be some more. Sit for a minute. Is there stuff still in the cellar? Have to check.

Walker stood by the foot of his bed looking around the room. Bed, dresser, chair by dresser, closet with door partly open and a red bathrobe thrown over the top of the door, pair of brown loafers on the left almost hidden by the bed, the little brown pine table beside the bed just big enough to hold a Dumbo-The-Elephant lamp with Dumbo flying around and around the shade wearing a wide smile and pointed yellow hat for all eternity. Eternally smiling. Eternally happy. As a boy, he had woken up to that sight every morning. As a man, he had stored the childhood lamp and bought a man lamp with a solid brass base and neck and a tan, rather severe, shade. It had not lasted six months before he found it ugly and tiresome and had rescued Dumbo from the box in the attic, brought him down, given him a new bulb and brought the happy smile and pointy little hat back to his bedside. Walker smiled now, thinking of that. Beside the flying friend was a Sony Dream Machine mindless showing the time in big green numbers: 5:33 AM. Good God. You'd think this was a week day. In front of the clock was an old take-out menu from Lings No 1 Chinese restaurant with a duck sauce stain on one corner. Ling made great sweet and sour chicken, Walker remembered. Not that gooey stuff you get most of the time. Ahh, breakfast time. Didn't have to worry, didn't have to think with sausage to fry and coffee to drink. That thought cheered him measurably. Might as well. Wouldn't get back to sleep anyway. Sausage and scrambled or perhaps poached eggs this morning. All those wonderful eggs swirling around in the water and plop onto crisp buttered English muffins and BAM. Salt and pepper, a little paprika for a little kick and then lots more butter.

Walker pulled on a pair of khaki shorts and a white t-shirt with a big, yellow smiley face on it and padded out of the bedroom and into the kitchen. Faint, predawn light shadowed the counters and the fridge, throwing darker shadows over the upper cabinets. He stood for a moment looking out the window over the sink into the back yard. Bare spots still showed where he had taken down Jen's swing set, where her feet had scooped a shallow indentation in the earth beneath the swings and at the foot of the slide that had almost rusted through by the time he took it down. Just to the right was the big bush where she liked to hide in a spot where nobody would ever find her. This had usually occurred after disappointment or even punishment when she decided to exact revenge on the cruel monsters that kept her enslaved. How many times had he stood out in the yard pretending not to know where she crouched in the hollow spot behind that bush. He would walk around mumbling to himself that she was gone forever and that he would never find her and that would make him so sad that he would never smile again and then he would hear her giggling behind the bush. "Oh, no," he would gasp. "I hear something, maybe just a teeney weeney something. Maybe . . ." and Jen would break into a gale of laughter and run out from behind the bush and into his arms. "Ooh Daddy, you're so big," she'd say and he would reply "and you're so small. You're my little china doll."

Just as well, he thought. Spending too much time moping around this house remembering and not enough time out of it getting on with my life. Jen had grown up big and rebellious and with no drive to even achieve a minimal standard of living. She got those genes from him, Walker supposed. His father had always told him well never godammed mind what the old bastard had told him. He had a child to carry on and, though he often rejected the thought, he was glad to have someone with his blood in her carrying on after he had shed his mortal coil. That is part of us all. Be fruitful and multiply.

Walker pulled a pot from under the counter and filling it with water, put it on to boil. He took a frying pan and, after retrieving them from a plastic package in the fridge, threw on a handful of breakfast sausage links. Blue flames licked the undersides of the pots. He would clean out the attic, give Zinny a call and then sit down to get some more done on his book. That thought encouraged him and, whistling tunelessly and rather tonelessly, he cracked three eggs into then boiling water and consigned two pieces of English muffins to the dark hell of the toaster.

Attic trolls are notorious for their nasty tempers and waspish ways. The one in Walker's attic was particularly so for he was as old as the house and had no reason to like Walker any more than he had the previous occupants. The fact that he was suddenly awakened from a sound sleep on one of Beth's old dresses when the door to the attic creaked open did not improve his disposition. A churlish troll was he and so would remain by guess and by God. "Christ almighty, you dammed fucking human shithead. May you lose more than just your house you great fat bastard." After uttering these pearls of wisdom, the troll retreated into the darkest corner of the attic. He did not like humans but he respected their power. One small female had almost torched him with a candle some years before. He wished the worst of luck upon whoever was venturing into his kingdom.

As if the cosmos was answering, Walker did immediately and severely strike his head against a resistant roof joist upon entering the attic and, upon cursing his fate and the progeny unto the tenth generation of all home builders, did then snag his pocket on a nail protruding from a wooden chest and, upon moving forward without acknowledging said happenstance, did rip his shorts the point where some expert tailor would need to attend them before he could use them during gainful employment.

Walker stood in the gloom holding the pocket onto his pants with one hand and groping for the light switch with the other. "Shit," he muttered. "Goddamned attic filled with goddamned junk. It's a wonder I didn't kill myself." His head throbbed where he had struck it. He found the switch and stood there in a semi-crouch rubbing the growing bump on his head.

What Walker saw that he remembered but did not take with him: One US Army dress green uniform with the insignia of a Specialist Fifth Class and the badge of the Big Red One. When he was a lot skinnier, couldn't get into it now. Had some good times back then. Drinking in the NCO Club, driving with friends off post to the local whorehouse in an old VW that he had bought from another spec 5 who was being transferred. Mooney was his name, he remembered. Yeah. Mooney. Not much of a car but it kept on running. Okay for two hundred bucks. It was all we needed back then. There was one woman who was so hot that he'd almost creamed when she skinned a rubber over his dick. Had to think about KP or some other nasty thought to keep control. Even so, happened once or twice but she never said anything. She was older, though. The younger ones were like sticking your dick in a bag of crushed ice.

One child's kitchen set composed of one sink, one stove and one refrigerator. Jenny wanted to be a cook when she was five or six. The set was on her Santa list, and, even though it cost a fortune, we bought it and he'd spent the whole of Christmas Eve putting the damned thing together. Santa did a lot of un-Santa-like cussing that year. Almost melted the tinsel off the tree.

One old trunk that Beth spotted at an auction and absolutely had to have. It was cavernous and made of canvas over wood with wooden slats reinforcing the outside and a huge circular brass lock on the front. It had stickers from England and France on it and some others too faint to read or partially torn off. The trunk and its contents were being auctioned as one item.

"Just think," she kept repeating, "there might be something really valuable in there."

"Oh sure" he'd argued, "like nobody ever looked in it before putting it up for auction."

"Well, maybe they didn't know a good thing when they saw it. I'm going to bid on it." And she stuck up her hand and we ended up driving home with it tied to the roof of the car and threatening to come undone and crush any car behind us.

And what had the seventy five dollar bargain contained when they'd finally got it home? (Careful, CAREFUL. Don't drop it. It's an antique.) There was a trunk full of dust and grime and some moth-eaten clothes that were too ragged to save and a copy of the New York Times dated July 14, 1947.

A Rosenthal china service for six with a floral pattern that Beth had liked for its understated simplicity and that now occupied several wooden shelves built down from the ceiling joists. Beth and he had saved for two years for that service. Beth had been working at the time and still it had been twenty here and ten there into the china passbook account, between unexpected expenses that all couples face who are owned by the bank, their children and their pets in that order.

What Walker saw that he did not remember: A large turkey platter in a blue country pattern with a large crack running through the middle of it, a yellow serving dish with a long-handled wooden spoon sticking out the top, a cardboard box with SONY on it from a long vanished stereo system(Walker jiggled the box just to be sure), a cardboard wardrobe containing a sea-green evening gown, two white men's shirts, one pair of corduroy pants(chocolate brown and way too small), and a small child's green velvet dress, one box with stuffed plush animals and what looked like a Barbie doll peeking over one side, a large aluminum roasting pan(yeah, okay there was that one Thanksgiving when we had both sets of parents over and everyone got tight and got along like oil and vinegar), a tricycle missing its seat, a huge trunk filled, Walker supposed, with items long forgotten, a hat rack with no hats and missing one of its pegs.(When did I last wear a hat? Christ, during some past winter I suppose.), a small box crammed with old letters tied in neat stacks and some postcards of tropical scenery (My parents, I guess, for we never had the money to travel anywhere that required a postcard), one game of Monopoly, one game of Chutes And Ladders, one game of Trivial Pursuit, one set of plastic poker chips (Sure, we used them that New Year's Eve when Stu and Jan came over. We got bombed and ended up playing strip poker. What a set of boobs. She said she could aim as well as any man and she ended up standing on top of the coffee table and peeing down into a large kitchen pot. Hit it too.), one oil painting depicting the face and upper torso of some long dead ancestor. He looked very grim (constipated, perhaps?). He was dressed in black with a wide, white stock collar. Very Puritan. Must have been damned uncomfortable to sit for a long period of time dressed like that. Maybe that was the point. Scourge the flesh for the benefit of the spirit. Thou shalt not do anything, anywhere at anytime but Walker would bet they did anyway, human nature being what it is, one stack of phonograph records dating back to the Andrews Sisters, Bing Crosby, The Kingston Trio and Johnny Mathis. Lots of good music there and nothing on which to play them. He remembered singing Tom Dooley as a kid. His mother would tell him not to do that because his voice would drive the help to quit.

Walker stooped slightly and walked slowly along the spine of the house, carefully avoiding the single, unshielded light dangling from its old and somewhat frayed cord, and looking to both sides at the boxes and old toys that were stacked there. He saw a small, pink sneaker, just one, a lonely orphan. He saw a scarf balled up alongside a cardboard box. Upon picking it up a delicate translucent bird of paradise spread its wings in the dusty air illuminated by the single bulb and a dim light coming through a cobwebbed window at the end of the attic. Jennifer probably took it from Beth's closet at some point, probably meaning to return it and then forgot. He was silent while stepping through time, through the litter and jumble, flotsam and jetsam of human lives. Walker could think of nothing to say that would break the silence but would not break something inside. The attic troll sniggered and twittered in the darkness.

And by the little attic window, Walker slowed to a stop. On top of a small chest, almost a suitcase, was a tin measuring cup full of ashes and cigarette butts. Beside it was a stack of teen magazines with pictures of handsome young men strolling confidently through the garden of life, singing prettily into a microphone or waving to adoring fans. There was an empty paper Marlboro pack and a small, almost delicate looking battery operated boyfriend. My God, he thought, how little we know of our children or them of us. This must be at least ten or twelve years old. Wonder if she confided in Beth about growing up and sex and all that? He moved the cup and the stack of magazines aside and, picking up the little case, placed it on top of a pile of boxes. It was just a little Hartmann brown leather suit case with brass locks and a good sturdy handle. Beth's, probably, he thought and flicked up the latches and raised the lid of the case. Bundles of letters neatly arranged in stacks, some tied with string while others were tied with string or yarn. The top letter on one stack was addressed to Tom Beauchamp her long past boyfriend. He felt somewhat awkward, looking down at the stash. He was, in a sense, intruding on a part of her life about which he knew nothing. Maybe best to throw it out with the rest of this stuff. He couldn't bring himself to do so, however, and picked up the letter. There was no envelope. Perhaps she had written it but never sent it. It was dated the year that she and Walker had gotten together and the script was in her small, neat hand that he would recognized anywhere. "*Tom—I have resolved the problem that you could not face . . .*

Walker sat in his chair and stared to his left at the tan-colored phone sitting on the little table. He should call her. He sipped at his drink and stared out through the living room windows at the mound of stuff that he had brought down from the attic and put on the curb. Out with the old, in with the new except I am now old or at least older and maybe I should be on the curb with all that stuff. He should call Zinny. The thought irritated Walker but he did not know why. He had been sitting there for an hour and still had not made the call. He had flat run out of choices. He knew it but knowing it didn't make him feel any better. From seven rooms to one room. Big change. His glass was empty. He swished the half melted cubes around in it. Call.

The phone rang several times on the other end and Walker was about to hang up with a sigh of relief as if he had been calling to tell someone that their dog had been run over. "Hello?"

"Oh hi. Is this Zinny?" Walker suddenly felt slightly queasy. He wished he'd refilled his drink before calling and looked longingly in the direction of the kitchen.

"Yes."

"Zinny, this is Johnny Walker. How are you?"

"Oh Agile. Hi." Her voice rose in tones of recognition and pleasure.

Walker felt himself relax slightly. "About the room? Is it still available?"

"Certainly."

"Well, if you are agreeable I would like to rent it."

"That's wonderful. Certainly, you can rent it." She sounded really happy as if he had just told her that she had a winning lotto ticket.

"Great. Thanks for the tour yesterday. It was great seeing you again. What a coincidence, heh? I couldn't believe it when I saw you standing in the doorway. It was one of those small world type things, you know?" Walker felt himself rattling on and shut his mouth before he managed to stick his foot in it.

"I know exactly what you mean. I think it was just one of those things that was meant to be. I am so glad you decided to take the room. When did you think you might be doing it? I can have the lease ready for signing and the room cleaned and ready whenever you say."

"Well, I could come over this afternoon and settle the money and paperwork, moving might take a few days. Maybe next weekend if I can rope my daughter into helping me." Life seemed simpler already and Walker wondered why he had ever hesitated to call. This would work out. Yes indeed.

Walker drove the little U-Haul van down Farmington Avenue. He was in a good mood. The next day he had taken off to attend the closing of the house. Today he was on his way to Zinny's bringing the small load of furniture and belongings to his new home. Once again he would have a clean credit record. He tried to think back to the last time he had no debt. Just after meeting Beth? Probably. Was single and living in an apartment smaller than Zinny's room. Just the basic expenses. Utilities, rent, food. Simple existence. Didn't know how happy I was until I look back on it. Things really snowballed after Beth told me she was pregnant. Boy, did it ever, and I never really noticed but just went along doing what I needed to do for Beth and then for Beth and Jennifer and one day bled into the next and now, whaddya know, but here I am, alone again, well almost, and cruising down the street with all my worldly possessions and debt free so raise a cheer for ol' Johnny, will ya? I had just enough in savings to give Zinny a deposit and, by the time the credit card bill comes due for the van, I'll have the house money to deal with it.

Walker looked to his right at Jennifer who was slouched down in her seat staring blankly over the dashboard of the truck. "Penny for your thoughts," he told her.

Jennifer shrugged. "Nothing special. How long is this going to take?"

"Not long. Relax, will you? The landlady's nice. You might like her."

"Is she a les?"

Walker was shocked and then suddenly amused. This child was nothing if not startling at times. Then he realized that she might say something really stupid to Zinny. "No, of course not. Please keep such remarks to yourself when we get there. I'll be living in her house and would like to have her as a friend and not an enemy." He tried to sound reasonable but it came out raspy and complaining.

"Relax, Dad. I won't dis your squeeze."

"And she's not my squeeze."

"Anything you say." Jennifer closed her eyes, looking happier than she had since she had appeared at his door, drawn by the promise of several twenties to fatten her wallet or that of Moses, Walker thought somewhat uncharitably.

"What have you got against the world, anyway?" Walker asked. "Nobody beat or abused you as a child. You had a roof over your head and food on your plate, toys to play with and clothes to wear, but you seem to think that everyone outside of Moses and maybe me are somehow against you and not to be trusted or even given a chance to be trusted. I mean we all go through a stage of rebellion in some form or another. When I was young, I thought I knew better than my parents about many things. In fact, my parents and I never got along, but that was because I never saw my father much except when he was mad at me and my mother never quite got the hang of motherhood after going through the pain and indignity of childbirth. I swore things would be different when I was a father, and both your mother and I were always there for you. I remember almost falling out of dozens of tiny, uncomfortable, chairs watching you in plays and recitals, and talking with your teachers. Can you picture me sitting in a chair meant for a fourth grader? But you never got past the counter-culture stage. What is so wrong with the life I lead and most people lead for that matter that you insist on living in a slum and knocking everything and everyone around me?" Walker thought for a moment and anger gained momentum. "You want respect, but you don't want to give it. Believe me, Jen, that respect is a two way street."

Jen didn't respond for a minute but just sat in silence slumped into the seat. "You just don't get it. You've got your little job and your little life, but it is totally meaningless. What have you accomplished with it all? I look around and I see a capitol filled with lobbyists trying to buy congressmen and politicians lining their pockets while mouthing a bunch of lies to their constituents. Everybody is out for number one and beggar their neighbor. Maybe we live a simple life, but we share with everyone and we do our best to live in peace and harmony with the world around us." She shrugged slightly and lapsed into silence. How could she possibly explain to her father how she felt? Pictures of high school years flashed across her memory. Hey, fatty. Want some candy? Move over, you whale, you're half in my seat. I saw your dad, yesterday. You look just like him. Get outta my way, you fucking tub of lard. She remembered the way the teachers looked at her as if she had done something wrong even when she got an "A" on her homework. She remembered all the times she had cried into her pillow, hating herself and hating the world for making her feel like shit. How could she admit even to her father that she woke up every morning dreading the day ahead of her. Only Moses had shown her any affection. Moses had not cared how much Jennifer weighed and only Moses had managed to ignite the fire in her body as they lay entwined at night.

Walker grimaced. "Yeah. It's not a perfect world. No doubt about it, but you can't run and hide and then bitch about everyone who takes what they are given and does the best they can with it." He really was being a hypocrite. After all, he had rejected his birthright and the life that went with it in favor of family, but he could hardly admit this to Jennifer.

"Yeah, well you walk your walk and I'll walk mine," commented Jennifer succinctly.

"Okay. Well, just keep in mind that I am not your enemy, that I am not totally clueless and that I love you and you can always come to me with whatever problems you have or want to talk about or whatever." Walker finished feeling lame and a little trite.

"'K?"

"'K"

They drove in silence for another minute and then Walker slowed and turned into the driveway beside the house, stomped on the brake and the truck jerked to a stop. Walker sat for a moment while heat waves fanned off the hood of the truck and the engine clinked.

"Hi, there Agile."

He looked to his left and saw Zinny standing on the front porch smiling down at him. Her face was shadowed so he could not read her expression, but her tone was friendly. A good start, he decided, and raised his hand in a casual gesture of greeting. "Hi, Zinny," he called out. "We have landed." He pushed open the door and stepped down onto the pavement. He heard the door slam as Jennifer got out on the other side and then she appeared in front of the truck.

"Fucking hot out here. Let's get this done, okay?" she complained.

Walker sighed. Why did he even bother to talk with her, to her, at her, behind or in front or to one side of her. He had a horse's ass for a daughter. Where did that gene come from? "Zinny, meet my daughter, Jennifer. Jen, this is my landlady, Miss Jones."

"Hiya."

"Hello, Jennifer. Nice to meet you."

"I gotta piss something fierce. You gotta bathroom in there?"

Zinny grinned and gestured her forwards. "Follow me," she said and disappeared inside the house with Jen walking with slightly hunched forward and with uneven gait in her wake.

Walker stood in the driveway staring up at the house and wondering if he hadn't made a huge mistake by hiring his daughter to help him. What must Zinny think? She was a librarian and single to boot. She was probably deeply offended by Jen's manner. He tried to put himself in her place but failed, coming to the conclusion that he might, over time, repair any damage done. He moved to the back of the truck and opened the door as Zinny came back out onto the porch. He lifted out a box of books and walked up to the porch.

"I think she made it." Zinny said as if announcing that the weather was fair that day.

"Good. Listen, Zinny."

She held up one hand to stop him. "You've a good girl there trying to be a woman. I think she'll be a good one."

"It's hard for me to tell sometimes," Walker admitted. "Still, I must apologize."

Zinny chuckled as she came down the porch steps and faced Walker, still holding the box in his arms and looking across it uncertainly. "Listen, Agile. Young people are like that. You and I were probably like that although selective memory allows us to forget most of our rudeness and arrogance."

"I was never that flagrant." Walker protested as he tried to remember back to all the things he'd said and done in his twenties. Maybe he had been, he admitted to himself. He thought of the time he'd flown into a rage and told his father that he was full of shit and should get his head out of his ass and take a look at the real world. Pretty flagrant, there, old man. Pretty flagrant.

"Nevertheless." Zinny thrust her chin out in an attitude of stubbornness and smiled. "If you and Jen need help, I'll be glad to pitch in."

"Why would you want to do that?"

"All part of the package," she replied. "For my first and best tenant."

"Yes. Okay. I'm glad you weren't offended." She took the box from him. "Heavy," he warned.

She winked. "I'm stronger than I look," and walked up the steps and into the house.

Jennifer reappeared on the porch. "Okay, Dad. Let's get this done. I got other things to do." She strolled across the lawn and climbed into the back of the truck.

Like spend all the money I paid you, Walker thought as he went to the back of the truck and took another box from Jennifer. As he turned towards the house, he saw the man standing across the street.

He was up the street about one hundred yards looking towards Walker. There was something familiar about him, the way he stood, the slant of his shoulders, like a relative that he'd not seen in years. Walker turned his head still trying to remember where he'd seen the man before and saw Zinny standing on the porch looking up the street.

Her face was set into long, vertical lines that outlined her nose and mouth, making her look stern and suddenly old. He saw fear in her eyes and something else, something animal like. It was there for only a moment before she came down the steps. "Here, if it's not too heavy, I'll take that one," she said.

"Who is that man?"

"Who?"

"The guy standing there up the street."

"No one." She took the box from Walker and headed back into the house totally ignoring the man watching them.

Walker thought to press the point but the look on her face discouraged him. Jennifer had been enough for today. He would not beard the lioness.

Not In Service

The light comes and goes for it is fickle and will not stay to play, will not shine on me for long before gone. I open my eyes and there it is, open them again and it is somewhere else. That is sad. I like the light. There was light when something happened but I cannot remember something warm and there was light then and now I am lying on something hard and cold and I see a brown, polished surface stretching out before me, Ethiopia, perhaps, and far away a chair. I try to roll over but my strength has deserted me and I lie there in the light waiting for something else to come along. I close my eyes and darkness spins me around hiding me but things are out there I know yes and with slithering tongues and white stuff bubbling and flying into the savage smoke of the night leaving me lying on the floor yes that's what it's called. How did I get on the floor? I have no answer so I lie still and open my eyes and let in the light with its shining and I say "Okay," and suddenly a big shadow blocks the light and a face is above my face and asking if I am all right and if I hurt anyplace and then someone grabs me under my arms and a monstrous face blocks out the light. It has huge, bulging eyes and a mouth that is reaching for me. I try and push it away but it turns into the frozen Chosin with commies running towards our little company and I know that we will all be killed and I wonder if Martha will ever know back home. I raise my hand and scream in terror.

"Does anything hurt?" the face sounds concerned. Is it talking to me? It has not eaten me and seems to be hiding a smile and so I say okay and I am warm there and I hear a voice I know for it comes every day and it is a good voice full of light and I remember it back when something happened. I can't remember but it was important and that voice was there.

"I think he must have fallen getting out of bed. I heard a thump."

"Oh my God. He usually lies there until I come for him. I'm so sorry you were disturbed."

I turn my head and there is a woman talking with the man who is naked except for underwear and a robe that has come undone in front.

He has a big belly with brown and gray hair around his belly button. The woman is looking down and away from him trying not to notice and the man sees this and quickly closes the robe and ties it shut. He seems uncomfortable, maybe embarrassed.

"I didn't mean to scare him," he tells the woman. I was awake and glad to help out."

I am sitting in a chair and the light is with me and my crotch feels warm. It is like the woman and part of me but apart, some fragment like when Zinny dressed up her favorite doll and brought her to church. When was that? Back in well anyway she did and it sat solemnly beside her in the pew with the prayer book on her lap but now the woman is doing something and suddenly I am naked and then something wet hits me and she is wiping me with a cloth, warm again but different, a different woman's kiss.

"Okay, Dad. You're all set. Look out the window. It's a beautiful day. I have to go but Rosa will be here."

"Okay," I tell her though I am not sure if everything is okay but there is light in the window so that is okay and she goes away and I stare out at the tree in the yard. The tree and me and the light makes three. Okay.

And my mind is now filled with a picture so vivid that it is real, a harsh flashing of forms and colors so harsh that I see spots in front of my eyes and there she is standing slim and straight in a blindingly white dress with waves of material forming its train and trailing back behind her. I turn to see Martha dabbing at her eyes and I look at our daughter now grown and soon gone and above her the windows of the church were filled with light of red and blue and green streaming down over the head of Father Conroy framing his white curls in a halo and beside her the man she would wed standing young and straight but not standing good, no, no. I know he is bad for her, sense it in my gut and try to tell her but she is in love and beyond my reach. There is something about him but I can't remember. Mark is his name, I think. Mark somethingoreother with sneers on his lips and darkness in his eyes thinking that he is a man among men, blessed art thou, oh ye sinner, along the trail of light, and he looks for rich helpings of treasure and pleasure. He is mean. I am a healer and see mean every day and I know the face of mean, the smell of it, the shadow it casts. I look at Father Conroy, now pronouncing, always a gift for gab, the Irish way. He can talk of you out of anything and then talk you out of it again.

"How you doing Doc? You looking pretty good today like maybe you have something good going on in there, know what I mean? It's going on a beautiful day out there. Maybe later, I'll get you down on the porch for a while. Would you like that? Bet you would. Here, let me raise you up and get you better like so. I had a bad back last year and I was laid up, you know what I mean, so I know how uncomfortable you can get just sitting there. Lord, lord, I had muscles hurting that I didn't even know I had."

There is a big, brown face full of white teeth in front of mine. A good face. I sense this. It is full of the spirit. Light hits it and is kept inside. It is a face of peace, a friendly face like some other faces I see but the names are gonegone gone. "Okay," I say and it is clear and loud with hope and expectation and the face goes away and behind me I can hear her humming and the sound of blankets and sheets coming off the bed. The sunlight comes through the window and kisses me and I say "Okay."

E2

Walker woke up feeling as if he hadn't slept at all. Cotton mouth and a dull headache reminded him that he had had one too many the night before. He closed his eyes but he knew it was just for show because he had to get to work, hung over or not. Feeling somehow cheated and somewhat surly, he swung himself up and out of bed, pulled his robe around him and padded across the room and then next door to the bathroom. This sucks, he groused to himself. I should have my own bathroom. Okay, no one but me uses it but it still sucks. I should find my own apartment. I mean really. I should be able to do better than one room. Of course, that would mean hardship for Zinny for a while but she could rent it out again. He stood under the hot shower trying to wake up and die right.

By the time he had taken his shower, shaved, passed a toothbrush across his teeth, Walker felt slightly more human than he had a few minutes before but only slightly. The thought of the work day ahead did nothing to improve his mood. Endless calls and endless hassles. Uggh. He slipped on the shirt from the day before. Didn't look too bad. He sniffed under one arm and grunted with satisfaction. Coffee time. Breakfast time. He cheered up slightly and went down the stairs and into the kitchen.

"Good morning, Agile." Zinny turned from where she was standing by the sink and smiled. "Sleep well?" she chirped.

"Not really," Walker replied and pulled a coffee cup from the overhead cabinet.

"Too bad. Tough night, last night? You look somewhat the worse for wear." She finished her glass of juice and sighed. "Lousy weather, too."

"Mmmm." Walker noticed the rain beading little rivers down the window over the sink. He had been so busy waking up that he hadn't even thought of the weather. The sight did little to improve his mood. Walking in the rain. Hell's bells, he thought.

"I bought some English muffins. They're in the bread box. Help yourself."

"Okay." Walker sipped cautiously at his steaming cup of coffee. His stomach stirred nervously at the mention of solid food, and he decided to stick with the coffee.

"Where is Rosalinda?" Zinny asked rhetorically and washed her glass out in the sink before putting it in the dish rack to dry. "She's rarely late." She crossed her arms across her chest and walked out of the kitchen towards the front door.

Walker sat down at the table. Almost Friday, he reminded himself. One day to go, well really two days since this one had just started. Had he been here only a few days? Seemed longer. How quickly our lives fall into a routine. We go and do the same day after day and never think twice and every once in a while something happens. All the cards get thrown up in the air and, after we finish picking them up, we start a new routine and go to work and go to sleep.

"Agile, I need a favor."

Uh oh. Walker turned as Zinny strode back into the kitchen. Her face was set into tight lines and her fingers moved nervously at her sides. She looked a lot older, suddenly. Time to get out of Dodge. He could almost feel his defenses rising, walls going up and cannons poking out. "Yes?" he asked, cautious, diffident, certain that he was not in the mood for favors but uncertain as to the nature of her request.

"Rosie's late. I have to go now or I'll be late. Can you stay here a few minutes until she gets here?"

"If I do that, I may be late. They frown on that where I work."

"My boss hates it too, and, because of Dad, I've been late more than a few times, and now there's talk of layoffs so I can't afford to bring my name to the top of his get-rid-of list. You don't have that problem."

"How would you know?" Walker found her question and the implied assumption irritating.

"Well I don't, of course." Zinny paused, "but you leave at the same time every day and there is nothing to keep you from doing that. I just thought . . ." She shrugged and smiled faintly. "Will you?"

"No."

"Please. I wouldn't ask if I didn't think it was really important"

"Sorry, Zinny," Walker finished his coffee and rose from the table. "No can do. Gotta get going." He pushed past her and rinsed out his cup in the sink. "Rosie'll be along any second." He knew that was maybe wishful thinking but he felt pushed into a position he didn't want to be in and resented it bitterly. Damn her to hell for asking him something like this. He hated her at that moment and wanted nothing more than to be out of the house and on the bus heading for work.

"Thanks for nothing," Zinny shot back bitterly. "It's not your problem, right?"

"Right." Walker told her. "I'm sorry you're going to be late but I'm not Daddy's day care." He opened the door and went down the steps to the driveway.

"Go to hell, you bastard," Zinny called out behind him, fear, desperation, anger and the ultimate acknowledgment of despair pushing her voice into a shriek that rang in his ears as Walker walked as quickly as possible away from the house.

Walker sat at his desk. He was wearing a telephone headset and staring intently at his computer screen as he typed "had caller reboot" into the call information screen in front of him. "Another reboot," he said to no one in particular. "Always get a bunch after the system goes down."

"and because users don't think," added Henry Clark who sat on Walker's right. "If something unexpected happens, the first thing they usually do is complain to the person next to them and then call us." Henry was not known for his patience and, on numerous occasions, had slammed the handset down onto the body of the phone after hanging up with a customer. Walker was waiting for him to jump the gun by a second or two and do that with a live customer still on the line.

"The old song and dance," agreed Walker as a light began flashing on his phone and his mind separated itself and went on an adventure while his mouth issued instructions long before memorized.

His bad mood had persisted and the system outage had only increased his desire to break something, yell at someone, kick a dog, chase a cat, so sure that the entire world would take on a dark smudge gray coating and flames would begin to lick up around the edges and smoke would billow up in his face as the end of the world appeared and that no matter what caused that final holocaust, someone would blame Walker for it. He could not think of a single thing that did not increase his temper. Politicians were fools. His job was awful. The weather was lousy and if it was lousy today it would, without the shadow of a doubt, be even worse tomorrow and here he was still plodding to work on the bus and putting up with the weather. Walker felt caught in a vise of his own making and his mood blackened more as the minutes passed. He thought of the man he had seen across the street from Zinny's when Walker was moving in. Somehow, the image seemed to fit with his current mood. There had been something about the man, the way he stood looking across the street at the house that had been really creepy. Even, now, with the memory of him, Walker felt creeped-out just like that time with Chuck Yarborough.

He sank back into his childhood when some really bad memories were not hard to remember. It was like going into a roadside diner and putting on a blindfold before you looked at a menu. If you felt in the mood for grease, it was not hard to find.

Walker had known Chuck Yarborough as far back as he could remember. The Yarboroughs lived in the same neighborhood and Carl Yarborough had done business with Walker's father. Carl was a self-made man and never hesitated to boast about that fact. His view of the universe, or least that part in which he played a minor and temporary role, started and ended with Carl Yarborough, his work, his play, his friends (anyone who agreed with him), his enemies (anyone who didn't agree with him or who came from a different tribe such as Jews, blacks, ragheads, leaches, tree-huggers, wealth-haters, bureaucrats, welfare recipients, wet backs, democrats, strong women) and innumerable likes and dislikes. Walker remembered him as a bear of a man who liked to show off his chest hair and his wife, probably in that order. Mrs. Yarborough, as if God had somehow decided to balance the scales, was a nice woman, or at least Walker remembered her as such. She had been slim and blond with a mile of white teeth which she beamed at everyone and anyone. She was always smiling but never said much. It would have been hard for her to do so considering the man she'd married. He boomed over her whenever Walker saw them together which, when he first met their son, was at a cocktail party to which they had invited his parents and himself. Mrs. Yarborough probably wanted a playmate for her son, Charles.

"Charles. I want you to meet Johnny Walker, Mr. and Mrs. Walker's son."

"Hi," Walker said and stood looking at Charles who made no reply. Charles, in fact, did not seem happy to see Walker and merely stood there staring at him with a look on his face that made Walker back up slightly into his mother standing behind him. Charles was already big, with a broad frame like his father. At the age of eleven or twelve, he probably topped one hundred pounds as did Walker, but Charles' weight was evenly distributed.

Mrs. Yarborough flashed another smile as she looked down at her son. "What do you say, Charles?"

Charles said nothing but just turned and walked away. "He doesn't say much," observed Mrs. Walker.

"No, but I can tell that he likes Johnny. Go ahead and go with him and you two get to know each other."

Walker's mother gave him a gentle push in the direction that Charles was walking. Feeling very shy and a little nervous, Walker trailed behind Charles as he disappeared through a door at the rear of the house.

The Yarboroughs lived in a huge brick colonial set back behind a large front yard heavily planted and through which the driveway ran in a semicircle in front of the mansion before wandering off to the left where there was a three car garage the size of a small house. Charles led Walker through a restaurant-sized kitchen where a tiny woman was chopping vegetables and went out the back door. When Walker followed him Charles was waiting. "Why are you following me?" he demanded with his hands on his hips and leaning aggressively towards Walker.

"Uhh. Dunno."

"You look like a weenie."

"Well I'm not."

Suddenly Charles relaxed and even smiled. It was a transformation that took Walker completely by surprise. "Call me Chuck. Only my mom calls me Charles. She's kinda dumb."

"I'm Johnny."

"Wanna see something cool?" Chuck smiled and without waiting for a reply turned and walked off towards the back of the garage. "C'mon."

They went to the back of the garage. Chuck opened a door there and led the way up a flight of dusty steps. At the top he turned to Walker. "Can you keep a secret? You gotta promise not to tell anyone."

"'bout what?"

"About anything."

Walker wasn't sure he should do this but he was curious. "Okay."

The space above the garage was one large rectangular space. Most of it seemed to be filled with assorted boxes, trunks, pieces of garden equipment and scraps of lumber. Overhead a row of lights hanging down from the ceiling cast everything in sharp relief and shadow. Chuck led the way around mounds of boxes to one end of the room where he had apparently cleared a space for himself. There was an old chair with the stuffing coming out of it next to a wooden crate on top of which was a lamp. Spilled around the chair were pornographic magazines. Walker stopped and stared down at them.

"Nice, huh?" Chuck had noticed the source of Walker's attention. "I found them in the back of my dad's closet. Chuck grabbed his crotch suggestively. "Hey, we can jerk off later. C'mon over here." Walker nodded as if he knew what Chuck was talking about. Chuck turned back and went over to the other side of the space.

"The gardener caught him and was going to take him somewhere and let him go but I convinced him to let me have him instead." Chuck pointed down at his feet.

Walker looked down and there in a medium sized cage was a large raccoon staring up at Walker with his two black eyes. He was a beautiful animal. Walker admired his sleek coat and nervous little front paws. "He's great," he told Chuck.

"You haven't seen anything," Chuck replied. His whole face had changed somehow. There was a light in his eyes that had been missing before, a look that was both malicious and excited. His thick body was almost dancing with anticipation.

"What do you mean?" Walker asked suddenly sensing that he shouldn't have made the promise. He had no idea what Chuck meant, and he found himself not wanting to know. Not at all.

Chuck held up a can of charcoal lighter fluid. "I'm talking Viking funeral, Johnny. Except this one will be on land." He held the can over the cage and squirted a stream of the fluid over the back of the raccoon that screamed and turned in a circle trying to find a way out.

"Don't," he told Chuck.

"Don't be a pussy," Chuck replied. Putting the can down, he picked up a box of matches and held them up. "Want to throw the first one?" he asked.

Walker turned and fled to the sound of Chuck's laughter and then the agonized screams of the raccoon.

"Hey, John. You got a call waiting."

Walker came back to reality with a start. Angrily he pushed the memory of that awful afternoon back into whatever hole in his psyche it had been hiding along with the stranger at Zinny's house and her reaction to him. He felt a stab of guilt at being caught dreaming instead of working and the morning progressed in a series of blinking lights, pushed buttons, mouse clickings and strange and sometimes not so strange voices in his ear. Hi my name is Leonard and Hi my name is Sam and is this the Helpdesk? I have a Hi my name is Charles and I need help immediately and Hi oh please I hope you can help me cause and Hi let me speak with your supervisor please. I need someone intelligent and Hi good morning how are you this Hi my screen went blank and I need to print something for a meeting in thirty minutes and Hi is this the Helpdesk? I've been transferred five times and you'd better fix this right now. No I did not touch that key and Hi I'm really new to computers and when I tried to turn it on and

Walker would talk in soothing tones and gentle modulations. What were you doing when you started and please move your mouse and click on the button and please don't do anything until I tell you to and please click shutdown and let your machine turn off and it does make a faint buzzing noise when it starts and that is okay and I'm glad to hear you're all set.

And on it went through the dark breaking hours of the morning with the pale sun shining in the green sky through the wall of tinted glass that was one side of the building. Walker rocked back and forth in his orthopedically correct chair while the calls came and went and the air hummed through the vents.

It was not until he glanced at the clock on his pc that he realized it was almost lunch time and that immediately woke his appetite and reminded him of the fight he and Zinny had a few hours previously. He had been so pissed off on the way to work, so sure that she had been trying to take advantage of him. Now, he felt like a fool. Walker leaned back in his chair and wondered what had possessed him to act that way. Okay, it wasn't cool to be late, but Zinny was right. He could count on the fingers of one hand the times he had been late in the past twenty years. Henry would have covered for him. He had simply been in a bad mood, stubborn and pissy like some great overweight ox. Walker sat stabbing himself, flagellating the emotions that he had treasured only hours before. Zinny had probably been late and that would be a big problem from what she had said. Idiot. Fool. It's a good thing you're on your own now because God help anyone who needed you for anything or depended on you for anything. Fucking selfish asshole. Walker sat steaming quietly looking at the minutes on his computer's clock slowly change. He would go to their usual spot for lunch. He would apologize for his behavior. He would do whatever it took. He just hoped it would be enough.

She had not been there; Walker sat and waited and feared for the worst. He hoped that she was just pissed and had stayed away because she did not want to see him. He sat in their spot and listlessly worked on a suddenly tasteless sandwich which immediately changed to a rock in his stomach. He could deal with that, at least he hoped that he could, but what if he had got her into a real shit storm and she had been laid off? Good Christ almighty. What then? Not only would he be responsible, but he was living in a house two rooms down from her. He would be the old sailor with an albatross hung around his neck. Water, water everywhere. Walker threw the remainder of his sandwich in the trash and strode off to the library, hoping against hope that Zinny would be out front, smiling and smiling. Nothing to worry about. Just borrowing trouble, he told himself, but somehow could not get rid of a sense of impending disaster.

F1

Zinny sat on the bus, a white face in a sea of black, dark brown, light tan, latte, strong coffee, almost white faces, many married to their cell phones, heads bowed in concentration as if they were part of some huge congregation with a God who called to them alone. Brown eyes stared out of the windows, at the seat in front of them, at the person across from them, at some middle space unknown to anyone else who was not black, poor and American. Zinny had grown up in this hood, played with some of her fellow passengers, watched her father treat others for various injuries and treated a few on her own stick for the past few years, but she knew that she would forever be an outsider, one that was known and respected, even liked, but still, at the end of the day, an outsider.

She accepted her position as she had learned to accept many things in her life with a measure of understanding of the inevitability of certain states of being that were beyond her control. Much, she thought, as the people around her might feel. She guessed it was like waking up in the morning. Something that happens whether you want it to or not, though most people kinda like the idea, but you have no control over it short of suicide, and when it doesn't happen, well you've got no say about that either.

That thought brought on more of her father and she shook herself emotionally. Enough already. Getting much too hung up on everything. Going to think your way right into a depression and you can't afford to lie in bed for days not caring about anything. There's your job and Dad, and now Agile. Oh God. Poor Agile. She'd bitten his head off this morning over nothing. So she was late again. Everyone at work knew the reason. They gave her as much latitude as possible, but oh no she had to make a federal case out of it with a friend whom she'd only known a few weeks and who was helping her keep her head above water with his rent. Suppose he decides to leave? Christ, Zinny, you stupid idiot. How could you lose control like that?

It had been a confusing time, of course. Agile had moved in and so there was someone else in the house beside herself and her father for the first time since her mother had died. Suddenly, everything felt different. There was a strange shirt drying on the back porch railing. He would be in the kitchen drinking coffee and listening to WTIC talk radio when she came downstairs. Sometimes, she could hear folk music coming from his room. It was not an unpleasant feeling, she thought, but simply a different one that they would all get used to in time. She looked forward to seeing him coming up the steps each evening smiling that smile of his and always with something cheerful to say. That is if he didn't move out and leave her back on square one, Zinny reminded herself, and whose fault would that be? Huh? She sighed and tried to think of something positive as they bus rumbled across Albany Avenue on its way out from downtown.

A few days before she had left her room to take care of Dad. She had still been half asleep and forgot completely to tie her robe and there was Agile leaving his room with a huge towel wrapped around him obviously on his way to take his morning shower. Zinny smiled at the memory though she had been mortified at the time. She remembered the heat of her blush as she had yanked her robe closed and muttered an apology and then pushed into her father's room where he had greeted her with a resounding "Okay."

Zinny leaned back in her seat and that moment flashed again in Technicolor through her memory. He had stood there, surprised, momentarily immobile, staring at her staring at him. There was a sparse growth of hair on his chest and a ladder of it running down between his breasts, over his navel and into the towel. Sitting there reliving that moment, she felt her breasts stiffening and a definite feeling of moisture between her legs as her imagination worked at what lay under the towel. She came back to the present with a jerk that startled the woman sitting in the seat beside her.

Silly, old woman, she scolded herself. There you are standing there with your robe open and your sagging breasts and pink undies with hairs sticking out the edges. Christ, what he must have thought. The stuff of nightmares. Even without this morning, she'd be lucky if he ever spoke to her again. Have to fix this mess tonight if possible. She was glad he was staying with them and not just for the extra money. She thought about him at different times during the day. The strangest things brought it on. The back of someone sitting at one of the desks, sunlight on the plaza, staring at a stack of books in front of her, sitting on the john. She always looked forward to seeing him at lunch and everything seemed much worse when they missed each other. Can't really put a name to it. Friendship, she thought. Definitely not love. Been there; done that; got the scars to prove it including an ex who just won't go away. She decided that she wouldn't call it anything but just enjoy it. Putting a name to it would probably ruin it anyway. Just be glad he's at the house and isn't too mad about this morning or catching her walking around *au naturel*, so to speak. Not that she was a prude or anything. It's been a long time though. Still, it's not something you forget.

"Whatcha thinkin, honey? You looks like you done been through something bad."

Zinny came back to the present with a nervous twitch of her head. "What?" She looked to her left and there was a tiny, little black woman staring at her. The woman had white hair straightened and curled. She wore a purple dress that sagged on her bird-like frame, but it was her eyes that amazed Zinny. They were large and brown and looked up at her with a wide-eyed amazed look as if the woman had not spoken in years and suddenly realized that she could still do so. A pair of thick glasses magnified the effect to the point where Zinny had to work at keeping from laughing in the woman's face.

"You be thinkin' of a man. I can see it in your eyes."

Zinny tried to think of something to say in reply and came up with nothing. What reply could she make in the face of the simple truth? "Yes," she admitted and felt a tingling run through her body and raise goose pimples on her arms. She hadn't said that about anyone except her father for years. It was a little scary but it felt right and she smiled at her fellow passenger.

"Thought so. You were a million miles away. Ah knows 'cause ah still thinks on mine even now." And the woman laughed, a gentle, low-in-the-throat sound like small waves on a sandy beach.

Zinny nodded and looked away towards the front of the bus. Her stop would soon be approaching.

"You de doctor woman."

"No. I'm a librarian."

"You know what I mean. Lots of folks gone to your house and your dad took care of them whether they could pay or not. Heard you do the same."

"Not really. Just Band-Aids and aspirin and an ear for listening to people's troubles."

The old woman reached over and patted Zinny on her wrist. "You gotta good heart, y'hear? Trust it." And then she got up slowly and pulled the overhead cord for the stop signal.

Zinny sat at the kitchen table over a cup of tea that had long since gone cold. The tea bag was still in it and the tea was the color of copper and probably just as strong. She had put her father to bed and had waited until she heard his breathing even out in sleep. There was no sound in the kitchen. Crickets chirped in the backyard but there was nothing else. Agile had been and gone, leaving only some crumbs on the table and a dish and a glass drying on the rack next to the sink. No note. No nothing.

She had spent the entire bus ride home coming up with various ways that she would tell him that she was sorry, that she had simply lost it that morning and he had been perfectly right to refuse. She had played various scenarios in her imagination. He was still mad. He wasn't still mad but he was stern and unyielding. He accepted her apology and they put it behind him. The last, of course, was the most attractive, and Zinny had spent most of her ride imagining how they would make up. Maybe she could take him out to dinner. Someplace cheap but not tawdry. The idea pleased her and she had come home in a good mood. The anti climax had been rough. She was ready to apologize but with no one to whom to apologize. She got her father ready for bed and then wished him good night and had come down to the kitchen to sit in front of a cup of cold tea.

Zinny glanced out of the window over the sink. The long, summer day sighed and swayed back beyond the shadowed teeth of nearby homes with the still life of approaching night. She pushed her tea away with an expression of disgust. Where would Agile be now, she wondered? With a woman, perhaps? She felt somehow betrayed and the feeling both surprised and confused her. Why should she care what he did or with whom? He was just renting a room and solving a financial problem. That was all. She pulled her shirt more tightly around her waist as if to reassure herself that the status was most definitely quo and that was that. She was still feeling pleased with that resolution when there were a series of loud thumps on the front door.

Walker sat at the bar at Mikes trying to pretend that all was as it had been, that he still walked over from his little red house, and was just another regular, a local and part of the tribe, a known quantity acceptable to all. It felt all wrong but he sat there anyway sipping at a beer and staring at himself in the bar mirror while Mike stood at the end, a huge and immobile shadow in the light coming through the front windows.

"So what brings you here? I thought you moved away." Mike wiped an invisible spot on the bar and threw his bar towel back over one shoulder.

"Who the hell d'ya think you are, Emeril Lagasse?" piped Buddy from his station at the other end of the bar.

"He could aspire to worse," Walker remarked.

"Ha. Some sissified cook waltzing around going "BAM, BAM"?

"His food is good," Mike retorted mildly.

"Yeah? So you gotta throw your towel over your shoulder like you're making crepes or something?

"Easier than throwing you over my shoulder, but if you think you would value the experience." Mike swung around and started to glide up the bar towards Buddy.

"Hey, hey whoaaa, there cowboy. I was just kidding around, you know? Is that any way to treat a regular paying customer?" Buddy put on his most aggrieved affect.

"Haven't seen any money recently."

"Okay. So I'm a little behind. I got a job with a landscape crew. I'll bring some in on Friday."

Mike returned to his usual spot. Walker looked to his left at Buddy and grinned. "Didn't want to play hero, I guess."

"Not a chance," Buddy shot back. "It would interfere with my drinking," and he finished his beer and banged the mug down onto the bar.

"Not too many hero's around now," Walker said.

"That's our problem. We got no real heroes today. Okay, maybe in sports with guys like Peyton Manning and that golfer, whatshisname, Tiger, but that's for those who follow the sport, right? I mean there's lots of people in this country probably never heard of Manning, you know? All we got today is a bunch of politicians who would steal the clothes off your back if they got the chance. We need another Neil Armstrong or John Glenn."

"Glenn became a politician." Walker pointed out.

"Yeah, but he was a hero first."

"He certainly fired up the public's imagination," added Mike.

"You know, I think the hero quality is in each of us," Walker said. "I think becoming a hero is an ordinary man in an extraordinary situation who manages to overcome his own limitations." He grinned at Mike. "Of course it helps if you're tall and straight and look the part. I think I could be a hero only in some kind of science fiction comedy situation."

"I don't know any heroes," Mike offered and wiped at the bar with his towel. "At least no live ones."

Walker stared down into his beer and saw nothing but yellow. He felt a heaviness in his gut, a sadness unidentified and of unknown origin that had slipped into his emotional woodshed and the darkness there. He shouldn't be here and he knew it but when he got back to the house he had been unable to stay there and face Zinny. What if she had been laid off? It would be his fault. He had sat on his bed and tried to read but quickly gave up the effort. He couldn't concentrate on the story and found himself reading the same page over and over. What was he going to say to her? What could he say? Cursing, he had taken his car over to Mikes but that had not improved his mood or solved his problem.

"I'd settle for simply not being an idiot," he mumbled.

"Woman problem?" Mike raised one eyebrow.

"I just got my back up at the wrong time," Walker admitted. "So now I have to step up and admit it and I've been putting that off and that just makes it worse." He pushed himself to his feet. "Time to face the music."

"Luck," Mike told him.

Zinny walked down the hall to the door. Probably Agile forgot his key, she thought and that reminded her to tell him where she had hidden a spare. Strange that he hadn't come to the back door, though.

"Okay," her father's voice floated on the air above the staircase.

"Damn. Now he was awake. It would be hell getting him down again. She wished whoever was at the door would disappear without making any further noise. "Who is it?" she called out but no one answered.

Zinny slid back the deadbolt. The door was pushed violently inwards. She stumbled back and there was Mark standing in the doorway. "Get out," she hissed.

He stood there grinning at her and weaving slightly back and forth like some great dark cobra. "After all that we've shared together? I'm shocked." He burped. "Shocked," he repeated.

"You're drunk."

"Not at all. I've had a drink or two but I am not drunk. You're such a tight ass that you'd say that of anyone after a single drink."

"You stink of whiskey."

"So what Miss High-And-Mighty?" He leered at her leaning forwards to grab her. "You still the frigid bitch you used to be or are you ready for a man now?"

"You're disgusting. Anyway, there is no man here."

"Bitch." Mark's eyes, glazed with drink shriveled to pig's eyes in the light of the hallway. "I don't see a 'For Sale' sign out front." Mark jerked his hand, thumb outstretched, over his shoulder.

"I rented out a room. I'll give you that money but you agree to get lost again and this time stay that way. All nice and legal. I cannot sell this house now or anytime in the near future. This is a take-it-or-leave-it deal. Use your brain for one of the few times in your life and take the deal." She crossed her arms across her chest and glared at her ex-husband, hoping that this would resolve the problem.

Mark held out his hand, palm upwards. "It'll do for a down payment."

"Down payment? The hell you say." Zinny backed up and shook her fist at him in a total rage. "You get the rent and that's it. Otherwise I call the police and have you arrested for trespassing and then I get a lawyer and a restraining order." She thrust her hand into her pocket, pulled out a wad of bills and threw them on the floor in front of him.

"You know what you can do with your piece of paper, Zin."

"Yes I do. I'll have the police stick it up your ass. This is as far as it goes. I don't know what kind of trouble you've gotten yourself into." Zinny paused as something dark and vicious flashed across Mark's face and she knew she had hit home. "You were always one for wheeling and dealing, always thought you were smarter than the average bear. You saw yourself as some clone of Donald Trump and when it didn't work out, you always had someone else to blame and then there was me standing there like a dummy for you to take your failure out on. How 'bout that time we took a vacation up to Vermont and you got us lost? Did you admit it? Hell no. It was my fault for talking to you when you were trying to drive and then when I shut up, you got mad and accused me of not giving you directions. You shafted everyone and anyone that you ever came in contact with. Remember when you promised Paul Telow that you would help him shovel off the driveway at the apartment building? You showed up with a shovel, announced you had to take a phone call and disappeared for the rest of the day. Paul was angry and rightly so. Told me you could take a running jump if you ever needed his help. These are little things, Mark, but there are lots of them. So who'd you try and screw this time?"

Zinny stood back, hands on her hips, leaning towards Mark slightly, and screamed at the man who had curdled her youth, whose excesses had exposed the weakness of his core, that soft, smelly area filled with fear and hatred of that fear and of those who might see and understand it for what it was and laugh at him and say oh what a maggot is this guy. She may have, in that same horrible moment, sensed her own weaknesses as well, the need to shrink back in the face of conflict, to withdraw into her own sense of Zinny as a blameless victim unable to control people or events, swept along with the other flotsam towards some great delta with myriad hidden channels and sucking stinking swamps. She had always sensed this within her, the sudden urge to throw a blanket over her head, and her time with Mark had only increased this need to hide beneath a bed or in a closet hoping that the bad things would go away. Now she forced herself to stand there in the hallway staring down her ex as if a total stranger had forced his way in.

Mark bent and retrieved the money. "What I do is none of your dammed business." Mark straightened up and stepped forward, reaching out with one arm to grab her, his face contorted and eyes bulging with rage and frustration.

Now, truly scared by what she saw in Mark's face, Zinny tried to back up and tripped over the loose corner of the old carpet. Her arms flailing for balance, she went over backwards as the front door opened all the way behind Mark.

The beer tasted like piss, Walker thought as he drove carefully across Hartford towards the house. Don't know why but everything feels different since the house sold and he'd moved in with Zinny well not exactly with Zinny but in her house anyway, not that he'd mind moving in with her. She's great. Got a body to make the dead rise, well his anyway, but she seems further away now than she did when he didn't even know her name. Wonder if she felt the same? Hope not. Bad enough one of them did. Can't forget that moment in the hallway seeing her with her robe open. What wonderful breasts, large, heavy, sagging just a little, the kind you can get your hands around and feel the nipples harden beneath your fingers. He'd never forget the look on her face. Too bad he didn't have a camera. If there was a fly on the wall, he probably had a hard-on. Slow down, there, or he'd end up with one even after all the beer. Careful now. Don't get into an accident or they'd lift his license for sure. Just take it easy. Nothing to do at the house but go to the room, read a bit and then fall asleep. Not a bad idea. Walker was tired.

Tired, yes a little groggy foggy beer full and even sad, Walker drove slowly down the quickly emptying streets along Homestead and then across Albany and into the hood beyond where the street was suddenly less well lit and guarded by oaks and maple trees along shadowed sidewalks fronting two and three storied houses with front porches like dark eyes glaring out at the pieces of colored metal floating by.

He had made the turn into the driveway that ran alongside Zinny's house before he realized that something was not right. Walker brought his car to a stop and sat for a moment trying to pinpoint what was bothering him. The house next door was dark with no car in the driveway. Nothing unusual there. There was a car parked on the street in front of the house. That was it, Walker realized, as he glanced at the car in the street and then back to the house. The front door was open and dim light from inside the house shown on the front porch. Zinny must not have closed it tightly and it had swung open a little. Walker got out of his car and walked across the lawn and up the porch steps to close the door.

"Oh no." Zinny stared at the figure in the doorway behind Mark. It was Agile. In the mood Mark was in, he wouldn't stand a chance. She scrambled to her feet, reaching out to grab Mark as she did so.

"What's going on here?"

Mark whirled around. "None of your fucking business asshole, so get the hell outta here."

"Agile, please go. It's okay," Zinny shouted to him.

"Get away from her." Walker, plainly terrified, nevertheless stepped through the doorway towards Mark.

Who promptly buried his fist into Walker's belly all the way up to his forearm. Walker's eyes bulged as the breath whistled out of him. His glasses flew across the entryway landing on the floor. Walker clutched at his stomach and sank to the floor with a low moan where he doubled up into the fetal position trying to regain his breath.

"You bastard," Zinny screamed and hit Mark in his side with all her strength.

Mark grunted, turned, and delivered an open-handed slap with enough force to twist her head violently to one side. "Get this place sold or tonight will seem like a tea party," he snarled and stalked out of the door and into the night.

Zinny, one side of her face already reddening, knelt over Agile who was still gasping and trying to uncurl his body. From above them came the sound of her life echoing through her ears as the years came and went came and went and smooth to wrinkled and brown to gray. "Okay" She looked up the stairs and sighed. Her father sounded almost happy. "Okay," he repeated.

F1

Walker knew he was dying but he really had no time to regret his demise as the breath left his body and his body lost its strength and the world around him blurred for a moment and then his face hit something hard and he found himself on the floor struggling for even a tiny breath, just enough to survive somehow until he could come up with another one.

Someone above him shouted something. Someone screamed. One more breath, he thought. His midsection was a giant flame that was consuming him, devouring his will to live. Another breath, tiny but there, and then another. His legs were like water. He could hardly feel them let alone move them. Vaguely sensed someone pushing at him, light stabbing into his eyes creating pinwheels behind the closed lids.

"Agile, can you hear me?"

Yes he could but could not answer but only moan came out. Trying to straighten out. Taking another breath, a little bigger this time. Might live, he thought. Might be okay. "Gauuugh," he managed to gasp. He opened his eyes a little and found himself staring along the floor at the blurred edge of the front door. Still partly open, he saw. Even after this fight it's still fucking open.

"See if you can straighten out a bit. It will help." It was Zinny's voice coming from above and behind him. Walker moved his legs a little and the pain eased somewhat and he was breathing more easily. "Oh Agile I'm so sorry. This is awful. If I help, do you think you can sit up?" He saw her face as big as a full moon appear near his and then go away. Then he felt her arms around his shoulders pulling him up with a loud grunt and then he was sitting on the floor staring around for his glasses. "Here." Zinny handed him his glasses and the world quickly resolved itself. His stomach felt as he thought it would have felt had someone stabbed him.

"Let me get Dad settled down and then I'll be right back." She gave him an encouraging smile and then disappeared up the stairs while Walker sat on the floor trying to decide if he could attempt standing up. That's what I get, he moaned to himself. *Try to help and get knocked on my ass. What a fat failure I am. They were all right with their sneers and their jokes and whispers and knowing looks and studied avoidance and everything they knew I looked like well I did and God help me I never had a chance and now I'm sitting here holding my gut and Zinny is probably wondering if she can find another boarder. What a mess. Some big hero charging to the rescue of the damsel in distress. Shit.*

Walker pushed himself backwards to the banister on the staircase and used it to stand upright on legs that threatened to give out at any second. Above him, he could hear Zinny's soft voice as she talked to her father. He felt his stomach heave and staggered down the hall to the half bath off the kitchen where he half fell over the bowl and donated an evening's worth of beer and chips to the porcelain god. He retched until there was nothing left and was on his knees in front of the toilet feeling more dead than alive.

He heard Zinny coming down the stairs and suddenly realized that, in his haste to get to the toilet and avoid vomiting all over the floor, he had left the bathroom door open. Jesus Christ, he swore. Walker could not think of a more humiliating position in which to be found.

"Agile where are you?"

Walker tried to push himself to his feet and had almost managed it when Zinny appeared in the doorway. "How are you doing?"

"I've been better." Walker tried on a small, rueful smile but was certain that it had failed. Actually, he was feeling a little better now that his stomach was empty and his lungs were working normally again.

"I'm going to call the police. He has gone too far this time." Zinny's expression would have frozen a snowman. She went into the kitchen and Walker heard the handset of the phone being lifted from its hook.

A minute of two later, the doorbell rang. "Wow," Walker muttered. "That was fast." He moved slowly towards the door as Zinny came out of the kitchen behind him.

The man at the door was dressed in dark pants, a gray jacket and nondescript tie. He was broad of body and of face with gray eyes under heavy black eyebrows. He flashed a wallet containing something silver. "Good evening, sir. I'm detective Erskins. You called in a report of domestic violence?"

Erskins stood in the little entryway and looked around him and then down at the floor where the rug was still balled into an untidy bundle by the staircase. He seemed somewhat surprised by his surroundings as if he rarely if ever entered someone else's home and wasn't quite sure how to react. He pulled a pen and a note pad from his jacket pocket and proceeded to get the details of Mark's attack. He seemed particularly interested in the amount of money that Zinny had used to try and buy off her ex-husband. Walker did not understand what that had to do with the attack but he stood by as Zinny and the detective talked. His stomach ached dully where Mark had hit him, and he was still feeling slightly nauseous. He wished the detective would finish up and leave. Walker wanted nothing more than to toddle upstairs and flop onto his bed. Finally, Erskins put his little pad away and turned to the door.

"What a night," Walker sighed as the door closed on the detective.

"Amen to that," replied Zinny and stooped to straighten out the carpet. "One thing is for sure and that is that I am going to make sure this carpet doesn't move anymore."

Walker was starting towards the stairs when the doorbell rang.

Zinny opened the door and then turned to Walker with a baffled expression on her face. "The police are here."

"There is nobody by that name on the Hartford force." Detective Sergeant Marvin Berliner looked as if life was slowly consuming him from the inside out. Tall, thin with a face etched in vertical lines and eyes recessed behind rings of puffy, discolored flesh, he looked as if he hadn't slept in a week. He had, however, a low reassuring voice and Zinny felt that she was standing on firmer ground now that he was standing in her entryway holding a notebook and looking around the inside of the house. "Can you describe this man to me. He may have been working with your ex-husband." Berliner jotted notes as Zinny described Erskins to him. "Maybe you could come in and work with the sketch artist," he finished and then moved on. "So you opened the door and found your ex husband standing here, is that correct?"

"Right. He was drunk and wanted money. I gave him what cash I had. We argued. I stepped back, tripped over the rug and fell down."

Berliner's expression implied that he had been through this same conversation a thousand times which he undoubtedly had. "And that's when Mr. Walker showed up?" He looked at Walker expectantly as if cueing a small boy for his part in the school play.

"Yes. I was coming home. I turned into the drive and saw that the front door was open a little so I went to close it."

"How did you see that it was open?"

Walker thought of mentioning his eyes but thought better of it. He had already been in one fight tonight and didn't need to get into another with the authorities. "Light from hallway was shining through the crack onto the porch."

Berliner nodded, his eyes lidded as if he was fighting to stay awake. "Coming home from where?" he asked.

"What difference does it make?" Walker felt his stomach begin to knot up again. "I was with friends."

"Sergeant, Mr. Walker was the victim of Mark's assault. He came through the door, saw Mark standing over me, assumed the worst and tried to help."

"Yes, ma'm. You said that. I'm just trying to get the facts surrounding the assault. That's all."

Walker felt a little foolish. Berliner was there trying to help. "No problem, sergeant. I was at Mikes, a bar at the corner or Boulevard and Caliban. Mike can confirm that." He smiled at Berliner while hoping that Zinny wouldn't be upset that he had been at a bar. Maybe she was sensitive about things like that. It was a little embarrassing.

"Any idea where your ex is staying? Any known friends in the area?"

"I really don't know. We've been divorced for about thirty years. I didn't even know he was in the area until he showed up at my workplace. How long he has been in Hartford and who he might know here I couldn't say. If he's staying with a friend it must be his only one. He was apparently almost broke until tonight at least." Zinny turned to Walker and said "I gave him the rent money thinking he would take it and go away."

Walker nodded his head in understanding. Good idea with a bad result. He wished he were up in his room lying on his bed with a shot of Jack in his hand and none of this had happened. It was like falling down the rabbit hole and finding himself as one of the characters in the book he was writing. Surreal. He definitely needed to do a major re-write. He stood beside Zinny as she talked with the detective and felt the warmth of her arm as it brushed against his and decided to hell with the Jack. What he needed was to be lying in bed with Zinny, not that he thought he would be able to do anything. He felt weak and exhaustion lay upon him like a blanket but just being next to her made him feel better, more able to cope. It had been a night from Hell and he was glad it was almost over.

"Okay, Ms. Jones." Berliner closed his notebook and looked at her. "I'll write up a report and you'll get a copy. With that, there should be no problem obtaining a restraining order. We will be on the watch for this guy in the area around here and run an extra patrol or two over next few days. That's about what our budget will allow, but I'll give you my card and you call if you see him again." He smiled faintly, really just a twitch of the corners of his mouth. "You've got a lot of support in this neighborhood I hear so you may find him before we do. Call anytime." Berliner turned and went through the door where his partner was standing and Walker and Zinny were left alone in the entryway.

And finally it was and he stood naked in his room rubbing his gut and looking at himself in the mirror over his dresser. He was definitely going to have a juicy black-and-blue mark there. Now that there was nothing in it, he was beginning to feel hungry again. Tough, he told himself. If you hadn't been such a fat ass in the first place, you might have stood up to Mark. Gotta stop thinking about food all the time. Lots of other things in life. Like sleep. Mumbling to himself, Walker got into bed and lay there willing sleep to come but it seemed that his mind was not about to call it a day.

It continued to be filled with the picture of Mark turning and coming at him. The man's eyes had been like chunks of coal with tiny, white dots painted on them and his fist as it came towards him had seemed to move in slow motion with an unstoppable and unspeakable majesty. It moved at him and he could do nothing to stop it. Onwards it came and a piece of him was destroyed as it did so.

F1

Morning light brought Walker back from the unknown, butterflying his eyelids and tap dancing lightly on the sheet that covered him. Momentarily, he thought he was in the old, red house and had even started to turn towards Beth's side of the bed before he realized his mistake. With a sigh, he relaxed back into his pillow before trying to swing his legs over the side and stand up. He groaned as the pain from the newly stiffened abdominal muscles went through him.

God Almighty dammed, last night, yes sir and you got yourself sucker punched but good didn't you oh and now you can't even get out of bed no but you'd better figure out a way 'cause you've got work in an hour and they won't want to hear that you're calling out 'cause someone hit you in the stomach. Wassa matta, honey? You feeling too sore? Maybe we should get someone else. What 'chu think? Oh and that someone would be entry level and much less expensive than yours truly and Walker would be truly fucked and plucked. Okay, let's try getting off this bed for starters. Use your arms and push oh Christ that hurts come on pushohjesuspush. Okay. He was on his feet. Score one for the home team. The very stuff of life. Triathlete of the year. Shit. Felt like someone hit him in the belly with a sledge hammer. He hoped Zinny was not around. Couldn't face her after last night. He should find another room, or better yet an apartment, and just turn into that quiet little fat man who lives up the stairs. The least peculiar man. Send Zinny a note and then quietly turn to dust somewhere else. Zinny will forget all about me. Tough having an ex like that, though. Christ, what she must have gone through when they were married and Walker thought he had it tough. Wonder what his problem is? Maybe something like the wife beater whose wife just takes it and takes it. Zinny didn't, though, and good for her. Best rid of that trash. No fair. Walker could'a hit Mark back if he'd known. Guess that's the name of the game. Defense is taking care of yourself when you don't expect to have to do that. Wonder what's in the fridge? Need food. Need coffee. Need all kinds of things but mostly he needed to stop standing here, get to the bathroom and pee like a fucking horse.

A few minutes later, showered, shaved, scented up, wet hair combed down, hands pink, chinos pressed, yellow shirt neatly tucked in, fingernails clipped, toenails on the to-do list, stomach empty, abdominal muscles sullen, Walker went slowly down the stairs and into the kitchen. Zinny was there, modestly attired in an ankle length chocolate brown skirt with white flowers printed around the hem. She was bent over with part of her head in the refrigerator. "Good morning," he greeted her with a cheerfulness he did not feel. "How are you this fine morning?"

Zinny, startled, came up suddenly and cracked her head against the bottom of the freezer door above the cavity of the refrigerator. "Oh damn." She whirled around while rubbing her head and saw him standing in the kitchen doorway. "Oh hi. You startled me. How are you feeling?"

Walker looked behind her at the refrigerator. A big bowl of cereal with cold half-and-half would be wonderful and maybe a cup of coffee to go with it if there was time, though he could get some at work if push came to shove though coffee from the pot here would definitely be better. He turned his attention back to Zinny and found her looking at him sympathetically. Christ, that was the last thing he needed. "Gotta go," he mumbled and headed towards the back door.

"Hey, wait a second."

"Can't. Running late," he told her with down head, down eyes.

"Like hell," Zinny snapped. "You're early if anything. How's the stomach feeling?"

"Okay." Walker rubbed his paunch and tried on a rueful smile that felt awful and must have looked like the grimace on a death mask. "Hurts a little. Sorry about last night."

"What?" Zinny looked at him in amazement. "You're sorry?" She pulled a battered wooden chair away from the kitchen table. "Sit down," she commanded and then in a softer tone. "Please, Agile." Zinny went to the other side of the table and sat down with a sigh.

Walker debated for a moment. He did not want to hear a critique of his performance of the previous evening, but common courtesy dictated he at least listen. He decided that he would not be churlish and sat down in the chair. He stared down at his belly where it bulged over his belt. He really needed to get serious about losing weight, he thought. It was becoming ridiculous and he was so tired of listening to the doctor lecture him that he had stopped going to the doctor. Okay, so that didn't make a lot of sense but that was how it was. He thought again of that big bowl of cereal and decided to make it a small bowl with no sugar. The resolution made him feel more cheerful until he remembered that Zinny was sitting across from him.

"Agile, I have no idea why you are apologizing for last night. You were the victim, remember? You walked in on a really nasty scene and got hurt. I'm the one who should be apologizing and I certainly do. I wish last night had never happened." Zinny leaned forwards towards Walker as her body was weighed down by the sincerity of her words.

"Me too," Walker admitted. "I tried to help out and just ended up making things worse. I saw him standing there and looking down at you and I didn't even think but just reacted and if I'd stopped for even a second, I could have called the police or run to the neighbors or done something useful instead of getting myself floored," he finished miserably.

"Nonsense," Zinny retorted more sharply than she meant to. "If you hadn't shown up, he would have beaten on me. He's done it before. He gets off on it, "she added bitterly.

Walker stared at her, slightly embarrassed by her admission but curious at the same time. Why had she married this man who was so obviously psychotic? Maybe he hadn't been then or hadn't seemed to be anyway. Had he been gentle and kind at some point, a wolf in sheep's clothing as the saying goes and preying on a much younger Zinny? It was hard to believe anyone could be fooled so badly yet she had married him for better or worse and then found out how much worse "worse" could get and run and run fast. She had that much sense at least. "So what did he want?" Walker ventured and then wished he hadn't. It was none of his business, really.

"Money. What else?"

"Has he done this before? Come to you for money?"

"No he just appeared in front of my desk a couple of weeks ago." Zinny pushed herself to her feet and turned towards the coffee pot. "Coffee?"

"That sounds wonderful."

She poured coffee into a chipped, yellow enamel mug with FLOWER POWER written on it and handed it to Walker before sitting down again. Walker poured a stream of cream from a small, brown creamer and then, remembering his recent resolution, put in a small teaspoon of sugar. "How much does he want?" he asked.

Shrug, mouth twisting down into lines of flesh alongside her lips. "Whatever he can force out of me, I guess. He wants the house sold and half of what it sells for or so he says, but restraint was never part of his vocabulary and what he probably wants is the whole shooting match."

"What about your dad?"

"Mark never gave a tinker's damn about Dad. When he realized that the great doctor was not rich and making a lot of money like most of Dad's peers, Mark decided that my father had conned him and so whatever happened was Dad's fault."

"You're kidding, right?"

"Nope."

"Wow." Walker took an experimental sip of his coffee. UGH. Needs more sugar. He put the cup down and looked at his watch. He needed to move his fat ass or he'd miss the bus. "Gotta go. You okay?"

Zinny smiled. "Of course. Have a good morning. See you at lunch?"

Walker took an apple from the fridge and remembered that he had not made his lunch the night before as was his habit. Thanks, Mark, he thought, and checked to see if he had enough cash in his wallet to buy a sandwich. "Right, lunch it is," he told her.

Zinny watched him leave and then rinsed out the coffee cups and went back up the stairs to check on her father. As she hustled to make his bed and change his diaper, she wondered what in hell she thought she was doing?

I must be out of my cotton-picking mind, she told herself. Isn't life crazy enough right now without feeling lost when Agile's not around. He's just a friendly guy, easy to be with and someone close to my own age that happens to be around and available. This is just stupid. I must just be horny and want to touch one doesn't belong to my dad. It's been so long solongsolongsolong. Christ, I've got to stop this. Here I am mooning over my boarder while my ex is going psycho on me. Stupid, stupid. I had better wake up and face reality. I have enough trouble without chasing Agile even if he is friendly and attractive. Oh sure. Fine time to decide he's getting too close when the man is lying and breathing and whatever just two doors down from you. He is just a boarder. Nothing more. I better keep my distance or I'll just get into more trouble than I'm already in. Agile doesn't love me. He doesn't even know me and if he did it would probably be just a play to pay less rent or something like that. Men are like that. Takers rather than givers. Remember back when you were just a skinny plain-faced girl with braces that kept you from smiling and a brain that worked better than most?

Her mind set her apart and made her geeky and untouchable, rebellious and miserable and so she was shocked into immobile silence when Bradley jock-of-the-century and twice as good looking sat down next to her on the school bus instead of his usual spot next to Susie Billington, beautiful and vivacious and full of herself, she of the perfect hair and the perfect clothes and the perfect shoes. Zinny sat there in a trance of horror and anticipation. She could not even look at him. She thought she must be in a dream and stared out the window trying desperately to find something sophisticated to say, something that would make him see her as she was instead of as she looked.

"Hi. Mind if I sit next to you?"

And she almost fainted and got so excited that she jerked around and dropped her text books all over the floor; instead of being cool and beautiful, she was nothing but legs and arms as she bent over and scrambled for the books on the floor beneath the seat in front of her. She could feel her face burning with embarrassment. "Oops. Sorry. Sure. Sit there. It's okay." She risked a quick glance at the young god sitting beside her and saw he had picked up one of her books and was holding it out to her. "Thanks" She took the book feeling like a simpering idiot and he smiled at her with those blue eyes and curls. She felt herself being shredded into little pieces that promptly blew out the bus window.

"I saw the seat was open and thought I'd say hi, you know?"

Zinny had stared at him as if he had just materialized out of thin air. "Uh, sure." It was the best she could do.

"They call you Zinny. That's a pretty weird name."

"My real name's Azalea."

"Oh."

They sat in an uncomfortable silence. At least it was for her. She should have said Alice or Sue. Would he get up and find another seat now? She rearranged the books in her lap and waited for that to happen.

"Have you heard the latest Beatles album?"

"Oh yes. They are so cool. I have "Michelle" memorized, I think." She was suddenly so excited that her mouth went dry. This boy, who had, heretofore, never acknowledged her existence, was actually talking to her. Real words. She looked at him sitting there and bestowing his status upon her and almost choked. "So how come you're not sitting with Susie?" Not that she cared as long as he was sitting next to her but it was the only thing she could think to say and, somewhere deep inside, a cynical little voice kept yapping at her that this was not good. She ignored it. She would have recited Milton if she thought it would keep him talking at her with his big, blue eyes.

"She's okay." Bradley shrugged.

Like she's okay but they had a fight? Like she's okay but, there's only dust bunnies between her ears? Like she's okay but she's the jealous type? Zinny was filled with questions she dared not ask for fear of suddenly watching that wonderful butt moving down the aisle towards Suzie who had turned around seemingly to talk with Rebecca Hickman sitting behind her but Zinny knew better. You bet she did.

"Hey, did you understand what old Coleman was talking about in math today?"

"Sure. It wasn't too hard." Mr. Coleman taught tenth grade algebra with a style and manner guaranteed to put the football cheerleaders to sleep. He wore wrinkled chinos and even more wrinkled white shirts and a tie that always seemed to have at least one spot on it. His black hair was graying and stuck out at odd angles around his ears. He spoke in a low monotone and his whole manner was one of bemused boredom. If she had not had an aptitude for numbers, she surely would have had a hard time learning the equations he explained as he scrawled them across the black board in his crabbed handwriting.

"Yeah." Bradley nodded his head and looked at her through the corner of his eye. "Ready for that test next Friday?"

"I guess so." She could already guess what the questions would be and had the answers for them. "Why?"

"I dunno," Bradley replied with studied indifference. "I figured maybe we could study together, you know? We live pretty close together so we could probably get together with no effort, you know?"

She knew then that he was not sitting next to her for her nonexistent beauty or for her outgoing personality, not for her smile or her *bon mots* but for the ameliorative effect she could have on his algebra grade, and although looking back on it she felt cheated and used, at the time she was more than happy to with the deal. Maybe she wasn't a Suzie, but God had given her a different weapon and she intended to use it. "Sure. That sounds great." She rode the rest of the way in silence, sitting on the bus but already imagining Bradley and her studying together. In her mind they would sit together over the textbook. He would understand the logic and smile at her in silent thanks. She would smile back and shrug it off as no big deal. Then maybe they would take a walk to clear their heads. Bradley would see the special inside part of her and respect and appreciate it and they would become close friends, maybe even boyfriend and girlfriend. Suzie would be in a fit of permanent rage. What a shame.

She showed up at his house in a glow. She was washed and brushed and dressed seven ways to Sunday. She had undoubtedly used up all the hot water in her house. Her hair was combed back in the casual pony-tail look that the other girls used. Her mother had helped her with just the faintest trace of makeup so that whatever she had in the looks department was enhanced rather than caked. She wore a new pink blouse and freshly washed and pressed yellow slacks. She felt beautiful and radiant and very nervous. Clutching her math text, she went up the concrete walk to his house and suddenly the door opened and there he was.

"Hi, Zinny" He smiled and pushed his hands into the pockets of his faded jeans.

"Hi, Brad." She smiled up at the young god perfect in his moment of nonchalant, hip slung, youthful arrogance, fear a word unknown from a territory not yet explored, sure of his life and the course he was steering through it. She felt secure in her own moment for such is innocence that fear is just a word and the loss of one is the discovery of the other but tragedy to come had not yet arrived as she went up the steps and Brad turned and followed her through the door into the house.

He started up a flight of stairs. "C'mon up. I've got everything set up in my room."

She followed him up the stairs and into a large corner room. Against one wall was his bed and on the opposite wall a large desk with his textbook and a pad of paper neatly arranged on top. An extra chair was just to the left of the wooden chair that he normally used. All the lights were on. The room was lit up and so bright that it almost hurt her eyes and she squinted a little as they entered. On the wall to her left opposite a window was a vented door, probably a closet. The window was large and sunny and looked out at a maple tree growing on that side of their yard.

"Nice room," she told him and put her textbook down on the desk.

Brad shrugged. "Yeah. It's okay." He sat down in the desk chair and she sat down beside him.

She was totally happy. She was working on something she liked and helping a boy whom, a few short days before, she had never imagined she would be sitting next to. Now she was actually sitting there talking with him and going over equations. There were a lot of girls at Hartford Public who would have given whatever they had to change places with her. For the first time in her life she felt special in her own right and not just because her parents told her that they thought she was. She watched him as he bent over his scratch paper, his forehead wrinkled in concentration, peach fuzz softening the outline of his upper lip. He would be shaving soon.

They sat there for what seemed like a few minutes but was actually about half an hour. He was intelligent and obviously wanted to do well on the next test but he had problems understanding the logic. They went over the equations and answers several times while she tried to come up with an explanation that would cause him to suddenly open his eyes wide in understanding. Instead, he just grew frustrated. Finally, he put down his pencil and stretched his arms above his head. "How 'bout we take a break?"

"Okay."

He smiled and relaxed his arms. One of them came down around her shoulders. She did nothing to remove it. Truth be told, she was probably feeling as if she had been selected to be his steady, or at least his steady tutor. She was not totally naïve even back then. They sat there at the desk for a minute. She couldn't say what was going through his mind, though in retrospect it was nothing good. She felt comfortable as if his arm was an affirmation of a friendship that she had never expected and, now that it had come to be, did not want to end.

Suddenly, his arm tightened and his lips were smashing down onto hers. She was so surprised that she did not react immediately. He was trying to force her lips open with his tongue and his hands were pulling at her new blouse. She panicked and struggled to push him away. "Wait. Stop it, Brad." Something flashed.

"C'mon, Zinny. Relax," he panted and tried to hug her to him again.

She pushed back as hard as she could, somehow breaking away from him at the same time that his chair went over and he was spilled onto the floor on his back. She stood up. Her blouse was torn and open in the front revealing the white cup of her bra. "Bastard," she screamed clutching her blouse and grabbing her book from the desk. "I hope you fail." She turned and ran blindly out of the room and down the stairs.

It was not until a week later that she learned the true extent of Brad's viciousness. April Conway came up to her in the hall and, pulling Zinny to one side, half whispered in her ear. "My God, Zinny. What were you doing?"

"What? What are you talking about?"

"It's like all over the school. Brad's going around with a big grin on his face and saying that he made you and showing a picture of you two kissing and your shirt half off. Jenny heard some of the jocks laughing and joking about some sort of contest."

Zinny sighed and pushed away that ugly period of her life down past the electric bill and the water bill and the tax bill and the health insurance bill and groceries and bus pass and Rosa and down past the thousands of mornings she had gotten out of a queen-sized bed with a dent only on one side of the mattress and the ceaseless if loving okay, okay, okay, okay what okay and past the vacation days spent sitting on the porch watching the street grow older waving at neighbors and waving at herself and her life while she tried not to think about the time when her father would pass and she would be sitting on her life alone. The front door opened and she heard Rosa's cheery 'Good Morning.' When it came to men, she had not chosen well and Mr. Walker was yet another example of that. Good thing there's yet time to back off, she thought. She would eat her lunch inside, today, and not risk seeing Agile in the courtyard. Somehow the idea did not please her but she reminded herself about the relationship between pain and gain. Determined to make the right decision this time, she went down the stairs to get ready for work. Men were a pain and, like poison ivy, best avoided.

E2

Walker stepped towards the church and then stopped and waited for Jennifer to get out of the passenger side and join him. He looked up at the towering pile of brownstone and glass that rose before him, solid, impenetrable, immune to the feelings of the humans who had built it, died, and left it for the following generations. They built it long after the original European churches and cathedrals went up stone by stone on wooden scaffolds with simple hoists and wooden pulleys to help them. Those were done for the glory of God and as testimony to the power of the king and his kingdom. What stood before him now was testimony to the wealth of the parishioners and their desire to have something massive to stand for their wealth and faith. He and Jennifer walked up the steps towards the large double doors that were now open to receive the stream of people dressed in black and blue clotting into small groups before finally entering the church.

Walker kept his head down and his thoughts to himself. *Low in the valley go I go I and treading the path of ancient rhyme and holding the weight of the passage of time go I go I to the end of days where dust blows over the floor of the church and prayers are all that's left to do, prayers for her passage to Heaven and may God smile down upon us. Stone and moan, stair and prayer to forgive from life saying sinner but really meaning human from he-who-hates-bacon now bless you my child; forgiveness, forgiveness but they never forgave and now molder in the fecund earth. I know her gimlet gaze and slash of lip remain and somewhere in the ether I hear her "Sit up straight, John, you pathetic excuse for a Walker. God is watching you and so am I so SIT UP." How I hated Sunday mornings spending time in between each of them. I kept hoping I would wake up with some horrible but quickly curable disease that would preclude my scrubbing and brushing and dressing in a suit and sitting like the Sphinx in a pew constructed as a device for the torture of murderers and rapists. I always had sit to my mother's left and as far from my father as possible and with any little movement not associated with a religious motion she would elbow me into stone-like attention. I sat like a soldier on parade. I would look forward at the people sitting ahead of us. There was someone with a canary yellow hat. There was Mrs. Farmer in her red one and Mr. Farmer with his shiny, black toupee. There was old Beedle, the choirmaster and the pastor in his robes. I felt like a marionette jerking up and down from prayers to hymns and back down again as the words of peace and trial rolled above me barely disturbing the somnolence of the assembled sinners.*

"Whatch'a thinking, Pops?"

Walker came out of his reverie and found Jennifer standing beside him popping gum and looking around as if she were at a country fair. "Remembering church back when I was a kid. It fed upon itself and it fed upon me."

Jennifer laughed. "Sure looks hungry now, Dad. Just swallowing a ton of people." She nodded at people still coming down the sidewalk towards the church. "Grandma knew a lot of people, I guess."

"Yes she did," he agreed. His mother had known many people or rather many people had known her for the act of knowing implies some sort of effort and Walker could not remember his mother ever making such an effort. She looked as good as she could by doing as little as possible for as long as possible and for as few people as possible. Standing there with his daughter, Walker's mind was suddenly filled with one of the strongest memories from his childhood. He saw his mother sitting on a white, wicker lawn chair under a huge umbrella with green and white triangles. She was dressed to the hilt in a yellow and white patterned ankle length dress and wearing a wide-brimmed Easter bonnet. She sat like a statue staring out into the middle distance while, behind her, a tiny Scots gardener worked his way along the flower bed.

He shook his head as the memory faded. His mother was a woman of erect bearing, imposing visage and one thousand poses. Children have a hard time visualizing their parents engaged in the sexual act. Walker found it impossible to imagine his mother engaged in sweaty, tongue-sucking, body licking bouts of good old fashioned fucking. He had never seen his mother sweat. Mother Nature knew better than to try. It was much easier to imagine her lying stiffly in bed next to his father like a corpse set out for a funeral. Walker turned towards the church filled with a vast feeling of desolate emptiness.

"Well? Are we supposed to, like, stand here all fucking morning?"

"Watch your mouth."

"No." Jennifer pouted and it was not a pretty sight. "These rags are hot. Let's get this over with."

"Behave, Jen. It won't take long," Walker told her reasonably.

"So you say." She turned and marched off towards the church.

He watched her back. The people, the tower, the daughter still his, by God, for he had raised her and, though she rebelled, she was as bound to his existence as he was to hers as all humanity is mixed in a tin cup and sipped through summer lips.

It was not until later after the echoes had faded from the towering stone vaults and pew filled nave and the somber mass had left the church, slowly made their way to the gravesite and then off to the reception that Walker had a moment to himself. It was not until he had thanked the preacher and stood solemnly by as people ate cake and tea sandwiches and drank gallons of punch, and murmured their stock phrases of sympathy for the passing of the old bat. It was not until he had dropped off Jennifer and had gone to Mikes and somehow driven back to Zinny's without killing himself or someone else, clomped heavily up the stairs to his room and flopped onto his bed that he started to shake and found himself unable to stop.

He curled into a ball and clutched his knees but it did not stop. His body continued to vibrate like a plucked guitar string. The steeple over people towered within him, a red sweater, a child smiling, a pendulous breast with a few black hairs on it, a lake at sunset, its glassy surface reflecting the sky, pine needles, a big gray rock, naked children playing doctor, wood with green paint peeling from its surface, Beth crying, Jennifer screaming, a broken child's tractor, pictures of Beth hanging on the wall of his study, pieces of orange, the Cheerios Kid, a Wheaties champion, an enamel tiger, Tiger Woods, much of his first draft in the trash, pieces of paper lying around like patches of snow, people crossing the intersection of 42nd street and Broadway, grey writhing masses moving in opposite directions, an umbrella turned inside out in the wind, Jennifer's first tooth and a visit from a fat tooth fairy, Zinny in the hall with her robe open, her father staring out the window, Beth lying on the bathroom floor clutching herself in agony all spun in a flash of neurons as Walker lay twisted and vibrating within the coil of his life.

He did not know why his mother's death should effect him so for he they had spend so many years apart and he had so many bad memories of her that he supposed he should have been able to jump up and do a jig for joy. This reaction was a part of himself that he had not known existed, a quiet, sorrowful part that had sat in silence all these years and now would not be stilled, would have the world know that maybe it had not been all bad, that there had been times when she had made him smile, or made him happy, times that he had thrust behind him as you would push a piece of scrap paper into a wastepaper basket. He stared from the bed across to the desk where a brand new, Ticonderoga No 2 sharpened and unused glinted in the light from the lamp; virgin lead should join with virgin paper. It mocked him for all that he had done and left undone and it spoke to him of a dream that Walker knew he should get on paper but would not, and, even if he did, he was sure it would seem like a sheet with cum stains the morning after speckled and stiff like his marriage if he cared to admit it in the presence of spirits who shouted "Fool, fool" at him even before it was proven. He sensed but ignored such thoughts for then he would be admitting his own inconsequence, and, he knew, consequence was an important part of man and Ticonderogas and the bread crumb trail behind as one walked along whistling bravely and hoping for the best and he would leave his prints, mark his spot, maybe, no, certainly for though she wasn't but still his by right of sacrifice and tears and giving and the getting of pain when those cherubic lips turned down and the big eyes turned empty, icy, lost within her own darkness. Disowning she would have, could have had she known and maybe, somehow, she did; easy to lay it all on blood and walk away dusting off the hands dust to dust but we are more than that surely more than predestination and the source of life. Yes, he had stuck his finger in the bottle right enough and it had not come out for skin or nought.

And then he was falling down and looking saw rocks with jagged teeth and gaping mouths waiting below him and he knew the terror that turns the bowels to water and could only scream.

"Agile. Agile"

Someone was pounding on him. The rocks, the rocks were . . . He felt cold and judged himself to be still alive and from above him someone was pounding on a drum and throwing spikes through his head as they did so.

"Agile, are you all right?"

Walker opened his eyes. He was on his bed in his room. The sheet and blanket were tangled around him so that movement was difficult. He recognized the familiar shapes of his desk and bureau, the chair with his mourning suit draped carelessly across its back, a different person, somewhat strange and formal, uncomfortable at best, who had somehow snuck into his room and then vanished leaving behind the black pants and jacket. Zinny, he realized. It was Zinny knocking on his door. "Yes? Yes, okay, I'm okay, thanks" he managed to say. His throat felt as if it was full of dust. He was not at all sure that his statement was true but anything to stop her from knocking at his door.

"I'm sorry." Her voice floated above and beyond the door, disembodied and unreal, a fallen angel wandering. "I didn't know if you were supposed to work, today. It's almost eight."

"It's okay. Give me a minute." He struggled vaguely with his sheet and finally made it to his feet and made a grab for his clothes. The left pant leg had some kind of stain on it but he drew it on anyway and followed that minor accomplishment with the shirt, cursing softly as he worked with the buttons. He opened his door and there was Zinny looking at him, eyes sad, and lips drawn down towards her chin. "Sorry to disturb you," she said and turned to go.

"Wait." Walker blinked, trying to clear the fog that was still rising from the marsh of his senses. "I'm the one who should be sorry." He felt that he was standing on the edge of a chasm needing to be totally sober and alert and was neither. Adrenaline came to the rescue. "I look like a wreck, I know." He tugged at his shirt that was bunched up under his left arm exposing a soft, white piece of belly. "I have today off. Gotta go talk with the lawyer so I'm glad you knocked. Really." He tried a smile and hoped for the best. At least she had turned back towards him. Not still walking down the hall towards her room. "I haven't seen much of you recently, how 'bout you? You okay?"

Zinny smiled in turn. How like this man to think of her in the middle of his own personal crisis. "I'm fine, really. Just busy, I guess." Remembering her resolve, she turned away again.

"I haven't seen you in the plaza during lunch. It's not something I've done, is it?" Walker persisted, stepping into the hallway as he did so.

"Okay," came the voice of her father from the adjoining room.

"Well I've been a bit busy. Working through lunch. Really crazy."

Walker nodded in understanding. "I've been down that road. Just as long as you're okay and not mad at me for something. The last few days, I don't know. I just got the feeling that you were kinda distant, you know? Like maybe I had a bad case of body odor or something. I don't know.

It was just a feeling and maybe I'm way out in left field." He halted, out of words, feelings banging up against a fervent desire not to make worse whatever might be wrong if anything but he couldn't risk pretending that everything was okay-dokey serendipitous. He sensed the distance in her, the act of avoidance as obvious to him as if he had invented and planned it himself and perhaps he had, in a sense, for he had often seen the same darkening mood within his wife and had known it in himself. We are social animals with a strong herd instinct, but the fear of rejection is an emotional storm that is always within us and tends to blow up into thunder and rain just when we feel the most secure. It is part of the obdurate stubbornness of the human spirit.

"Why should I be pissed?" asked Zinny wondering how he could have sensed her fear. She had been acting totally normally, she thought. Nothing unusual in act or manner. Work had been upon her, and she had buried herself in its folds with maybe only the slightest feeling of guilt at the thought of the empty bench in the plaza and her friend and boarder sitting there munching on his sandwich.

Walker shrugged. "Okay," he ventured.

"Okay," came the echo from her father's room. The two friends, not quite strangers, almost lovers looked at each other for a moment in complete silence and then burst simultaneously into gales of laughter.

"Okay," gasped Zinny as she bent over trying to catch her breath only to collapse again in a hooting cawing spasm of pent up relief from fear and self loathing that left her barely standing looking up at Walker.

Walker had fallen back to lean against the wall next to his door. He swiped his arm across his face to catch the tears of merriment. "Oh my," he managed. "That was just perfect. You have today off as well?"

"Yes." She muffled a last chuckle and then tried to look serious. "I thought the funeral was very nice," she told him as she turned into her father's room. "Very dignified."

"You were at the service?" gaped Walker, completely dumbfounded by the revelation.

"Yes. Left work for an hour or so and went."

"Why?" he asked her back as she bent over her father and thrust a hand expertly into his pants to see if he needed a change. He found it hard to understand how someone who had not even known his mother would take time off from work to go to her funeral. It was like a nun attending the funeral of a murderer and she had not come to the reception so had not wanted to sign the book or see him or be seen by him. Perhaps she had a time crunch and had to get back to her job, but he thought it strange, nonetheless, a nice gesture but definitely strange. In Walker's world, random acts of thoughtfulness had not occurred very often.

"Just curious, I guess." Zinny mumbled as she straightened up. "Saw the obit and decided to go. She must have been quite a woman."

"She was a bitch," replied Walker with some bitterness. "She and my father were much more interested in being rich and famous than being parents. I was simply living proof of American family values and parental fecundity. We had not spoken in years and at the end I barely knew her."

"What a shame." Zinny sounded truly regretful. "My parents were just the opposite. Dad was never interested in making money, just caring for those who did not have much or none at all."

Walker nodded as much to himself as Zinny and watched while she got her father arranged in his chair. "You'd think there'd be some kind of balance."

Zinny gave a little shrug of her shoulders. "Well, you know balance, like religion, is so subjective." Zinny turned towards him with her face smiling eyes soft. "I always thought Dad had it right, but Mom never did." She walked within his face, her eyes within his thoughts. "I'm sorry if I haven't been around. I guess I'm not used to having friends, especially male friends."

Walker wondered why Zinny had said that. She had not needed to. He was glad that it wasn't some action of his, some relation-busting gaffe that he had unintentionally committed, but she had opened up to him, if only in a very small way. He felt both flattered and slightly embarrassed that she had done this, as if she had suddenly pulled up her blouse and shown him a tattoo on one of her breasts. How should he respond? Just ignore it or maybe come back with a little bit of himself? Perhaps he should just tell a lie or a half truth, something that would not be misinterpreted or that would cause her to shy away again. He should say something quickly, though, or she might think him a fool or worse.

Beth had often thought him one, he knew, maybe always for he had seen it in her eyes even if she did not tell him directly, heard the implications in her speech when she was talking with friends or even strangers and thought he was out of hearing range. This had hurt the worst of all. Friends could always shrug and laugh it off, go on their way with their opinion of him unchanged and, in some perverse human

242

way, even strengthened as if in reaction to her verbal barbs and jabs, her conversation quickly forgotten but strangers would carry Beth's opinion like a contagious disease spreading it in ever wider circles and Walker would never know why he did not realize some goal for which he was striving because a stranger denied him or why someone he didn't even know treated him with a stiff rudeness born of self-righteousness and fear, for we all have the fool inside of us be we presidents or paupers and we know that it can come out and turn us into objects of ridicule in a moment. They would be as water bugs setting off ripples that join one another and breaking the glass of the pond's existence. Walker hated it when he thought his wife was doing this. It drove him inwards in a fuming silence and fed on itself and became harder and harder to break. Now, of course, he had to find a way.

"Uhh." What a comeback. Great sweet Jesus Christ on a crutch. Walker felt the first cold finger of panic in his gut.

Zinny walked past him and started down the stairs.

"Wait." Walker turned and started after her. "Zinny, wait up a sec."

She kept going. Walker followed. Why was he always talking to her back and, when he found himself face to face with her, could only make monkey noises. "How about dinner tonight? Can you get someone to be here with your father?" He stopped as she continued down the stairs, clop, clop, clop, clopityclopityclopity head up clop shoulders back clop clop and he counted the canyon echoes back and forth between his eyes and skull clop. The silence was killing him by smothering his senses. He wanted to scream, jump up and down, anything. "We could go early," he ventured. His tongue had become a foreign object that had been jammed into his mouth. Inchoate madness.

Zinny stopped but did not turn. Hope flared up and Walker continued down the stairs. "Sound good?" he asked her.

She turned and looked at him with the expression of a deer on the edge of a clearing, a rabbit in short grass, but there was more in her eyes, he thought, a cloudy, dull uncertain light in them that he could not fathom, understanding only that she was not going to stamp on his feet or slap his face. Her face changed in tiny ways as thoughts danced across it but Walker could not think of what it was that he thought she was thinking. Fuck it, he told himself.

"All right," Zinny said, smiled a little on the wistful side and went down to the first floor and then along the hall into the kitchen.

Zinny stared out the kitchen window and realized that she was doomed to repeat history. After resolving not to get involved, here she was going on a date with Agile. It made no sense. She did not know why she had accepted, only that, having done so, she felt better about things. Still, the fact that she would cave so easily bothered her and she could not help but remember her college days.

"C'mon, Zin. It'll be a blast."

"No."

"Then what?"

"I've just started a good book."

"Bullshit, girl."

"No shit."

"Get a life."

Suzi Compton was ragging on her again for the umpteenth time. Zinny was tired of the constant back and forth over her social life, of lack thereof. What was the big deal about dating anyways? Suzi and all the other girls in the dorm made a big fuss over it. They spent hours getting ready, choosing the right clothes, gossiping up and down the corridors about one man or another. Zinny found it all boring. Boys were boys. So they had different equipment. No big deal.

Suzi was a big girl, not fat, but broad with a pleasant face of broad lips and a slightly snubbed nose and big brown eyes that always seemed to dance from point to point, person to person as she talked incessantly about all the myriad events in her life both big and small as if they were balls on a shelf of an overstuffed closet just aching to fall down on the head of some unsuspecting soul. "You can't just spend all your time sitting at a desk buried in a book. It's not normal. It's crazy, in fact. All work and no play and all that jazz."

"I like books."

"I know, and you're scared to go on a double date with me."

"I am not."

"Eddie is cute and he says his friend is too. C'mon, Zinny. Have some fun for a change."

Remembering that moment, Zinny still had no idea what caused her to weaken. Perhaps it was Suzi's accusation that Zinny was scared to go on dates. Nobody likes to be thought a coward, especially when one is young and willing to challenge anything and anyone in their path. Perhaps it was her innate curiosity, the piece of her that was feline in focus and intensity and unable to pass something without knowing it. It could have been just plain cussedness or a combination of many emotions that had bubbled to the surface over time combined with the unusual heat of an early May day. "Okay," she said, and turned towards the closet for some clean clothes.

What a nightmare. Even now, decades later, the memory made her shiver. The double date had started smoothly enough with a dinner that cost more than Zinny had wanted to pay but was pleasant enough and she found herself relaxing a little and even enjoying the conversation. Eddie, Suzi's date, turned out to be a good looking college junior who paid attention to his date and had a store of funny stories that kept everything going. Fred was her date and he seemed to be even more shy and uncomfortable than Zinny. He was tall, and very thin, with tufts of dark blonde hair that stuck out at odd angles that gave him a half awake appearance. His eyes were enlarged behind coke bottle glasses. He would look at Zinny and smile and then look down at his plate and then back up and say something like "This is pretty good, huh?" and then at his plate again. He had a slight stutter which probably explained his lack of conversational ability. Zinny thought that Eddie had brought Fred as Suzi had convinced her to come. This did not bother her for she felt safe with Fred and did not mind when she tried to talk to him and his only response was to smile and nod his head.

It was on the way back to the campus that the evening went bad for Zinny. Eddie was driving since it was his car. Suzi sat beside him and Zinny and Fred were relegated to the back seat. Suddenly they turned off onto a dirt road. They thumped and bumped along a short distance and Zinny was about to ask what was happening and where were they going when they stopped. The road came to an abrupt end at the edge of a field. Just as abruptly, Suzi and Eddie had locked lips. Zinny watched in amazement as they swayed back and forth in the middle of the bench seat and then Suzi's head disappeared and Eddie's moved back against the driver side door.

An arm came around her neck and suddenly Fred's tongue was all over her face. It was as if he were licking an ice cream cone. One hand groped for her breasts and the other found her hand and jerked it down into his lap. "C'mon, Z Z Zinny. Just a k . . . k . . . kiss," He gasped and she found herself looking into his bulging eyes behind their thick lenses. It was like having a frog in her face.

"Get off." She struggled to break away from him but there was no space and he seemed to be everywhere. "Fred, dammit to hell." She yanked her hand back from his lap.

"Just a l . . . l . . . little bit, Zinny. Relax." He grabbed her hand and pushed it back down. She felt flesh, and, looking down, saw that he had somehow managed to get his penis out of his pants. It was sticking up through his fly, white with a big, blue vein along one side and trembling slightly. The mushroom head was large and had a purplish tinge to it . . . "C'mon. Hold it. Just a little. C . . . c . . . c'mon," he gasped, his eyes bulging behind their lenses, his face turning a bright red and his breathing coming in gasps.

From the front seat came the sound of a sigh from Suzi and a groan from Eddie. Fred tried to flatten himself against her pushing her back into the corner formed by the back seat and the rear door. Trying to push him back, her hand brushed against his cock and Fred stiffened as if he had been shot. "Oh God," he shouted and came all over her new skirt and his clothes and the back seat.

Zinny watched as the neighbor's grey and tan cat glided across the back yard on his way to explore some distant land. For having taken place so long ago, the memory was extremely vivid. She had come away from that night hating Suzi for dragging her into it, hated the thought that someday a man would lie on top of her heaving and puffing with bad breath and hair all over and sweat dripping down. UUUGH. She became again one with the little girl holding it in until she was certain no one was around before going to the bathroom, and then carefully covering the seat with toilet paper before sitting down and the same little girl who would run screaming to her mother when she spied a tiny house spider on the wall of her room. Zinny sighed and crossed her arms across her chest, pushing back such memories into whatever part of her sat in the darkness humming softly and grinning and waiting for the next time, almost salivating there in the dark where fear grows on trees.

So now she was doing it again, getting involved with a man, knowing that it would lead to nothing but fear and self loathing. It wasn't fair to Agile but she'd agreed and now it was done. Stupid idiot, Zinny seethed. Get through this evening somehow and then just leave it like that. Nice dinner. Thank you very much. Bye now. Agile was just horny. He didn't love her. He probably didn't even like her. She wished he had never caught her in the hallway with her robe open. Stupid, stupid to forget she was no longer the only sentient being in the house.

Well it was done and nothing to be gained from standing in the kitchen worrying about it all. It was nice of Agile to make the invitation. Maybe she should have kept walking but she hadn't and somehow it seemed all right. Maybe even she was looking forward to it. From deep within her, though, a screechy little voice reminded Zinny that the next man she had been with after Fred had been Mark.

Garage

Mark McGuigan had no generosity of spirit; he had no spirit at all. Perhaps he had been born with that lack. There are those who display emotional black holes from the time that they can walk. His mother had been, at best, a post against which his father thrashed out his failure in life and, when that had become insufficient, his son. Yet it cannot all be blamed on parental dysfunction though that comes first to mind. There are children that were born into to loving parents with the desire to teach right from wrong and watch them grow into solid citizens but who yet lack basic tenets of those moral signposts by which we survive as a society. Mark had been one who, upon being whipped by his father, had turned and kicked his dog, and, when the dog refused to come to him after that, put rat poison in the dog's food.

His was a world of real or believed insults, slights, affronts, rudeness and rejections. The streets he walked were the dusk of a winter storm, early and cold with rims of ice forming in the stinking scum filled potholes that he did know that he had created, did not recognize as part of his landscape and therefore must have been created by those who saw him through eyes of jealousy and contempt. Those who would forever be smaller beings stuck in their own mediocrity.

He heard the clackbang of the screen door and, a moment later, she appeared carrying a cardboard box and walked along the driveway to the garage. She looked so small and scrawny; the box was almost as big as she. He felt that he could be by her side in a second or two and break her into pieces without breaking into a sweat and the urge to do just that was strong within him.

Mark stood within the shadow of a car parked across the street from the house and watched as she went in the small door on the left side of the garage and disappeared. It was all so unfair, he thought. Those who didn't have a dammed clue had it all while those who knew the score had to bow and scrape and beg for fucking crumbs from the fucking table. It was as if someone had planted the bitch in front of him and then stood back and waited for him to snap at the bait. Her old man probably had a good laugh at him throughout it all. He had never liked Mark, and had done everything in his power to make Mark fail so that good ol' dad would be able to tell his frigid cunt of a daughter and that wet rag of a mother that he had warned them. What a joke. Always whining about how terrible he was and how bad her precious Azalea had it. Enough to make a saint puke, and it wasn't as though he wasn't good to them or their precious daughter. It was not his fault that his luck had run badly; plans made that should have yielded success had been thwarted by bad luck and those who conspired against him. Goddamned bosses are all the same. Work your ass off for peanuts and you get nothing but show up five minutes late and that's all she wrote. You're fired and don't come back. Christ, they don't even pay for the time you spend eating lunch but have a drink or two on your own time just to smooth things out and they're on your ass like butter on bread. Nobody had ever cut him a break but did that cunt and her self-righteous bastard of a father ever think about that? Fuck no. Over the side with him. So long, sucker. Don't take too long to sink, thank you very much.

The woman came back out of the garage and walked along the driveway towards the rear of the house, this time without the box. He looked up at the house itself. The middle window on the second floor was lit up and another window on the right hand side towards the rear. The old man and that fat prick of a renter, probably. Mark felt in his pocket for the wad of bills reassuring himself that it was still there. Chicken feed, he knew. She had to do better than that or he would find himself anchored to the bottom of Long Island Sound. Still, he would have to send the money off as a good faith payment that would keep him healthy for a little while longer.

It was simply the curse of the McGuigan luck. Like the song said if it weren't for bad luck he wouldn't have any luck at all. He should have been living the good life right now, set in a nice apartment with a good looking woman and a servant to cook and clean. He should have been a lot of things. Anchors Aweigh in the fourth at Belmont had been the closest thing to a sure thing that he had ever known. The gelding was a twenty-five to one shot only because a new jock was on her and the track was a little soft but a hard bump in the first turn had creamed her and she finished second to last and he, Mark Mcguigan, was hung out to dry but good. Who could've known the nag couldn't handle the rough stuff at the rail.

The light at the front of the house winked out. Mark noted the time, turned and walked down the street neither fast or slowly, just another person out for an evening stroll before retiring. Zinny had better come up with his share of the house or he would be retiring that senile old fuck of a father. He wondered what Lisa was doing at that moment. Then he wondered who she was doing it with. The thought nagged at him. He needed to get the money and get back to her before she got restless. Give her dad the money. Keep Lisa happy. Mark scowled as he got into his car. This time, everything had to work like it was supposed to. This time it would.

Not In Service

Light is around round and round by the window blasting in around me. Let the show begin in fragmented rays ahh Joseph who aren't in heaven yet remembering back when you played the violin at parties with your mother sitting so straight and proud and father in his evening clothes big mustache drooping down and all their friends smiling and clapping. All hail America land of the brave land of bureaucracy. Stay sick, woman. Do not wander off because your insurance has been denied by some duckbill reading cost figures in an office. All hail brave statue. Welcome the throng that then can beg and starve at your feet. We who are about to die should do so without fuss and not cause you undo expense. Ah liberty your torch burns low and lower still the expectations for, though made of foreign clay, yet now you would turn away those who aspire. Ah beauty, you shriveled old hag leaking self-righteous juices lapped by foreign minions and praised by wooden heads without memory or wisdom. Yes, and the girl I should know who she was or is or will be.

She came with tears on her cheeks and a black eye too ahh who did this to you? What happened? The face goes away again and then there is another face dark and scowling, with the eyes of a child denied and outraged that it should be so and now so sullen and unformed in a man's face. Ah the children all go out to play and we did too. There was Squinty and I can't remember who else but we had fun and sure we fought and wrestled and ran into each other and tried for the girls but there was never any malice. Malice towards none but there he is again the man with the boy's face looking like he never had fun, like he knew that the world was out to get him okay and paranoia in the heartland oh heart oh heart oh my heart is still beating but I don't know why cause all is just light or dim or not light like the boy-man's eyes no light there and it was then I knew okay yes there was trouble down below where the ants crawl in and the ants crawl out. Ha I remember that much but the woman I don't know, familiar though, I think but she . . . wait there were tears and bruises but

I knew yes okay and pain. When she was a little girl she used to come into the treatment room, start up at me with huge serious eyes as if she had accidentally spilled grape juice on her new pinafore and say 'Father, I really do think I deserve an ice cream.'

The light is fading. It is getting dark outside the window and street lights like giant fireflies are coming on showing the snaky grey street with dots of cars lots of dots and blue and red and tan across the street where the man is standing like a tiny, squatty little lump but that lump is familiar, yes it is. I feel I should know the man, the way he stands, the way he hunches over as if he were sneaking a peek at his shoes. I thought I knew him but now it's gone. Seemed familiar. I'll write it down, yes a piece of paper and what was that I was thinking what except that what oh well.

"Time for bed, Dad." A voice floats over my shoulder like a summer zephyr, cooling and beautiful. It is like an echo without body or source. The window has gone black now. That voice I know, or knew or . . .

There she is now in front and I see her face and her lips are smiling and her tired, sad eyes of the valley where the creek runs down under the willows and the bank collapses down to the deep pool and eyes of the sky when God pulls a coat of many colors across the sky and mist forms in the valleys and hides in the canyons. Her eyes are red and tucked behind pouches of discolored flesh. "Okay," I say.

And suddenly there is a young man in my mind running through vast, green spaces, running down from a porch towards the black, speckled lake that has little waves running north to south now after the front has passed over running down hair flying back and arms pumping and then of the end of the dock in a flat dive for it was still shallow there feeling the rocks on the bottom kiss his chest and then older playing doctor in the boathouse with cousins and yet later sneaking down to look at pictures of naked women working his hand up and down, feeling the pubic hair brush against his fingers up and down and up and out with visions of breasts standing taut in the shadows.

And now I am sitting on the pot, the woman standing off to one side and the urine sliding out of me and yes, yes the other too and then I feel her hands on me helping me rise and the feeling of paper on my butt feels good okay and then across the floor step step oh so careful for the light is full of tricks now and the bed is there in front of me with cool sheets yes okay and the pleasures of the harbor yes and a daughter running towards me laughing 'Daddy, Daddy, I fooled you.' Yes yes you did you certainly did and then the prize of a little plush kitten with brown fuzzy fir and little glass kitten eyes and thank you,. Daddy oh thank you okay yes.

And night covers all me all around me inside and outside and I lay in the night and I feel a part of it all that cannot be seen but felt yes I can still feel even though I do not know what well anyway yes okay there I am light and dark and darkly lighter on my little wooden sled going down down gliding down the snowy slope snow in my face laughing and laughing.

E2

Walker glanced at his watch and grimaced. The concrete wall on which he sat was unyielding and his ass was beginning to ache from sitting there. He had to be at the lawyer's office again to deal with his mother's estate in an hour but still he sat hoping that Zinny would show up and fearful that she would. It was maddening, he thought, that he could not simply shrug his shoulders and walk away from something that was not his business, not his responsibility and involving someone about whom he kept telling himself he didn't give a damn. It was absurd that he should sit here risking being late for an important appointment just because Zinny was off doing God Knows What and leaving him to get sores on his ass for her. He would have changed the ending of the night before if he knew how but the beginning flowed and glowed in memory

Started off so well too. He was so glad she had accepted that he'd gone back into his room and then hummed his way into his clothes feeling almost like a kid again. Double times down the stairs and went down to the kitchen for bacon and scrambled and English muffin. Thomas makes the best, no doubt. He'd made reservations at Max's Oyster Bar, he thought. Figured it would be good. Zinny always has some fish in the fridge. Told me once she liked sea bass. Good for the teeth, he thought. Lots of iron too. Big place, that Max's and loud but you don't really notice after a while. Boomy, though. Sounds like you're talking into a drum but really good food. He liked their scallops sizzling in butter and spices and then onto a plate and brought quickly to the table still bubbling. Just making reservations made him hungry. Later, with the mail came a letter from his boss expressing sympathy for his recent loss. Showed how much he knew about Walker. Well he'd had to take time off and explained why. Big deal. Zinny looked great in a green dress that showed off her figure. Standing there in the hall, she glowed and he swore she had a real aura about her though that could have been the lights in the living room; He was hungry as well. Standing above her on the stairs was like Christmas, yes, when he was little and the big hall was all green and sparkling with lights and candy canes and ornaments. She looked good enough to eat and maybe later oh do stop you horny asshole. He walked down the stairs to join her and the memory of her breasts peeking out of her robe almost brought him to a standstill flashing like a fire in his mind. Yeah, fat chance, asshole. What would she want with you? You who were never very smart, never very motivated, with just enough of both to make a living and that's about the extent of it. So now you live in a one room walk-up and dream of being a hero to the woman down the hall. What a crock.

Hi he said and she turned and smiled and he smiled back just like the white folks do and he gestured towards the back door. My chariot awaits he announced and she giggled with the sound like a gently C major riff on an old Steinway. They had one when he was growing up but no one ever played it. Dad just got it to show off, he guessed. Sometimes he would finger the beautiful ivory keys listening to the tones up and down te la la upanddown upandown black on the half tone falala and Zinny walked towards the door and he shadowed behind watching the sway of her hips and rear pushing up and down beneath the green of the dress lalalalala salad fixings with lettuce leaves moving up and down and cherry tomatoes jiggling and cucumber slices in the shadowy parts and pepper parts hiding beneath them. Upandownand up and drive to the restaurant. His parents used to go out to the Hartford Club and sometimes take him and he remembered walking up the hill from the parking lot staring at all the shiny cars. He liked Lincolns the best. They were big and low and totally cool and Zinny and he got to Max's and Zinny sat there across from him looking great and the menu lay on the table in front of him beckoning him onwards with the silent siren song of hunger and the golden promise of Jack Daniels sitting behind his eyes like an invitation from the White House. The whole evening seemed as if they were simply actors in a one act play:

ZINNY: [green dress with white lace collar modestly covering long unsought breasts. She looks at him and smiles obviously meaning it. *Yes he is a nice man isn't he?*] This is lovely [she looks around at people flowing past them and rapidly filling up the huge room] Have you been here before?

AGILE: [gray jacket over a maroon tie on a white shirt] Oh yes [with the air of one who owns part of the business. *of course it was the Panda Inn Chinese restaurant back then]* You look great. That dress becomes you [*and*

255

how. He leans forward slightly and sings softly to the tune of 'My Darling Clementine'.

> In the cavern
> Down at Max's
> Trying hard to order wine
> But the waiter just ignores me
> Walks right by me every time

ZINNY: [Clapping her hands and laughing gaily]. That's wonderful. Where did you find that?

AGILE: [showing his pleasure that his ditty is well received and shrugging modestly] I just made it up. [*need a zippy follow-up but suddenly I can't think of a thing to say*]. This is so nice, I mean sitting here with you. [He gestures around them. Across the aisle from them sit a man and a woman, a man and wife from the way they interact without talking. The man has white hair combed straight back across a bald spot and wears a dark blue blazer and a blue and red striped tie. The woman is a bleached blonde beached on the shores of life. She wears a lemon yellow jacket over a ruffled white blouse. She has large breasts obviously firmly held in place and that must have made her appear slightly lopsided naked. Next to them a single skinny man bent over his plate as if in prayer. To the other side was a family with two screaming kids with sauce smeared mouths and clutching fingers in fork city] Looks like everyone is having a good time.

ZINNY: [She nods and fiddles with her napkin, folding and unfolding it, placing it in her lap and then back onto the table to the right of her place] It was nice of you to ask me, Agile. I mean really but this place is so fancy and expensive. We could have gone somewhere else for a lot less. [She twists her napkin and looks uncertain as if wondering whether she's said the wrong thing]

WALKER: [He smiles]

HAROLD: [A waiter glides up to their table. He is tall, perhaps six feet or an inch higher, and thin with black hair slicked back unfashionably and narrow hands with long, skinny fingers that gripped two menus as if they were a life raft] Good evening, folks. My name is Harold and I will be your waiter tonight. May I start you off with a drink? [He opens the menus and hands one to Zinny and the other to Walker]

WALKER: Jack Daniels on the rocks, please.

ZINNY: I'll have an ice tea.

HAROLD: [nods his head and smiles] Very good [He turns in a precise, almost prissy fashion, and hurries off towards the bar]

ZINNY: So why did you ask me? [Her tone is light but her eyes are serious and deep]

WALKER: I thought you looked like you needed a break what with Mark attacking you and your dad and everything. I don't know. You seemed distant somehow. All those little smiles disappeared. I know I was feeling a little down [Walker smiles ruefully] so I thought we could have a little fun for a change. [Walker leans towards her hoping that she will remember his trauma of the other night, sympathize and agree that the evening out was indeed a good thing]

ZINNY: [She nods her head once as if to acknowledge his words without judging their content, a quick jerking motion up and down] The past few weeks have been interesting. [Her lips twitch in an attempt to smile] So what family do you have? You know all about mine already.

WALKER: Just the daughter whom you met. [*How much should I tell her? Too much detail too soon could be bad. Jennifer is still my daughter. I helped raise her. Even when she does stupid things that piss me off. Yes, even so. So maybe the person playing the fool has the last laugh. She's got a lot of her mother in her but when she stops running away from herself she should find solid ground. Wonder why Zinny never had kids. Mark being her husband would certainly be a good reason but that was long ago. She must have known men since, but obviously never one she could bring herself to trust again. Maybe she does have kids. She never said one way or another.*] She's going through a rebellious stage right now as you know.

ZINNY: I liked her. She's a little rough around the edges but time has a way of smoothing those out.

WALKER: And you?

ZINNY: Just Dad and me now. No kids. [Zinny looks down into her lap and then back up at Walker. Harold appears bearing the drinks on a small tray. He puts an ice tea in front of Zinny and a Jack in front of Walker. They sit in silence as he does this as if they were discussing a national security secret]

HAROLD: Are you folks ready to order? [He pulls out an order pad and stands expectantly, pencil at the ready]

ZINNY: Oh dear. [She picks up her menu] Uhhmmm. I'll have the sea bass.

WALKER: Something to start with? Salad perhaps?

ZINNY: [Shakes her head and smiles] No. I'd run out of room.

WALKER: [Nods] *Better skip the Calimari myself then.*

HAROLD: Good choice, ma'am. It's excellent.

WALKER: I'll try the pork chop.

HAROLD: Very good, sir [He makes a notation on his pad and walks away]

WALKER: Choice or chance? [*oh hell, that was stupid. It's none of my business I should tape my fucking mouth shut. Might look strange but I'd be far better off. Hope she doesn't just get up and walk out*]

ZINNY: [*Calmly as if discussing the weather*] Both, I guess.

WALKER: Never mind. None of my business. [He takes a large sip of sour mash and feels the warmth spread throughout his stomach. *Did I offend her? She doesn't seem upset sitting there so prettily sipping her tea. I don't know but somehow this seems important and I don't know why. I want her to enjoy this. Really get into it and into me. I'm starting to sweat. Like a dammed river beneath my arms.* He takes another sip]

ZINNY: You look so serious, suddenly. Surely things couldn't be that bad? [Her voice is light, trying to tease him out of whatever he is thinking]

WALKER: Didn't mean to.

ZINNY: Serious thoughts?

WALKER: In a way. [*what can I say? I think I'm booting this whole conversation and no matter what I say, I get the feeling that I'm just getting myself into ever deeper shit*]

ZINNY: About what?

WALKER: [Shrugged but does not reply]

ZINNY: About me? [She pauses as if debating something within herself] You've met the reason in person. Never got close to another man after that. [She smiles at him] So don't think twice about asking about kids. It was a fair question. So how did you end up at my house? It was such a huge coincidence. I couldn't believe my eyes when I saw you at the door. [She laughs and Walker grins in return.]

WALKER: [*Yeah, it was just one of those small world happenings that constantly confront our view of reality twisting it ever so slightly in different directions like a gigantic taffy pull and highlighting the minute quality of our lives. We who live each day feeling that we are so important in nature's scheme of things suddenly find ourselves tripping over each other like so many*] *bb's being poured down the barrel of a child's gun]* I thought I was seeing things as well. I had to sell my house. I looked around for an apartment but couldn't find one I liked at a price I could afford. Finally, when I was almost forced into a hotel, I saw your ad and thought well why not. It would be better than a hotel and give me time to find a place I really liked. [Walker's reply trails off as Harold approaches the table with a large tray suspended above one arm. He lowers the tray onto a folding stand and then places a plate in front of Zinny and then in front of Walker]

ZINNY'S FOOD

Grilled Chilean Sea Bass fillet: Shades of brown and black with grill marks plainly showing against the white of the china plate, the top layer of flesh already flaking off the surface and wisps of steam rising from it. A freshly cut cross section of lemon bedded on a cross hatch of parsley served as garnish. The fillet is lightly caressed by a white wine and caper sauce that subtly enhances the flavor of the sea bass. Nestled next to the bass is a mound of mashed potatoes and a small thicket of green beans also steaming. [Green beans were always one of Zinny's favorites. As a small girl she remembered stacking them up into lean-to's on her plate and then devouring her temporary shelters with great relish, slowly nibbling from one end of a bean on her fork to the other end. *Dad thought it was cute. Mamma was much less thrilled and demanded that proper manners be observed at the dinner table. Eat a bean, change the scene I used to sing to myself over and over]*

WALKER'S FOOD

Panko Crusted Pork Chop: The chop was so large it must have been either a double thick chop that the chef had split down the middle or the porker who had unwillingly donated it had been large enough to turn an eighteen wheeler into road kill. It took up most of the plate and glistened with panko breading and oil. He could smell the scent of basil and thyme and had to restrain himself from attacking the plate like a starved animal. [The sight of it brought memories of Bridgette's leg of lamb that he had known as a child. Garlic gently inserted under the skin. Salt, pepper and rosemary liberally sprinkled and then the leg was basted while cooking until the skin was golden brown and crunchy.]

WALKER: [Looks up from his plate at Zinny's] Everything okay?

ZINNY: Oh yes. [She looks up and smiles] It's just so much. I don't know how I'll fit it all in but it's delicious. [She puts a forkful in her mouth as if to prove her statement]

WALKER: [He watches her chew slowly, almost rhythmically. Her lips glistened slightly and a faint blue vein pulsed on the left side of her neck. He cuts a piece from his chop and pushes it into the pile of mashed potatoes and then carries the result to his mouth] So you never remarried?

ZINNY: No.

WALKER: Ever come close?

ZINNY: [Her expression becomes thoughtful and she stares into the middle distance somewhere over his head] No.

WALKER: [*What a waste of a beautiful woman.* He cuts another bite off his chop. It tasted of pepper with just a hint of garlic. He chews slowly and nods in appreciation of the feel of it on his tongue.]

ZINNY: What are your plans? [She daintily separates a forkful of fish brings it up halfway to her mouth] Surely you won't be happy with just a single room forever? [She brings the fish to her mouth and chews slowly while looking across the table at him]

WALKER: [*I don't know what I might or might not do. Shit. I just got moved in and settled into a new routine. Suits me just fine right now. Got my books and writing when I'm not tearing it up and the little TV. CSI is great. Love Grissom. Good character with some depth and color. Unusual for TV shows. The old house was full of memories that I am better off losing. Too many memories. Got enough to carry around, maybe more than I should have to. The lone black hair that grew out of Beth's left breast just above the aureole ZIP Jennifer running up the stairs laughing in a game of hide n seek ZIP lugging a huge picnic basket up the side of a fucking mountain as we searched for the perfect picnic spot wishing Beth would drop dead so that I could put the dammed basket down while Jennifer ran back and forth saying c'mon Dad don't be so slow ZIP turning over on my side with my back to Beth and masturbating while the sound of her snores filled the bedroom ZIP the sandbox out back that I built and Jen had piled up the sand into a huge mound, placed Mrs. Jingles, her raggedy Ann doll, on top of it and then sat for hours simply staring at the stupid doll ZIP mowing the front lawn in August while all the heat from the Sahara seemed to settle in around me sucking the life from my flesh and desiccating my soul ZIP [Beth emerging from Lake Totomac with the sun setting behind her throwing a glistening coronet around her shadowed figure]* No plans. Happy to be where I am to tell you the truth. Sometimes it's not the amount of space that we have but the amount of living that we are able to put into it. I feel as if the room is just right for me. *[Hope I didn't overdo it and let my mouth run off too much. She doesn't seem to be withdrawing.* Walker looks down at his pork chop feeling relieved somehow and less alone, warmer and more complete]

ZINNY: Well I'm glad. God knows what the situation would have been without you. Your rent money is a lifesaver. I feel as though you are part of my little family and have been for a while even though it's only been a short amount of time. That's not a good thing for you, though. I'm sorry for all the trouble. [Zinny stops suddenly, as if embarrassed by such a revelation, and then smiles and looks down at the fish on her plate as if to identify from where her next forkful should come] If you need something and you see it in the house or in the kitchen, you know, just help yourself. *Mi casa su casa.* [Zinny tries to adopt a tone of light-hearted gaiety but it doesn't work. Her worry shows clearly on her face]

WALKER: [Gravely] Thank you. Have you heard anything more from your ex?"

ZINNY: No, thank God. Maybe the rent money was enough for whatever he needed to do. I don't know. I just hope he's gone. *[and a hope is all that it is. He will be hanging around and making life miserable until he either gets what he wants or gets arrested. Dammed if I'm going to spoil the evening by bringing up that point.]*

WALKER: [Looks around for Harold who is nowhere in sight] Amen to that. Been there. Done that. Got the bruises to prove it. Maybe the police will keep him at arm's length. Ahh there you are. [Walker looks up as Harold glides to a spot six inches from Walker's end of the table and four and one half inches from Zinny's end]

HAROLD: How is everything?

ZINNY: Delicious [Zinny murmurs and pats her lips with her napkin]

WALKER: [Points at his glass]

HAROLD: Another, sir? Certainly [Harold neatly removes the empty glass and vanishes.]

ZINNY: [Takes another bite. *I have no idea why I chose fish. I hate it. It reminds me of Mark. He loved fish of all kinds except the kind I cooked for him and whatever that was it was not good enough. It was cooked too long and had become mush. It wasn't cooked long enough. Did she have any idea how sick a person could become from eating raw fish? There was too much salt. There was too much pepper. Had she mistaken him for some wop greaser? Mark had complained volubly and loudly about almost everything, particularly after he had pressed her for money from her dad and her father had claimed that he did not have it.* She pushed at the pieces on her plate and looked at her star border, and yes, she had to admit it, her friend. *Fat little man obviously enjoying his meal with a twinkle in his eyes and lips glistening with pork fat and whiskey like some small, greasy Santa traveling incognito. Why should I enjoy sitting here with him?* [She looked down at the now cooling piece of fish on her plate and felt her stomach rise slightly in rebellion] *Well he had gotten between Mark and her, or at least tried to when most people would have backed the hell out the doorway and taken a long walk down the street full of self righteous confidence that, after all, it was not their fight, not their argument, and that they had not paid for their room only to be involved in something like that but he had not done that, had come in and tried to change something he perceived as being wrong not because he had stood there and thought it out and said oh my god there is trouble here and I should do something, maybe call the police, maybe run down the street screaming, maybe standing there and watching me being creamed by some strange man but because some part of him deep inside caused him to step in and try to keep Mark off of me, and that is something of value, something that I have never felt before and, God knows, may not feel again and God, I do believe I love him or at least part of him or maybe all of him not for what he is, maybe, but for what he's not and that doesn't make any sense but I am not up to making sense right now. It was like I had someone in my corner dabbing at the bruises and issuing instructions with machine gun rapidity. Never knew that feeling except from my parents and oh it feels good, really good and I have no idea why I feel this way. What is it about Agile? He is almost a complete stranger, after all. What did he like besides Jack Daniels? Liquor has done nothing except turn my life into a nightmare. Agile drinks it as if it were water. At least he doesn't smoke. Uggg. Can't stand the smell. He reads a lot and that's definitely a good thing. Chalk one up for the gipper]* You seem to be enjoying yourself.

WALKER: [His mouth is full so he just nods back at her] Mmmmm. [He winks at her]

ZINNY: [*What was that? I can't remember the last time anyone of either sex winked at me. It is such a friendly gesture as if we are together on some adventurous journey. Yeah, right. Don't be so naïve, girl. The man is just an old letch*]. Zinny bursts out into laughter at the sheer incongruity of it all and the pleasure of being out with a friend. [*Damn, I haven't felt this way since high school when the football team won the All State championship and all the kids were going nuts dancing in the parking lot behind the gym yelling and screaming as the bus pulled in, cheerleaders flapping their pom-poms and pushing their tits out towards the players, freshmen in the back looking lost and sneaking cigarettes in the shadows, seniors slouching around and trying to look cool and all knowing and I was yelling and screaming along with the rest and feeling as if I belonged, not to a club exactly, but like I was where I was supposed to be doing what I was supposed to be doing and everything was somehow RIGHT and here I am laughing like a crazy woman but it too feels right. Right as rain. Yes indeed, but, oh my, he is maybe thinking that I am laughing at him*] You have a great wink.

WALKER: Why thank you Zinny. Just for you. Can't remember the last time I did that.

ZINNY: I'll bet you say that to all the girls [Zinny speaks in a little girl voice, flutters her eyelids at Walker and imitates a shy maiden by holding her hands up in front of her mouth and turning her head slightly downwards and to the right]

WALKER: [grins] Only dem what's eatin' wid me and dat be you [He points across the table at her] Seriously, though, you're the first person I've broken bread with besides my wife and daughter since I was a young man. It feels a little strange but very nice. Thank you.

ZINNY: I'm the one who should be saying thank you.

WALKER: Then let's resolve that neither of us needs to say it.

ZINNY: [Claps her hands and laughs]So resolved. Friends don't need to say thank you for something like this anyways. [*Okay, so what to say next? Oh well, in for a penny as they say whoever they are.*] So what do you think about the election? I think Obama will put this country back on track, don't you? I mean, he's young and progressive and cares about the middle class and that would be a real switch from the current administration that just seem to want big oil and war. [*Well, he looks as if he is interested.*] Look at the mess Bush made of the economy and McCain is the same way. Everything for the rich and nothing for anyone else. What does he care? That snow queen wife of his is probably worth millions.

WALKER: Really? When the Republicans wanted tighter controls on Fannie Mae and Freddie Mac, it was the Democrats, Dodd and Franks, who refused to hear of it. Let's face it, Obama says he's for change but not all change is for the good, right?

ZINNY: Well I think Obama will change things for the better [Zinny stabs at a piece of fish on her plate with conviction]

WALKER: [He is appalled and his expression shows it] I can't believe you mean that. Change for the better with Wright and Ayers and that Palestinian professor as role models? This smooth talking, college educated, Teflon coated radical has an agenda that you seem to be just ignoring or minimizing. I mean McCain is not running well but at least he has no desire to turn the American economy on its ass. I think Obama wants to organize a community on a national scale. His team is running a great campaign. People are tired of war and any change seems good and most of us don't bother to ask what kind. McCain's team is running his campaign with the usual Republican ineptitude and so now people making good money are going to be the bad guys while those paying no taxes at all are going to be the good guys. I know he says that everyone making less than two hundred fifty grand will be all right but I have little faith in that promise. You're joking, right?

ZINNY: No. I believe that he has the interest of the nation at heart. We do need to end the war, and change a lot of other things too. We need to change from an oligarchy by big business back into a democracy.

WALKER: I think Obama is heading way left of democracy. Look, he's only been in the senate a few months. He has no experience in economics and foreign policy. He was a candidate reared and bred by the Democratic machine in Chicago. [Walker runs out of words as Harold glides up to the table and starts to remove the dishes]

HAROLD: Would you like me to pack that, ma'am? [He holds her plate of sea bass up for her decision]

ZINNY: No thanks. It was very good though.

HAROLD: Would you like coffee or the desert menu? The double chocolate cake is excellent.

WALKER: Mmmm. [*Good. Let's get off the subject of politics. So Zinny is a big time Democrat? So what? He'll probably win and that will be that. Better or worse. So don't get into a big argument with her. Shut up and deal the cards, asshole]* Irish coffee and the chocolate cake [Harolds makes note and turns towards Zinny.] Let's agree to disagree on politics.

ZINNY: Gladly. [She nods happily. *Who would have thought that Agile would be a Republican? He certainly doesn't seem to be rich or a fat cat.*

Well, fat, okay but definitely not a cat. How strange. Still, one man's ceiling is another man's floor. She looks at Harold] Nothing for me, thank you. [Harold smiles and turns away] Do you think the economy will recover soon? [*This should be a bit safer topic, I think as long as we don't get into the politics of it all]*

WALKER: Well let's think on that for a moment. Banks, insurance companies and investment firms got caught holding huge amounts of investments and collateral the value of which could not be determined and so, under accounting rules, had to be written down to zero. Whoops. Required capital reserves disappeared. Creditors started calling in loans. Almost overnight, the financial services part of the economy was kaput. Combine that with a housing market that is in the gutter due to lax underwriting standards for mortgages and subsequent high default rates when people who could not afford a house in the first place got a loan anyway and then walked away when their ARMs rate shot up. I think we'll be sucking wind for quite a while. The government's borrowing or printing almost a billion dollars to keep the wheels of industry or at least Wall Street turning. God only knows what effect that will have on us all for years to come. [*Uh oh. I lost her. She looks like I used to feel in Algebra class. Eyes have that glassy look and she is nodding politely and probably hasn't heard a word I said. Well, she asked. Yeah, you dumb shit, but you didn't have to give her your economics 101 lecture in the middle of a good dinner.* He waves his hand back and forth in front of Zinny's face] Hello. Earth to Zinny. Are you there?

ZINNY: [Her head twitches and her eyes regain their focus] Sorry. Guess I spaced out a little bit there.

WALKER: Penny?

ZINNY: For my thoughts? Not worth the price. [She smiles, an almost imperceptible movement of her lips]

WALKER: [*I don't think I've ever seen anyone look as beautiful as Zinny does at this moment in the light of this restaurant dining area for it is much too large to be called a room].* Okay. I won't push but sharing can work wonders.

ZINNY: [Nods. *What the hell should I tell him? The truth, the whole truth, and nothing but the truth? It would surely ruin a wonderful evening that has been special from the moment I said yes but which scared the shit out of me just a moment ago. It would be better if Agile knew, of course, but this is just not the moment to tell him]* Well, I've been thinking of the times we've

265

shared, when we met and how we got to know each other. It all seems a bit like a fairy tale, doesn't it, or a TV soap where *deus ex machina* is taken as a God given right. [Zinny runs out of words, feels a blush coming to her cheeks and almost knocks over her glass in an effort to take a gulp.]

WALKER: You're right. It does, but I'm sure that thought didn't cause your face to tighten up and become so serious. This evening's been so nice that it just seemed a shame that you would have thoughts like that.

ZINNY: [Her face showing her relief.] Thank you, Agile. [She reaches across the table and pats the top of his left hand gently with her right hand. *It feels so smooth and warm. The hairs on the back are like silk.* She withdraws her hand quickly, feeling slightly embarrassed by the contact.]

Walker came back to the present with a start, the characters of Zinny and Walker exiting the stage, the lights dimming and the audience murmuring as they moved slowly towards the exits. The plaza around Walker ebbed and flowed with people, clumping and separating like beads of mercury. Zinny had not appeared and he was out of time. Memories of the previous evening would have to suffice, he thought, but at least they were good ones right up to the end that is.

When her hand touched his it was if she had tazered him. His whole body suddenly felt hot, the skin on the back of his hand seemed to burn, and goose bumps erupted on his arms. Far beneath the hard working organ that was his stomach, his penis woke up and stretched slightly. Walker shifted in his chair and beamed at Zinny as Harold put cake and coffee in front of him. *Wow. She must be carrying a load of static electricity or something. Dammed near blew my circuits with just that one touch. Wonder what a kiss might do? Probably never find out but you never know. Things look promising.* Walker picked up his fork and attacked his cake with gusto.

She still looks so serious sitting there watching me eat as if it were an action she has not seen before or maybe as if I were a doll that she has seated at a table and with whom she is about to share high tea. I wonder what's worrying her? Not me, I hope. Mark, maybe. That psycho is enough to worry anyone. She should be worried about him. The creep should be in jail, but no, he's running around demanding money from her and now she's got him on her shoulders as well as her dad. He's like a tornado that suddenly appears out of nowhere and destroys everything in his path. I felt the same way when Beth was sick and Jennifer was just starting to rebel and I was caught between my job and Beth and Jen. Probably didn't do a good job there. Hell, I know I didn't. Everything I did back then seemed to push her further away like reversing the polarity of a magnet. Still, she's grown now for better or worse. Looked good at the funeral. Too heavy like her old man. Ahh Beth, I do miss you so. May you be happy and pain free now wherever your spirit has come to rest. We had some good times and time dims all the rest.

Walker finished his coffee with a satisfying slurp and raised his hand in an attempt to get Harold's attention. "Shall we depart?" he asked her.

Zinny replied with a smile. "We shall."

They were silent on the drive back to the house, enjoying one of those moments when both people are comfortable with themselves and each other and the glow of a good meal prepared by someone else is paramount. Walker looked to his right and found Zinny looking at him. Simultaneously, they both smiled almost shyly and turned back to look at the road ahead. *Damn she makes me happy just sitting beside her driving down the road. Haven't felt this way in years. Like, I'm almost giddy. Is that a real word? Maybe when I first met Beth, I felt this way but it was so long ago I can't remember. That's awful. I can't even remember how I felt about my wife. I mean I remember some things but not others. Should be able to remember how I felt way back then. I remember how her breasts gleamed with sweat as she rode me that first time but I can't remember if she came or not. I came. Man, I thought I had broken something I came so hard and for what seemed forever, but I can't remember how her face looked while she slept and that says nothing good about me for sure. Shit I should be able to remember every detail of our life together. Laughter, fights, tears, exhaustion, jealousy, the whole panoply of our lives should be there but it just seems to have melted away with just little chunks sticking up here and there. Jen with the chicken pox, Beth with a new hair-do, my promotion to senior analyst, moonlight after I blew out the candles on our fifth wedding anniversary cake and she clapped her hands and shouted how beautiful, oh beautiful, the thrill when my first little story got published in a mystery magazine, standing over my father's grave wondering how Miami was doing in the playoffs while my mother stood black draped and plain saying to everyone how he meant well, God knew he meant well, alarm clock failing and coming in late to work where the hell have you been sorry, sorry, fuckyou very much your royal assholeness, walking with Jen and Beth down a dirt road in Vermont and watching a huge red and yellow hot air balloon rise majestically over the pines, Jennifer's face-splitting grin when she graduated from high school after promising us for two years that she would drop out and sell herself on the street rather than listen to absurdly dull people yak about such dead subjects as algebra and American history, Beth's first severe stomach pains when she would retch herself dry in the bathroom and then put it down as the flu, sunrise coming through the tree in the front yard and turning our living room into roses and golden, a plate of steaming angel hair pasta with a thick rich carbonara sauce over the top and a mound of freshly grated parmesan, a porterhouse steak rare with herb butter and mushrooms sliced thick and sautéed in Campari white vermouth and Cabot butter, Zinny sitting in Max's this evening looking so fine.*

Walker turned onto their street, blinking rapidly as his mind came back to the here and now, to the car and Zinny and the big, dark shadow that was her house with a light on in her father's room midway along the second floor. Okay, Walker thought, and smiled a little. Okay. 'Home is the sailor home from the sea.'

Zinny sat staring straight ahead at the dark shadows of the garage as the motor died and Agile moved to undo his seat belt. She wanted desperately to move, get out of the car, turn the radio on, turn the radio off, undo her seat belt, fart loudly, anything at all but all she could do was to sit very still staring out. *What now? What if he wants to well it's been so long could I . . . I mean do I want to? Well, Agile's a nice guy. I like him. Okay, Zin, admit it. Maybe even you love him but what if it is like back then and oh God what will I do what can I do that would not turn him away and the rejection would I mean for me or for him and then what cause then he's here and oh, it gets so dammed complicated and what if we, well then it would be okay but years ago there was one and he came to kiss me and I went all stiff and I couldn't I mean I tried but this is different, isn't it? Agile is different, something rare, not like the other so I hell I don't know Christ.* Zinny pushed away the darkness, forcing herself to undo her seatbelt fingers feeling cold and foreign as if they were robotic pincers in some sterile lab. She suddenly felt overheated. Sweat popped onto her forehead. Slowly, almost painfully, she got out of the car and turned to face Agile across the span of the car's roof. His eyes were black dots in the light from the street lamps. She walked around to his side of the car. "Thank you, sir," she told him and made a pretend curtsey. They walked up the steps to the back door and into the kitchen.

"I better check on Dad. Rosalinda has to leave at eight and we did stretch the evening a bit." Zinny smiled and pushed past him on her way to the stairs. Walker followed.

"Did you leave money for Rosalinda?" he asked. "I didn't think of it," he admitted.

"No worry." Her answer floated down from the second floor. "It all gets squared away."

What the hell does that mean? Walker went up the stairs while Zinny disappeared into her father's room. Should he just stand in the hall feeling like a nun at a bachelor party or should he just go into his room and leave her be? The decision was made for him when Zinny came out of the room looking down at a plastic bag into which she was stuffing a diaper and ran into him.

"Whoops." Zinny found herself looking into a pair of large, brown eyes that showed momentary surprise and then laughter. They seemed to shine out at her.

"No harm." Walker put his hands on her shoulders to steady her. "It really was a wonderful evening," he told her softly and brushed her cheek with the fingers of his right hand. The flesh felt slightly warm and soft under his fingers. He brushed at it gently and the lines around her nose and mouth smoothed momentarily and Walker caught a glimpse of the young woman Zinny had once been. Her face was inches from his and he leaned towards her seeing acceptance in her eyes and something else as well.

Zinny felt the brush of his fingers on her cheek as if they had been a branding iron. She felt hot and then chilled. The skin on her face tingled and her crotch itched as well. His hands tightened around her shoulders and she felt as if her insides had melted somehow and dripped down into her groin.

Funny it should itch so. Hasn't felt like that for a long time since that library intern who wore those super tight pants. Couldn't afford ones that fit properly, I guess. Itched then too and stained brand new panties and had to throw them out. What a waste. Body goes one way and mind goes another. Riding on a big black horse on a Merry-Go-Round up and down up and down. Felt sick and Dad had to get me to the bathroom. His hands are so soft. Wouldn't think that of a man. Mark was hard. Scratchy beard. Always mad at someone. Yelling. Shoving it in my face suck screaming cursing me or all of life maybe. Needed to scream into a mirror. Not likely. Raised better than that. No sense using gutter language. Still, it fit him. Can't think of him any other way. Pretty. Mom said Zinny you are pretty maybe not outside but inside and that is much more important. Truisms R Us okay, Mom but now I am scraggly and old and plain as a broken shoe lace and my breasts sag and my ribs show and I'm a little bowlegged and certainly hairy and God, why would he want to hold me even for a second? Out of pity, I'm sure. I felt him watching me all evening and the people around us too but Agile had eyes on me and me alone. It's always the eyes. They follow me like tiny shadows dancing and dipping but he's a nice guy. He has kind eyes that seem to hold me to him. Wouldn't hurt anybody. That's what I like about him. Well, okay, if I'm being honest, one of many things. His arms feel so strong and warm. No. No. This cannot be I cannot be trusted, not pretty pretty not again oh nonononono. Cannot be. Bad, Zinny you are ugly and all he wants what all men want OH NO think I'mgoingtobesick oh god notherenotnow. Please not now oh . . .

Sobbing, Zinny pushed herself away from Walker, turned and flung herself into the bathroom leaving him standing in the hall staring at the bathroom door.

Feeling tired and somewhat depressed, Walker lay on his bed. He had lost count, had he ever bothered to keep one, of the times he had asked himself what he had done wrong. Yes, he had held her. She had run into him and he had steadied her, Walker told himself with some self righteousness. He had brushed her cheek and it seemed as if they would share a kiss and suddenly she had gone all stiff and fled into the bathroom. Women. Impossible creatures. Really. A man would never collapse like that.

Not In Service

Light again and then dark where little sounds live creaking somewhere a soft pop like bubble gum bursting pink onto surrounding mouth flesh ah double bubble trouble with dark is the faces I can't see their faces only shadows hardly even that but know they're out there silent quickly in front and then gone like everything else is gone except sometimes a picture in the light like a match struck in a dark room and then a face comes and I am in motion and there is food sometimes and then gone and darkness with the warmth of sheets wrapped around for protection I hear the sound again, a creak of wood, a step outside perhaps on the porch. So lightly she stepped and so radiant her smile. No, not beautiful took after me I suppose but she radiated happiness lit up like a light bulb on on on on Oh Daddy I love him so and I would like your blessing oh God what was I to do when I saw nothing in him but darkness and hate.

It is getting on getting on the window in front of me is holding its hand over the light. Shadows dance the walls onestep twostep sway and dip and turn and turnandswirl backwards and forwards turn and sway. I need to piss. "Okay," I say as the shadows climb on the walls dancing and jiggling like the old timey movies staccato action dedumdedum. They are my friends turning this way and that mocking the darkness and the light showing the shapes inside of us all as we roll like dust bunnies along the floor of our lives but suddenly there is a different shape, a shadow not familiar yet I feel I should know it. I should. One shadow among many oh I am old so old and okay I say as I sit and watch the shadow creep along the wall to my left.

And I feel cold like once I was naked no that was before but cold like winter on the back and I wrap my arms around shivering and then a face comes and I see death empty of all feeling dark and cold eyes flat as a snake dark and cold unblinking without remorse no thought no mind like a king of old overlooking the field of bodies dead and dying and who has won sire oh we did for sure yes but how can you tell my Lord. Because

I am still alive and what has been gained on the field in front of us my Lord? Why death and only that. "Okay," I say and watch the face tighten into slits and lines empty of all.

"Keep your trap shut, you old cheapskate or I'll fucking shut it for you. Understand?"

"Okay," I say.

F2

Zinny stood before the long display case filled with various types and cuts of meat. In the beef section were sirloin steaks, filets of beef, rib eyes, and flank steaks as well as packs of hamburger meat and smaller ones of cubed steaks. There were top round roasts and bottom round roasts, thick cut London broils, chunks of stew beef, and ribs both country and spare ribs though she found herself in the pork section when she saw those. Packages of pork chops stared pinkly up at her. Large roasts dozed quietly to one side. Then, of course, there were the sausages, pork and turkey, small and large, breakfast and dinner, bratwurst, weisswurst, Kielbasa, stuffed with cheese, stuffed with apple, begging for attention before passing the shopper to the huge pink cheeks of the hams. Just thinking of all the meat in this one case, and the thousands of cases across the country staggered her imagination. How many tons of food on the hoof had to be put to sleep every day to feed the populace and provide this kind of selection? It made her feel a little uneasy as she studied the case. She resolutely turned her thoughts in a different direction.

She should foxtrot with the turkeys, waltz with the top rounds, cha-cha with the Cornish hens, passé doble with the fat back, rhumba with the tilapia and quick step with the salmon. She smiled at the thought of the meats and fish dancing down the aisle on their way to checkout heaven all to a Latin beat. Cha-cha with the tuna but her amusement ended abruptly and she stood in the wide aisle at the back of Stop & Shop frowning at the meat case while people flowed past her in both directions. The afternoon was almost over and she was no closer to her goal than she had been ten minutes previously. They watched and stared. Ahh the eyes.

It had seemed like such a good idea at the time. She needed to take vacation time or she was going to lose it. She wanted to do something to reassure Agile that he was not to blame for the fiasco of a few days past. Zinny's scowl deepened at the thought of that horrible moment. How could she have done something like that? Right out of nowhere as if some monstrous being had flicked a switch and turned her from a woman into a staggering tower of vomitus. Why? Why? Why? She asked the question but there was no answer, at least none that she could see. The whole evening had been a fairy tale; the food, the drink, Agile sitting across from her smiling and chowing down as if it were his last meal on earth. Sitting there with him, she felt a sense of peace, of being whole and complete that she had never felt before, at least since becoming an adult. Coming out of the restaurant, she had known deep down in herself that Agile was real, not some dark handsome figure in some book but totally himself, emotionally complete, kind, considerate, certainly generous, as solid and comfortable as a favorite old shirt. He made her feel safe, more sure of her spot in the scheme of things, more comfortable with her life.

As an adolescent, Zinny remembered, she had been absolutely, positively, dead sure right on certain that she was ugly and destined to be an old maid at the age of seventeen, and only her father's insistence that she accompany him when he went as a volunteer to the local nursing home brought her out of her self-imposed torture chamber.

"Well, Azalea, you may think that you've been dealt a bad hand but I think Mr. Wilson, here, would gladly trade places with you." Her father brought her into a room occupied by a human skeleton who stared at her through drug glazed eyes as he contorted his body back and forth beneath the covers.

Zinny quickly looked away feeling slightly ill and guilty at the same time. Her father was right, as usual, but, with the determined stubbornness of a seventeen-year old, she was dammed if she would admit it. Tears blurred her vision and she turned away and walked quickly down the hall towards the front door. She and her father spoke not a word on their way home and he never referred to it again.

Zinny stared at the beef case. Agile ate pork the other night. *Couldn't feed him that again. Steak, maybe? Never knew a man who didn't like steak. Haven't known many men, though. Suppose he hates steak. Could say the same for anything here. Just have to take a chance and pray. Hate it, hate it not knowing, worrying. Shouldn't do that but can't seem to help it. C'mon, you silly old woman. Pick something and be done with it.*

Zinny stopped muttering to herself, took two determined steps to the case and picked the thickest rib eye steaks she could find. Wheeling abruptly like a British guardsman in front of Buckingham Palace, she marched to her cart, dumped them in, and marched down the nearest aisle towards the front of the store, weaving in and out around other shoppers and their carts. She was a thin, almost stick-like figure so obviously alone, part of all and yet solitary and aloof somehow, looking straight ahead with a blank, sad, blasted stare that never quite made contact with the people around her and they, in turn, moved themselves and their energies from her path staring at her from the corners of their eyes. Mothers reached out reflexively to touch their children, not even to pull closer, but simply to touch as if in reassurance of the solidity of the flesh and the trust and protection of the family. One woman reached behind herself without looking and caught the shirt of someone else's child. Zinny calmly pushed her cart past both as they stood and glared at each other.

The heat of the late summer afternoon melted her mind and she had to force herself to walk across the softened asphalt of the parking lot. She wondered if the steaks had already begun cooking in their plastic containers within the plastic shopping bag with the recycle message on it.

How should I cook them? Broil, I guess, since the old grill finally rusted out. Don't know if I would remember how to get it going anyway. Mark was always after me for burning the meat. Came at me with his spatula once. Still have the scar. Sorry, but no t-shirt this time. Bastard. May it was in May I think or maybe early June. Fire lapping at the steaks. Mushrooms frying in some butter will be good, better with some white cooking wine in there too. Think there's an old bottle in the back of the pantry. Those potatoes I brought home last week. I think Agile will like those. Can't wait to see his face. He'll be grinning and rubbing his hands together the way he does and I'll pour him a glass of Jack. I wonder if there's any of the wine left. I could join him for a glass. Maybe I should stop at Barclay's liquor superstore. Jack and Merlot. Just the ticket. Like the Bobbsy Twins. Jack and Merlot, Zinny and Agile. Wow. I haven't felt like this in a long time about a man, not after Mark, but I do, sweet Lord, I do and I don't regret it for a moment, not a second. Wonder what Dad would think if he could still think probably like Agile I'm sure he would yes for Agile is gentle and unassuming and smart. Don't know exactly the work he does but I just know he is. Maybe Dad already knows in his own way but he can't express it. He's seen Agile, after all and I bet he knows more than he can say donch'a, Dad cause you always saw into me a little deeper than anyone else even Mom you just were able to peel back that extra layer and take a peek. When I was a kid and came home crying with a bruised and bleeding knee you saw that the tears were not from the pain but from the frustration of not being able to push Eddie Dickinson down as he pushed me and later when I was going through my nightmare with Mark you told me that my house had far too many doors in it and I should get out and avoid running into them.

It was rush hour when Zinny pulled into the liquor store on Albany Avenue and the place was packed. Social Security day, she thought. People were streaming in and out and lined up to buy lotto tickets. She brought out her cell phone to check with Rosa at the house. Dead battery. Damn. Should she try another packie? She sat for a moment watching the customers entering and then leaving with bottled oblivion shouldering their way out the door with the usual brown paper bags. The crowd thinned momentarily; Zinny saw her chance and walked into the shop behind an elderly black gentleman with a violently yellow jacket.

Zinny slowed to a stop in her driveway and sat for a moment before getting out of the car and retrieving her bags of groceries and liquor. The air conditioner made it comfortable, more so than her room that had a fan that succeeded only in moving the hot air from one part to another. Agile would be home in a little while and she had things to do, but it felt so good to just sit in the coolness and do nothing. She couldn't remember the last time she had a moment like this. She wished that her childhood swing was still in the back yard. Back and forth, up and down. She shook her head and opened the car door. Such fantasies had no place here and tonight would be special, she hoped. Besides, she reminded herself as she heaved the bags out of the back seat of the car, she wouldn't fit in the swing now anyways.

"Rosa?" Zinny called as she entered the kitchen. There was no answer. Zinny put the groceries down on the kitchen table and went into the hallway. "Rosa?" Silence. She must have left early for some reason but when that happened she always called. Zinny remembered the dead phone in her pocket. Damn.

Zinny went upstairs and stuck her head into her father's room. "Hi, Dad. Everything okay?" He didn't answer but he was sitting in his chair staring out the window as he normally would. She decided to get the potatoes going and then take a quick shower before Agile came home.

Their skins came off in long brown and white strips as if they had suffered severe sun burn. Zinny lay down the little peeling blade and ran water into the sink to peel and wash the little white mushroom caps and let the peels be gathered by the drain filter. Agile should be home anytime. She smiled softly to herself that she should regard his arrival as some form of being home. Well, why not? He had no other place that she knew of and he was there every day. This was home.

"Therewashomehometherewashomehomeyhomehome," Zinny murmured to herself as she went up the stairs to shower and change. She heard the scrape of her Dad's chair on the floor and a soft "Okay."

The hot water beat down upon her and she welcomed it, raising her arms and turning to face the spray that stung her face reminding her of the rain that trickled from her face and dripped from her chin when child Zinny used to walk home in the rain from the bus stop head up and arms raised into the warm, gray wetness, smiling and feeling invincible until she got home and her mother hustled her into a hot shower for fear she would get sick walking in the rain like a simple turkey coming in soaked with her slicker held over one arm and her hat in her hand it simply defied description and Zinny's mother was infuriated by such behavior on the part of her daughter but in the rain she had found release, a freedom from self and present, thoughtless and tactile, a physical moment in temper and affect, but the mind healing in effect, a time when she truly felt part of something much larger and with which she could not dispense.

Zinny came back to the present, head lowered, water streaming down her body over her the soft slopes of her breasts down her stomach and on through the thick mass of pubic hair past her legs to hiss softly on the shower floor. She rubbed her breasts slowly with one hand and felt the gently tingling that spread warmth throughout her body. Embarrassed and irritated that she should feel that way, she stopped and turned to rinse off the soap. Perverse old woman, she thought. She had no business doing that but even the rough brush of the towel as she stepped from the shower and wrapped one around herself felt good. Well, so what, another inside voice demanded? Since when is feeling good a bad thing? You like Agile, okay, maybe love him, so stop mopping your emotional floor and move on.

And so she did, quickly dressing in a pair of tan slacks and a teal shirt with a pair of tan slip-ons and then moving into the hall and left into her father's room. He was sitting in his chair as usual, rocking slightly backwards and forwards, staring vacantly out the window to the street outside and the houses opposite them.

She watched the back of his head. He had a full thatch of white hair that stuck out at odd angles making him look as if he were in some science fiction movie where the hero is subject to electric shock. Once a lion on the plain, strong and proud, protecting her from all, guarding her health with his knowledge and love, always there with quiet comfort and wisdom when she hurt her body or soul. Once families had cared for their young and elderly in the same house. Multi-generational families were common as was a morality that included God, patriotism, rectitude and honesty in one's dealings with others and humility and self-depreciation when dealing with oneself. Zinny sighed softly so as not to disturb the scene. Now, the elderly were shipped off to assisted-living facilities and convalescent homes where they are stacked one on top of each other in tiny spaces that cost their families or, less frequently, insurance companies tens of thousands a year. There they pretended to be happy and socially well adjusted in the community room with the big screen TV and the wii systems while they lived through the balance of their lives. Some of them undoubtedly were but Zinny had seen people trapped in their beds or their wheelchairs who, she had been told, never received visitors or family. They were the effluvia of a society that had transformed from agrarian to technocratic. Perhaps Obama would be able to help with his talk of health care for all but Zinny had her doubts.

She had not dismissed the idea of a nursing home lightly. After all, how would she cope when her father became bedridden and unable to totter from the bed to the bathroom? Would she have the physical strength to deal with that? Would Rosa be willing to carry on? She had gone around to some of these places. They all seemed very nice, modern, clean and the residents, depending on their physical condition, engaged in various activities ranging from barely awake vegetables to burly bodies holding tennis racquets and golf bags. She watched them as some young, chirpy woman showed her around pointing out this feature or that benefit and how the underpaid, overworked staff just loved the residents who loved them back and, golly, out there in back is a little putting green and picnic area and in the main room two bowling leagues compete over ice tea and wii and there's a gym for the more active residents or those going through physical therapy and yes there was something for all and family members could come and visit whenever they liked. Zinny came to realize, though, that some people never got visits and others saw family only on holidays. They were on alien ground far from the homes they knew or even the home of a son or daughter and on the faces she passed in the halls she felt the shadow flitting behind the eyes, pulling at the ends of the lips, flickering with the memory of the past, of children growing and then suddenly gone and busy with their own lives and maybe illness and weakness where there had been none before and now sterile corridors with smiling young things bringing strangers who studiously avoid looking at the tubes and wheelchairs and bedpans and screens, who wear frozen, desperate smiles on faces set with concern and the question is this the right place will he like it will she like it oh God have we really come down to this?

Zinny had decided it was not for her or her father. They would somehow find a way to stay where they were, in his house where he belonged and if she was forced to rent out a room and give the money to Mark so be it. She would find some other way to make ends meet. She eased into the room and put her hands gently on her father's bony shoulders. He jerked forward in surprise and then twisted to his left to see who was behind him. Recognition lit up his face momentarily and then he became confused again, but, just for a second, he had known her. Zinny felt it. There was hope. Always hope. Stem cell research. Lots of promise there, she thought. "Just be patient another minute, Dad, and soon we'll have some supper. Good stuff tonight. I got some steak. I know you like that. It used to be your favorite and Mom would do her scalloped potatoes. I always looked forward to those meals and I still remember them. Do you remember? Somewhere inside that head of yours?" Zinny moved around to his front and could not help herself for her world, serene a moment before, broke into pieces and she knew a fear so deep and pervasive that she could only stare while hearing an animal-like sound that she did not even recognize as her own.

E2

"I see you haven't collapsed yet, dearie."

She was a mountainous pile of flesh and clothing, a picture of purples and yellows, rose rainbows, curling lines of showers across a moor, rainbows and oxbows, bangles and bracelets of silver and tin, fake jewels and starry skies smeared with mascara and lips and lipstick from beyond, or maybe behind the Moulin Rouge pursed as if in pursuit above chubby fingers with each nail painted a different shade of green so that they looked as if they had started in an outhouse and finished in an Irish pasture.

Walker knew that he must be dreaming, knew for certain that such a creature could not long exist on this drab part of the planet but it all looked so real. He could see a bead of sweat under her right eye and there was a faint scratch mark on her forehead. Dream or not, he could not avoid it, could not wake up, could not do anything but stare at her as she sat with chubby fingers tapping lightly on the bar, dark to light, teal to virgin forest.

One hand shot out and one finger tapped his hand, a cool touch, light as a sun beam, a dust bunny, a smile and it caused him to look up into the blackest eyes he'd had ever seen. They were the black of a windowless room when the light is turned off, the black of a train tunnel at night, a black darkness without beginning or end, without cruelty or mercy but just there, limitless and immense in its understanding. He stared into them while her finger kept up its steady tapping rhythm, fingeronhand tap tap pause taptaptap.

"Collapsed?" He asked. What on earth was this creature talking about? He was in no danger of collapsing except perhaps from laughter at the appearance of such an amazing apparition.

She stopped tapping on his hand. "You are looking for something and the search is tiring you," said purple mountain majesty in a voice that reminded him of a train whistle, low and very throaty. Her statement was so trite that he wondered if maybe he had dreamed up a fortune teller who had forgotten to change into street clothes before charging into his subconscious after a long day of uttering such phrases to people unable to rely on their own instincts to guide their decisions and actions.

"I am searching for nothing, thank you." Walker told her, perhaps a bit stiffly because he wondered what he was supposed to be searching for and that thought irritated him. Even his goddammed dreams were asking questions that he did not want to answer, or was perhaps afraid to do so.

"Buy a lady a drink?"

"After such an opening line, I should buy you a glass ball." Damn. Suddenly now they were sitting in Mikes, or someplace that looked a lot like it. That's the subconscious for you. Totally flexible.

"I do not tell fortunes." She began tapping an icy calm finger on my hand again.

"Okay, sorry. You look the part, though."

"I am fortune."

Yeah, right, he thought and his mother was one of the three hags working on a length of string. "You are fortunate, then." he told her. This woman was just too much.

How much was she:

Greater than thirty years but less than seventy.

Greater than two hundred pounds but less than four hundred.

Greater than the Lesser Antilles but lesser than the Greater Antilles

Greater than one hundred dollars but less than one thousand dollars.

Greater than 60 degrees Fahrenheit but less than ninety degrees.

Greater than the sum of her parts but less than some.

Greater than chapter but less than verse.

Greater than most but less than some.

Greater than bad but less than good.

"She loves you and that throws her into confusion and despair. Give the gift of understanding but beware, beware" Purple Mountain rocked back and forth on a barstool that seemed in constant danger of either tipping over or collapsing entirely under her immensity. She started tapping at him tapping tapping.

"John, wake up, man. Wake up before Fetterman comes through and catches you dozing."

Walker came back to consciousness with a start. God, it had been a dream, but what a dream. He stared at the screen in front of him and tried to collect his thoughts. "Thanks, Sam," he said and rubbed at his eyes.

Almost quitting time, thank God. He felt tired. His head ached and his ears felt slightly numb from the pressure of the headphones. Another day down the tubes. Another day deeper in debt, but he was not in debt, he reminded himself. In fact, for the first time in his life, he had money in the bank. That thought cheered him considerably and he rose from his chair and stretched comfortably before beginning the process of shutting down the various programs he used during the course of his work day.

Instead of getting on the old F1 immediately, maybe he would take a stroll and shop around a bit. The daydream, or whatever it was, still stuck in his mind like a paper torn in pieces and each piece sticking to a different spot in a slightly different way. Zinny had withdrawn into herself over the past week since their dinner together. He could not honestly feel that she was avoiding him but she stayed in her room or in her father's room when not at work. It was as if he were alone in the house except for occasional sounds from her father's room. A sense of ennui had enveloped him; she had somehow departed with no explanation or even a postcard from Honolulu. He sulked, then hoped, then ignored, then depressed, then shrugged against that for which he had no answer and answered only to himself that he did not know her, had never really known her and so could do nothing about her present state. A small gift might help her back to smiling again.

He turned to Sam Jenkins, a stocky man with a head of brown curling hair and a red face that usually was smiling. He would have been a great salesman, Walker thought. Sam had a quality over the phone that people trusted instinctively. Many of the calls Walker got were from people wanting to speak with Sam and only Sam. Loyal fans, by God. Somewhat unusual in this line of work. "Are you married, Sam?"

"Yep. The old ball and chain," Sam replied and smiled to take away any hint that he did not like his present estate.

"I'm thinking I would like to get a gift for a friend, but I don't quite know what to do. I was married for a long time and I knew what my wife liked but now it's like starting all over again." Walker shrugged his shoulders. He was prepared to kneel at the feet of the master.

"When I find myself thinking of a gift, I usually drop back ten yards and punt. If I get her clothes, they either don't fit or she hates the style or color and will throw them in the back of closet. She collects glass horses, but they can be very expensive, so usually I get her a nice card with gooshy words 'cause she likes gooshy words and some totally ridiculous little trinket to go along with it. She knows I love her and this package seems to confirm that feeling whenever she's mad at me or needs a lift for some other reason." Sam started to close down his machine.

Memory of some of the fights he and Beth had flashed just behind his eyes and he nodded sympathetically at Sam. Maybe he should stop obsessing over this gift. She wasn't expecting it, after all. He could just walk out of work, get on the bus and come back to the house as usual. Serve her right for acting like some panic stricken teenager. It wasn't his fault she'd had a bad marriage. Beth hadn't always liked her presents either.

Walker went through the double glass doors and into the corridor where the elevators opened and shut with monotonous clicks and whooshes. He knew that he would not be going home immediately. The idea of a present would not go away, and the fact that he could now afford one made it stronger yet. He walked through the double doors and out onto Constitution Plaza, a huge sterile expanse of concrete surrounded by offices. Trees and plantings were strictly visitors there. What would she like? She was a librarian and treated books like food but mysteries or romances, "War And Peace" or "Lady Chatterly's Lover", "On The Beach" or the "Naked and The Dead", something from the past or maybe a Lee Childs or John Grisham? He had never seen her with a book at the house, and that seemed strange now that he thought about it, but then he had never been in her room. There were a few old books in the living room that looked as if they hadn't been touched in decades. The chance that he would buy her a book that would only be added to that collection seemed pretty good. He walked off the plaza and up to Main Street frowning, lost in thought and suddenly he knew. Cheerful again, he whistled the Colonel Bogey March as he strode down Asylum towards a jewelry store.

Walker stepped off the F1 and turned to look back into its interior. The driver, a woman named Betty, seemed to be enshrined in a circle of light from the overhead lamps in the driver's compartment. Light ringed her hair, turning the red blonde strands into a halo.

"Take it easy, John," she said and smiled which increased the halo impression by a factor of two, Walker thought.

She's such a nice person, pretty, intelligent, vivacious. She's one of those rare people on whom others depend. One of the strong ones that keep going no matter what and always manage a smile at the end of a run. Helluva job. I doubt I could do it. Think she said her husband has Alzheimer's. Sad way to go and hard for her. Don't know how she does it well yes I do cause I did it with Beth onedayatatime onestep one step and Zinny is doing it for her father. Do what we must, heh? In God we trust. I'm hungry. Seems like a year ago I ate lunch. And that dream or vision or whatever it was. Did I leave some turkey in the fridge? Make a nice sandwich, now with maybe a slice of that tomato that was on the window sill and some mayo, oh yes indeed. Hope she likes the music box. The little girl twirled around with such a fetching smile I couldn't resist and with a catchy tune. Couldn't quite put my finger on the name of it, but it is one of the Musak favorites for sure. Ah when we were young and going round and round. She should like it, but maybe I should test the waters first. See what kind of mood she's in. Definitely don't want a repeat of the other night. Good Christ almighty. She tightened up like a coiled spring.

Lagging slightly behind a short shadow from the evening sun, Walker went slowly up the street carefully holding the small silver box from the jewelry store in his left hand.

F1

The kitchen was quiet, slightly dimmed by the early evening light and looked as though it could have been a painting depicting the Americana of the 1950's. Walker put his gift down on the table and looked around. Zinny must be home. There was a pot of potatoes bubbling away on the stove and a big package wrapped in butcher paper on the counter by the sink. It was marked "Steak" and Walker's stomach rumbled. She had the day off and it looked as if she had plans for the evening. Next to the steaks was a brown paper bag. He peered into the top and saw the Jack and Merlot. Wow. Things were indeed looking up. He was about to pick up his gift and head for his room when he heard her scream.

It was piercing and sounded as if she were being tortured. Walker bolted out of the kitchen and up the stairs to the second floor. "Zinny," he called. There was no response but he heard scuffling noises from her father's room. Oh God, he thought. Not her dad. Please not her dad. He knocked but there was no answer. He pushed on the door and it opened.

Zinny was kneeling on the floor in front of her father, her arms folded across his knees and her head resting on her arms. A piece of paper lay on the floor to the left of the chair.

"Zinny, are you all right? What on earth happened?" Walker stopped, unsure or what to do and suddenly afraid of doing the wrong thing. Was she sick, tired, dead oh no surely not. She had just screamed and what a scream, a scream straight from fifties sci-fi and horror flicks. He stood his ground, but suddenly wished he was standing in his own room holding a glass of Jack and a good book, serious, well written, entertaining, a King novel perhaps. "It" popped into his head for no apparent reason. What a great book. Good versus Evil. Go turtle. One of the two basic themes of all writing. What time was it? He thought to look at his watch but that was ridiculous with Zinny kneeling on the floor beside her father.

She looked up at him and he had never seen such desolation on a human face. "Hi, Agile."

"More trouble?"

Zinny nodded. Reaching out her hand, she picked up the piece of paper and then struggled to her feet. She silently handed it to Walker.

SELL THIS HOUSE

Walker looked at the words crudely printed in black Magic Marker on a piece of copy paper. He looked at them so long and hard that they blurred and he could no longer make out the letters. So Mark was back. Big time back. Finally, he looked up from the sheet of paper. "Where did you find this?"

"Taped to my father's chest."

Jesus Christ on a crutch. What kind of psycho was this guy? This was totally unreal as if they were stuck in a drug store novel being moved here and there and put into creepy scenes by someone else. "He's just trying to scare you," Walker ventured, not at all sure that he was right, but hoping to put some life back in Zinny's eyes.

"How would you feel?" Zinny asked.

He'd be scared, Walker had to admit. Scared shitless. Still, he thought it impolitic to admit it under these circumstances. He shrugged and looked at Zinny miserably. "I don't know," he temporized.

Zinny got to her feet slowly and turned to look out the window. "He's out there somewhere."

"Probably long gone by now. Just trying to throw a scare like I said."

"Maybe, but I will have to sell this place." She turned to face him, her face broken into shards of desolation, her eyes reflecting the hopelessness and sullen resignation of the lost and forgotten who had no further recourse to dreams or futures or any of the normal life music that keeps us dancing.

God, I didn't even feel like that when my dog, Banjo, died when I was twelve and I knew with certainty that only a boy that age can achieve that I had lost the best and only friend I would ever have. "No you don't. The police are bound to catch him and arrest him for assault." *Sure they will. The psychotic fuck can't hide out forever.* "Spread the word. You've apparently got juice in this area. I've seen you in your little outpatient clinic on the weekends." He held out a hand. "C'mon. Nothing's as bad as it seems. If nothing else, I've learned that much and I noticed when I came in that the Merlot fairy has paid us a visit and left her mark in the kitchen."

"Oh, no," Zinny began to explain.

"Ah. Ah. No talk. Else the spell is broken and the bottle in the kitchen turns to vinegar before we can get to it. If memory serves me, the fairy had company on her flight through the house. A male fairy named Jack. Whodathunk it?"

Zinny looked down at her father who stared vacantly in front of him out the window out of mind and time out of. "Okay." She crumpled up the note and threw the paper into a small trash basket by her father's bureau.

Walker watched Zinny out of the corner of his eye as he got the steaks out of their paper womb and seasoned them. He tested the potatoes and took them off the heat. She sat at the table, a glass of wine in front of her untouched. It was as if she were simply going through the motions because it was the easiest thing to do and she was in a state so fragile that anything else would have been impossible. A deep sense of loss filled him until he felt a physical pain in his stomach. He stood motionless at the kitchen counter waiting for the pain to pass sensing deep inside that it would never, not completely, and some part of him knew it. "C'mon, Zinny. Talk to me. Okay, we may not be brother and sister but we've become friends, at least I consider you my friend, maybe more," he admitted feeling his cheeks growing hot. He busied himself mashing up the potatoes and turning on the broiler. "You don't have to sell this place. For what reason? Mark? Like I said, he won't be around forever." He poured two fingers of Jack into a water glass and walked to the fridge for two cubes of ice. Behind him was silence heavy on the room booming around him in its nothingness. He sat down across from her and took a slug of his drink. "Hello. Earth to Zinny. Come in please," he intoned through his nose as if over a loudspeaker.

She smiled, faintly but it was there. "You don't understand, Agile, but thank you for trying. Really."

"Make me understand. Talk to me. I'm a good listener. Really I am." He tried to make a humorous remark out of it but failed. They stared at each other. She had a faint shadow of hair above her upper lip and there was a tiny indentation in the skin just to the left of her left eye that was staring directly at him as if she was seeing something that she had never seen before and was trying to understand it. She raised her glass and took a sip without looking away but then did, looking down at the table as she lowered her glass.

"Mark was simply a catalyst," she said in a voice so low that Walker had to lean forward until his face was less than a foot from hers. "A reminder that things had not been going well for a while. I didn't want to admit it to myself or anyone else but that is the truth." She sighed. "I don't know. Maybe it's time. Maybe not. You're not to blame for any of this. You just got sucked in."

"Did it ever occur to you that I might want to be "sucked in", as you say. That maybe we came together by chance but since then we have shared a lot, good and bad. I regret Mark, needless to say, but I regret nothing else. Not meeting you. Not this house. Not your father. Not sitting here with you." He reached out and put his right hand over her left. "None of it," he told her and found himself meaning every word. It surprised him a little, and then he felt good about it; he thought that he had said what he felt and to hell with the consequences.

She nodded as if accepting his little speech. Maybe she simply knew he was speaking the truth. Maybe she felt the same way. "Living with someone who is gradually losing his memory is not easy. I mean it doesn't happen overnight. There are little things like forgetting to take out the garbage or forgetting that he had already brought in the paper. A shrug. A chuckle. Senior moment. No biggie. But it gradually gets worse until you wake up one day and find that the person who sired you, who loved you through it all, who was a rock in your life, is now forgetting to eat and not recognizing his surroundings and then not recognizing you. That, maybe, is the hardest. You have suddenly become a stranger. But it is not a sudden shock. And you think well okay I can handle this and you adjust and go on and your life gradually changes and you find yourself changing sheets at five in the morning before getting yourself ready for work but that's okay and you adjust and go on and every couple of weeks you take the pile of bills and do the best you can but the paycheck doesn't move much and your expenses keep climbing. Rosa is wonderful and gives a lot of time free of charge because she and her parents were patients of Dads, but I have to pay her something and at this stage of my life I realize that I am not going to burn bright within the state library system and won't be making much more than I am now so I thought maybe renting out a room would cover the shortfall but I am seeing that although it does so there are other problems." She fluttered her hands in front of her face as if waving away flies. "In the end, of course, it becomes a physical problem. I guess the mind controls the body and when the mind goes, the body eventually follows. Dad is increasingly unable to walk. I think he suffered a mild stroke a couple of weeks back and now it's all I can do to get him out of bed and clothed and changed. Soon, that may not be possible. I just don't have the strength and Rosa can't be here all the time. He loved this house and I love this house, but I need more help and a nursing home may be the only answer." She raised her glass, avoiding his eyes, and took a delicate sip as if they had been discussing the differences in fine bone china. She seemed composed, perhaps relieved that the problem was finally out in the open while afraid of how Walker might react.

Walker was suddenly filled with a light such as he had not known since his wedding day. The idea had come as Zinny had been explaining and he had not really listened to the end of her explanation. It would be perfect and the irony did not escape him. His mother probably would have a hemorrhage be she in heaven or hell and that would be icing on the fucking cake as far as he was concerned. Man, talk about perfect. He was a dammed genius, yes he was, and it was only with an effort that he sat there while Zinny finished and sat there sipping at her Merlot.

He beamed at her across the table, lifted his glass and raised it in her direction. "I'll buy the house."

Zinny gaped at him. "What?"

"I said I'll buy the house," Walker repeated feeling better about it with every passing second. "I mean it. My mother left quite an estate. I thought she'd probably leave it to some charity but she left it to Jen and me. So I could buy the house. We could pay off Mark. You and your Dad could stay right here with me. It would be as much your house as mine, you know. More because of all the years and living that you and your family have put into it. I mean you wouldn't really be losing the house. Not really, you know? From the moment I stepped through the front door a few weeks back, I felt at home. It was like the house I sold, only larger. It felt friendly and lived in and I breathed a sigh of relief when you said I could rent a room. So I would be glad to take over the mortgage and all that. You could chip in only what you could afford. We could pull this off and everyone would win. You'd have the money to have someone come in every day and help with the nursing chores. It's perfect." He took a sip of his drink and broke out in a grin from ear to ear. "Whaddya think?"

My God, I think he means it. "You're joking, right?"

"Not at all. Think about it. It solves all the problems that you face and that I face. I took this room thinking that I could then take my time and find a place that I really liked since, no matter what I found in the way of an apartment, it was going to cost me an arm and a leg. Now, suddenly, I can afford more, and I find myself living in a place that I really like. This house. With you and your dad. It's perfect."

"Agile. It's sweet of you. It really is." *And if he's really serious I won't be able to stop him since I really do have to sell this place and get Dad where he can get the kind of help I can't provide* "but we are old enough to know that such things rarely work out in real life. Suppose you got tired of sharing your home. I wouldn't blame you. Living with someone who's handicapped is no easy thing. I guess you know from your wife's illness, but you should remember it because Dad can get loud, not often but it happens, and sometimes the upstairs smells of urine and shit and there's always the atmosphere of chronic illness and the smells of laundry and disinfectant." She made a face, pulling down the corners of her mouth. "and I'm not always easy to get alone with as you know."

"Fair enough." Walker nodded in agreement "and if that happens I sell the house back to you on terms you can afford and we go our separate ways. I'll put that in the sales contract if you like. Sorta like a pre-nup." He took a sip from his glass. "Now, how about I see to seasoning up those steaks. They look fantastic."

"Agile, really, I think that . . ."

Walker held up a hand to stop her and rose from the table. "Nuff said. Let's do something to celebrate. I know." He held up a finger as if he had just come up with a novel idea. "We can eat. I'll call it supper. What d'ya think? Catchy name or what?"

Zinny couldn't help herself and broke out into a smile. "Very catchy. Let me get the rest of dinner going while you work on the steaks."

Suddenly, there was a loud crash from the back stoop and then the door flew open and Mark tiptoed into the room on feet that barely touched the ground. He was being almost held in the air by the massive man behind him whose huge hand was holding Mark by the back of his shirt.

"We saw this piece of shit coming out the back of your house. Heard someone was causing you a problem. This the guy?"

Zinny was speechless, mind and body paralyzed by the shock of Mark's sudden appearance. She stood by the sink, holding a fork in one hand, eyes wide and mouth describing an almost perfect "O".

Walker, too, was taken aback but was quicker to recover. "That's the asshole, all right."

"Fuck you." Mark started but was quickly silenced as the giant behind him shook him like a rag doll. His whole body shook and his head bounced from side to side like a marionette with strings cut. "Quiet, mothafucka."

"Thomas. What on earth?" Zinny remembered that she was holding the fork and quickly put it down on the counter behind her.

"Hey, Zinny." The giant grinned exposing a gold left front tooth that glinted dully in the kitchen light. He loosened his grip on Mark's shirt and Mark stood on his own two feet, obviously badly frightened but trying hard not to show it.

Zinny felt a wave of relief run through her. "Agile. The gentleman behind Mark is Tom, Cool Blade, Thompson. He's the eldest son of a man with whom I played when I was a kid. We played baseball, as I remember."

"Hi, Tommy." Agile smiled and nodded in greeting.

Tommy smiled again. "Whassup, Zin girl? Got this here honky been shadowing your house. Heard he wasn't no friend, understand? So whatchu want?"

"Zinny, please. I know you don't like me but if I don't get the money, I'm a dead man."

"Zip it." Blade slapped Mark on the side of his head rocking his whole body.

God. This could be the end of it and I didn't make it happen. Just a word or two and Mark is gone, gone, gone like the summer breeze and he would deserve it yes he would but look at him standing there trying to pretend that he's in control even with Blade standing behind him. Okay, he was a shit but I probably didn't help much either. You gotta take some of the blame, lady. I could have been more understanding or maybe just less judgmental and I couldn't sleep at night if I thought I had anything to do with another man's death, but what about Agile and his offer. I wasn't lying to him. Things are getting to the point where I need help and it's about time I admitted it. Been whistling past the graveyard for too long. So what now? I just tell Tommy to make him disappear? Then what? Could I live knowing that I had caused something like that?

Zinny felt as if she was moving in slow motion as she turned back to the counter, opened a drawer and took out a scratch pad and a pencil. She tossed them across the table towards Mark. "Write down your mailing address. If I sell the house I'll send you some money. You never come back here, never call, write, text or tweet. Do you understand?"

Mark's eyes gleamed. "I need fifty thousand."

Zinny had seen that look before. Even now, stripped of all pretenses, he was padding the take, or at least trying to. "Take what I send, Mark." She looked past him at Tommy. "Know what I need?"

Tommy nodded and casually put Mark back on Mark's toes again. "You hear the lady? You come back here, you be one dead honky mothafucka, hear? You bother her again, just know that I got friends all over the place, hear?"

Mark nodded. Blade wheeled around and pushed his burden out the kitchen door as if he had been a sack of rags.

Mark fell down the back steps onto the concrete walk that led to the driveway. For a moment he lay there completely disoriented. His mind swirled as his eyes tried to regain focus. He was at Zinny's. That was right. He had been in the back trying to see if there had been any reaction to his message. The blimp had come home and gone in the kitchen door. He thought he had heard her scream and that had filled him with glee. Suddenly he had been hoisted in the air as if by magic. Something huge and powerful had grabbed him and then he was in the kitchen jerked around like a rag doll.

He got to his feet slowly, feeling for anything that might be broken or strained. Nothing badly hurt, thank God. Slowly, Mark tottered down the driveway towards his car. He was, in fact, rather pleased at how things had turned out. Zinny was going to send him a lot of money. He believed her. One thing about his ex wife. She was completely honest. If she said she would send the money, he would receive it. He would give some to DiNapoli, of course, but not all of it. He could say that he had only been able to get whatever he gave the old man. Hell, Mark was in tight with the old man's daughter. That should count for something. Maybe he would say that Zinny had refused to give him anything but the rent money. DiNapoli might go for that. Sure, and with Lisa behind him, and Zinny sending him a wad of cash, he would be on easy street. Things were definitely looking up in spite of the bruises to his body and dignity. Wincing slightly, Mark was reaching into his pocket for the car keys when he felt movement behind him.

Turning around, he found himself facing a man of whom he had only heard, and had come to believe was just a fiction. Even shadowed by the fading light, Mark saw the man's eyes, and wished he hadn't.

"We need to talk," Artie Tagliemo said.

"b . . . 'bout what?" Mark stuttered as he tried to maintain some semblance of dignity. "Who are you?"

"No one you want to mess with, little man," Artie replied. "Did you get the money?"

"Not yet."

There was a faint click and a sharp-looking six inch blade appeared before Mark's face. "Really?" Artie whispered. "You came down that driveway looking like a cat who'd caught a mouse. "You wanna know something? I would enjoy cutting you into little pieces, *capesce?*"

"DiNapoli will get his money," Mark replied trying not to look at the knife or at Artie.

"You bet he will, 'cause you're gonna go back in there and give them the boss's address."

"What?" The thought of meeting Blade again terrified Mark. He felt his bladder release a warm stream down his legs. "I can't do that. There's huge fucking black in there who will kill me."

Mark felt the tip of the knife pressing against his throat. "Do it now," Artie told him and pressed one of DiNapoli's cards into one of Mark's hands. If the boss doesn't get the money, I will find you. Do we understand each other?"

Mark nodded and made his way slowly back up the driveway towards the back door of the house praying the Blade was not still in the kitchen bullshitting with Zinny. He was but a dim shadow in the dimness of the dusk. Artie nodded to himself and got on his cell phone.

Conjunction

Walker was working on a chapter or, more truthfully it was working on him because all he had was a chapter number and a sense that he had run the characters into a concrete wall and should chuck the whole dammed thing and start over again but it was two years work and so he sat in the chair pretending to work but really just running back over the whole series of events of the past few hours.

He was the proud owner of another house, in theory if not in fact. He hadn't thought of buying another house so soon, had not thought about buying a house at all, and was only beginning to think about finding a bigger apartment. The evening had settled like comfortable shawl around the shoulders of the earth. There was the hum of the crickets, the occasional beep of a car. The humidity of the past week had lessened and a small breeze came through the window in front of him. All in all, Walker found that he had no regrets. Rolling it over in his mind, looking for some flaw in his reasoning or in his reaction he could find none. The look in Zinny's eyes when he had made his offer made it all worthwhile even if it had not been a good investment. She had been about to refuse it. He knew that and then Mark had entered the equation and suddenly, she had gone ahead and said okay and that had made him feel great as if some hidden force had been conquered, had slunk away in sulking silence leaving only peace in its place. Sitting at his desk looking out over the street, he wondered what would happen now. From renter to owner and Zinny from owner to tenant. Life was indeed strange. He shook his head and tried to focus on the screen in front of him. He picked up the glass on the desk but it was empty. Well if ever there had been a night for celebration it was tonight.

With Mark and Blade gone, he and Zinny had simply stood and stared at each other unsure of what to do next. Then Mark had come through the door again, looking around fearfully for Blade. He handed the card to Zinny. "Send the money here," he said, turned and beat a hasty retreat back into the darkness.

Walker had finished his drink as the adrenaline in his system dissipated leaving him feeling tired and somewhat flat.

"Supper?" Zinny asked and held up the potato masher that she had forgotten during the confrontation.

Walker nodded his head and grinned. "By all means. Victory dinner. Let me at those steaks."

And what a wonderful dinner it had been. They had eaten the steaks and drank the Jack and Merlot. They had shared little grins and smiles throughout it all. One would catch the eye of the other and a glass would be raised and a sense of understanding and friendship would pass between them. As Walker sat at his desk, he reflected that, in a sense, they had felt like two soldiers who survived a fierce battle while all around them was death and destruction.

Walker picked up his glass and walked out of his door on the way to a refill when Zinny appeared in the door of her bedroom

"Hi there," Zinny said.

"Hey." Walker turned towards her. *Wow. Who is this woman and what has she done to Zinny?*

Zinny had on a long white kimono-like garment with the painting of a sun coming up on a lake and a gnarled tree bending in from the left as if bowing to the new born day. A row of large buttons colored to blend into the picture ran down the middle. Her hair was washed and shining. She stood very erect and had a serious expression on her face.

Shit. What has happened now? She looks as if a new disaster has taken place. And what's with the threads? Like some heroine in one of those Japanese ninja films. She is so beautiful, though. If she raised her arms, I think the whole world would kneel at her door. "More trouble?" he asked. "You look really tense."

Zinny shook her head and walked towards him. "Dear Agile. I just wanted to thank you for all you've done. I don't think anyone has ever extended that amount of concern and generosity since my childhood." She reached up with one hand and touched him lightly on one cheek. "It was really very special."

"You're welcome," Walker replied. "I thought it was the right thing to do for both of us and I was just sitting here thinking it over and I still think it's the right thing to do. So get a hold of a real estate agent and get an estimate of the market value and we'll go from there."

Zinny stepped in close to him and lay her head on his shoulder. For a moment they remained like that, two silhouettes in the fading summer light.

Now what? I don't want to send her into the bathroom like the last time. Should just stand here and enjoy the smell of her hair and the feel of her body. How long has it been? Too long by far. Beth used to smell like this when she had just taken a shower and dried off and smelled like a garden on a Spring morning yes she did and looked as beautiful as well and usually she would walk past me, climb into her side of the bed and go to sleep but every once in a while. Walker brought his arms around Zinny in what he hoped was the lightest of caresses, barely touching her robe enough to stir the fabric. He felt her stiffen and dropped his arms in alarm.

Zinny shook her head as if perplexed by some hidden problem and looked into his eyes. "No, Agile." She pressed against him while pulling his arms around her waist.

He felt her body trembling and imagined he could even feel the staccato beating of her heart beyond the soft press of her breasts. He looked down into her upturned face and felt her lips press against his.

It would have been okay, well, it is okay because she said so and because there was not choice, not really, not and keep intact a significant part of what each of us valued in the other but at that moment, of course, neither knew which is just as well. I felt her lips against mine and then her mouth opened and the warm coil of her tongue swished inside my mouth and I was so totally lost and never wanted to be found again. It was a Delphic moment as I found my mind wandering through generalities that seemed of vast importance where flashes of form and color blended as our tongues met and the settlers circled their wagons while the Indians showed their wampum and I pressed against her body, feeling her breasts flatten against me and my dick stiffening, all ready to give and receive that for which we are born. I felt her hand sliding down under my stomach until it found my dick and rubbed against it up and down until I had a raging hard-on and thought in momentary panic that I might come right then and there. Desperately, I pushed away oh so gently and with a vast ocean of regret and we faced each other's eyes, lips parted slightly, face tightened in lust. Zinny was breathing quickly in shallow gasps as if we had suddenly been thrust into an airless room, her eyes deep without light filled with a desperate determination, a chaotic sense of finality and I lowered my hands until I felt her ass cheeks soft and straining against me beneath them as they tensed and then relaxed. She looked at me with an expression so serious that she might have been researching the proteins inherent in Irish sea moss and then reached up and touch my cheek with one hand stroking quickly and softly and then dropping to the buttons on the front of her garment. She undid the first and then moved down to the second and then to the third while I could do nothing but stand there like a statue watching as the cloth parted, a porcelain statue in an earthquake as if my body would shatter should I move a fraction then, trancelike, I moved to unbutton my shirt as well as Zinny moved down button by button until her robe was open to her waist. Slowly, with the movement of a breath, with the decision made and mind and body moving as one, she reached up to the top of the robe and pulled it away from her shoulders letting it drop in a curving mass around her waist.

Agile finished unbuttoning his shirt and drew it off. His chest was not as fat as I had imagined. There was a patch of brown hair in the middle of it. Almost as if I was watching a stranger do it, I moved one hand across it feeling the loose wiry texture of it as the hairs moved between my fingers. This is crazy. I don't need to do this. There is still time to back away and run out and hide but no, Azalea, you are a grown woman standing close to a wonderful man and you can do this, you can do this and I felt every muscle in my body become tense as panic rose like a stick shoved down my throat and Agile wavered and floated in front of me. Not Mark. Not Mark a voice inside shouted out, cried to be heard and understood and was heard and I stood there and felt his hands on my breasts and they were warm and solid and my nipples came up beneath them and I reached down for his belt while my heart felt as if it would explode and my mind was filled with dread and momentary images of Mark, his face contorted in anger, coming at me across the bed his hands clenched but I stood there yes I just stood there and looked at Agile and saw the searching question in his eyes and I would answer yes and I would be with him, and forced myself to relax, forced my stomach to be still for it would not be my master not this time no no and his pants fell down and there he stood in plain white briefs tucked beneath his belly like a giant bandage holding everything together, a bandage that had a notable bulge in its center and he reached out and undid the next button on my kimono and it joined his pants in a gentle pile at my feet and all I could see now was his face inches away, five o'clock stubble just beginning to show at eight o'clock and his eyes that seemed to be focusing on *something behind me but probably saw a blur since he was without his glasses. His mouth closed on mine and his tongue probed my mouth, met mine in a wet embrace that seemed to last forever and that sent shivers running up and down my body. I could feel moisture running down the inside of one thigh. We pulled apart and I hooked my thumbs into the top of my panties and pushed them down as Agile did the same with his. He was uncircumcised. It was not long but thick and stood out from his body and its thick patch of pubic hair with the head just poking through the foreskin. I felt a shock as my whole body tightened with pleasure.*

She was so lovely standing naked in front of me. The evening light turned her skin to a soft alabaster. She stood straight and very still. Her eyes filled my sight, so calm and maybe even happy. I touched the skin of one breast and felt her shiver slightly as she gently ran a finger down the length of my dick. I put both hands on her and moved her breasts ever so gently. Zinny sighed and moved against me. Her nipples were taut beneath my hands. I went to my knees and buried my face in her pubic hair, feeling the soft mass of it against my nose. It grew down the inside of her thighs and back towards her ass. She sighed softly and spread her legs a little. I pushed my tongue into the moist darkness of her and heard her breath catch as her legs trembled. I knew we would not be able to hold back for very long.

Without speaking, almost without thought but guided by the base instincts of the foundation of the race, Walker got to his feet took Zinny's hand, turned and they walked over and sat down on the bed. The room around them was softly shadowed by the summer evening light. The desk, the chair, the bureau and bookshelves all seemed to be part of some late nineteenth century photograph in shades of brown and gray, of people looking sternly ahead alert for their destinies. There was no sound but for the creak of the bedsprings as Walker shifted slightly and put his right arm around Zinny who turned towards him as they kissed away the light. She pushed him gently and Walker fell back onto the bed and rolled away slightly to allow Zinny room to lie beside him.

She stared down at him with an expression Walker could not read. She appeared sad, but not really, more thoughtful or a little scared as if she was a deer at the edge of a field sniffing the air for danger, afraid and yet not afraid. She smiled then and lay down beside him putting her arms around him and molding her body to his. He felt her breasts against his chest and the soft brush of her pubic hair against his thigh as she rolled towards him. He had a raging erection and pulled her to him feeling the soft pillows of her buttocks. She stiffened again, then

"Everything okay?" he asked softly.

Zinny nodded but did not speak. Instead she rolled over on top of him until she was kneeling over him staring down into his eyes and rubbing her hands across his chest pulling slightly at the hair there and then stroking his belly up and down up and *downandupagainandohgodwhatareyoudoingtome* and raising up slightly she put her right hand down between her legs and softly held his cock *jesusohjesus* and guided it into her and settled back down onto his hips just as *Beth loved me yes she did even though she came to me after and needing someone and there I was oh bethbethbeth I always loved you*

And he went limp. Walker felt himself suddenly soften and pushed up trying to regain the feeling but it was no use. His cock had died a sudden death and would not be coaxed back to life. He felt a darkness settle upon him, a depression that was at once part panic and part regression for he felt that somehow he deserved the moment, maybe not for what he had done in the past but for that which had left undone in some way, had not been what he should have been, had not made the right decisions in some way that he could not understand but felt as a weight within him nevertheless.

Zinny rose slightly, inched backwards towards his feet and put the malfunctioning part in her mouth sucking on it while she gently rubbed his balls but that effort failed as well and, after a couple of minutes, she yielded to reality and lay back down beside Walker, her head on his shoulder and one arm draped across his chest.

"Sorry," Walker said to the ceiling unable to look at Zinny, feeling his failure as a twisting pain in his gut, filled with embarrassment and remorse.

With instinctual wisdom to woman born, Zinny did not respond immediately but simply lay there reassuring by her simple presence, silent in the face of the unknowable and her own feelings of relief and disappointment. "Sorry for what?" she replied finally.

Walker blew air through his lips in answer.

"Listen," Zinny continued. "When Mark had too much to drink, he couldn't keep it up either but he blamed me and then came after me with his fists." Zinny stroked his chest with her hand. "I love you, Agile, and after this, I love you all the more."

Walker turned his head to stare at her and smiled. "Make a hell of a pair, don't we?"

"Functionally dysfunctional," Zinny said with a throaty chuckle.

They lay there in the fading light, two bodies through the window patterned in light and shadow like a crossword puzzle light on dark but no words for the down and no words for the across but only the two of them weaving their lives together and apart filled with desperate conviction that the morrow would somehow outpace the present.

Outside the window, they heard the hum of a car passing on the street below, the creak of some part of the house adjusting itself. From her father's room came the faint sound of a body shifting.

"Okay"

The End